MIST DRAGON

THE DRAGON MISFITS BOOK 5

D.K. HOLMBERG

ASH PUBLISHING

www.dkholmberg.com

1

Flying with the massive iron dragon left him with a feeling of calm, and Jason Dreshen enjoyed the way the wind swirled around him. Rather than with wings beating at the sky the way most dragons flew, the iron dragon propelled himself forward on bursts of heat and energy, something that made him special and unique.

The calm was disturbed by the strange burst of dragon power that had drawn him here. Jason wasn't even sure how to describe it, other than power. It had flooded him, nearly overwhelming him, and then had faded.

It was enough to know Lorach moved.

Jason and the iron dragon circled over the forest, patrolling the outer edge of Dragon Haven. There was movement. These days, there was often movement around Dragon Haven, though most of the time, that movement came from the Dragon Guard in their attempt to ensure the safety of their community. Cherise and Olar, the rulers of Dragon Haven, asked that of the Dragon Guard, recalling them from their fight as leaders of the rebellion, worried about what Lorach would attempt next.

He'd considered going to the Dragon Guard to share with them what he'd detected, but he had a feeling they wouldn't listen. They were convinced they didn't need to listen. Not to him. He wasn't Dragon Guard, despite having protected Dragon Haven repeatedly.

That didn't keep Jason from doing what he could to offer his unique protections. Given his connection to the misfit dragons and the fact that the dragons he had bonded to were so different from the others within Dragon Haven, he could do more.

A flicker of movement caught his attention, and through the connection he shared with the iron dragon, they veered toward it. Both he and the dragon had noticed it at the same time.

Jason connected to the iron dragon's eyesight. Learning that he could do so, attaching to the dragon in a way that allowed him to see what the dragon saw, had given him an advantage that others did not share. He saw the world as flashes of orange and red, layers of heat that stretched over the forest. There were some aspects that were lighter in color, such as the forest floor, and even the trees. Other aspects flared brighter within the dragon's eyesight: squirrels and other small creatures that navigated through the forest. Larger animals, like the deer that scurried at the first sight of the dragon. Other dragons blazed even brighter.

Eyesight like that made the iron dragon an incredible hunter. He didn't have enough of a connection to other dragons to know whether they shared something similar, only that the iron dragon did.

The ice dragon, another dragon misfit that Jason had bonded to, shared his eyesight in much the same way, though everything Jason could see through the ice dragon was a little different. Cooler. The ice dragon searched for movement almost more than he did heat, though he *did* see gradations of heat. It made everything appear different.

As they neared the location on the forest floor where he had seen the movement, Jason couldn't identify what it was. He tapped on the dragon's side. "What do you think that was?"

The dragon rumbled. "Nothing tasty."

Jason chuckled. The dragons were ferocious hunters and the iron dragon in particular had a way of moving through the trees that made him especially deadly. He could slither through the trees so unexpectedly that he never went hungry.

"Not tasty, but it wasn't anything to be concerned about?"

"I've seen no other dragons."

Jason stared into the distance, his gaze drawn toward Lorach. Since his escape, there had been signs of movement out of Lorach, but they had not attacked. There was no evidence that Lorach even came toward them. It was a matter of time, though. Jason, along with others within

Dragon Haven, knew that Lorach would eventually bring forces to bear upon Dragon Haven. They blamed the rebellion—and Jason in particular now—for what had happened to them. More than that, Jessica, the person who essentially led in Lorach, would stop at nothing to overpower Jason and claim the misfits.

"They have to be out there," he said.

"The others have kept watch. We do not need to do this."

Jason smiled slightly. By *others,* he knew the iron dragon meant the dragons of the Dragon Guard. They patrolled, sweeping through the forest, keeping concealed as much as possible with the illusion Jason had cast upon them, making them appear to outsiders as nothing more than large birds. Perhaps birds that were out of place, but birds nonetheless. They would look like eagles or massive sparrows or other birds that fit within the forest. Jason tried to make sure they were as appropriate for this space as possible, though that wasn't always easy.

"The others are patrolling, but I feel as if this is something I need to do."

"You need to trust that they are capable," the iron dragon said.

Jason smiled to himself. He was right, but that didn't make it any easier.

"You have other business you need to be doing anyway."

He chuckled again. The iron dragon urged him in ways that the ice dragon didn't. There was a heat within him, along with some irritation, though Jason knew it was only because he wanted to help. "By other business, you mean understanding my parents."

"You know what business."

"I know what business, but I have a feeling you don't know what business," Jason said.

The dragon rumbled and turned suddenly, veering away from the outskirts of the forest edge, taking them back toward Dragon Haven. He led them away from Lorach and away from danger. It was probably for the best. Jason had no interest in battling with Dragon Souls from Lorach, though if he did, he knew he could free dragons. He had done so before, at least until Jessica had learned to counter the effect of what he had done. With her newfound skill, Jason worried that he would not be able to save more of the Lorach dragons from slavery.

"You don't need to turn back quite so quickly," Jason said.

"I need to hunt. You need to do the same."

"If I need to hunt, then—"

"Not that kind of hunting."

In the distance, the outskirts of Dragon Haven came into view. There was an illusion over the entirety of the city, masking it from any outsiders, though to Jason's eyes, the illusion shimmered, fluttering slightly so that he could see beyond it. It took very little for him to make out the outline of the city through the illusion itself. He held onto that illusion, tugging on the power of it, and tested it. For a moment, some aspect of the illusion flickered.

Jason sat upright, frowning. "Did you see that?"

"I see nothing," the iron dragon said.

Jason frowned. The illusion was such that it masked everything within Dragon Haven, concealing even the heat of the dragon's eyes. He borrowed from the iron dragon again, using his connection to look down and see if there was anything that he might uncover within the city, but as he did, he found nothing. Through the dragon's eyes, it looked as if it were nothing more than a stretch of forest. Perhaps a stretch where there was an absence of other movement, though Jason had hesitated at the idea of forcing more heat through the illusion to avoid the likelihood that a dragon might decide to hunt here and uncover Dragon Haven.

As far as he could tell, the illusion held. Some aspect of it didn't feel quite right, though. Despite his ability to see down below him, to make out the illusion, he worried why he had seen a flickering.

This was all that stood between them and discovery. If Lorach decided to send a squadron of dragons their way, sweeping over the forest, it would be a simple matter for them to find Dragon Haven without the illusion.

Or maybe not. That might simply be Jason's arrogance. Dragon Haven had survived without his presence for decades. Centuries, even. The city itself was old and remained from a time long ago when dragons were revered in this part of the world. The artifacts set throughout the city, many of them sculpted in the shape of dragons, suggested that. The people of Dragon Haven all shared a similar philosophy: All wanted to help the dragons, and none wanted to see them trained the way the Dragon Souls would do. Both groups had the same powers, though, which limited what Dragon Haven could do against Lorach.

They circled for a moment over Dragon Haven, and Jason continued studying the illusion, watching to ensure that there was no change to it and testing whether there was anything more that might have indicated a flickering of power. He saw nothing. It should have relieved him, and he supposed that it did, but he also wanted to ensure that the illusion was solid.

He called upon the power of the forest dragon, feeling her distantly. His connection to her was different than the one he shared with the iron and the ice dragons. Whereas those dragons readily lent him strength, the forest dragon didn't often do the same. She had power that she gifted to him, though with a reluctance. Much of the illusion Jason utilized came from himself, almost more so than it did from the forest dragon. He used that now, trying to borrow some of her power, knowing that if he were to do so, the effect would be far more significant and would force the illusion to take greater hold over Dragon Haven.

"Are you done?" The iron dragon snorted, twisting so that he could look over at Jason.

Jason chuckled to himself. "I think so."

"I would have you leave me."

They descended, crashing through the illusion. Knowing that it was there gave Jason the ability to anticipate where it would pass over him, but it still was a bit jarring going through what looked to be the forest and suddenly seeing the city spread out below him. The entirety of Dragon Haven consisted of domed-roof buildings, all made of stone, and it was massive, occupying the space in a clearing within the forest. Somehow, the forest had grown around the city and did not appear to have tried to grow over it. It was a marvel Dragon Haven had never been discovered before.

They came to land in a small clearing on the outskirts of the city. It was a space designated for dragon landings, large enough for a dozen dragons to cluster, all of them capable of taking riders, but it was also large enough for the half-dozen or so small dragons that frolicked. Because dragon eggs were rare, the younger dragons were prized. They had all been rescued from Lorach before they had been trained, which allowed the people within Dragon Haven to establish a connection to the dragons to help ensure they never suffered the way that dragons within Lorach did.

Jason climbed down from the iron dragon's back and patted him on the side, feeling the heat flowed, though not dramatically. He had always managed to withstand the heat coming off the iron dragon and now was no different. He could feel that energy shifting along the dragon's side, practically slipping along the surface of his body. He had considered the dragon a construct of molten metal, though he didn't know if that was an accurate description.

He did seem to be made of metal, which was why his method of flying was so different.

The dragon slithered off, drifting into the forest. He moved quickly and, unsurprisingly, he could move just as quickly along the ground as he could through the air.

Jason looked around the clearing and was surprised that there were no other dragon trainers out. Three of the small hatchlings frolicked near one end of the yard, but there were no other dragons present. He hadn't paid attention to whether the dragons were startled by his arrival with the iron dragon, though he suspected they were not.

Dragon Haven was built centuries ago, and by people who revered the dragons, the artifacts scattered all throughout the city fascinated Jason. Some were sculptures, markers of power that the dragons once possessed, and others were in the style of the buildings themselves. Many buildings were made of stone, though with curves that didn't exist anywhere else. None seemed made of wood—or any that were had long ago decayed.

Dragon Haven was a massive city, far larger than the population who occupied it now. Those who did were all part of the rebellion battling with the people of Lorach, striving for the freedom of the dragons.

He headed into the city. There were others out, though many were people Jason didn't know. Dragon Haven was large enough that there were often people he didn't know, but he was often absent from the city as well, which made getting to know the people a little bit more difficult. He made his way along the cobbled street and found himself meandering along the outskirts of the forest. It was as if he avoided going into the city.

In reality, that was part of what he was doing. He was aware enough to acknowledge that he had no interest in visiting with his mother, especially as she was the person he avoided most. He felt betrayed by her, though he knew he shouldn't. After wandering, Jason found himself at the edge of the forest, the city behind him. He stared toward the trees. This place was so much warmer than his home. When he had grown up living in the northern mountains, suffering with the cold and the ice, he had come to terms with what it meant to survive there. He had grown skilled, competent, even, at survival. In order to thrive in his village, that was a necessity.

The only difference now was that Jason recognized that what he had been doing was not living. Even now, he wasn't entirely sure that what he was doing was living. It felt as if he were singularly focused, tied to helping dragons, which perhaps was not necessarily a bad thing.

"I think you've been avoiding me."

Jason turned to see his mother standing behind him. She was dressed in clothes befitting Dragon Haven: a loose-fitting pale blue dress cinched at the waist with a leather strap. A pouch hung over one shoulder, and he could imagine that she had it filled with medicines and herbs that she had collected outside the city. As a healer, his mother would have been valued in any place, not the least within Dragon Haven. Jason's connection to the dragons, and the power they lent him to heal others, could only go so far. It couldn't be used to restore everyone, even though the power often felt limitless.

"I haven't been avoiding you. There are things that I'm responsible for."

She nodded, her hands clasped in front of her as she watched him. It was strange for him to see her like this after she had been so long incapacitated. She looked... well. He had spent so much time trying to ensure that she survived, that she was cared for, and now that she was upright and active and alert, he knew that he should be pleased that he had helped her, but he couldn't shake the feeling that he'd been misled his entire life.

"You've always been the responsible one."

"That was Father," he said, turning away.

She joined him at the edge of the forest. "It's easier for me to collect some of the medicines here."

Jason glanced over. Her graying hair was pulled back into a braid. The wrinkles along the corners of her eyes were deeper than he remembered, and there was a hint of a frown etched across her face, something so familiar to him, along with the determined set to her jaw.

"After he was gone, you took over his responsibilities. Neither Kayla nor I would have survived were it not for you."

Jason nodded. "I did what I needed to do," he said.

"And he would've been proud of the man that you've become," she said.

Jason looked at her. "He taught me what I needed to know."

"Did he?" She started to reach for him but withdrew when Jason stiffened. "I wonder if perhaps we made a mistake bringing you there."

"You didn't bring me there. You had me there."

She nodded. "I suppose that's true."

"You suppose?" He had wondered when he was younger how his mother had learned the different healing arts that she had mastered. There weren't many within his village who had her same knowledge of medicines and herbs. It was possible she had learned some of it in Varmin, the larger city down the back slope of the mountain, though he had never known for certain. She didn't speak of it. Now he understood why. "Why that place?"

"You would like to do this now?"

"Is there another time?"

She started to smile, but it faded quickly. She watched him before turning to look back out toward the forest. "I have been trying to talk with you for weeks. Ever since you learned, you've avoided me."

"I haven't been avoiding you." Distantly, Jason was aware of the iron dragon as he moved through the forest and felt the heat of their connection. Within the iron dragon was a sense of anger and rage that always seemed to boil beneath the surface. That anger stemmed from what had been done to him when he was younger, the way that he had been captured and held within cells deep beneath the ground, and it was that anger that bonded him to Jason. Because of that connection, he could use the heat of the iron dragon. "There has been much I've needed to do. The last few weeks have been filled with preparations for dealing with Lorach. Jessica knows about the dragons now, and she *will* bring the Dragon Souls to us."

"They have known about Dragon Haven for years," his mother said softly.

"Known about, but they haven't known how to find it."

"You have protected it." She glanced up at the sky. From this vantage, the illusion was translucent. Few within Dragon Haven knew it even existed. There was no need. It was better for the people of Dragon Haven to believe that the city itself was protected, and they didn't need to know that he had placed the illusion to offer an additional layer of protection. It would only make them scared. "From what I understand, you have control over powers we didn't fully understand within Lorach."

"By that, you mean illusion."

She glanced over at him before nodding. "I learned enough of it," she started. "We had to, for us to remain hidden."

"I gathered that much," Jason said.

"I figured you had. We hated that we had to hide it from you and your sister, but we thought that it was necessary."

"Why, though?"

"To ensure your safety. Had we not, you would have been targeted."

Jason pointed to one of his eyes. "What about this? You didn't cover this."

She shook her head. "Placing an illusion over ourselves was fairly straightforward, but placing it over someone else..." She shook her head again. "Especially when you were away from us. It became more difficult. You had some talent, but other than the enhanced eyesight it permitted you, we never really worried about it. There were few in the north who understood it, anyway."

"It made me different," Jason said.

"There were many things that made you different," she said softly.

Jason grunted. As much as he wanted to deny it, there was no point in doing so. He was a misfit, no different than the dragons that he worked with. He, like the dragons, did not fit in.

Even within Dragon Haven, Jason didn't necessarily fit in. He tried, and with his connection to the dragons, he was allowed to remain, and more than that, he was trusted to work with others here, if only so that he could help them understand the dragons better, but he still wasn't like them. Jason didn't know if he could be. Perhaps he never would be.

"Did he ever know I could use this power?"

His mother shook her head. "I would be lying if I told you he knew. That I knew. Neither of us believed that it was possible. Not without having the opportunity to connect to a dragon."

Jason closed his eyes. He could feel the distant ice

dragon flying high overhead. His energy was there, circling. He had to do nothing more than focus on the ice dragon and call to him, and he would come. He would prefer to be with either of them than talking about this with his mother, but he had avoided it too long.

"I don't know that I ever would have learned about my connection were it not for one of the misfits. And because of Father, I had that opportunity."

She looked over at him. "I don't know how much he knew that he was helping a dragon versus harming a Dragon Soul."

Jason remembered his conversation with Therin and how he had believed that Jason had come across the egg by chance. Knowing what he did now of his father, and believing that he had been involved in placing the egg, left Jason wondering if perhaps it had been more coordinated than he had realized. If only he had the opportunity to talk to Therin, to question him and see what he might really have known.

If he were really looking to the past, wishing he had an opportunity to speak to someone who was dead, he would wish for a chance to speak to his father. That opportunity was gone, and now he had to piece together aspects of what he might have been able to learn from his father. It was more difficult than Jason could imagine.

"What happened?" When he had first learned that his parents were Dragon Souls, he had been shocked to the point that he hadn't questioned, not like he wanted to. His mother had offered him answers, but they were more placating answers, not real in-depth responses. Given how she had been sick and had recently recovered, Jason wasn't sure if she would be able to offer him the answers that he wanted. Now, looking at her and how vibrant and alive she looked, and having heard from others within the city that she had taken to wandering the forest and collecting various leaves and roots and herbs for her medicines, he had to believe that she was well enough to answer questions. "Why did you leave Lorach?"

She shook her head slowly. "Many people leave Lorach."

"How many Dragon Souls leave?"

She took a deep breath, letting it out slowly. "Not many," she said softly. "We weren't as powerful as some." She shrugged, glancing over at him before turning away again. "Strong enough, though. We had a connection to dragons and had been training with them. We were learning what those connections meant, but neither of us had ever progressed far enough to be sent out on missions to face the rebellion."

Jason looked behind him toward Dragon Haven. "You didn't have to fight anyone here?"

She shook her head. "I think if we would have, coming here would've been harder for me, but also for them."

He shrugged. "I'm not so sure that's true. The people of Dragon Haven are far more forgiving than you would give them credit for. There's another who came to Dragon Haven and has been welcomed."

"Maybe," she said. "I think if we would have been

responsible for harming others of the rebellion, or the Dragon Guard, we may not have been welcomed here quite the same way."

Jason grunted. "Henry was."

Her brow furrowed. "I haven't seen him," she said softly.

"No? He hasn't really been difficult to find. He has a distinct appearance. Between his beard, and…" Jason frowned. He supposed that Henry wouldn't be dressed in the same furs as he had been dressed in when Jason had first encountered him. Henry would wear clothing more suited for Dragon Haven. "Anyway. Between his beard and his connection to the dragons, I suppose he should be easy enough to find."

His mother let out a long sigh. "I haven't seen him. I don't know that he would even recognize me, though I knew him."

"Why?"

She turned to Jason, shaking her head. "Some things are not for me to share."

Jason frowned. He knew Henry had had a difficult time within Lorach. The scars on him were a testament to that, but other than his time serving as a Dragon Soul, Jason didn't know all that much about him. It was because of Henry that Jason had come to Dragon Haven, but there would have to be more about him. More secrets.

"You should go to him. Tell him."

His mother shook her head. "And what would I tell him?"

"I don't know. That you are like him. That he's not alone." Jason thought about his experience with Henry, and what the old Dragon Soul had gone through. He had suffered. Within Dragon Haven, Henry was unique as the only person—or had been, prior to Jason's mother's arrival—to have escaped from Lorach. "You could even help with the dragons. They could use somebody who has a connection to them."

She tensed. "I don't think they would permit that."

Jason frowned. "Why don't you think so?"

"I might have a connection to the dragons, or have had one, but for me to find that again is… Well, I suppose that it's impossible. I have lost it. That time is behind me."

"It doesn't have to be," Jason said.

She took a deep breath, drawing herself up and turning to him. She still hadn't unclasped her hands. There was a tension within her that surprised him, mostly because he suspected that tension was because of him.

For so long, Jason had wanted to do whatever he could to protect his mother and sister, to allow them to survive —and thrive. They had struggled and had barely held on, especially after his father's death.

Learning now that his parents had been Dragon Souls, and they had come to the north willingly, escaping from Lorach, changed things for him.

Perhaps not significantly, though. He never would have learned about the misfits had he grown up in Lorach. He might have ended up as a Dragon Soul.

The idea gave him pause.

"I've wondered what Father would have said to me had he learned what I could do with the dragons," Jason admitted.

"I suspect he would be proud of you," she said.

"Proud?"

She nodded. "One of the things that we felt was that the dragons deserved more. While they are well cared for in Lorach, there is something off about the training methods they use. There were quite a few people within Lorach who felt the dragons deserved more. When you first encounter one, when you realize just how intelligent they are, when you see the power within those dragons, you come to understand that they are more. They deserve more." She looked over and fell silent for a moment. "Of course, you already know that."

Jason nodded. "I know that."

She chuckled, shaking her head. "I should be more careful. I don't need to lecture to you about the dragons."

"It's interesting hearing you talk about them in that way," he said.

"Why is that?"

"Only that everybody within the village feared the dragons. It was difficult for me to get over that."

"For good reason," his mother said. "Considering how the dragons were controlled by the Dragon Souls, it was safer for you to fear them. It was safer for you to believe the dragons should be feared."

Jason shook his head. "That's just the problem, though. As people fear dragons, it makes it more difficult to rescue them. It makes it more difficult for us to create a time where the dragons can live freely." He thought of the ballistae the village possessed, and how the villagers were trained to use them on dragons, attempting to hurt the dragons if they came too close to the village itself. In Jason's lifetime, they had never been fired at dragons, and he knew that it had been generations since they had been, but there were those within the village who felt dragons deserved to be targeted.

"Is that your goal?" she asked.

"Is what my goal?"

"To free the dragons?"

Jason took a deep breath, letting it out slowly. "I want to ensure the dragons aren't forced to serve. If that means freeing them"—and as far as he knew, that was what it was going to take, and thankfully with his connection to the dragon misfits, he could do so—"then that is what I will do. I have already freed dozens of dragons from Lorach. I intend to do the same again."

She watched him, and the frown on her face faded, if only for a moment. "I believe you," she said.

Jason snorted. Even though she believed him, he wasn't at all sure it even mattered. Not anymore. All that mattered was that he would do what was necessary to help the dragons. All that mattered was that he would ensure they were allowed to fly freely. If it meant sending them all to Dragon Haven, then so be it. These lands were sparsely populated as it was. They wouldn't pose a danger. Still, having flown with the dragons as much as he had, he knew the world was enormous. He had seen only a small slice of it. With as many dragons as existed within Lorach, what might it be like were they to all scatter, flying freely?

He thought of what David had once shared with him, how the people of Lorach were reassured by the idea that dragons were trained and could not use their destructive power against the people of Lorach. Would others grow to fear dragons the same way if dragons weren't controlled?

He pushed those thoughts aside. Fearing what might be was not going to keep him from what he knew needed to happen.

"What happened to the dragons you were to bond with?" Jason asked.

His mother watched him for a moment, then finally shook her head. "It doesn't matter."

"It does. You were progressing within the Dragon Souls. You were going to learn their secrets. You were training to work with the dragons. Something changed."

"*We* changed," she said softly.

As Jason watched her, he realized that she wasn't going to share with him. Perhaps it didn't matter, but Jason couldn't shake the feeling that it did matter somehow. In order to know about himself, to understand his parents, he might need to know.

She offered a sad smile. "I hope you don't hate me for what happened."

The irritation within him faded. "I don't hate you. I don't think I could hate you."

"I haven't thanked you for everything that you did for me when I was... Well, when I wasn't well."

"You're my mother. Of course I was going to help you."

She pulled him toward her and wrapped him in an embrace, and Jason breathed in before softening for a minute. Still, he couldn't shake the feeling that he needed to better understand more about his parents, more about what had happened and why they had left, and perhaps the only way that he could would be by going to Lorach. It was the one thing he didn't think he could do. Not while Jessica was there and ruling.

It was even more reason for him to remove her—and her influence—from Lorach.

2

The ice dragon circled high overhead. Most dragons could fly high in the sky, piercing clouds and streaking through the upper reaches of the sky, but the ice dragon had a unique ability of doing so more easily than other dragons. He could soar beyond places that other dragons would dare go. Most would find the air too cold and thin, but the ice dragon seemed to thrive on that, which didn't surprise Jason, given his origins.

He clutched the dragon's back, squeezing the spikes on his spine, holding on to him. Bending low, he pressed himself up against the dragon, almost for warmth. The dragonskin he wore kept him as warm as possible, though his connection to the iron dragon augmented it, keeping him protected in ways that the dragonskin would not.

Jason breathed in, trying to fill his lungs. The air was thin, and it was difficult to catch his breath, so he was thankful that the dragon did the work. Were he to have to fight, Jason doubted that he would be able to do so.

He stared down toward the ground, borrowing from the ice dragon's eyesight, and could make out contours flowing beneath him. There was some aspect of the ground that made it easier to see through the ice dragon's eyes. He wasn't looking for gradations of color as he would with the iron dragon. All he searched for now was movement. The ice dragon was skilled at looking for that.

"Have you seen anything?" he asked, barely getting the words out.

The ice dragon roared softly, a rumble coming from him. "There is nothing," he said.

"Nothing?"

"There is nothing."

Jason focused on what he might observe, but he still did not see anything. He wasn't nearly as skilled at looking through the ice dragon's eyesight as he was through the iron dragon's. Not because his connection was any less, though there were times when he questioned which of the dragons he was most bonded to, but because of the way the ice dragon's eyesight worked.

Thankfully, seeing nothing was a benefit. He didn't necessarily want to encounter anything, not out here. It was his way of searching and ensuring that Dragon Haven was safe. He had hunted like this with both dragons. Not just the iron dragon, using his eyesight to look for movement, but also with the ice dragon, hoping that by staying connected to him, he could search for Dragon Soul movement.

In the time since speaking with his mother, Jason had found himself avoiding Dragon Haven. Perhaps he should not, but he had questions, and every time he got close to the city, he worried that he would encounter his sister. She deserved answers as well, no differently than Jason did. He would find it challenging to keep from her what he had uncovered, along with his suspicions about their parents.

Something had happened to the dragons.

More than ever, Jason felt that to be the case, but even as he learned more about his parents, and learned more about where they had been and what they had done, he still didn't know enough.

He should have asked her more about Lorach. He should've asked her about how to navigate through the city, through the people, and should have asked her about what she might know about Jessica and her parents and all of the Dragon Souls, only he had not.

What more would she know that Henry did not?

He sighed and continued to focus over the side of the dragon, looking out into the distance, straining to see if there was anything that he might be able to see. He looked for movement, but he also looked for anything that might be out of the ordinary. He didn't necessarily need to lean off the dragon to see, either. He did it because he wondered if there might be something that his own vision might reveal, but he could make out nothing.

He patted the ice dragon's side. "We could head north."

He could feel a hint of amusement within the ice dragon; it came with a soft, rumbling roar. The dragon streaked away, and it took very little time for them to reach the northern mountains. They slowed, circling overhead, and Jason took that opportunity to look out over the mountainous landscape. There was a time while he had been living here that he had believed that the mountains were everything. It was easy enough to think that they went on forever, an endless rolling mountainous landscape, despite knowing others who had descended all the way down the mountain and come back. He could see the mountains now before him, the way they stretched outward, a jagged jaw of rock and snow-peaked mountains. They grew ever taller the farther Jason and the ice dragon went, until the snow covered the entirety of the mountains. Wind whistled this high in the sky, and the ice dragon descended, moving low enough for Jason to feel the wind whipping along his cheeks, to feel the bite of the snow and ice, and to recognize the power that existed here and just how different it was from Dragon Haven. He smiled at it. It wasn't home, but it was no longer as fearsome as it had been when he had been growing up. He knew there was a way to protect himself, and he knew that there was something more beyond here, so he no longer worried the way that he once had.

Jason wrapped himself in the warmth of the iron dragon, using that to protect him. He held onto it, keeping himself warm, which he found ironic, considering that when he had lived here, there were times when he had questioned whether he would ever truly be warm. They had no firewood, nothing other than the dung they burned.

Still, he had survived. The cold had made him stronger.

He didn't need to suffer now. Why should he when he could use his connection to dragons to ensure his own safety? More than that, the ice dragon provided a protection to the cold that he didn't have otherwise. Jason could use that protection, and he didn't need to fear the cold the way that he once had.

They circled, moving lower and lower, closer to the ground, as he continued staring. He caught sight of his village.

"I didn't say we *had* to go there," Jason said.

The ice dragon grunted. "You wanted to return. That tells me that you wanted to come here."

"I don't know if this is where I wanted to come or whether I needed to come." He sat up, borrowing from the ice dragon's eyesight as he looked down at the mountainside. He could see the wind, something he found interesting. By looking out through the ice dragon's eyes, he could make out swirls and patterns along with the current in the air. Jason no longer felt the cold, as if it had taken a few moments to adjust to it. "I questioned why they came here," he said.

"Would you have had them go elsewhere?"

"I don't know." He'd given it some thought since

learning about his parents. Riding on the dragons, flying with them as they hunted for signs of movement out of Lorach, gave him plenty of time to think. So far, he hadn't come up with much. "They came here because they were running from something," he said. "They had to have been, or why would they have been willing to come so far and risk so much? Otherwise, why come to such an inhospitable place?"

"Is it really so inhospitable?"

Jason smiled to himself. "Perhaps not now, but when I was growing up, it certainly was."

"You became the person you are because of this environment," the dragon said.

Jason knew that was true. He knew that had he not grown up here, he wouldn't have been strong enough to have withstood what he had. It was because of what he had gone through that he had learned what it would take to tolerate the rigors and violence of the Dragon Souls. He had come to the same conclusion. Much like the ice dragon, along with the iron dragon, his environment had shaped him, fueling him in a way that created the man he had become.

"It doesn't make it any easier," he said.

"Life is not easy," the ice dragon said.

Jason chuckled. "You don't have to be so pragmatic."

The dragon roared softly. They circled around the top of Jason's old village before streaking away to the north. "A place like this brings someone a certain pragmatism."

Jason grunted again, chuckling. Perhaps that was true.

The dragon was doing what Jason should've done. He had moved on.

They swept along the mountainside, and gradually they found themselves heading back toward Dragon Haven. Jason looked into the distance, watching the landscape shifting. It went from the mountainous terrain surrounding his old home to a rolling hillside, and finally to the dense forests that would eventually lead to Dragon Haven.

All the while, Jason looked out through the ice dragon's eyes, borrowing from him to see what was out there. There was a flicker of movement.

He tapped on the ice dragon, who followed the movement. It brought them to a small open hillside with a rolling grassy plain near it. Jason peered down from the side of the ice dragon and tapped on his back, asking him to land. When they did, he climbed down and approached the dark blue dragon that he'd seen.

The dragon was curled up on the ground, wrapped around a soft mound of freshly moved earth. Jason had been tempted to tamp the earth down when he had come here to bury David but had felt as if that were not necessary. More than that, he felt as if the dragon didn't want him to.

The dragon looked up, holding his gaze on Jason. "Do you come here often?" Jason asked.

The dragon rested his head again, and Jason realized that he was looking toward the fresh grave. "I come here to mourn," the dragon said.

"I'm sorry," Jason said. He took a seat on the other side of the grave, looking at the mound of earth. "I wish I had a chance to know him better. He seems like he was not the man that I knew him to be."

"He was the man you knew him to be. He sacrificed himself on behalf of the dragons."

Jason took a deep breath, letting it out slowly. He thought of when he had first encountered David and the fear that he'd had of finding a Dragon Soul, and what that might mean for him. He thought of how David had been the one to help him gain a certain understanding of the dragon pearls, learning about them at a time before he truly understood the nature of his connection to the dragons. Over time, David was the reason that Jason had gained an increased understanding of dragons. David was the reason that Jason had begun to grow more powerful.

Perhaps he should have taken more time.

"I've been looking for movement out of Lorach," Jason said.

"They are preparing," the dragon said.

"Preparing for what?"

"Preparing," the dragon said.

Jason frowned to himself. He had no idea what the dragons and Lorach would be doing, only that he didn't doubt that they were readying for something. With enough time, he expected that Lorach would find their way toward them. Jessica was skilled and powerful, and more than that, he knew she was angry at him.

"We are preparing, as well," Jason said.

The dragon looked up, holding his gaze for a moment before turning his attention back to the grave. Perhaps the dragon knew that Jason made an empty promise.

It *was* empty. They were preparing, and the Dragon Guard had been searching for signs of movement out of Lorach, but nothing they did was going to be enough when it came to preventing Lorach from attacking them. Everything that they did was focused on sweeping along the border, trying to ensure that Lorach wasn't there. That did nothing to stop their arrival, though.

That simply wasn't the way the Dragon Guard operated. They never had. They had worked in these lands, dealing with the threat of the Dragon Souls for years, and had battled with them in their own way, but they had done nothing other than delay the Dragon Souls. If Therin had been able to find them in Dragon Haven, Jason had a hard time thinking that Jessica, with all her cunning and creativity, would not be able to do the same.

"If there's anything you can offer that would help us know what we might need to do, you'd have my thanks."

The dragon didn't look up.

It was more than just what the dragon might be able to offer. He had never been trained by Dragon Souls, so far as Jason knew. When he had first encountered David and this dragon, Jason had learned that he had not been under the same influence. The dragon had not been tormented. It was the first time he had come to realize that David was different, though he had known it. He should have known more about what David had done and what he had been willing to do, and he should have known more about the fact that David had refused to attack him, and more than that, had refused to betray the people of Dragon Haven.

Some of that came from the oath that he'd taken, but some of it came from the man himself. It came from his willingness to find a trust within the dragons and his desire to help them.

"Are you afraid we will destroy the dragons?" Jason asked softly.

The blue dragon glanced over at him. "You would not," he said.

"Good. I don't have any intention of harming any dragon. I want to rescue as many as possible."

"Not all are like you," the dragon said.

"The Dragon Guard won't harm the dragons, either."

The blue dragon watched him, and yet, even as he did, Jason realized that the dragon questioned. He doubted. There had to be something that he could say to convince the dragon, only he wasn't sure that words would be convincing enough. It would need action. It would require time.

"I intend to free as many dragons as I can."

The blue dragon breathed out a heavy breath. "There will be too many for you."

"Then I go at them in smaller groups," Jason said.

"There will be too many for you," he said.

"You don't know that. You don't know whether or not I can get to the dragons and free them." Jason forced himself to be confident in that, even though he didn't necessarily feel it. He might have had he not failed recently. Jessica had learned a way of overpowering him and had found a way to reclaim the dragons that he had rescued. If she could, then he suspected she could teach the other Dragon Souls to do the same. It would take more effort on his part. It might be more than he could accomplish. "You could help. I have offered my protection to you."

"I will carry on what he wanted."

Jason looked at the gravesite. "What did he want from you?"

"To live," the dragon said softly.

Heat radiated from him, though nothing like the iron dragon.

Jason had seen dragons mourning before. He had heard their song, the sadness that they cried out with when suffering. He could see the pain within the blue dragon, and he recognized the agony with which this dragon still suffered. He suspected it would be a long time before the dragon moved past it.

Perhaps he never would.

As Jason looked at the dragon, he realized that he could not ask it to help. The dragon needed a chance to mourn, and he deserved an opportunity to come to his own decision.

Still, he was a free dragon. He was powerful—powerful enough that David had recognized that and had worked with him. There was value in that, especially when it came to dealing with the threat of Jessica.

"If there's anything that you can do to help, I would appreciate it. If you can find me, then…"

Jason knew that he didn't need to finish. The dragon watched him, breathing out again before resting his head once more.

Jason stared at him for a few moments before getting to his feet and making his way over to the ice dragon and climbing onto his back. Once he was seated, they launched into the air, cold surrounding him once again. Jason embraced the cold, clutching the ice dragon, feeling that cold surge through him. He breathed out a sigh and looked down at the blue dragon as they circled higher into the air.

"How long will he suffer like that?"

"Only he knows," the dragon said.

"Would you do the same were that me?"

The dragon roared, shaking everything within him, and icicles streaked off him. "I would kill the one responsible," the ice dragon said.

They banked and had started toward Dragon Haven when a strange pressure built. Jason frowned, sitting upright on the dragon, and motioned for him to turn. It brought them back toward the mountains, heading over the forest, and from there to the rolling plains that stretched to the base of the mountain.

Jason stared through his connection to the ice dragon, using that to find anything that would permit him to know what he felt, but he couldn't tell what was out there, only that there was some sense of power.

"Do you feel that?"

"I feel something," the ice dragon said.

They needed to get lower. Up high like this, Jason didn't think that he could see well enough, and he needed to descend to understand the power. Maybe it was nothing more than the energy of another dragon, though he couldn't shake the feeling that it was something else. If that were the case, then he wondered if perhaps it might be a dragon.

He hadn't abandoned his desire to find more dragon misfits. That was still necessary. The last dragon misfit he had encountered had been the storm dragon, but before that had been the jungle dragon—who had died before Jason had an opportunity to help him. He believed there had to be more misfits out in the world. Therin had not simply placed a handful of eggs. He would've placed many.

"Could it be one of your hatch mates?"

The ice dragon rumbled, and Jason could feel a surge of power as he attempted to probe outward, as if testing whether or not he might detect one of his hatch mates. More than Jason, the ice dragon hunted for them. Had he found any, Jason would've expected the ice dragon to have shared that with him, but there had been no word of the hatch mates, which meant that there were either no more or they were scattered beyond where the ice dragon had looked.

They banked again, heading lower to the ground, moving closer and closer to the pressure that Jason detected. As they lowered, he borrowed from the ice dragon's eyesight again. This was a time when using the iron dragon might've been beneficial. With the iron dragon, he would have radiation heat and could have seen whether there was anything more down there than what he could tell otherwise. With the ice dragon, it was simply movements, layers of color.

What about his own eyesight?

Jason had dragon sight. He could use that.

He peered off the side of the ice dragon, closing his normal eye. As he stared, it took a moment for his eye to adjust, but then his breath caught. There were a dozen bright surges of color down in front of him. It was so bright that he knew exactly what they were: Dragons.

There were far too many dragons for them to be the Dragon Guard, especially out where they were. The Dragon Guard wouldn't have ventured this far away, not risking themselves like this. No, that meant that these were Dragon Souls.

"We need to be careful," Jason said.

"You wanted to help them," the ice dragon reminded him.

Jason nodded. There were a dozen. A dozen Dragon Souls, along with their dragons, might be more than he could attempt to free, but if Jessica weren't there, maybe he had a chance.

"Stay above them. Don't let them know you are here."

The dragon roared. "They won't."

They ascended again, and Jason shifted, peering off the

side of the ice dragon. He held onto one of the ice dragon's spikes, gripping it tightly. There had been a time when he had feared that he might break the spike off, but he had found that the ice dragon was in complete control of whether those spikes came free. He could shoot them, but he also could grant them were it necessary.

Jason looked down, studying the ground. He could see the dragons as surges of light far below, looking something like a cluster of stars on the ground. He focused on the power within the ice and iron dragon, calling it to him. It took a washing of power, and he thought that he could add a hint of the energy of the forest dragon to it, using that to mingle the two and hopefully save these dragons. They would toss the Dragon Souls, but Jason had long ago decided that it did not matter to him.

"Be ready," he said.

He borrowed power, pushing it out from him. As it pressed downward, he could feel a resistance. It came from the dragons, and though he pushed downward, he hoped that the dragons wouldn't recognize the source of what he was doing. Not until he was done. Jason continued to press, feeling that resistance.

He leaned over the edge of the dragon, looking down as he continued to call upon power, trying to see what he could from this vantage.

There was nothing.

"We need to get closer," he said.

The dragon roared.

Getting closer put them in danger, but he wanted to

free these dragons. They were sweeping along this grassy plain, but they were heading closer to Dragon Haven. If they got much closer, they would find the city.

Jason needed to free these dragons. If he didn't, there was a real possibility that the Dragon Souls would find them and would know what they were doing and how to uncover them. He needed to defend against them merely so that they could ensure that Dragon Haven remained safe.

Jason took a deep breath, holding onto it as they descended, getting closer and closer to the dragons. He peered over the edge of the ice dragon, watching them. He could see their brightness growing larger, looming closer.

As they dropped, he continued to push power out, borrowing from the ice and the iron dragon, mixing with it the energy of the forest dragon.

Something was off.

Maybe it was the resistance that he attempted to grasp, but he couldn't shake the feeling that some aspect of his connection felt off.

He tried again, forcing more power out, toward the dragons.

It met resistance, which didn't surprise him. He expected that resistance and expected that Jessica would've trained the people of Lorach to handle anything that he might do, but this was unusual.

Then there was another sort of strange pressure.

Jason tapped on the ice dragon, and they stopped their descent, circling. He looked down and could see the glowing orange of the Dragon Souls, but something about it felt off.

"Do you detect anything?"

The ice dragon roared softly, and Jason knew he didn't.

What was it that he detected, then?

Was it just the Dragon Souls?

Could it be Jessica herself?

He wouldn't have expected her to come out here by herself. Not with a dozen dragons, not to face the possible threat of Dragon Haven. Jessica was too clever for that. She would've sent the full force of the dragons out were she to come. Whatever this was would be different. Perhaps just as powerful, but different nonetheless.

Jason pulled on the energy within him, and he held off on borrowing from the forest dragon. That power was useful, but not so useful that he thought he could use it now. Instead, what he needed was to call upon the others, those dragon misfits that could heal. The Dragon Souls dragons needed that healing.

Jason had to force as much as he could, and he pushed downward, letting that energy sweep away from him, toward the orange lights that he saw in the distance. In doing so, he could feel the resistance, and focusing now as he did, getting closer, he pressed as much power as he could downward, forcing that power away from him.

Finally, the resistance began to ease.

Then something pushed back on him.

Jason forced even more, pressing with everything that

he could, summoning the cold through the ice dragon, sweeping it downward. Maybe the problem was that he was trying to target too many dragons at one time.

He shifted his focus, looking down and trying to focus only on one dragon at a time. When he had helped heal the dragons within Lorach, he had handled more than one at once, but perhaps with whatever Jessica had done, teaching the Dragon Souls how to defend themselves, he wasn't going to be able to use that power in the same way.

By shifting that focus, targeting only a single dragon, Jason pushed outward. He felt the resistance, but this time, it started to slip past. He forced even more and could summon more power. He had to borrow it, and he had to call it from the ice dragon, letting it shoot from the sky overhead, borrowing the energy in its purest form.

It streaked toward him and through him—as Jason was mostly just a conduit—and down toward the ground. He added as much power as he could from the iron dragon. Perhaps it would be easier with the iron dragon here, but as he forced that power downward, he felt the resistance fading.

Something pushed back against him again.

There came a shriek.

Not a roar, but a shriek. It sounded painful and horrible, and it tore at Jason's ears.

He jerked his head back, and the ice dragon moved with him.

The pressure upon him continued to build, ripping upward.

They weren't going to be able to do this.

Jason tapped on the ice dragon. "We need to go back," he said.

The ice dragon roared softly. There was a hesitation within him, mostly because the dragon didn't want to leave any other dragons behind if there would be anything they could do to help them, but Jason doubted they could. Not like this. There were too many together.

The ice dragon climbed, circling quickly. As they did, there came more pressure.

He could feel it pushing against him.

They reached the higher atmosphere again, circling once more, and Jason stayed there, looking down from the dragon's side, staring at the ground, and couldn't tell whether the other dragons were still there. As he peered from the ice dragon's back, he searched for signs of those dragons but found nothing.

They had disappeared.

That shouldn't be possible. They could've flown away, but Jason thought he would've seen something. More than that, he would've expected the dragons to have given chase, but they had not. It was as if they had abandoned Jason and the ice dragon, ignoring them.

Something was off, and Jason feared he needed to understand what it was before Lorach began their attack on Dragon Haven.

3

As they circled toward Lorach, Jason peered over the edge of the ice dragon, looking down at the ground, mixing his dragon sight with what the ice dragon saw, though he couldn't make out anything more than what he had noticed before. The land beneath him had no movement. Ever since pulling away and leaving the large grouping of dragons, Jason had found nothing. Not that he had not tried. He wanted to ensure there was no further movement, that the Dragon Souls had not come toward them, but he had seen nothing more. He still believed there was something taking place; it was just a matter of figuring out what it was.

"I don't know how much longer we should stay away," Jason said.

"Will the others have expected you back?"

Jason shook his head. He hadn't revealed to anyone else where he was going, only that he was hunting. They had come to know that he would go off on his own, and so far, no one had objected to him doing so—mostly because when he did, there was nothing that could be done to stop him. He wasn't one of the Dragon Guard, so he didn't have to answer to them. Given that the dragons he flew with were not dragons from Dragon Haven, there was no reason to worry about angering them, either.

"I feel like we need to find something," Jason said. "The Dragon Souls wouldn't have abandoned their search."

"What if they haven't abandoned it?"

Jason frowned, looking down. "What do you mean?"

"What if somebody deflected them?"

He didn't think so. He had felt the resistance that was down on the ground, and had felt the way that the Dragon Souls were pushing against him. That couldn't have been somebody else. That had to be the Dragon Souls, working against him.

He just had to find where the rest were.

In the distance, Jason could barely make out the outer edge of Lorach. They were high enough that he didn't worry about the people of Lorach knowing that they were there, but he was still careful. He didn't want to have anyone from Lorach—especially Jessica—realize that they were patrolling and watching for movement. He could see a faint glow through his dragon sight, though it wasn't bright enough to know whether what he observed was anything to be alarmed by. He saw no sign of the dragons, though were he to fly farther, they would. The dragon pens were just beyond the border of Lorach, outside the city where the people of Lorach wouldn't fear them.

"They were moving," he said to himself.

"We saw several, but Lorach has many more dragons," the ice dragon reminded him.

"What if they have them all scattered and hunting?" Jason asked. "Jessica could be sending waves of dragons out to find us."

He turned, looking toward Dragon Haven, though they were far enough away he couldn't make out anything of it. He scanned the horizon, searching for anything that might give him an idea of what would be out there, whether there were dragons to fear, but he saw nothing. Had there been anything out there, Jason would've expected to have come across it by now.

"Somehow, we have to stop her," he said.

"Stop her, or stop the dragons?" the ice dragon asked.

Jason ran his hand along the slick surface of the ice dragon. It wasn't cold, though he was pressed up against a dragon made of ice. The dragonskin he wore offered some protection and trapped some of the heat within him, but even that probably wasn't necessary. Jason had never needed protection around the ice dragon. "I want to free the dragons, not stop them."

"Not all dragons will be freed," the ice dragon said, his voice coming softly and filled with a hint of sadness.

"Do you really believe that?"

"I believe you want to save as many as possible, but I also believe it will be difficult for us to do so."

"They aren't going to succeed," Jason said.

The dragon rumbled again. "I fear for the other dragons."

"You fear for them as much as you fear for the misfits?"

The ice dragon turned his head, looking at Jason as they circled. "There are few who worry about us."

"I do," Jason said.

"As I said. Few."

He took a deep breath. "What if we had a way of helping others like you?"

"That is what you intend to do," the ice dragon said.

"What if it's more," Jason said, thinking it through. When he had been in Lorach, he remembered Jessica telling him about Therin and his goal of creating more misfits. Jessica knew something about their creation, even if she had not revealed it. That had to matter somehow. "What if we knew how to create dragons like yourself?"

There was a part of Jason that wondered if that was even something he should do. The misfits were misfits. They were unlike other dragons, but that didn't make them less than the other dragons. In some ways, Jason found the misfits to be more powerful than the traditional dragons of the Dragon Souls. By connecting to them, by understanding them in the way that he did, he had found something unique and beautiful and powerful. If he could do the same with more misfits and create others, then perhaps they wouldn't have to be so different. He could imagine what the ice dragon would think if there were a dozen like him. Perhaps the same with the iron dragon.

Even the forest dragon. Would the world be a better or worse place if he did that?

Was it even something he should be doing?

There seemed to be an ethical aspect to it that Jason considered. Therin had forced these dragons to become something different. How many eggs had not survived in the attempt to create misfits? Of course, the standard way of creating dragons was by keeping them near other dragons, which ensured that they all were uniform. Maybe the dragons were meant to be misfits. Maybe the dragons within Lorach were the misfits.

"I don't know," the ice dragon said.

"Have you thought about it?"

The ice dragon turned away from him and roared softly, a heavy rumbling. "I have considered it before, but I don't know."

Jason couldn't help but think about what it might be like for there to be other dragons like that in the world. He couldn't help but think about how useful that would be, and how much easier it would be for them to counter Lorach. That was what this was all about, after all. They needed to find a way to stop Lorach, to ensure the safety of the dragons, and to free them. If they could have that connection, and if they had some way of binding to the dragons, then perhaps he could do that.

He was getting ahead of himself.

He didn't fully understand what all was involved in the creation of the misfits. All he knew was that Therin had taken eggs—something that Jason found surprising, especially given how rare the eggs were—and had put them in places where they would struggle without any additional help. It was a wonder that so many of the misfits had survived. How many eggs had not?

Or maybe they had survived but the egg had not yet hatched.

There was simply so much about the gestation of dragons that Jason didn't know. Perhaps he could not know.

"I guess I don't know either," Jason said.

They continued circling, never getting close enough to Lorach to pose much of a threat, neither of them wanting to reveal their presence. As high in the sky as they were, he didn't think they would, but he couldn't tell, either.

"Perhaps it's time for us to return," Jason said.

"And do what?" The ice dragon roared softly and swooped even higher, as if shooting toward the sky, trying to move beyond Lorach.

"It's time to come up with a plan for Lorach. A real plan."

They had spent enough time thinking and talking and not as much time preparing. Jessica would be doing something. Having seen the dragons, he knew that she would.

He continued to stare, focusing on what he could make out of Lorach, and for a moment, he thought he saw a cluster of dragons, but this high up, it was difficult to tell. Even borrowing from the ice dragon, he couldn't see very easily. If he came with the iron dragon, he might be able to see more, but he also had difficulty with that idea. The iron dragon couldn't fly nearly as high, which meant they were more likely to be observed. It was easier to scout and spy from as high as the ice dragon could fly.

He tore his gaze away, and they turned, making their way back toward Dragon Haven. As they flew, Jason peered over the edge of the dragon, borrowing from the ice dragon's eyesight and adding his own dragon sight. He stared at the ground, searching for any signs of movement. Other than a stray herd of deer, he didn't see much. The ice dragon wasn't in the mood to descend low enough for Jason to get a better vantage, either.

As they neared Dragon Haven, the ice dragon streaked through the illusion, giving Jason barely an opportunity to detect whether there was anything off about it. He tested it, nonetheless. It seemed solid, but as he ensured that it was still intact, they came crashing to the ground.

He looked up at the sky, focusing on the illusion, but couldn't see it. It was there. He could feel it, but he couldn't tell if it was as solid as it needed to be. He thought that it was, but if not, he didn't know how much more he could pour into it to ensure its stability. He had already pushed as much power as he thought that he could into it.

Climbing off the ice dragon's back, he looked over at him. "What will you be doing?"

"Hunting," the ice dragon said.

"Hunting for Lorach, or hunting for your hatch mates?"

The ice dragon stared at him, and there came a surge

of power from him. Within the ice dragon, Jason felt the connection that the ice dragon shared with others. It was strange to be so aware of it, but it was a bond that had formed between the ice dragon and the iron dragon and the forest dragon, going all the way to even the storm dragon, though Jason didn't share in that connection. The ice dragon wanted to have a better understanding of the other misfits and wanted to connect to them.

"Hunting."

"Good luck," Jason said.

The dragon rumbled softly before pulling his wings in and launching upward. It was a strange sight to see from the ground. The ice dragon had taken to flying with a different technique than he had before. Now he used the cold, the ice, and shot upward as if sliding on a sheet of ice lightning. It was powerful and amazing and something that Jason wished he could learn how to do.

Pulling his gaze away when the dragon disappeared through the illusion, he looked around. There were four small dragons here today. Two were little green dragons, one was a red dragon that he knew William had been working with, and another was a pale yellow dragon. They had looked over at him when he had landed with the ice dragon, but now that the dragon was gone, they turned their attention away. Jason watched the dragons for a while. It was interesting to see them frolicking and to notice how carefree they were. At this point, the small dragons feared nothing. There was no reason for them to, though. They'd not experienced the threat of the Dragon

Souls, not the way that so many of the older dragons had. These dragons lived a life where they were practically revered. Certainly protected. There was no danger to them the way that there was for the older dragons.

Jason took a deep breath and turned to see William watching him. His friend's bright red hair stood on end, and he was dressed in a black jacket and pants that had dragon scales worked into them, though Jason didn't think they were dragonskin.

"I haven't seen you around much lately," William said.

Jason flicked his gaze up, where he could still feel the sense of the ice dragon as he circled. "I've been busy trying to chase down any sign of the Dragon Souls."

William shivered. "That's probably good," he said. "When we were there..."

He didn't need to finish. He had been through quite a bit and had been trapped by Jessica, no differently than Jason had. Unlike Jason, William had been unable to escape on his own.

He didn't seem the worse for it. William always liked to say that he was lucky, and considering everything that he had been through without any real connection to the dragons, Jason had started to believe him. When he had shared that with David, David had questioned, only because he seemed to think there was something to it.

"Have you found anything?" William asked, glancing over at the dragons as they played behind Jason.

"I thought I did, but I lost it."

"The Dragon Souls?"

"They aren't close," Jason said.

At least, he hoped that they weren't close. Now that he wasn't sure where they had gone, he worried that perhaps he had missed something. If they had come this way, Jason thought that he would've seen them, but he had not. He and the ice dragon had circled for long enough to have uncovered something, and the fact that he had not left him thinking that perhaps he didn't need to worry about them getting here. Not yet, at least. Eventually, he did worry that there would be some danger from those dragons.

He would have to figure out why he couldn't rescue them. He had felt the resistance within them, and if it came from something Jessica had taught them, Jason was going to have to find a way to overpower it. He would need to do so to free the dragons. The alternative was… It was unthinkable.

The alternative meant that they couldn't defeat Lorach. It meant that they were going to have to hide. If Lorach kept coming toward them and was determined to find Dragon Haven, Jason didn't know if he could stay hidden well enough for long enough to protect the dragons.

"I'm sure others will be glad you're back," William said, grinning at him.

"Others?"

"You know. Sarah. She's been asking about you, though I get the sense her parents don't like it when she travels with you."

Jason shook his head. Cherise and Olar might rule in Dragon Haven, but they also were protective of Sarah. Mostly because any time that she had gone off with Jason, she had put herself into danger. Sarah had a responsibility to Dragon Haven, and it was one she would not be able to fulfill if she ended up injured because of him.

"I think after her captivity in Lorach, they have been much more protective."

"She doesn't like it," William told him.

Jason snorted. "Knowing her, she probably doesn't. Where is she?"

"With them. They have been meeting with the Dragon Guard." William shivered again. "They scare me a little bit. If I didn't know they were on our side, I would probably be even more frightened of them."

Jason patted him on the shoulder. "You don't need to fear the Dragon Guard. They work with us."

"They remind me of the Dragon Souls. Maybe they don't torment the dragons the same way," William said, twisting so that he could look deeper into the city, as if he were going to see one of the Dragon Guard, before turning back. "They still make me nervous."

"What about you? What have you been doing since we returned from Lorach?"

Jason spent so little time within Dragon Haven these days, preferring to travel with the dragons, searching for evidence of Lorach moving toward them, that he hadn't visited with his friend the way that he should have. He regretted it now.

"Working with the dragons." William nodded to the younger dragons behind him. "Before you go and tease me, I know that I don't have the same connection you do. That doesn't mean that I can't work with them. Besides, I feel like I'm getting through to them."

He smiled at one of the dragons, and Jason turned to see him looking at the red dragon. He was a little bit larger than some of the others, though not nearly large enough yet to ride. At least, Jason didn't think so. The dragon had strength, though. He could feel it emanating from the dragon, a particular surge of heat and energy that suggested the dragon would be mighty one day. When he was fully grown, Jason could imagine this dragon helping the people of Dragon Haven in ways that were hard to predict now. Eventually, the dragon would have to connect to others who could use that power and would be able to draw upon it. When that happened, William would no longer be able to work with it the way that he did now. He suspected that would bother his friend.

"I'm sure you have been," Jason said. He sighed. "I'm going to meet with Cherise and Olar. I need to see what they are planning to do about Lorach, and be a part of it."

"Why wouldn't you be a part of it?"

"Well, mostly because I am not one of the Dragon Guard, but partly because I think they see me as a little bit of an unpredictable element."

William chuckled. "You *are* that. Of course, I have a

little bit of experience with something similar. I could go with you, if you want."

"I don't think that you need to. Besides, it looks like you came out here for a reason. Your dragon needs you."

"He's not my dragon," William said, shaking his head as he looked across the yard. "He's just one that I have been working with. I work with all of them, really."

"That one is the easiest for you, though."

William nodded. "How did you know?"

"You have a fondness for it. I can see it in your eyes."

William smiled. "Maybe I do. That one amuses me. Did you know that the dragons have different personalities? I never would've guessed that before, but they do. Some of them have a sense of humor, and others are a lot more serious. This one is a little bit of both, depending upon his mood. He can be frustrating, but I think he does it intentionally." William made a face as he looked over at the dragon. "I'm going to get through to him."

Jason followed the direction of William's gaze, and he chuckled softly. "I think you've gotten through to him already."

"Do you?"

"I do, and I think you're probably right. He probably is doing it intentionally. Have you asked him?"

"I talk to the dragons all the time, but they don't talk back. Not like they do to you."

"I think eventually you'll be able to hear them."

"That would make all of this a lot easier," William sighed.

Jason didn't know what made one person more sensitive to the dragons speaking to them than another. All he knew was that some people were, and others were not. He could listen to the dragons and speak to almost every dragon, though he knew that wasn't the case for everybody.

He glanced over at the dragon and wondered if he might be able to encourage him to speak to William, but decided that William needed to work that out on his own. It would be better for him—and it would mean more, anyway.

Jason clasped William on the shoulder and headed past him, moving along the streets of Dragon Haven. He made his way toward the main building within the center of the city. It was taller than most of the other buildings, though it had a domed roof like every other. He stopped in front of the main entrance. It had a wide arc at the top of its double door, with dragons made of a metal print pressed into the door, a design that showed the celebration of the dragons within Dragon Haven. Jason often wondered what this city must've been like at its founding. The people who had lived here back then had idolized the dragons, though the people who lived here now still did. He wondered what it might've been like when dragons were numerous, flying through here and more openly. He believed there was a time when that occurred, even though it wasn't the case now.

He headed into the building, making his way through the halls, passing sculptures and paintings and other decorations, all depicting the dragons. Lanterns glowed in the walls, all of them shaped like dragons. He reached the throne room and paused. There was no movement and no sound, but he knew that others were there. He could hear them inside, but surprisingly, he could also feel them.

Jason waited a moment before stepping inside. Once inside, he found Sarah sitting on what appeared to be a throne alongside her parents. She shared much of the same look as her mother, the same golden hair, the same eyes, the same strong chin. Her father had dark hair and a solid, muscular build. Both of them were connected to dragons, though not, from what he had seen, nearly as powerfully as their daughter.

Cherise and Olar were speaking to one of the Dragon Guard when Jason came in. Max was a large, dark haired man with a powerful chin. He dressed in dragonskin, the leathers seemingly cut for him, and his dragon bone sword sheathed at his side gleamed in the lantern light. There was something imposing about him. He understood why those within the city would feel afraid of the Dragon Guard.

Sarah's parents looked over at him, frowning.

"I'm sorry to interrupt," Jason said.

"What is it?" Olar asked.

Jason glanced over at Max, then looked at Sarah for a moment, holding her gaze. She studied him, a question in her eyes. Jason debated what he needed to say. He had come here thinking that he would help talk about the plan for what to do about Lorach, though now that he was here, he questioned the wisdom of that.

From what it seemed, they were planning without him, anyway.

"I saw a dozen dragons from Lorach."

Olar leaned forward, gripping the sides of his chair. "Nearby?" He glanced over at Max. The Dragon Guard frowned.

Jason shook his head. "Not near here."

Olar breathed out, a relieved sigh escaping his lips as he relaxed.

Jason turned his attention to Sarah. He knew that she would take what he said thoughtfully, even if her parents didn't. "There was something off about the dragons. I tried to free them—"

"You tried to do *what*?" Max demanded.

Jason turned to him. "I tried to free the dragons. I have freed many before, unless you don't remember."

Max glared at him. "Yes. I seem to recall that you have created a difficulty for us. You put a target on us."

"As if the rebellion wasn't a target already," Jason said.

"A target, but you have created a renewed urgency. We had avoided pressing the attack."

"For what reason?" Jason asked, glancing from Cherise to Olar before turning his attention to Sarah. "The dragons need to be freed. I seem to think that was the intention behind all of that, wasn't it? That's the purpose of Dragon Haven."

"You would lecture them about the purpose of this place?" Max asked.

"Enough," Cherise said. "What is it about these dragons that brought you here?"

Jason sighed. "I've been watching for movement out of Lorach. Jessica will try something. I've seen that."

"I know that you have," Cherise said, her voice low and dangerous.

They were still angry with him. It wasn't his fault that Sarah had gotten caught, though he wondered if they would even believe him.

"She must have figured out how to teach the Dragon Souls to protect the dragons from me. I wasn't able to overwhelm their resistance. They *are* moving, though. I wanted to come to you to come up with a plan for dealing with them."

"We are coming up with a plan," Cherise said, looking at Max. "The Dragon Guard have continued their patrol. They will ensure Lorach does not pose a threat to us."

Jason should be comforted by that, and there was a part of him that was, but he couldn't shake the feeling of what he had noticed. He couldn't shake the strangeness of the power that had pushed upon him when he had been there before. There had been something, and within that was power. A resistance. A way for Lorach to overwhelm even what he had done.

Therin hadn't known how to do that. That Jessica had developed that much so quickly suggested that she was more of a threat than the others here would give her credit for. Jason was going to have to convince them.

"At least let me be a part of it," Jason said.

Cherise looked over at Olar.

"It wouldn't be the worst thing," Olar said. "With his connection to the others—"

"No," Max said. "He has not worked well with us. We are not going to risk our dragons, and my people, because he has brought these strange dragons to us."

"These strange dragons have allowed us to free others," Jason said. "If it wasn't for the misfits and me, Dragon Haven would have been destroyed."

"It is because of you that Dragon Haven was targeted," Max said. "You are the reason that we have returned from our patrols. Were it not for you, we would still be much farther north of here, drawing the attention of Lorach away. It's because of you that they even know that Dragon Haven is anywhere near here." He turned to Jason, and one hand fell to the hilt of his dragon bone sword. "Do not lecture me about what you have done for this place. I have been fighting on behalf of Dragon Haven for longer than you have been alive."

Jason arched a brow. Max didn't look that old, but maybe he was wrong.

"I'm not trying to be your enemy," he said. "All I'm trying is to help."

Max grunted. "You have helped enough."

"You would rather risk the dragons than work with me?" He looked over at Cherise and then Olar before finally looking at Sarah. "You would rather sacrifice the chance of freeing more dragons just because you don't want to work with me?"

Max stared at him. "As I've said, it's because of you that we are in this predicament. We will fight our way out of it. The Dragon Guard have plenty of experience dealing with Lorach. We will draw their attention away."

"And if that doesn't work?" Jason asked.

"If it doesn't work, then so be it. Then we will return and fight."

"By then it will be too late," Jason said. "Jessica will be arranging her dragons. She will figure this out. She will come for Dragon Haven."

"It's settled," Cherise said, turning to Jason. "We trust that the Dragon Guard will ensure our safety. Do not fret."

Jason grunted. "I'm not fretting. But I will keep searching. I will watch for movement out of Lorach."

Max sneered at him. "Why don't you go back to searching for your precious misfits?"

"It's those precious misfits that allow the dragons of Dragon Haven to be freed." He nodded to Sarah. "If you don't believe me, then ask her. She knows just what I've done. She knows just what the dragons are capable of doing. And she knows that those dragons are going to be the key to stopping Lorach. Not you. Not the Dragon Guard."

Jason turned and made his way out. He knew that he shouldn't, but frustration filled him. At the same time, he couldn't deny that what Max said was true. He had been responsible for some of this. It was because of him that Dragon Haven had been targeted. It was because of him that Therin had found it. Just because Jason had uncovered the misfits didn't excuse him from everything else that had taken place.

It was going to have to fall upon him to try to ensure that nothing worse happened.

If that meant finding other misfits, patrolling for Lorach, ensuring that the Dragon Guard did not do anything too foolish to draw the attention of Lorach, then Jason was going to do it.

He just had to figure out how.

It would start with watching. It would start with understanding just what Lorach intended. It would involve him patrolling even more.

He was willing to do it. He just wished that he didn't have to do it alone.

4

Cold wind whipped around Jason's face as the dragon soared through the air, a hint of mist streaking off the ice dragon, dampening Jason's cheeks. He held tightly to the dragon's back, clinging to the small spikes the ice dragon had formed. By using those spikes, Jason had a handle, a way to maintain his grip, and it was enough that he could cling to the dragon and not fear falling.

They dipped, angling toward the ground at a rapid rate, the speed leaving the wind streaking into Jason's eyes, making them water. "Now you're just showing off," he said to the dragon.

The dragon rumbled, a sound that was more amusement than anything else. "How is it showing off?"

"You're trying to see if you can dislodge me." Jason clutched tightly to the spike, squeezing the ice as it flowed from the dragon's back. "You aren't going to succeed."

"You had better hope not."

Jason laughed.

The dragon twisted, angling toward the ground again, diving toward the snowcapped mountain peak.

"Is there any reason you chose this location to travel?" Jason asked.

"I thought it would be intriguing," the dragon said.

"What's intriguing about it?" Jason asked, quickly adding an illusion around them so that was there anyone watching, they wouldn't necessarily see a dragon and a rider. All they would see would be a massive hawk. In this part of the world, that would be strange enough, but at least it wouldn't draw the same sort of notice that a dragon would.

The ice dragon snorted again, seemingly amused by Jason's desire to create an illusion around them.

"You know it's necessary," Jason said.

"Only because your people are fools," the dragon said.

"Only because my people have been attacked by dragons."

"In what lifetime?"

The question lingered, coming through the air on a gust of wind, but almost as much inside Jason's mind. In what lifetime *had* his people been attacked by dragons?

It had been generations, as far as Jason knew. In that time, his village had never seen a dragon attack. They had prepared for one, believing they needed to have the ballistae to defend against the possibility of an attack, but never had the actual need to use them.

"You're right," Jason said, his mood suddenly souring.

"Just because I'm right doesn't mean it matters," the dragon said to him.

Jason grunted again. He thought that it mattered a great deal.

The dragons had been forced to hide, but what would happen if they found others like those within Dragon Haven, others who appreciated the dragons for what they were, recognizing them as a part of the world rather than something that needed to be removed from it?

Jason let out a frustrated sigh, and he stared at the swirling snow all around them, watching as the dragon launched himself up and then back down. The change of direction was impressive. The enormous dragon had gained significant skill ever since Jason had begun flying with him.

There had been a time when he'd traveled with the ice dragon and feared whether or not the dragon would be able to carry him. Of course, Jason remembered the very first flight they'd taken, when the dragon had barely been able to use his wings and when the snow that had streamed off him had been something different.

"What are you hoping to find?" Jason asked.

"Others," the ice dragon said.

It was the first time the dragon had admitted that to him in this particular place. They had hunted here but never had they looked for the hatch mates. Perhaps that was only when Jason was with the dragon. As far as he knew, the dragon hunted for his hatch mates at all times.

"If we can understand what Therin did to create you, then we can help others." And there *would* be other dragon misfits. Jason didn't believe they had found all of them. There would have to be more.

The ice dragon breathed out a hint of cold and arched back up into the air, streaking high overhead. "Perhaps," the ice dragon said.

They took to the air, gaining altitude quickly.

Jason sensed the ice dragon's emotions, recognizing the sadness within him. He understood it. The ice dragon wished there were others like him. How could he not? The ice dragon was unique. All of the other misfits were unique. They suffered because of it.

There was a bond between them, all of them misfits, though there was still something that kept them apart. The only shared connection they really had was Jason and a willingness to work with him, fight on behalf of him, and to search for other hatch mates.

He said nothing as they circled, flying ever higher, reaching the altitude where the air became thin, the cold biting. It would've been intolerable were it not for Jason's connection to the iron dragon and the heat he could summon through him.

He leaned forward, embracing the ice dragon. The contact between them was potent. Though Jason embraced it, he wasn't sure if the ice dragon did as well. Perhaps being a dragon wasn't enough. The ice dragon wanted other ice dragons. How could he not?

Up high like this, there was a sense of darkness. It

hung over everything like a cloud, a blanket of night. Moonlight trickled out, spilling out over the sky. Up above the clouds as they soared, Jason felt the energy all around him, some sense of power, but it was different than the kind of power he possessed through the dragons. What he sensed from up here was a power that came to him from everything in the world around him.

"It can be peaceful," he whispered.

"Yes," the dragon said.

"I will help you hunt," he said.

"You have helped."

"I can help you continue to hunt," Jason said.

The ice dragon snorted, cold spilling from his nostrils. "There might not be much that can be done. The others may not have survived."

Jason thought of the lost jungle dragon. There might be others that had not survived, hunted and attacked because they were different. It saddened him, and he sensed a similar sadness within the dragon.

They circled, flying in the thin air above everything else. Every so often, Jason reached through his connection to the dragon, borrowing his sight, and looked down upon the world to see what existed below him. There wasn't much he could make out from where he flew, though occasionally he caught glimpses of snowcapped mountains and swirling snow. He sensed contentment within the dragon when he saw the snow and the wind and the inhospitable conditions.

Surprisingly, it was a contentment that Jason shared, at least in a way. Having grown up in a village where snow and ice were a frequent companion, something was refreshing about it. His sister didn't share that emotion. Not anymore. Kayla had adjusted to her time in Dragon Haven, coming to grips with the change, entirely happy to abandon the village.

"You've been quiet," the ice dragon said as they flew. "You have not wanted to speak of him."

Jason chuckled. "Sometimes, I forget just how much you can recognize my emotions."

"As you can recognize mine," the dragon said.

"Yours aren't nearly as easy as I wish they were."

"Neither are yours," the dragon said.

Jason smiled again and leaned over, looking down upon the world below him. "I don't know why he never would have told me what he was."

"Perhaps he could not."

"Why did he choose our village?"

"Perhaps he did not."

Only, Jason didn't think his father had been sent to the village by the Dragon Souls. He had no idea what role his parents had, only that his power was gifted to him by his parents, and they must have known what they could do. His father, at least, must have known.

"You've avoided seeking answers," the ice dragon said.

"I haven't avoided it."

"You've hunted."

"Because it's been necessary," Jason said.

He felt as if it were necessary. After the attack in Lorach, he felt as if he needed to better understand what they faced. He had helped dragons. Countless dragons. By freeing them from Dragon Souls, Jason had changed the dynamics of the rebellion. For the first time, the rebellion teetered toward overthrowing the power of Lorach.

Only, first they had to stop Jessica from controlling other dragons. It was why *he* hunted.

"We need more misfits," he said. "And we need to find them before the others do."

"The Dragon Souls won't be able to find the others," the ice dragon said. "They aren't patient enough."

Jason laughed a little bit. They started to descend, heading through the clouds, and when they poked free, the snowcapped mountains loomed in front of him, closer than he had expected. The ice dragon banked, twisting off to the side, forcing Jason to dig his heels in and grip the icy spikes more tightly. Water beaded around his hands.

"They aren't patient, but they *are* determined. I wouldn't be surprised if they're persistent, as well."

Persistence was the key, at least when it came to the misfits. Partly that was trying to understand just where to find the misfits.

"Besides, knowing Therin as she did, I suspect she'll know how to find them. Especially now that she's seen how powerful you are." And different. She wanted both. "Which is the other reason I've been hunting."

"That is not the other reason," the ice dragon said.

He sensed a bit of amusement, mixed with irritation —at him.

"You don't want me to find them? If she traps them and uses those dragons against us, then—"

"You need to better understand yourself before you go chasing this sort of power," the ice dragon said.

Jason grunted. "I understand myself well enough."

He fell silent as they circled around one of the snowy mountains. Down here, the brunt of the wind and the swirling snow crashed into him, the snow feeling more like needles that burrowed into his skin. He had to maintain his connection to the iron dragon to ensure it didn't harm him. The ice dragon seemed to feel that pain—and seemed amused by it.

"You don't have to take such joy in tormenting me," he said.

The dragon chuckled, the sound disappearing into the wind as they banked, turning and heading off to the west. They flew, staying low and close to the ground.

As before, Jason reached through his connection to the dragon and used the ice dragon's sight. He wasn't able to make out much of anything, though every so often, he caught blurring movement. After the third time catching that movement, he motioned to the ice dragon.

"Do you see that?" he asked.

"Of course," the dragon said.

"What is it?"

"Food."

Jason laughed. "To you, everything is food."

"Even you," the ice dragon said, turning toward him and snapping his jaw.

Jason laughed again.

They twisted, turning and heading farther to the west. They stayed low, swirling through the increasingly warm air, as moisture dripped from Jason. The moisture turned to ice that glistened off the ice dragon's back, gleaming along his surface. As they flew, the ice dragon twisted again, streaking toward the sky, toward colder air, and then back down.

Each time they went toward the sky and the colder air, Jason could feel why they did it. Heading to the upper atmosphere replenished power within the dragon, just as he recognized how the warmer air stressed him, challenging his ability to withstand the more temperate climates.

"Why do you do this to yourself?"

"I must be able to accommodate it," he said.

"You don't have to."

"If I am to stay with you, I do."

There was the key. The ice dragon *wanted* to stay with Jason.

They dove back toward the ground again, and movement in the far north caught his attention. It caught the ice dragon's attention as well. The ice dragon twisted, veering off toward what he had seen. They streaked through the air.

The ice dragon was a fast flyer. Perhaps one of the fastest of the dragons. In colder weather, the ice dragon was probably unrivaled. Even in the warmer air, he was still incredibly fast. The only dragon Jason had seen that surpassed the ice dragon was the storm dragon. Thankfully, the storm dragon had disappeared, led off by the forest dragon, and no longer a threat. At least, Jason hoped that it was no longer a threat.

As they neared, Jason recognized the blue dragon. What was he doing coming back?

"Can you speak to the dragon?" Jason asked the ice dragon.

The dragon snorted. It came as a heavy rumbling that echoed through the air. The wind tried to tear some of that sound away but wasn't able to take all of it. "No, but I think it's unnecessary."

The ice dragon slowed, readying for the arrival of the other dragon. The blue dragon had no rider ever since David had fallen. Jason wasn't sure if there could be one. Perhaps he wouldn't accept any again. If he did, it would have to be somebody who was skilled—possibly even powerful. Would such a person be allowed to make a connection with him?

"What is it?" Jason called across to the dragon.

"Come," the dragon said.

"Did you find Jessica?"

The blue dragon breathed a streamer of flame. "Come."

He veered off, heading back in the direction he'd come. Jason tapped on the ice dragon, and they followed. Every so often, Jason tested to make sure that the blue dragon wasn't tainted, that he hadn't been influenced by a Dragon

Soul, but each time he did so, he found a resistance to Jason's magic. Some of that resistance had to come from what David had done, though some of it seemed to be natural, innate to the dragon itself. It was a strange thing to be aware of, stranger still that he could feel just how powerful that resistance was.

Perhaps the training David had used with the dragon had given him that resistance. Jason wasn't sure, but then he hadn't known enough about David. The Auran had remained a mystery to him up until his death and remained so even now.

The dragon started to slow, and so did Jason and the ice dragon. They dropped down near a river with water rushing through and waves burbling along, and the blue dragon settled down near it.

Jason climbed down from the ice dragon's back.

"Look," the blue dragon said.

Jason shook his head, staring at the river. "What am I supposed to look at?"

"Look," the blue dragon said again.

The blue dragon headed into the river, and Jason followed.

The water rushed past him. It forced him to brace himself, holding on to power from the other dragons. Were it not for the energy of the ice dragon and the heat of the iron dragon, Jason might've been swept along by the current.

Of course, he doubted that the blue dragon would have allowed that. Even if he had, Jason could have used the power from the dragons he had connected to to break free. He felt the power and energy within him.

As he waded after the dragon, looking down to see just what it was that the dragon was trying to show him, he still didn't see anything.

"Do you see anything?" he asked the ice dragon.

The dragon snorted. "No."

"Look," the blue dragon said.

Jason stopped when the other dragon did, looking down.

The only thing he noticed was the changing of the water, as if it were swirling around some obstacle in the river. "I'm not sure what you want me to see."

"Look," the dragon said.

Jason continued to stare into the water. He still didn't see anything.

He tried a different tact.

Turning to the dragon, Jason tried to connect to him and borrow from his sight.

He didn't have a connection to the dragon usually, but by standing close to him, he hoped the dragon would allow him to connect. If he did, then Jason would be able to see what he wanted him to see.

Perhaps that was what the dragon was trying to urge him to do anyway. Jason connected, and he looked through the dragon's eyesight. It was different than what he saw with the ice dragon, different even than what he saw with the iron dragon. The water swirled around, creating a rippling of waves around an obstruction beneath him. At first, Jason thought what he was seeing was a rock, but that didn't seem to be the case.

It was too round. Almost perfectly round.

Understanding dawned on him.

"An egg," he whispered.

5

The water swirled around the egg, and he tried to grasp just what it was that he was seeing. The egg was enormous, standing on end and reaching easily up to his waist. As the water rippled around him, the water looked clear, almost translucent. The sunlight glistened off the surface.

Jason backed out of the river, crouching near its edge, looking out into the water. "That's what you wanted me to see?"

The dragon shook himself, heat radiating from his body so the water that had been on his scaled sides suddenly turned to steam. "You saw it."

"I saw it, but the egg wasn't intact."

From what Jason could tell, the egg had either already hatched or had been damaged, and the dragon hadn't survived. If the former were the case, it meant the river dragon or water dragon or whatever this one would be had already disappeared. If that latter, then it was one more egg that hadn't survived.

"Have you seen where the dragon went?"

"No," the blue dragon said.

"I don't know how we will find it, then, unless we find something strange with water that we can't otherwise explain."

"We must hunt," the blue dragon said.

"Jessica is going to be hunting, too," Jason said.

If she uncovered a freshly hatched egg, it would be dangerous. Jessica might have already identified the dragon misfit. What would she do with a river dragon? It depended upon the power within the dragon.

"I didn't realize you have been looking for these dragons," he said to the blue dragon. "Will you continue?"

"Yes. The others search, too."

"Others? Are there other dragons looking?" Jason looked from the blue dragon to the ice dragon, but neither of them offered him an answer. "What others are looking?"

"Others."

Jason frowned. If not a dragon, there weren't many others the blue dragon would refer to. It meant Lorach. Jessica. She searched for eggs.

"Is that what she's doing? I thought she's searching for Dragon Haven."

"She does both. You must be careful in case she succeed. I will hunt, and you must hunt." The dragon shook himself again, then launched into the air, circling for a moment until he disappeared into the cloudy sky. Jason hesitated, but then he connected to the blue dragon.

He didn't know how long he would be able to do so, or whether the blue dragon would prevent him from reaching the connection, but as he connected across the distance, he could look down to see where he stood next to the ice dragon, and he had a sense of the blue dragon he didn't have otherwise. It was almost as if the dragon permitted him to know him.

Then Jason tore that attention away. He didn't want to maintain it any longer than he should. The dragon allowed a certain amount of connection, but he didn't want Jason to hold onto it.

When he was gone, he turned to the ice dragon. "What do you think a river dragon will be like?"

"Is that what you will call him?"

"Are you sure that it's a him?"

"Perhaps not," the ice dragon said.

"There aren't many females, though, so maybe we'll get lucky." He stared at the water, thinking about a water dragon and what it might look like, the way that he might fly—or swim. It was possible the dragon wouldn't fly at all.

"He may not have survived," the ice dragon said.

"All of the others have survived the hatching."

"All of the others you have found have survived. There were probably others that did not."

Jason hadn't considered that, though it did make a

particular sort of sense. “I suppose it’s good the blue dragon was willing to hunt.”

“I will look as well,” the ice dragon said.

“Good,” Jason said. “We haven’t found a misfit for a while.”

As he headed toward the ice dragon, the dragon shook himself, and spikes streaked off his back. When they struck the water, they floated for a moment before sinking.

“What was that about?” Jason asked.

“A plea for the dragon to come to us,” the ice dragon said.

“Will it work?”

“I don’t know.”

Jason turned toward the river, and he watched where the water swirled around the egg, wondering what it must’ve been like for that dragon. Within the river, there would’ve been no shortage of food. In other places where the dragons had hatched, it wasn’t quite as easy to feed.

When the ice dragon had hatched, Jason had assumed that he must have needed to hunt in the mountains, searching for game, but the more that he had been around the ice dragon, the more that he had begun to wonder if perhaps what he fed on wasn’t so much animals as it was the cold itself. That cold seemed to fuel the dragon in a way that nothing else did.

He climbed onto the dragon’s back. “We should return.”

It was time to get back to the city. He didn’t know

what the Dragon Guard might be up to, but without being able to be a part of it, he couldn't linger too long. The Dragon Guard intended to marginalize him, and that was something Jason was unwilling to do. If Lorach was involved, he was the best equipped to deal with it.

He wrapped his arms around the dragon's neck, embracing him, and they streaked into the sky. They reached the thin air before dropping back down to the ground.

"What will you do?" Jason asked.

"Hunt with the other."

It was good the ice dragon and the iron dragon got along well enough to hunt together. "Let me know if you find anything."

The dragon let out a breath of cold air and then launched himself into the sky. Jason watched for a moment until the dragon disappeared above the top of the trees, parting through the illusion. When he was gone, the illusion formed around him, leaving empty sky.

Outside Dragon Haven, Jason had secured an illusion around the ice dragon so that he would look like an enormous raptor, but he had wondered how long he would have to hold onto that. At some point, he hoped the illusion would become unnecessary, that a time would come when the dragons were accepted and not feared. It was the same thing that all the dragons felt. None wanted to have to maintain an illusion. They wanted to fly freely.

Jason looked around the clearing. There were no young dragons here today. Three of the dragon instructors were nearby, watching Jason, nodding when he turned his attention to them. They weren't trainers. They would never refer to themselves as trainers, not after the Dragon Souls considered themselves to be so, because using that word would admit they were similar to Dragon Souls. They helped raise the young dragons, trainer or not.

He headed through the courtyard, passing through the gate and into the streets of Dragon Haven. The sun shone down overhead, and he opened up the dragonskin jacket he wore, releasing some of the stored heat inside. He probably didn't need dragonskin, not anymore, though there was some element of protection to it that was more than just what it offered from heat and cold. Having the dragonskin protected him were he attacked. Plus, there was the added benefit that it had once been David's. By claiming the dragonskin for his own, he had a connection to the lost man.

The main building was much larger than the surrounding ones. Even though he knew it to have only a single level, it arced higher overhead, as if there were multiple stories. Once inside, the halls were wide and vast, and the dragon relics were far more prominent. As Jason reached the entrance to the main building, he paused, tracing his finger over the outline of a dragon etched into the wooden door. Most doors within this building had a similar symbol engraved upon them.

Jason headed through halls until he reached his room. Pausing at the door for a moment, he rested his hand there, feeling for any sense of heat that might be on the other side. He didn't detect anything.

When he pulled the door open, he found the room empty. He had thought that his sister might be there, or perhaps his mother, but neither were. That wasn't altogether surprising. Closing the door, Jason strode through the building, heading toward Sarah's room.

There was a dragon carved on her door with its wings spread in a ferocious roar, as if it were preparing to launch into the sky, readying to throw itself high up into the air. Jason looked at the carving, as he did each time he came to Sarah's room. He suspected this dragon mattered to somebody at one time. He wondered if this one had ever been trained, forced to serve, or if this dragon had been allowed to be free.

Given what Jason had gone through before when he had tried to come to Sarah and her parents, he didn't know what sort of response he might find this time. Perhaps they would send him away, chastising him as before, but finding another misfit seemed important.

Besides, his time away from the city had shown him how lonely it could be. He knew he couldn't do this on his own. He could not defeat Lorach by himself. It would take all of Dragon Haven. It might take the Dragon Guard, regardless of whether or not they wanted him to work with them, or whether he wanted to work with them. He might not have a choice in the matter.

He hurried until he found Sarah. She was in her room,

sitting at a desk, bent over as she read. He knocked on the door before poking his head in.

"Jason," she said, looking past him before smiling. "Close the door."

He stepped in, closing the door behind him. "I'm sorry about the other day," he said.

"You don't have to apologize. I understand. The problem is, I also understand why my parents have been so..."

"Uptight?" Jason offered.

She chuckled. "I suppose uptight. *Concerned* might be a better way of saying it. They worry about me. When I told them how I was captured by Jessica and held, they suddenly saw everything that they had been working for falling apart."

"Others can lead in Dragon Haven."

"Others can, but others don't have—" Sarah seemed to catch herself before shaking her head. She took a deep breath, glancing down at the book on the table alongside her. "I'm glad you came back."

"We found something," he said.

"We?"

"The ice dragon and me."

"Just the two of you?"

"Well, I have been out scouting with the misfits, much like I told you and your parents. This time, it wasn't even one of the misfits that helped me. It was David's dragon."

She frowned. "We haven't seen him."

"I have." He told her about encountering David's dragon while it was mourning, and she frowned.

"We've never seen dragons behave like that for somebody."

"I have a sense that David and the dragons have worked together for a long time. I had a sense that they viewed David as quite a bit different than most people, but considering the way that David was willing to work with this dragon, and how different that was from so many others, it doesn't surprise me that the dragon would have felt a considerable sense of loss."

Sarah watched him. "You felt it, too."

Jason shrugged. "I suppose I did. I didn't get to know him. I wished I would have, but…" He shook his head. The last thing that he had said to David had been unimportant. And here David had helped him, going against his sister—his family. "They have another kind of power within Lorach," Jason said.

"You told me that, but we've never known anything about it."

"Maybe not, but that's probably because no one has been able to use it. I had a sense from David that he was surprised I could."

"You can use many different dragons differently than the rest of us, so I guess that isn't too shocking."

"They called it the dragon source," Jason said. "Does anything strike you as familiar?"

Sarah glanced down at her book before looking up at

him again. "No. Maybe my parents would know something more, but I don't."

Jason took a deep breath, letting it out. "I suppose that would be asking too much."

"What happened to this misfit that you found?"

"I didn't find him. I found an egg."

"Where?"

"It was in a riverbed not too far from here." He didn't want to tell her that it was far enough away that he doubted that the dragon would be able to make its way to Dragon Haven. "I didn't find any sign of the dragon, though I tried."

Sarah frowned. "That's unfortunate. The dragons that you have found really are powerful. They could be helpful."

"Your parents don't seem to feel that way."

"My parents do recognize what you've done for us, Jason. It's just that they also need to make sure that they are working as well with the Dragon Guard as possible."

"I can draw the attention of Lorach," Jason suggested.

He had thought about it while traveling with the ice dragon. He could have the misfits travel with him, and together, they could trigger enough power that maybe Lorach would think that they were in the opposite direction than they really were. With as quickly as the ice dragon could fly, it wouldn't even be that difficult.

"What Max didn't want to tell you is that it's already too late," Sarah said. "They've started moving."

"Who has?"

"Lorach," she said. "They have seen considerable movement."

Jason frowned, thinking about what *he'd* seen. There had been movement of dragons, but nothing he'd call considerable. "I've been watching for it, but I haven't seen anything more."

"They have somebody in the city. Lorach has been sending dragons out in small groups. Small enough that I suspect even you won't recognize it. It allows them to sneak out of the city, and then..." She shrugged. "I think they are much more concerned than they're letting on, but I can't blame them. If Lorach is starting to move and sending their dragons this way, we have to be ready. We don't have enough strength to withstand their full might."

"I know we don't," Jason said. "But with what I can do, I have to believe that we can stop them."

He would've believed that much more firmly had it been a week ago. He would've thought that he could overwhelm what Jessica might do with the dragons, but now...

Now he no longer knew if that was the case. The problem was that now he didn't know if his way of helping protect and heal the dragons would even be effective against Lorach.

What a difference only a few days made.

He wasn't going to tell Sarah that, though.

"I've been telling my parents the same thing," she said. "We will stop them."

It fit with what Jason had seen. If Lorach were moving —and he suspected she was right and they were moving—

then it was time for him to start making preparations. He needed to be ready for the possibility that they would face a dangerous threat.

He was going to have to fortify the illusions around the city. He would have to connect to the other misfits. If he could, he would need to even find this river dragon, use its power if he could connect to it.

If only he had some way of finding the storm dragon, but any attempt to do so had been thwarted, mostly by the forest dragon. She protected the storm dragon from Jason, but also from anyone who might attempt to use it. The storm dragon feared others, and for a good reason. The storm dragon had been used and attacked.

"Try to bring me in," he said. "I need to be a part of this. A direct part. Not going off on my own the way that I have been, but I need to be involved."

Sarah nodded. "I keep trying. Believe me. But even if they don't formally pull you in, you need to keep doing what you're doing. It's important. I know that you want only to protect the dragons. Even if no one else believes that, I do."

"No one else believes that?"

"Well, Henry does, but to be honest, the Dragon Guard don't give much credit to him, either. So I guess you don't have to think that you are the only one picked on." She forced a smile, but it did nothing to make Jason feel any better. "And William. I know he believes you've been doing all you can to help the dragons."

Jason stood quiet, saying nothing.

Sarah studied him. "Have you found anything else about your parents?"

Jason blinked a moment. "Not really," he said. "I talked to my mother."

"That's a start," Sarah said.

"A start, but she's hiding something still."

"If she was working with Lorach, then it's not altogether surprising that she would hide something from you."

"I just wish that I knew what it was. She's hiding something about her time in Lorach. About the reason they left."

"Maybe they were forced to do something that she doesn't want to remember." She shrugged. "Henry doesn't like to talk about his time in Lorach, either. I know there's more to what happened to him than what he lets us know."

Jason nodded. The people in Lorach had suffered. Not all of them, but enough. He had seen the scars on Henry's back, so he knew that he had been through quite a bit.

"I just want this all to be over," Jason said.

"It will be. One way or the other."

Jason grunted. "I don't like the sound of that."

"We *will* stop them."

He held his gaze on Sarah for a moment. He could tell that she wanted to help him, that she wanted to say something so that he could be brought in, but for now, maybe he had to deal with the fact that he was an outsider.

Until he proved himself even more, though Jason

didn't know what more he might need to do, he was going to have to deal with that feeling.

"I'll keep looking."

"Let me know what you find," she said.

Jason nodded. He stepped through the door, closing it behind him, and stared at it. There was a time when Sarah would've offered to go with them, when she would've fought to go with them, and that she didn't now bothered him. Perhaps it shouldn't. She did have responsibilities within Dragon Haven, and they were responsibilities that he didn't share.

That didn't mean he couldn't help.

There was much that he could do. Much that he needed to do.

It was time to search for Lorach again. They weren't going to be surprised. And if it came down to it, Jason would ask the other dragon misfits to help draw Lorach away. He would protect Dragon Haven, even if it didn't want to defend him. It was his responsibility, much like taking care of his family had once been his responsibility. If there was one thing his father had taught him, it was that he was to fulfill his obligations.

6

There was nothing about this part of the forest that struck Jason as unusual, and nothing that left him feeling like the river dragon had come through here, though he'd looked. He patrolled, the iron dragon nearby, slithering through the trees and radiating heat that washed away from him, streaking through the forest and leaving Jason's skin flushed.

It wasn't so much an unpleasant heat. When it came to the iron dragon, Jason wasn't sure if there was an uncomfortable heat, at least not for him. Not only did he have the dragonskin that offered a level of protection, but the iron dragon glove also helped, protecting him in a way that kept him safe from the dragon's heat.

"How long do you intend to be out here?"

Jason looked over at William.

He held onto a branch and tapped on the ground as he walked, his long hair standing up straight from his head, giving him a wild appearance. He bounced a dragon pearl in his other hand, though as far as Jason could tell, William didn't have any way of connecting to the energy within it. Jason was acutely aware of the power within that dragon pearl, feeling that energy as it flowed through it.

The dragon who had given William the pearl trailed behind, making his way through the forest. He was the small red dragon Jason had seen William with earlier, a juvenile, but from the power within him, Jason suspected the dragon would eventually be powerful.

"Long enough for me to see if there's anything here."

"Why are you so convinced that there's going to be something out here?"

Jason glanced over at William. His black hair stood straight up like usual, and crystal blue eyes flashed with curiosity as they looked around. "Because of what I've felt from Lorach."

"What have you felt?"

Jason squeezed his eyes shut, thinking about that pulse of energy. He had never detected anything quite like it before, but having seen the movement from Lorach, he knew there had to be something going on, but the issue for him was figuring out what that was and how he was going to go about stopping whatever they planned. "It's hard for me to describe. I don't even know exactly what it was. Power, but not the kind of power that I've ever felt from Lorach before."

William started to laugh before cutting off. "What sort of power have you felt from Lorach before?"

Jason breathed out. "When I was held there —"

"We were both held there, Jason."

He looked over at William. It was easy to forget that they both had been trapped in Lorach. Jason's experience had been different than William's, but perhaps he had been in more control, which would have made him less terrified. "I know we were both there. I'm sorry. When we were trapped in Lorach, I felt the power of the Dragon Souls, but there was something from within the palace itself as well. David didn't get the opportunity to ever explain it to me, but I have a feeling that whatever Jessica intends is going to be tied to that."

He wasn't sure. Not yet. But he had to believe that it was something that he had not yet experienced.

"What exactly do you expect to find here?"

"I don't know. I'm hopeful that I can find another dragon misfit. Maybe even the river dragon. Whatever it is…"

Whatever it was, Jason had to hope that it would be enough to stop Lorach.

He had thought he might be able to uncover some energy that would suggest one of the dragon misfits, but he hadn't felt anything. Jason swept his gaze around the forest, focusing on his connection to the iron dragon, using not only his link to the forest and the trees and the energy that was here but also borrowing from the dragon's eyesight.

He wound through the trees, following the sense of the iron dragon. There was an ongoing sense of energy and pressure here. It was pleasant. Perhaps it was the warmth, or maybe it was being out with the iron dragon and walking through the forest with a friend, or maybe it was merely the fact that Jason could feel the dragons all around him, those back in Dragon Haven along with those that he was connected to, but despite the fear the Dragon Guard had, Jason felt comfortable. He knew he should not.

With that relaxing sense around him, Jason continued to look through the forest, wandering with William, holding onto the awareness of the iron dragon. He found the sense of the forest remained empty to him.

Not completely empty, though.

There was something here. Jason could feel power here, was aware of an energy within the forest. William wandered, weaving through trees, and Jason found himself following his friend. Every so often, the small dragon with William would sneak up behind him and would slam into his back playfully.

Jason smiled.

It was the kind of behavior he would once have never believed possible for the dragons. It was almost friendly. Of course, Jason understood the dragons were friendly. His experience with the dragons suggested they were more than just friendly. They wanted much the same as he did. They wanted to be able to live freely, and not to fear the danger of people chasing them, hunting them. If the dragons had the opportunity to live freely, then they could thrive.

They reached the edge of the forest. From here, the land sloped down, disappearing into a valley. He lingered at the edge of the trees, looking with William, the iron dragon drifting nearby and the small red dragon with William.

"Do you detect anything here?" William asked.

"No," Jason said. "Just the forest."

"I just thought—"

The sound of thunder came in the distance.

Jason turned to the iron dragon and frowned. "What was that?" he whispered.

"It was not the storm dragon," the iron dragon said.

"Are you sure?"

The rumbling came again, this time closer. Jason couldn't tell, but it reminded him too much of the storm dragon. Why would it have come back? They should have been protected from the storm dragon—or the forest dragon.

Jason still didn't know where the forest dragon had brought the storm dragon, and as he had no connection to the storm dragon, he had no reason to believe that he would ever know unless the forest dragon shared. There were many things about the forest dragon that Jason appreciated, but she was not forthright. If she felt she needed to protect something—and given what had happened to the storm dragon, Jason believed she would think she needed to protect him—he would not know.

The rumbling came again. If not the storm dragon, then could it be Lorach?

Jason looked over at William. "I need to go explore this," he said.

"I can come with you." William nodded to the red dragon. "He would let me ride him."

Jason studied the dragon. It was small, and he didn't know if the dragon was large enough even to fly, let alone carry someone. "Are you sure?"

William nodded. "I've been practicing."

Jason climbed onto the iron dragon's back, and William climbed onto the red dragon.

With the undulating movement the iron dragon used to fly, he took to the air, pulsing upward, propelling himself into the sky with the power of his heat within him.

Jason swiveled so that he could see William and the other dragon as they started to ascend. It happened slowly, much more slowly than Jason and the iron dragon, but gradually they began to spiral up, taking to the air and joining them.

The dragon was mighty, though small. Perhaps Jason shouldn't be surprised that the dragon could carry William. William grinned at him as he followed, and Jason shook his head, turning away, and they streaked into the distance.

They headed toward the sound of the rumbling.

Jason tried to gauge where it came from. He feared the storm dragon. The dragon could be unpredictable, and though he didn't fear the dragon, not as he once did, he feared what that dragon might do to other dragons if it got close to them.

Jason could feel energy within the air, and the iron dragon surged toward it.

The small dragon William rode was far faster than what Jason would've given him credit for. He streaked through the sky, carrying William as the valley dipped below them.

The iron dragon stayed low, soaring above the treetops.

In the distance, he noticed something. At first, it looked almost as if it was just the wind rustling the trees. The dragon slowed, hovering, and Jason raised his hand to motion to William to keep him from arriving too quickly.

"What is it?" William asked.

"Look at the trees," Jason said. "It looks as if a wind is gusting through here, but I don't see any or feel anything."

Beneath them, the trees trembled. Something big was coming through the forest.

"What do you think it is?" Jason asked.

When Lorach had traveled through the forests before, it was nothing like this. They would travel by dragonback, not thunder through the forest the same way the iron dragon had done. Something was coming here. Something big. Something dangerous.

"I don't know what you're looking at," William said.

Jason smiled as he'd been talking to the iron dragon.

"I can't tell," the iron dragon said. "Not from up here."

"Do think we could tell if we flew higher?"

"Possibly," the dragon said.

Only, Jason knew the truth. The trees were dense, which made being able to see through them difficult. Even from an altitude, it would be challenging to be able to make out what was happening in the forest below.

"Wait here," Jason called over to William.

The iron dragon circled higher, and Jason looked down toward the forest, toward the trembling trees, using the dragon's sight. What he could tell were gradations of color, orange and red reflecting the energy down below. Jason couldn't see anything beyond that. The trees were too dense to be able to make anything out, the canopy blocking him.

The tops of the trees trembled, though all the trees swayed rhythmically, as if something were snaking through the forest.

Jason looked over at William. "We need to go down there. I worry there could be a misfit down there." Worse, if it wasn't a dragon misfit, that meant it was Lorach. Maybe *this* was what he had detected, though when he had felt that strangeness before, there had been no sense of a rumbling, not like he recognized now. It didn't feel like the storm dragon, but could this be where the forest dragon had brought him?

Jason closed his eyes, trying to focus on the connection between himself and the forest dragon, but there was some aspect to it that felt clouded as if she didn't want to connect fully to him.

He didn't know why she wouldn't want that, though perhaps it was time to visit with her again and ask. He patted the iron dragon. "We need to circle behind it." Looking over at William, he said, "If you want to head back to the city, I won't blame you."

"I'll stay with you."

They veered around before starting toward the forest floor. The iron dragon carried them quickly, descending toward the treetops, streaking down to the ground. When they reached the canopy, Jason braced himself, and the iron dragon plunged between the trees.

It was something of a gamble.

Jason had learned that when dealing with trees or any other obstruction like that, it could often be a gamble with the dragons as to whether they could even pass through. Dragonskin had its advantages in that they were protected from danger of whatever might be there, but they also didn't know whether there would be space enough for them to retake flight.

In the case of the iron dragon, Jason was not as concerned. There was something different to the way he flew, the way he undulated with heat, that allowed him to propel himself upward, shooting the power behind him, but he worried more about the small dragon William rode. It was possible that the dragon would be trapped within the forest. He might have to find a clearing, space enough for him to stretch his wings and take off, unlike the iron dragon.

They plunged to the ground. This close, he could feel

the trembling. It wasn't too far from them. Jason climbed off the dragon. The iron dragon snaked off, and Jason followed him.

William climbed down from his dragon. "You're going to walk?"

"I want to be ready if there is something strange here."

"Dragon strange?"

"I don't know if it's a dragon," Jason said.

"What else would it be?"

"I don't know, but everything that I am detecting is—"

The rumbling came again, this time near him. Jason backed toward one of the tree trunks. He focused on the iron dragon and what he could see through the iron dragon's eyes but didn't see anything.

There was only the heat, but in the forest, it was difficult to make out much of anything. The colors of the trees all blended together, making it difficult for the iron dragon to navigate effectively. The iron dragon saw the trees as small beams of heat light and could generally avoid crashing into them.

Could whatever was in the forest and coming toward them do the same thing? Dragons had similar eyesight, as far as Jason had determined. He focused on the energy around him. It was something he'd come to realize he could do. It allowed him to test for dragons.

And it was.

He couldn't tell whether this was one of the regular dragons, one of the dragons he'd freed from the Dragon Souls, or whether it was one of the dragon misfits. After having seen the river dragon, at least seeing the evidence of the river dragon, Jason wanted nothing more than to find more misfits. He hadn't expected to find any misfits this close to Dragon Haven, but perhaps that was because he hadn't been looking well enough. If this was one of the misfits coming toward Dragon Haven, maybe it was coming toward Dragon Haven because of him.

"Do you see anything?" he asked the iron dragon.

"Not yet," the dragon rumbled.

"What about your dragon?" Jason asked, turning to William.

"How would I know?"

"You ask," Jason said.

William turned to the small dragon and frowned. "Would he tell me?"

"If you ask nicely." Jason headed over to the small dragon. He remained crouched, his wings tucked in. Jason raised his hand to the dragon.

He sensed something coming from the small dragon: uncertainty. The prospect of coming here, that he might not be able to escape, left the dragon unsettled.

"I'll make sure you return when this is over," Jason said to the dragon. "For now, I need to know if you can see anything."

The dragon turned his head toward him, the bright glowing eyes looking at him, orange burning within them. Heat streamed from his nostrils. He nudged Jason.

"I know you can talk, so you might as well get on with it."

There was power within every dragon, and he had only to reach it, to find that energy, to see if there was anything that he might be able to uncover from that dragon.

The ground rumbled again, closer.

"Do you detect anything?" he pressed.

"I can feel something," the small red dragon said.

Jason smiled. "Good. What is it?"

"It feels as if it's everywhere. Beneath me."

Jason frowned, focusing on that rumbling, but didn't detect anything. Perhaps the red dragon was right. They were focusing more on what might be pushing up through the trees, but what if that wasn't the case? Maybe it came from beneath the ground.

The dragon looked over at him. He was uneasy.

Jason turned to William. "You need to get the dragon out of here. It has nothing to do with you or the dragon's ability to stay here. I just worry that you won't be able to take off again."

William looked over at him, then at the dragon as horror dawned upon his face.

"I didn't even think about what might happen when we tried to leave," the red dragon said.

"You can head to the clearing up there," Jason said, motioning into the distance. He couldn't see anything, though he could feel a space between the trees, mostly because he could see the iron dragon up ahead.

"If there's something here, I can help," William said.

"I believe you could, but I think there's something more you can do by returning to Dragon Haven. Alert them there's something out here and send people to investigate."

"What about you? You shouldn't stay here, either."

William wasn't wrong.

"I'll be right behind you," he said.

Jason motioned for the small dragon and patted him on the side. The dragon looked over at him. There was something in his eyes Jason couldn't quite make out. Was it irritation? The dragon wasn't angry with him, but perhaps it was the fact he couldn't do what he wanted.

William climbed on the dragon's back, and they headed through the forest, away from Jason. After a moment, he felt the dragon taking to the air, the power of the small dragon as it circled up and into the sky.

He stayed there for a moment and pushed through a connection to the dragon, borrowing from that dragon's sight. Having spoken to the dragon allowed him to connect, and now connected, he could feel his energy, and he thought he might be able to borrow enough to use that connection were it needed.

The trembling of the trees persisted, but it was fainter than it had been.

He turned to the iron dragon. "Do you detect anything else?"

"Nothing more than what we already have," the iron dragon said, emerging from the forest.

"There was *something* here, but what was it?" The

rumbling came more faintly. It drifted away, becoming distant. "It was a dragon. I'm sure of it."

"Probably," the iron dragon said, rolling his neck forward and rubbing up against one of the trees.

The trees shook. When they did, Jason realized something. Seeing the iron dragon pressing up against the tree didn't cause the tree to swing in the same way as he had seen from above. Whatever had been causing that trembling had caused the ground to shake beneath them. It had come from someplace deep.

Jason stood in place for a few more moments, waiting for the rumbling to return, but it never did. It was as if the rumbling had disappeared completely. That left him troubled. If Lorach had some way of finding them, of moving through here and then disappearing…

Dragon Haven had stood for decades. Probably centuries. They had remained hidden, serving as a rebellion working against Lorach for longer than Jason could even understand. He didn't want to be the reason that something happened to Dragon Haven. Unfortunately, ever since he had come to the city, things had shifted. He was the reason some things had changed.

Letting out a sigh, he knew he had to be careful. Everything wasn't one of the dragon misfits, regardless of what he wanted to believe.

"Let's go," he said to the iron dragon.

He climbed onto the iron dragon's back, and the dragon began to pulse with heat, starting from deep within him, radiating from his tail all the way up to his neck in rhythmic energies that surged through him as they coursed along his body. Then they launched themselves into the air. The sudden explosion of power carried them up and above the trees. From here, Jason swiveled, looking below him, searching for anything that he might be able to make out from this vantage, but saw nothing.

There was nothing. No trembling to the trees. Nothing other than the forest below him. With a feeling of frustration, he turned, and they headed toward Dragon Haven.

7

Sarah found Jason and William within the courtyard. Her brow was deeply creased, her jaw was set, and she strode toward him with a determined pace. She had her hair pulled back and a loop of gold set atop her forehead.

"She's dressed formally," William said.

She was, which troubled him.

More than that, he was troubled by what he and William had just experienced. If it wasn't Lorach, then what was it? They had not found the river dragon, though Jason doubted that he would find that dragon very easily. He wanted to, if only so they might know if it would help with the imminent Lorach threat.

"I need you to come with me," she said to Jason before glancing at William. "Not you."

Jason frowned. "Which is it?"

"You. I need you to come."

"Why?"

She shook her head. "Something happened."

"What?" Had something happened with the dragon that they had detected? "Is it the Dragon Guard?"

She shook her head. "Not the Dragon Guard. This is something else. My parents wanted you to come."

Jason glanced over at William before turning to Sarah. "Your *parents* wanted me?"

"I know. I've been trying to have them bring you in for the last few days and all of a sudden, they had me come out here chasing you. I don't know what it's about, only that they wanted me to get you." She turned William. "I'm sorry. They don't need you."

William shrugged. "I don't mind. I can stay out here with the other dragons, anyway."

Jason sighed. Something was going on, and it was something that he didn't know about. Maybe it was Lorach, but perhaps not.

They hurried through the city, reaching the main building, and Sarah held onto his arm in the hallway. Jason glanced at her. She looked straight ahead, her golden hair flowing around her shoulders. She looked regal, every bit the appearance of someone who should be a ruler, though her isolation in Dragon Haven would prevent her from ever genuinely ruling.

They strode through the hallway, and movement in the distance along the hall caught Jason's attention. He slowed, looking at the Dragon Guard. Three of them marched through the hall, all armed with their swords, pale white blades made of dragon bone and heavy leathers cut from dragonskin. They were impressive, even though Jason knew they used the same sort of power that he did.

Jason couldn't help but be amazed by the Dragon Guard. They were powerful, but not nearly as numerous as needed to put up a real fight against the Dragon Souls. Still, they had served as the face of the rebellion for a long time. Without the Dragon Guard, Lorach might have destroyed the rebellion—and Dragon Haven—a long time ago.

The Dragon Guard marched in front of him, disappearing along the hallway. When the sound of their boots on the stone disappeared, Jason shook his head, tearing his attention away and turning back to Sarah.

"I don't recognize any of them," Jason said.

"No," Sarah said, leaning closer to him. A heavy frown wrinkled her features, and she pulled on her pale yellow dress, slipping a hand into her pocket. When she did, the distinctive energy of power pulsing from a dragon pearl flowed from her.

She squeezed her eyes shut, opening them again, and they marched onward, reaching the throne room. She paused for a moment, nodding to two soldiers standing on either side of the door before striding inside toward her mother and father.

Cherise and Olar were seated at a table. Cherise wore her golden hair twisted back behind her ears, braided and pinned up. She looked much like Sarah, only a generation older. She had strands of gray sweeping through her hair and faint blue eyes that were not nearly as piercing or bright as Sarah's. Jason wondered if Cherise had ever been able to summon dragons the way that Sarah could. She must have some potential, otherwise, Sarah wouldn't have developed it.

Her father, Olar, sat alongside Cherise. He had dark hair and no silver in his eyes. He was dressed distinguishably in a crimson jacket, his hair brushed back, his deep brown eyes darting at everyone within the room. He was more on edge than Jason had seen him before.

Henry sat near Olar, his hands resting on the table, dressed in the heavy furs that Jason had first seen him in. He was every bit as disheveled as he'd looked when Jason had first encountered him, but his bright silver eyes glared at the man sitting across from him.

"Who is that?" Jason whispered.

Sarah shook her head, glancing at her parents for a moment before turning her attention back to studying the man. "I don't know. I knew the Dragon Guard had arrived, but I didn't see anyone else come with them."

Jason wasn't sure that he was a Dragon Guard. He had a piercing stare, bright silver eyes, and a sharp jaw. He was slight of build, not at all burly like Olar or Henry. Still, there was something quite intimidating about him. Although he wore dragonskin jacket and pants, it was nothing like the dragonskin Jason wore, as if it came from some other land. The cut was completely different, the style of the jacket sweeping and wide, leaving the lapels open. The scales glittered, almost as if they caught the light in a way that allowed them to shimmer. Heat radiated from him, an energy that Jason could feel, a power that pressed outward almost overwhelming him.

The man turned toward him, regarding Jason. "Sit," the man said.

"Who are you?" Jason asked.

The man grunted. "Is he always like this?" He spoke the question to Cherise and Olar but held his gaze on Jason.

"Most of the time," Henry muttered.

"Good." The man leaned forward, regarding Jason with that bright-eyed stare.

Jason crossed his arms over his chest. "Are you going to tell me who you are?" Sarah reached for him, but Jason didn't let her get too close. He didn't want to argue, but at the same time, he knew better than to be intimidated. He had been through too much and had done far more for the people of Dragon Haven than this stranger had.

"My name is Lorren Daven."

Jason shook his head. "Am I supposed to be impressed?"

"Perhaps you should be."

When Sarah sucked in a sharp breath, Jason glanced over at her. "Do you recognize him?"

She stared at the man, and it was a measure of her surprise that she pulled a dragon pearl from her pocket. It was a pale yellow dragon pearl, and Jason could practically feel the connection between the dragon pearl stretching from her to its dragon. It was a trail of energy that stretched away from her, out of the throne room, out of the building itself, and to the dragon situated out in the yard not far from them. It would take very little for Jason to reach for that same power, stretching across that distance, and call for the same dragon energy.

"He was supposed to be dead," Sarah whispered.

Lorren grunted. "As I am not dead, I am here. Lucky for you."

Jason looked around the room, surveying the others in the room with him. He had seen the three Dragon Guard in the hallways, but there were no Dragon Guard in the room. How many had returned to the city? From what Sarah had said, it must've been enough to raise attention. When Jason had returned, riding with the ice dragon, he hadn't noticed any Dragon Guard. There had been no sign of dragons, nothing that would indicate riders having come through.

"Sit," Lorren said again.

Jason glanced at Sarah, and she nodded. He shrugged, making his way around the table until he found an empty seat next to Henry. Sarah joined her parents, sitting between them. It created a strange sight. All of them were situated in a way that allowed them to look at Lorren, yet he seemed completely at ease.

"Now that I'm seated, what do you want with me?" Jason asked. "I presume you're here because of me."

Lorren watched him. There was a brightness in his eyes that glittered for a moment, and he shifted, leaning forward a bit more. The dragonskin scraped along the table, creating a strange sound. "I understand you're the one who hunts for dragon misfits."

Jason's heart started to pound. "I search for them. Not hunt. They need to be protected."

Lorren regarded him another moment. "Have you found any recently?"

Other than the river dragon, Jason hadn't uncovered a misfit dragon in months. It left him worried whether there were any more, and he certainly worried that he had overlooked others. Knowing Therin and his plan, it was entirely possible that he had left other dragon eggs scattered throughout the known lands.

"I'm not sure it matters," Jason said.

Lorren grunted. "Oh, it matters. And I've returned to see if perhaps there is anything you might do to help."

Jason quickly glanced at the others, pausing a moment to stare at Olar and Cherise before turning his attention back to Lorren. "If you think there's a dragon misfit, then I'm happy to help."

He had traveled with the Dragon Guard before, but he began to wonder if Lorren was a part of the Dragon Guard. He flicked his gaze to the back of the room and the hidden figure. Somebody like this would offer them a different way to defeat Jessica. As Jason looked around the chamber, he didn't see anyone else watching Lorren the same way. It seemed almost as if they were concerned.

Why would they not want to involve Jason?

He needed the light to be a bit brighter and to know who was hiding there.

"I have found activity that leaves me questioning whether or not it is one of these so-called misfits. It's dangerous. Much as I hear *they* are dangerous."

Jason turned his attention back to Lorren. "The dragon misfits are real. And they have been mistreated by Lorach."

"As I have seen," Lorren said.

"Seen?"

"The dragons. The misfits. And Lorach. I dispatched a dozen of them recently, leaving them—"

"What do you mean you dispatched them?" Sarah asked.

Could Lorren be responsible for what Jason had detected? The dragons had been there—then gone.

"I removed the threat," he said, his tone making it clear he would not discuss it any further.

"Which misfit have you seen?" Jason asked.

He found it strange that Cherise and Olar had been silent. That troubled him. Something about Lorren left them uncomfortable. He could see it on their faces. He could see it in the stiffness of their posture. He could even see that same discomfort in Henry, which was unusual in itself. Henry rarely was uncomfortable. Having trained with the Dragon Souls, the only time Henry had been nervous was when he had felt the need to return to Lorach. Even then, Henry had done what was necessary to protect the dragons.

"All of them."

Jason pulled his gaze back to Lorren. "I don't think so."

He crossed his arms over his chest, watching Lorren. "If you would've said that you had seen the ice dragon, I wouldn't have been surprised. He tends to be quite visible —when he wants to be. Otherwise, he's no more visible than a cloud." Perhaps a fast-moving cloud, but even that would be difficult for anyone to see with the ice dragon flying as high as he could. "If you would have said the iron dragon, perhaps I would have thought you had seen him. He can certainly be noticeable. Made of what appears to be molten metal, when he's flying at full speed, he glows so brightly that he looks like the sun." The idea of it made Jason smile even now.

Cherise and Olar sat silently watching him. Sarah was stiff between them, though he noticed that she clutched a dragon pearl tightly in hand. He didn't think she'd need the dragon pearl but didn't want her to do anything that would get her into more trouble with her parents.

Jason recognized the uncertainty within Henry. He might look as if he were comfortable, but it was an act. If nothing else, he realized a truth from Henry. This man worried him.

Jason leaned forward, looking at Lorren. He *truly* looked at him.

His gaze darted from the dragonskin to his face and to his overall demeanor. Jason had assumed he was one of the Dragon Guard, there was something different about his dragonskin. Not just the cut of the fabric, but the scales looked different, as if from a creature resembling a dragon but not quite the same.

Who was this person?

Sarah recognized him, and he needed to understand why.

"You're not with the Dragon Guard," Jason started.

Lorren shook his head. "No."

"Then why are you here?"

"As I said, because I came to decide whether I could use your help. But first, there is something I must show you."

Could he have known about the river dragon? It was possible the river dragon would have moved, and Lorren might have discovered it. If that were the case, then perhaps Jason needed to take it easier with Lorren, though there was something about the man that left Jason unsettled. There was a darkness within him.

There was something that was almost dragonlike about him.

Perhaps that was what troubled Jason the most. It wasn't anything else about him; it was that inability to be able to interpret what he might do and what his intentions were.

Lorren leaned forward, resting his elbows on the table. "*I* have another misfit."

8

Jason followed Lorren out into the street. In this part of the city, the street was wide. It stretched out toward the courtyard where dragons were trained, at least in the manner that dragons were trained within Dragon Haven. It was a different sort of process than the dragons of Lorach suffered through. Jason could see the dragons in the distance, and he could feel the power coming from them, however faintly. They passed one of the massive dragon sculptures, and Lorren merely glanced over at it. Was that a sneer on his face?

Henry stayed with Jason, and Cherise and Olar trailed a few steps behind, as if they didn't want to get too close. Sarah maintained her position alongside Jason. Every so often, she would look at him. There was a hint of worry in her eyes.

Jason still hadn't identified the other Dragon Guard at the back of the room, but he thought that he understood why there would have been one there. If Lorren was *not* with them, they would be present to ensure Cherise and Olar were safe.

"Who is he?" Jason asked Henry as he followed Lorren. He claimed to have another misfit. That mattered—and was something that Jason hadn't expected and still didn't know whether to believe. "And why did you think he was dead?" he asked Sarah.

"We thought Lorach finally caught him," she said. "He'd been with Dragon Haven, but thought to attack Lorach on his own. They trapped him. Or so we thought."

It was just what Jason intended as well. At least he better understood her fear for him. She didn't want Jason to end up captured like Lorren. Would that be how Jason would end up if that were the case?

"Lorren had been outside of the rebellion for a long time, though he fought against Lorach on his own. Even when he was here, he was dangerous. It was before my time, but the Dragon Guard are clear on what he did. Does." Henry watched him, and Jason had a distinct sense that Henry pulled on power through a dragon pearl as he followed, as if to be prepared for anything.

"Aren't we all dangerous?"

"He's dangerous in a different way. Ruthless. He's been known to slaughter both Dragon Soul and their dragons to prevent them from attacking."

That was what Lorren meant about dispatching the dozen dragons.

The stiffness he saw from Cherise and Olar made a

particular sort of sense. They respected the dragons in the same way Sarah did. That was the entire purpose of Dragon Haven. It was a place where the dragons could be safe, protected, and it was a place where the dragons were revered. Somebody like this, somebody who didn't view them the same way, who was willing to attack the dragons, to cut them down simply to prevent them from being used, could be no different than the Dragon Souls.

Or from him.

Despite his protestations, when he'd dealt with the storm dragon, Jason had been willing to bring down the dragon if needed to save other dragons. Was that any different than Lorren?

"If he has a dragon misfit…"

"That still doesn't mean we can welcome him," Henry said. "When I was in Lorach, there were stories of his brutality. It made it easier to find those willing to fight the rebellion. Who wouldn't want to stop someone so willing to slaughter both man and dragon?"

Concern began to build in Jason. Who was this man?

"What about the Dragon Guard?"

"They followed him. They didn't arrive with him," Henry said. "They realized he was heading to Dragon Haven and attempted to stop him, but he overpowered them. He's been here before, Jason. Your illusion might prevent someone who doesn't know where to look from finding us, but someone who does…"

Jason frowned. The illusion should be powerful enough to deter even a determined person, but that was a different issue. "How did one man overpower the Dragon Guard?"

"How did you overpower as many dragons as you have?"

"Are you saying he's connected to the dragons in the same way?"

If that were the case, then maybe Jason could learn something from Lorren. There might be an opportunity to get answers about the nature of his abilities. There was an element to them that was different than those of a Dragon Soul. He could use the power of the Dragon Souls, and he could connect to the dragons. He could use the dragon pearls, but he had more of that same magic within him. If Lorren had that power, they could use it *against* the Dragon Souls.

"I see that look in your eye," Henry said.

"What look is that?" Jason asked, trailing after Lorren.

"The look that says you want to know if you could work with him."

He looked over at Henry. "If he fights Dragon Souls, how could we *not* work with him?"

"Didn't you hear what I said?"

Jason sighed. "I heard you, but I also recognize we might need somebody willing to do what it takes to stop them. With Jessica…"

He didn't have to finish. They knew what Jessica had been willing to do, the way she'd been willing to attack the dragons, to force them to serve. With her power, and the control she possessed, all dragons were in danger unless Jason managed to free them.

"At what cost?" Sarah asked, turning to him. "You've saved the dragons, rescuing them and freeing them. It's because of you that we finally have an opportunity to save dragons that have been captured and trained for as long as they have. Without you—"

"Because of him, I have a fleet of dragons," Lorren said. He barely looked over his shoulder, and yet there was a hard edge to his voice.

"What do you mean a fleet of dragons? If you've trained them the same way as the Dragon Souls—"

Lorren suddenly turned to him. "What would you do?" He was about the same size as Jason. Slight of build and certainly not imposing by his appearance, but the power that suddenly flowed out from him, an awareness of energy that burst from him, left Jason thinking he needed to be careful with this man. Lorren watched Jason, a hint of amusement lingering in his eyes. "What exactly do you think that you will do, Jason Dreshen?"

If this was somebody who had power the way it seemed he did, then he didn't want to fight. He might need to use him—and his connection to the dragons. Still, he wasn't about to allow somebody to harm the dragons.

"Have you attempted to train them like the Dragon Souls?" Jason asked.

"No," Lorren said.

"That's all I ask," Jason said.

"That's all?" Lorren grinned at him. "Perhaps you

should be asking other questions, Jason Dreshen." He spun and, rather than heading toward the clearing where Jason thought he'd go, he headed into the forest.

Jason frowned, debating for a moment before veering off and following him into the trees. The others stayed with him. Cherise and Olar remained quiet.

"What's wrong with them?" Jason asked Henry.

"Lorren had been with Dragon Haven long ago. He's rumored to have killed the dragon Cherise worked with years ago."

"He killed her dragon?"

"The dragon had been claimed by one of the Dragon Souls. Lorren refused to allow it to be used, and so he slaughtered the dragon." Henry turned and stared at Lorren. "At least, according to rumor. Who knows if that's true or not."

"It's true enough," Lorren said. He glanced over at Cherise, and she clenched her jaw, staring at him. "She doesn't want to admit it, but she failed to adequately prepare her dragon for what it might face. I tried to warn her, but she wouldn't listen. None of them listened."

"Is that why you're here?" Jason asked.

"I'm here because of you," Lorren said. "I have my sources—especially in Lorach—and have heard of these misfits. That is why I've come."

They continued through the forest. This part of the forest was incredibly dense, and the trees rising up around them created a difficulty in navigating through here. They took a small path, and no one spoke. A little bit of sunlight drifted through, though not so much that it warmed much of the forest itself. The air still had a humidity to it. All in all, it was far more pleasant than Jason's home.

Sarah stayed alongside him, finally grabbing onto his arm. She leaned close to him. "He makes me uncomfortable."

"I think that's his intention," Jason said.

"I've heard stories about him when I was young." She looked up at her parents and then over at Henry. "They're the same kind of stories Henry has been telling you, but more than just what he did to my mother's dragon. He's taken on Dragon Souls by himself."

"So have we."

"Not we. You," Sarah said. "But you took on Dragon Souls with just a single dragon. He went against an entire squad of dragons. Fifty. With no misfits. And he emerged unscathed."

"Not unscathed," Lorren said. He turned and pointed to his cheek. A thick beard covered his jawline, but beneath it, Jason could make out a long scar running along the jawline. "Not at all unscathed."

Jason frowned. "You were able to take on a squad of dragons all by yourself?"

"With enough training, anyone could have done it."

"Anyone?"

Lorren glanced over at Cherise and Olar. "Perhaps not anyone."

They glared at him. They disliked each other, but did that matter?

Jason had been looking or a way to defeat Lorach.

This man had it.

They headed deeper into the forest.

"How?" Jason asked as they walked.

Lorren looked over. "As I said, anyone with half a connection to the dragons could have done it. Lorach uses the same patterns. They are predictable."

"Maybe they had been. I don't know if they are anymore." Especially now that Jessica led them. She had changed tactics on them.

He noticed movement on either side of him. As he peered into the trees, he realized Dragon Guards followed. They were moving in the shadows, trying to avoid being detected, but moving so quickly, they weren't able to hide their movements.

Jason turned his attention back to Lorren to see him sneer at the Dragon Guards moving in the darkness. He knew they were there. Nothing else about his demeanor changed, though.

"Where are you taking us?" Henry asked.

"You don't know?" Lorren asked.

"No. Are we supposed to know something?" Cherise's voice had a sharp edge to it, as if she wanted to shout but feared yelling at him.

"Then you are a fool," Lorren said.

Jason frowned, but an awareness he hadn't noticed

before started to press upon him. The longer they walked, the more he became aware of it. It was a strange pressure that continued to build around him, leaving him unsettled.

It took a moment to realize what he detected, though he didn't know why it should trouble him. When he understood what he felt, the sense of it was there, burning within him.

A dragon.

As Jason focused on the dragon, he couldn't tell what kind of dragon it was. It wasn't any sort of dragon they were accustomed to finding.

Could Lorren have found a misfit?

He'd mentioned the misfits, but Jason thought the ice dragon would have said something had he found another. As Jason followed the sense, energy continued to build. He looked around but didn't see anything.

"Are you there?" he whispered.

He squeezed the iron dragon glove, feeling the pressure of the dragon within his hand and the surge of awareness that flowed between them. By holding onto that awareness, he could feel the energy building within him, the connection forming, the bond that existed between them suddenly solidifying.

"I'm here," the iron dragon said, the connection forming within his mind.

"There's another one here. I need you to help me know where they are."

Sarah frowned at him. "What are you doing?"

"I'm talking to the iron dragon," he said.

"You can do that even when he's not here?"

"I'm connected," he said, holding his hand out to show her the iron dragon glove. The glove covered his hand, the metal always warm, though not unpleasantly so. He had grown accustomed to having its presence on his hand, along with the connection that it permitted him to share with the iron dragon.

As he watched Lorren, he noticed a stiffness that made Jason wonder if he detected what Jason was doing, possibly even an awareness of how he communicated with the iron dragon. He ignored that feeling, focusing instead on the energy of the iron dragon as he followed Lorren. The iron dragon had been off a ways, though not so far that he would not have been able to return were Jason to need him.

"There is something," the iron dragon rumbled within his mind.

"I don't see it, though I feel it," Jason said.

"Similar to the storm?"

Jason didn't think so. With the storm dragon, there had been the rumbling and the thunder and the chaos of the storm clouds that fueled him. This was something else. As Jason looked around, he couldn't make out what it was, but he felt confident it was another dragon misfit.

A faint mist swirled around the trees.

Jason had seen a mist within the forest before, and given the humidity of this place, he wasn't altogether surprised, but there was something unusual here. He stopped near one of the trees with traces of mist swirling around it and leaned down. There was something almost tangible about the mist. He focused on it, taking a deep breath. As he breathed in, that moisture flowed through him, and something constricted. He coughed, trying to push it out, but couldn't.

Panic set in, only for a moment.

He embraced the power of the ice and the iron dragon, letting that magic flow through him. Together, the two dragons created a healing wave of energy that worked through him. It dispelled the mist.

He straightened, looking at Lorren. "What are your intentions here?"

Lorren watched him. "I told you to follow."

Jason shook his head. "No." He motioned to Henry to halt and noticed him reaching into his pocket, grabbing for dragon pearls. At least Henry would be prepared. Cherise and Olar paused, looking from Jason to Lorren, a question in Cherise's eyes. When she turned her attention to Lorren, hatred still burned there.

Sarah stopped behind him, hesitating for a moment, staying close, but Jason could feel the power she was pulling and recognized her concern as well.

"What is it?" Henry whispered.

Jason stared at the mist swirling around the trees before turning his attention back to Lorren. "I've been feeling something for a little while now." He nodded to Lorren. "He has an arrogance about his power and what he claims we should detect. We're overlooking something."

Lorren watched him. They didn't have all the answers about him, which bothered Jason. He had come because he claimed to have a misfit he wanted to show Jason. Wasn't that it?

Why bring them out here?

Unless *that* was where the misfit hid.

"There's energy within the trees," Jason said. "I can feel it."

"I should hope so," Lorren said. "Seeing as how you are supposed to be the great dragon expert."

Jason looked around, ignoring Lorren. "It's the mist," he said, nodding to Cherise and Olar. They were near a tree where the mist swirled. "It's not natural. Stay away from it, and don't breathe it in. If you do, it seems to be controlled by something." He nodded to Lorren, keeping his gaze on him. "I suspect it's his dragon."

Henry frowned. "You're saying he has a *mist* dragon?"

"I don't know. Whatever he has possesses the ability to control it."

"Very good," Lorren said, turning toward Jason.

The mist began to swirl around him, filling the space in between the trees, sneaking through the area. It moved rapidly, spinning. The mist dragon reminded him of the storm dragon in a way. The agitation. The power. Could Lorren have been responsible for the storm dragon, and not Therin?

Jason prepared his power, holding on to the energy from the iron dragon along with the ice dragon. He also readied for the possibility that he might need to create an illusion. He could tilt reality enough to control things, shifting the nature of what everyone saw around him. When it came to Lorren, Jason thought he needed to be prepared for doing something like that now.

"What is your intention?" Jason looked around him, noting the mist continuing to build. "There are a handful of Dragon Guard in the trees. You won't be able to harm Cherise and Olar."

Lorren smiled. "And then there's you." He took a step forward, and the mist started to swirl with him. "A man who claims power. A man who has connected to lost dragons," he said, tipping his head as he taunted him. "A man who claims he can rescue dragons from Dragon Souls and can bring them back rather than needing to destroy those that have been tormented."

"I *can* rescue them. If you are familiar with the dragons, you have seen what I can do."

Lorren snorted. "I have seen what you can do. And I have felt it. Do you think what you do has no repercussions?"

Jason glanced over at Sarah for a moment before turning his attention back to Lorren. "We do what is necessary to free the dragons." Sarah clutched her dragon pearl, and he could feel her calling upon the power within it, prepared to use it.

"You probably did not recognize the consequences of your actions. You have put more than just your dragons into danger. All dragons are in danger with what you do. Lorach was content with their stretch of land. Or had been. Now they look elsewhere. Now they move when they had been quiet. Now dragons suffer—truly free dragons and not those you claim to have freed—that would not have. The Dragon Guard managed to keep Lorach confined, which was enough. Until you." He watched Jason. "Now I have to finish what you cannot."

The mist continued to swirl, and a shape was taking form within it.

A dragon. It *was* a misfit.

The iron dragon neared. Jason could feel him and quietly urged him to stay hidden. If nothing else, he wanted to have the iron dragon ready to act if necessary, but he didn't want to target the mist dragon.

Jason focused on the energy of the ice and the iron dragon, combining that power, and poured it toward the mist dragon.

It faded.

This dragon seemed to have a natural immunity to Jason's abilities.

How would that happen?

There shouldn't be any way for the dragons to ignore the power he used.

How could he overpower them?

He altered his approach. Using the forest dragon, he tilted reality just enough to solidify the mist dragon, then added his connection to the iron and ice dragons, bonding the two in a way that permitted him to focus that power. The energy struck the mist dragon, but then it slipped away, tendrils of it fading, slipping from the dragon.

Lorren watched him. With a wave of his hand, the mist dispersed, as did Jason's power. He lost control over the illusion, along with his connection to the iron and ice dragon.

Sarah gasped. Jason suspected she had lost her connection to the dragon pearl as well.

He was powerful. Not only that, but the dragon was powerful.

Lorren turned to Jason, the mist swirling around him. "You thought you were the only one who had connected to the so-called misfits. Unfortunately, you were mistaken."

With that, the mist streaked toward him.

9

Jason backed away. The iron dragon might be getting closer to him, but he reached for his connection to the ice dragon. He could feel the ice dragon flying high overhead, drifting within the upper atmosphere, the cold calling to it. He borrowed that cold, and with a surge, he summoned ice lightning. It was the only energy he thought might be able to counter Lorren.

Jason braced himself for the eruption of energy. When it slammed into the ground, he felt it crash toward the mist dragon. The ice lightning crackled around the mist dragon, and it solidified it. Surrounded by an ice ball, the dragon could no longer move.

Jason held out his iron dragon hand, the heat already beginning to radiate.

"What are you doing?" Jason demanded.

"I intend to see what your dragons are capable of." Lorren backed away, and the mist continued to swirl.

He looked around, the power from his connected dragons filling him. "Try that again, and you will see what I will do to protect my dragons and me," Jason said, turning to Lorren. Heat radiated off him. In the distance, he could feel the iron dragon slithering closer.

Lorren started laughing. It was a wild and crazed sound, but he grinned as he turned to Jason. "Lovely," he said. With a wave of his hand, mist started to swirl from him.

Jason embraced the ice dragon, and he froze it. "What are you doing? If you oppose the Dragon Souls, then we can work together."

Lorren turned toward the mist dragon and focused on it. There was a strange glowing sense, almost a pulsing that came from within the ice ball that surrounded the mist dragon. Jason summoned the power of the ice dragon again, and another bolt of ice lightning streaked down from the sky, crashing into the mist dragon. Another layer of ice surrounded the mist dragon.

The others around the forest remained quiet, staying off to the side. Sarah clutched a dragon pearl, but her parents simply watched, their gaze focused on Jason before darting to Lorren. No one acted against him, though. They waited for Jason to do so.

And these were the people who would have the Dragon Guard act against Lorach?

They couldn't even act against somebody in their own city.

"Keep an eye out for anything else," he whispered, warning the ice dragon.

If this man was willing to attack them in Dragon Haven, he worried it might be a distraction, a ruse to try to come at them from a different angle.

He shifted his focus to the energy of the forest dragon. If she were willing to come, then perhaps she would be able to help this dragon, the same way that she had helped the storm dragon.

He turned to Lorren. "You don't have to do this," he said. "I felt what you were doing to me."

"What I did to you or what you did to yourself? I believe you were the one who attacked this dragon. I could've warned you that was a mistake."

"We both want the same thing. We both want to stop Lorach."

Jason called upon another ice lightning bolt, and it slammed down from high overhead, crashing into the mist dragon, adding yet another layer.

Within that ice ball, the mist dragon continued to pulse, and there came a steady energy pushing against what Jason held onto. In time, he suspected he wouldn't be able to maintain his connection to this dragon. Eventually, it would fade, and the dragon would escape. Strange, considering that mist was water and the ice dragon had control over water.

Unless there was something more to the mist than he understood.

Could this not even be a mist dragon? He thought

about the river, the spray, the way the water had swirled. Could it be the river dragon?

He'd seen the egg. He thought he understood the power that dragon would have. That meant this wasn't the river dragon. He didn't know which dragon it was, whether it was mist or not, but he believed that it had been hatched for longer than the other misfits.

The stories about Lorren made sense. How he'd disappeared. How he attacked Lorach. Even how he had killed Dragon Souls. All of it fit. "You hatched a dragon misfit long before these others," Jason said, realizing the truth.

Lorren stared at him.

Jason took a step toward him, still holding the power of the ice and the iron dragon. He was readying to use the power of the forest dragon, though with the power Lorren had over the mist, and the control he had with it, he couldn't help but wonder if he had some way to dismiss that power.

The mist was the key. There was something about it that felt… different.

More than how it was not one of the misfit hatch mates. It felt foreign in a way Jason had never felt from dragon misfits before. The energy in it was off—and painful.

Lorren needed Jason for something. That was what he said.

Was it the connection he shared with the misfits?

A different idea came to him. "Were you the one who taught Therin?"

Lorren's face clouded. "He abused my trust."

The power of the mist continued to swirl from him, and he could feel the dragon attempting to struggle against the way that he was held, but Jason maintained his connection to the ice dragon. With the ice dragon flying as high overhead as he was, connected to the biting cold, he had almost infinite stores of power. Jason served as a conduit, little more than that, but he could add his own touch to it.

"Why did you come here?" Jason asked.

"Because I needed to see if the rumors were true about you. I needed to know if you trained these dragons."

Jason swept his gaze around him briefly. The iron dragon was just out of eyesight, behind the trees. He could feel him, though. "I haven't trained anything. I'm connected to the dragons and use that connection to free them."

"What about that," Lorren asked, nodding to Jason's hand.

Jason raised his iron glove. "This was a dragon pearl that formed around my hand. It's much like the other dragon pearls I've been granted."

"You've been *granted* them?"

"The other misfits granted me a connection to their power."

Lorren watched him for a long moment. There came a pressure in the air, and Jason readied for a possible attack. A hint of a smile curved Lorren's lips. "I believe you."

With that, he waved his hand again, and the mist shattered the ice surrounding the dragon. The mist dragon suddenly swirled out.

Jason readied another ice lightning strike, feeling power building from behind him from the other Dragon Guard. The iron dragon was there, readying to attack, and even somewhere overhead, he could feel the ice dragon preparing to descend.

Unsurprisingly, he didn't feel the forest dragon. That was simply how she worked. She wouldn't reveal her presence unless absolutely necessary.

There was no attack. The mist swirled and then retreated, backing away.

Lorren watched him.

"What are you going to do?" Jason asked.

"I had to know whether or not you forced the connection. Given everything I'd heard about you, it seemed almost impossible to believe. And then there were these dragons. They seemed freed, but I couldn't be sure whether or not they truly were freed. With Lorach moving, I knew I had to take action."

"I've done whatever I can to ensure their safety."

"Interesting," Lorren said. "If what you've done is effective, I no longer need to slaughter them."

"You shouldn't have slaughtered them in the first place," Jason said.

"It was a mercy. Trust me when I tell you the dragons do not care."

There was a dark streak of cruelty within Lorren. How could he think that the dragons wouldn't care about being slaughtered? But there was what the ice dragon had said to him, a practicality that suggested he wasn't wrong about it.

Lorren glanced over at the mist dragon. Something passed between them. Jason could feel it. The dragon disappeared, fading into the forest, as if settling out like mist flowing around the trees.

"I have seen what I need. Now it's time for us to talk. There is much we can offer each other."

They weren't that dissimilar. Lorren was a misfit, just like Jason. He might take a more dangerous approach to the dragons, but that didn't mean they couldn't work together. "Just like that?"

He glanced at the trees. "You can tell the ten Dragon Guards they can follow us back to the city."

Jason looked over at Henry. "There were ten?"

"I don't know. I wasn't the one who deployed them."

Lorren turned and started marching back to the forest, heading back the way they'd come.

Jason had no choice but to follow. He didn't know how to even react. The ice hadn't stopped Lorren. It had done nothing. Lorren had been too powerful for Jason. He marveled at the power of that dragon, the way Lorren could use it, and he marveled at the energy within him.

They marched quickly back toward the city, and when they passed through the border of the forest, the iron dragon was there, slithering toward the clearing and watching all the way. High overhead, Jason was aware of the ice dragon, swirling, power pulsing out from him.

Other dragons were there.

Jason wondered how they had been alerted, though he suspected that the Dragon Guards had somehow managed to do so. Perhaps Henry had a hand in that as well, though Jason wasn't sure whether he could trigger a warning to them. As they headed through the streets, the dragons followed. Lorren never looked up, though Jason suspected Lorren was utterly aware of the dragons and chose to ignore them.

He followed Lorren back into the throne room, and he took a seat at the table, waiting for the others to file in and sit. The Dragon Guard took positions around the inside of the room this time.

"I don't know that they're going to be able to do anything," Jason whispered to Henry.

"Probably not, but I think it makes Olar and Cherise feel better," Henry said.

Jason leaned over to Sarah, frowning. "I don't like this. Lorren might—"

Lorren leaned forward, glaring at him. "Lorren might what?" When Jason didn't answer, he shook his head, staring across the table, seemingly ignoring everyone else. "You asked about Therin, and I will tell you what happened." Lorren leaned forward. "I found him wandering. Alone. Covered in furs much like Henry now wears," he said, nodding to Henry. "Yes, I know you." He sneered at Henry. "I know what you are."

"Were," Henry said.

"And much like Therin, that wasn't always the case."

Henry frowned, his jaw clenching. He squeezed the dragon pearl a moment.

"At first, I didn't know whether I could trust him, but I believed him a wanderer. He told me about trying to find dragons. I questioned him, tormenting him, wanting him to break. I believed he was a Dragon Soul."

"Do you do that to everybody who comes to you?" Jason asked.

"Only if I don't trust them," Lorren said. He looked over at Henry before turning his attention back to Jason. "In all that time, he didn't break. I began to believe him. I believed that he merely looked for understanding of the dragons. He wouldn't be the first person I'd found. He had a connection to them. I was able to determine that quite early. How was I supposed to have known that he was a Dragon Soul?"

"You would've known," Henry said.

"As they knew with you?" Lorren asked, glancing at Cherise and Olar before turning her attention to Henry.

"I have made no attempt to hide who and what I am," Henry said.

"Only, you haven't been as honest as you could be, either," he said to Henry. "Do you think I have no contacts within Lorach? I have to know where they're moving the dragons somehow." He paused, letting his words settle a moment. "Did they know how you used to work with the dragons? Training them, I seem to believe you called it. They understand what happened and how you acquired those lovely scars on your back?"

Henry leaned forward, tension within him.

"I imagine you haven't told them about how you were once well known for your torment of the dragons."

"I never tormented the dragons," Henry said.

"You were a Dragon Soul. That is all you do."

Jason could see the rage boiling within Henry, and knew that if he didn't do or say anything, there would be no opportunity to calm this down. "We are talking about Therin," Jason said.

"Yes. Therin. Indeed. He came to me, and he wanted to understand the dragons. He traveled with me for the better part of three years."

Jason glanced over at Henry for confirmation of what Lorren said, frowning at him. "Three years?"

"I don't know. It could have been a while ago. Therin had disappeared from the city for a while, and rumors spread about it, though… I don't know," Henry said.

"How long ago was this?"

"Nearly ten years ago," Lorren said. "He came with me, and he learned from me. We traveled extensively, seeing much of the lands beyond the borders of Lorach. He gained my trust, slowly at first, but the longer we were together, the easier it became to trust him. He fought alongside me. He killed alongside me," Lorren said, looking at Henry.

Jason couldn't imagine how Therin could have been buried so deeply within what Lorren was doing that he would have been able to kill other Dragon Souls. Of course, this was Therin. Therin had been willing to do whatever it took, to betray whoever he had to, to do what he thought that he needed to do.

"What else?"

"We traveled. We saw. We began to learn."

"Began to?"

"I had already learned quite a bit at that time, and I shared what I knew with Therin."

"About dragon eggs."

"Yes."

"About how they could take on the traits of their environment," Jason said.

"I found eggs as we traveled," Lorren said. "Finding eggs in the wild is rare. Females are difficult to find, which is why I went hunting Dragon Souls. If I could trap some of their females, we could learn from the eggs."

"What do you mean that you trapped them?"

"Exactly what I said. A trap is a trap," Lorren said. "And I brought them with me. My dragons were more than willing to mate."

Jason sat back, aghast at what he was hearing. "You held the dragons for mating purposes?"

"Is it so different than what the Dragon Souls have done? You look at me as if I'm some sort of monster, and yet, all I do is what must be done to conquer them and free them."

"It doesn't sound as if you want to free the dragons. It sounds to me as if you want to control them."

"There is a cost to freedom," Lorren said.

Jason didn't know what to say. There might be a cost

of freedom, but was that the cost that he wanted to pay? He couldn't help but feel as if what Lorren was telling him, what this man was willing to do, was beyond what Jason was willing to do.

He thought of what he'd seen in Dragon Haven, the way the dragons had been freed, the way that they were revered, protected, and how the people of Dragon Haven celebrated them. Was that not what the dragons should be?

"I see the way you look at me. It's certainly better than other lands where the dragons were slaughtered for their bones," Lorren said, glancing back at the Dragon Guard. Jason's gaze drifted to their dragon bone swords, the slender blades stronger than steel. "In those lands, they were stripped of their flesh, their blood boiled off, leaving nothing but their bones."

"Why?" Sarah asked, leaning forward.

Jason looked at her, then glanced at her parents. They'd been silent.

"Because the bones carry power. Some can access that power, and they draw upon it, using that energy to rule. I would see the dragons freed. I would see them unleashed upon the world. And if they can't be freed, then…"

Jason squeezed the iron dragon glove, tensing it in frustration. "Then you would destroy them?"

"If necessary."

"There are other ways," Jason said softly.

"I have been doing this far longer than you, Jason Dreshen," he sneered.

“Tell us about the eggs,” Henry said.

Lorren grinned at him. “Are you trying to protect him? From what I was able to see, he doesn’t need any protection. He is quite capable.”

“The eggs,” Henry said, glaring at Lorren.

“Yes, well, the eggs have presented a bit of a challenge. When we finally managed to acquire some eggs, I decided it was time for us to determine whether or not we could uncover the truth of whether the dragons truly did take on the traits of their environment.”

“How?” Jason said.

“Perhaps nothing quite as profound as what I suspect Therin did. He used his power in a way that was more demanding than anything I ever had done.”

“Demanding?” Jason asked.

“He placed the eggs into much more challenging locations. I thought they needed to have something more similar to the nest where the dragons would have raised them. How would I have ever known they could tolerate such extremes?”

“You sound as if you respect him,” Sarah said.

He turned toward her, looking past Sarah and smirking at her parents. “I respect his curiosity. How could I not when he went looking for knowledge and information, searching for a way to push the boundaries of what we know?”

“He tormented the dragons,” Jason said.

“He tormented nothing. He took the eggs. How is that torment?”

Without what Therin had done, Jason wouldn't have had the ice dragon, the iron dragon, or the forest dragon. None of those dragons would've existed.

Only, what would they have been instead?

He didn't know.

By taking on the traits of their environment, they became something else. They became the misfits, but they also had been essential in bringing Therin down. Good had come out of their existence.

If Jason were able to use the power of the dragons, if he was going to stop Lorach altogether, even more good would come from it. How could he feel any other way?

"That's how you formed your mist dragon," Jason said.

"That's how I formed one of them," Lorren said.

"One?"

"There are three mist dragons." How would you get the same misfit from a different set of circumstances? There was something to what he said that felt off.

The words settled in the room, leaving Jason uncomfortable. Three of those dragons. And he'd struggled with one. "What other misfits do you have?"

"I don't refer to them as misfits, though perhaps that is what they are to you," Lorren said, leaning toward Jason.

"I don't use it as a term of derision," Jason said. "I am as much of a misfit as they are."

Lorren grinned at him. "Do you really believe that?"

"Yes."

Lorren chuckled. "Perhaps you are. There are three

mist dragons, and there are five smoke dragons. There are seven earth dragons. Or there were."

Jason blinked, staring at him. So *many*.

The rumbling in the forest he'd detected with William made sense. That had to have been an earth dragon. Or more than one. "Where are they?"

"They are with me. Safe."

Henry grunted, and Lorren looked at him.

Henry shrugged. "I don't think they are safe with you."

"You can think what you want," Lorren said.

"If you know how to create these dragons, then share it with us," Cherise said. She held Lorren with an icy gaze, as if she were summoning the power of the ice dragon.

"The last time I shared it, it was abused."

"If you can keep creating these dragons, we can use that to overthrow Lorach," Olar said.

"That is all you think about?" he asked them before turning to Jason. "They are unique, but Lorach would turn them into something else. Weapons."

Was that so different than how Jason had used the misfits?

He watched Lorren, more troubled than he had been before.

Stopping Lorach was on Jason's mind, but it was more than that. The misfits. And they wouldn't even be misfits. They would just be dragons, only a different sort of dragon.

"Not all of them are as potent as what you saw in the forest. The smoke dragons are weaker. It was a mistake. I didn't know they were going to be unwilling—and unable—to be of much assistance. The earth dragons are bound to the ground, unable to fly. That, too, was a mistake. The only ones I've been able to create that have been of any use to me are the mist dragons."

"You came here for the others," Jason said.

"I wanted to know what Therin did."

Jason frowned, looking from Sarah and Henry to Lorren.

Were he honest with himself, it was what he wanted as well.

The misfits with him *were* lonely. The ice dragon longed for another like him, as did the iron dragon. Jason suspected the forest dragon did, too. How could they not?

"I came to study these dragons and work with you, Jason Dreshen. Think about what we can learn from each other. Envision what sorts of dragons we can create, how many of the different types, and the benefits they can provide to our world."

"You came to ask if I would allow you to study these dragons," Jason said.

"At first. Then you described them." He looked around the others. "And I've seen that *you* are responsible for Lorach moving again. Unfortunately, my plans have changed. I might have come to ask," Lorren said, sitting back in his chair. "But now, I will not."

Jason started to understand the threat. "You aren't going to command me. Others who have tried have found it doesn't go so well for them."

Lorren chuckled. "I do like the confidence, and given what I saw from you out in the forest, I think some of it is warranted."

"I'm just trying to help the dragons," Jason said. "And if what I can tell of you is correct, then we want the same thing." Jason hoped he understood what Lorren was after, though he started to question whether or not he could. This was a man who had a very different experience than Jason when it came to the dragons. One that had involved fighting with not only Lorach, and the Dragon Souls, but also with people from dragon Haven, and a willingness to attack those who had wanted nothing more than to provide protection for the dragons.

It was protection it seemed to Jason that he wasn't entirely open to.

"What if there is no help for the dragons?"

"I can show you. I can show you what we can do to save the dragons. I can show you—"

A burst of energy began to build.

"This is not necessary," Jason said.

Lorren frowned at him. "What exactly do you think is happening here?"

"You. What you intend to do is not necessary. I've heard you killed the dragons. We don't have to do that. I've discovered a way of saving them."

"Saving Dragon Soul dragons?" Lorren shook his head. "Perhaps I was wrong about you. Perhaps you won't be of any help."

"Help with what?" Jason said.

Lorren shook his head. "It's because of you I had to return. And it's because of you that Lorach finally has knowledge I've attempted to keep from them." He smiled tightly. "But I know what to do about such things. I know how to handle people like you. And I know how to ensure that Lorach does not gain the power of these dragons." He took a deep breath. "Because I will hold onto that power. You contained one dragon. And you contained him because I chose to allow it. What if I were to bring all three of them at you? What if they were to suddenly appear here?"

As he said it, the mist began to swirl.

10

Jason began to call upon the ice dragon. As he focused on the energy coming from the dragons, he could feel the mist as it swirled around others in the room. Even with his connection to the ice dragon, he didn't know if he would be strong enough to stop him if Lorren decided to attack.

The question he had now was *why*.

What did Lorren need to prove? He'd demonstrated a connection to the mist dragon, and to other misfits. What more could he want to accomplish?

"What are you doing?" Jason asked.

The mist began to force the Dragon Guards back, and Lorren squeezed them until they were pushed back against the walls. The mist came deeper into the room, swirling around Cherise and Olar. Finally it wrapped around Henry, holding him. Henry clutched a dragon pearl in his hand. It glowed, but it didn't do anything.

"I thought we could work together," Lorren said. "Unfortunately, I think Dragon Haven"—he spat the name—"has corrupted you like it corrupts so much. Now I will have those dragons."

Power reached Sarah, and Jason lunged toward her, wrapping her in a barrier of ice along with fire coming from the iron dragon.

She looked over at him. "Can you do anything?"

"I've been trying," he said.

"How can he do this?"

"I have no idea," Jason said.

He held that barrier out, continuing to squeeze, pushing it away from him, but there was too much power here. He could feel it squeezing upon him, mist continuing to swirl, threatening to overwhelm him.

He added the energy of the forest dragon, calling to her, focusing on his breathing as he did. He *shifted* everything.

This time, he shifted it so it brought them into the north, into the cold in the mountains. If Lorren was going to bring them to mist, then he was going to counter it by creating cold so bitter, the mist was nullified. Jason formed that cold, created that storm, and it swirled through the room, the wind picking up. Sarah braced herself. Cold started biting, the ice tearing at everything.

Jason surged with dragon power.

He let energy explode into the room and then called upon enough cold to freeze the mist. He barely had to summon the energy of the ice dragon when he did. It crackled, and then he waited for the ice dragon to control it.

The mist somehow held.

Lorren grinned at him. "An impressive trick, but one I taught Therin."

Jason could feel the touch of the forest dragon. There was the illusion that Therin knew, and there was that which the forest dragon granted to Jason. "You don't know this trick."

He solidified reality.

There is a difference between creating an illusion and altering reality through the power of illusion. With his connection to the forest dragon, Jason could do both. The storm raged, now much more real than it had felt before. The wind picked up, the ice now something real, tearing through here. Somewhere nearby, someone cried out.

Jason ignored it, holding onto the storm, the wind, and the power.

He called upon the energy of the ice dragon, letting it fill him, and he called upon the strength of the forest dragon. He squeezed them together, binding them in a way that allowed him to create a connection. Within that power, he held it and created something the mist dragon wouldn't be able to overwhelm.

Jason solidified the air around him. Everything froze. Even those who were with him were frozen. The only one who wasn't was Lorren.

Jason took a step toward him. "What are you doing?" he asked, standing in front of Lorren. "Why do this?"

"Since you drew Lorach out, now I will finish it. To do so, I need those dragons," he said.

"Not like this," Jason said.

He maintained his hold. He could feel the mist dragons attempting to influence him though he ignored them, pushing outward. He could keep reality shifted, but he'd used everything within him to do so.

"If you wanted to understand the dragons I'm working with, then you could have asked. What you're doing is something different altogether."

The energy from the mist dragons still pressed upon him with enough force that Jason strained. Even connected as he was to the three dragons, there was almost too much working against him.

He didn't know whether Lorren had access to more dragons than what he admitted to. He might have drawn upon the energy of the smoke dragons and the earth dragons, using that connection to overwhelm Jason.

"Release your hold on the dragons," he said.

"I will when you do," Lorren said. He stood casually, almost comfortably. "You aren't going to be able to win."

"Why must it be like this?"

"Because I have taken your measure. And you play at something you cannot fully understand."

He surged again. Power exploded from him and toward Jason. The energy was significant, a sharp explosion that blasted away from him, striking Jason. It was the power of the mist, but it was the power of something else.

He was drawing upon other dragon's energy.

Jason thought he understood. The dragon pearls of the freed dragons.

As he felt the power coming from Lorren, he recognized some aspect of it. It wasn't something he could necessarily see, but it was a power he could feel. It flowed from him, from deep within him, a connection to energy that Jason had felt before. He knew those dragon pearls.

Could he connect to those dragons?

He focused on the sense. It was different than what he felt from the dragon mist. This was the heat energy of the dragons coming to the pearl. He used his connection, that which formed between him and the other dragons, and forged a connection to those dragons, sending a question.

A faint stirring was the answer. All he wanted was for the dragons to know he was here. If the dragons understood that, perhaps they would withdraw their support of Lorren.

Then the power around him started to fade.

Jason moved forward. Power filled him, but he grew increasingly tired. He wouldn't be able to hold out much longer. Now that he knew the secret to Lorren's power, he might not need to.

Lorren watched him. "What did you do?"

"I alerted the dragons that you intended to hurt me."

Jason glanced around the room. The mist remained frozen, as did everyone else within it. He held them, isolating them within that power to ensure they were secured, but also trapped in his illusion.

He altered it.

He stared at Lorren. "You won't be able to use the power of dragons I freed. I rescued them from the Dragon Souls, and I will not allow you to torment them or turn them against me."

Lorren reached into his pocket and grabbed for something. It was another dragon pearl. Jason focused on the pearl. As far as he could tell, it was a different dragon pearl, one from a dragon Jason hadn't freed.

There was something he could do.

He focused on the ice dragon, the forest dragon, and the iron dragon, using the combination of energy to connect to that dragon pearl. A connection formed.

Power surged, answering him—and not helping Lorren.

Lorren glared at him. "This isn't over," he said.

"You don't have to wage a private war against everyone who works with dragons. You don't have to fight us. We're—"

"You're trying to save the dragons of Lorach, and yet you don't know anything about the power that exists in the world."

"I know enough," Jason said. "And I've learned I can work with the dragons. They can be saved." Jason looked at Lorren and frowned. "You are the reason those dragons disappeared," he said softly.

Lorren turned his attention to Jason, staring at him. "What dragons would those be?"

He spoke to Sarah. "When I came to your parents, I told them how I had felt the other dragons, and I didn't know what happened to them, only that I had seen the Dragon Soul dragons. They disappeared." Or so he had thought. Could that resistance not have been coming from the Dragon Souls as he'd feared? Jason had worried that Jessica had taught the Dragon Souls how to fight in such a way that he wouldn't be able to restore the dragons, but maybe it was Lorren. Having seen how powerful he was, he couldn't help but think that perhaps that was what it was.

"The dragons beyond the mountains. That was you."

Lorren glared at him. "The dragons must be used in the right way."

Hearing that told Jason all he needed to know about Lorren. His wasn't a desire to help dragons at all. Why would the mist dragons allow themselves to be used by him?

Unless they didn't know any better.

Could he connect to those dragons and share the truth? As he tried to form a connection, he failed. He retreated.

"You don't have to be like Therin," he said. "I spent enough time with him to know him."

"You don't know him like I knew him," Lorren said.

"Probably not. You traveled with him for years, and I only traveled with him for a day, but I battled him for long enough that I understood him." He sensed a hesitation within Lorren, and Jason thought to use it. Maybe he could get through to Lorren. "I was the one who killed him," Jason said.

"He's not gone," Lorren said.

Jason sighed. "He *is* gone. We fought. He tried to use illusion against me, he tried to use one of the misfits against me, but when I got through to the misfit, I separated Therin from the illusion and killed him."

Lorren looked around. "This is more than just illusion."

"That is my connection to the dragons," Jason said.

Lorren stared at him. "He's really gone?"

"He's gone. We have taken the fight to Lorach. There are fewer of the Dragon Souls with dragons remaining. With enough time, I'm convinced we can stop the Dragon Souls entirely."

That was the goal, but Jason wasn't entirely sure what he wanted. He wanted to prevent Dragon Souls from using the dragons, but there was some part of him that questioned whether that was what he really needed to do. Reaching for the dragons, to connect to them differently, might be more critical. By using what he knew, he had to believe that he might be able to get through to the Dragon Souls, and perhaps even help them come around.

Lorren might not come around, though. With his attitude about the dragons, and what he was willing to do with them, he had to wonder if there could be any way of turning him back.

What would it be like if the world was filled with dragons and those who could connect to them, but where they were all free? It seemed almost impossible to believe.

Lorren watched him, and Jason waited for him to say

something else. Lorren moved his hand. With a swirl of sharp mist, he disappeared.

Jason released the illusion. Sarah surged forward, looking around at him, as did Henry. The others gradually came back around, the illusion releasing more slowly.

"Where is he?" Henry asked.

"Gone," Jason said.

"Are you sure?"

"No."

That was the part that troubled him. Lorren could be anywhere. With his ability, the way he could connect to the mist, he might be able to hide among them. And if that were the case, then Jason had no idea how they would keep track of him.

The sudden disappearance troubled him, but more than that, he couldn't shake the feeling that as much as he might not care for Lorren, and as much as he had no reason to trust him, if Lorach were coming for Dragon Haven the way they all believed, Lorren might be a part of it.

How could they control that, though?

Given what Jason had felt while out with the dragons, he suspected that Lorren was powerful and likely dangerous.

He needed to be careful.

They all needed to be careful.

Lorren wanted the dragons.

"We have to find him," Jason said. Either to find a way

to work with him… or to stop him. Jason hoped it didn't come down to that.

"We have other things to be concerned about," Henry told him.

"We might, but we also need to know what he's doing. It might make a difference between us succeeding and not."

"What do you think he's up to?"

Jason shook his head. "I wish I knew. Unfortunately, I have no idea."

11

Jason reached out with his connection to the dragons, trying to probe for Lorren, searching for where he had gone, but there was nothing. The other man had disappeared altogether. He looked up at the treetops, searching for any sign of the mist dragons, though he saw nothing. What would his smoke dragons or earth dragons even look like?

Would they be dangerous?

Jason headed slowly to the forest. The iron dragon followed him, but there was no sign of other dragons.

"What do you think you're going to find here?" Sarah asked.

William was near her, once again with the small red dragon. The dragon seemed far more confident this time than Jason would've expected from him, though of course, perhaps the dragon was more confident knowing what they might encounter.

"William and I came across something when I was here before."

"You told me you thought it might be a dragon misfit."

"Right. We thought it came through the trees, but I don't know if that was it at all."

"What was it, then?" Sarah asked.

"What if it was in the ground?"

Sarah's eyes widened. "One of his."

Jason nodded. "That's my concern." William looked at them with confusion. He hadn't been there for Lorren's show of strength. Jason didn't think William could fully understand what had taken place. "When Lorren attacked, he mentioned having several misfits. Dragons he had somehow created. Three of them. The mist dragons, which he used to attack. Smoke dragons. And earth dragons."

William's breath caught. "You think we came across one of his earth dragons?"

Jason nodded. "The timing is right and it fits with what we know of him. He might have surrounded Dragon Haven." He looked over at Sarah. "I would expect he had preparations."

He'd tricked them into bringing them into the council chamber, and had separated Jason somewhat from his connection to the ice dragon—at least initially. Lorren might have thought Jason needed proximity to the dragons to use their power, much like he would have required proximity to the mist dragons to use theirs.

"So if these were earth dragons, what are you hoping to find?" Sarah asked.

"A trail," Jason said.

They headed to the forest, returning to where they had detected that strange undercurrent of energy before. As they neared it, Jason couldn't feel anything.

"We need to be careful," Sarah said. "It's dangerous to go after him."

"Even after what he did?"

"I know what he did, but I don't want us to go after him. As long as he leaves Dragon Haven alone, what does it matter?"

Jason held her gaze before looking at the red dragon with William. "I don't have the sense that he's going to leave Dragon Haven alone. He wants the dragons."

"That's not the reason you're going after him, though."

Jason shook his head. "He wants to stop Lorach. We could do it together."

"Even after what he did?"

"What did he do but try to wrest control of the dragons? He failed. I still think we can find him, and then convince him to work with us, not against us."

"I don't know if you're right," Sarah said softly.

Neither did Jason.

That was what troubled him.

He followed the same path they'd taken when they'd been here before, heading through the trees. "When we were here before, the treetops trembled. It was as if something moved through here that slammed into the trees."

Sarah looked up. "And you think *that* was this earth dragon? I've been around many dragons over the years, and none of them could damage trees without harming themselves."

"Show her," he said, motioning to the iron dragon.

The iron dragon rumbled, and power flowed from him. He rammed into one of the trees, and the branches trembled, shaking overhead.

"That's just one tree," she said.

"Can you show her more than one tree?" Jason asked

The iron dragon spread his wings and rammed into the trees, shaking them. Even as he did, it still didn't make the ground tremble the same way as when they had been here before.

"We have to figure out where the earth dragons could gain access underground. Lorren has them around us somewhere," he said.

He recognized the tracings of power that existed, and even if he didn't know where they came from or how to reach them, Jason knew that power had to be there.

The iron dragon remained near him, power coming from him. It trembled the ground, creating an echoing sensation. At first, Jason wasn't sure what the dragon tried to do, but gradually he recognized it. He used his power to connect to what was beneath them.

Sarah connected to her dragon pearl, trailing after him. He didn't feel anything more within the way that she was holding onto that power. He could feel the sense of energy and the connection to the dragon.

"Do you detect something?" William asked, running up alongside him. The red dragon chased after William, something playful in the way he did.

Jason couldn't help but smile as he watched the dragon.

"I think the dragon detects something, though I'm not exactly sure what it is. I can feel some energy there."

The energy coming from the iron dragon surged, suddenly significant. A reverberation came beneath him from someplace underground. The dragon moved ahead of him, and Jason followed.

He came upon another ridgeline and stopped. A river rushed in the distance. Jason lingered for a moment, staring down. This was where the iron dragon had led him. Was it a coincidence that he had come across an egg in the river, and now he stood in front of this river?

"What is it?" Sarah asked as she came up behind him.

He didn't think that it was the same river, but he couldn't help feel as if there was something unusual here. "This is where the trail leads," he said. "There's something down there." Turning to the iron dragon, he asked, "Can you see what's down there?"

The dragon rumbled, then launched off the ledge, hovering in his unique flying style.

"I can't get over how strange it is watching him fly," Sarah said. "It's the way he glows, I think."

"His glowing gives him a connection to the power within him." Jason smiled as the iron dragon descended along the rock wall. "I remember when I first started working with him. He couldn't fly at the time. I wasn't sure if he would be able to learn. There was something different about him, the metallic wings and how they moved, that made it so that I wasn't at all sure about what he could do. It's just that he had never had a chance to stretch…"

Jason stared at the iron dragon, an idea coming to him. It was one he hadn't considered before, though he should have.

"What is it?" William asked, joining him at the edge of the ledge looking down. The dragon with him perched at the rock line, leaning forward and breathing out with a streamer of smoke that drifted toward the river.

"I've been looking for other misfits, thinking about how to find them, but I haven't given any thought about whether there's been any trend among the misfits we've seen." He looked at the iron dragon. "They haven't been beyond a specific distance from Lorach."

"That's true," Sarah said, crouching down and staring at the river. "All of them are within a day by dragon."

"That makes sense. Therin would want to make sure he could check on them," William said.

"What if that's not it?" Jason asked.

He looked at the dragon flying below him and had a different idea. "We've been assuming Therin took eggs from Lorach to do these experiments, but from what Henry said, he wouldn't necessarily have been permitted to do that. At least, not with many eggs. They're too valuable." Which meant there might have to be another source for eggs.

"Where would he have gotten them?" William asked. "Did he take them from Dragon Haven?"

Sarah shook her head. "We would have known. And if they're not from Dragon Haven—"

"Some of them might be from Lorren," Jason finished.

"That's why he's come?"

Jason stared at the iron dragon. It made more sense why Lorren had been so angry at the misfits—and why he'd believed there was something about them he was owed. It was because they had been his eggs, as much as a dragon egg could belong to someone.

"Why would he have done that?" William asked.

"I don't know, but I think we have to find out." Jason didn't know what it would involve, only that understanding the egg and the way the misfits formed might be the most important thing he could do for the dragons—other than freeing them from the Dragon Souls.

"We could return to where the other dragons were hatched and see if there's anything to help us," William suggested.

That didn't feel right to Jason.

They need to find Lorren. Not go searching for where the dragons had hatched.

"We've spent plenty of time in your homeland," Sarah said. "Not that I wouldn't go back if you think it's going to be beneficial, but I don't know how much more we're going to find there."

Jason shook his head. "I don't even think that's where we'd need to go. Therin didn't place that egg. As far as he was concerned, that egg had been stolen from him. He went looking to see where it had gone. It was the others, though. The iron dragon. The forest dragon. The jungle dragon. The…"

"The what?" Sarah asked.

He looked over at her. "The storm dragon. I know so little about him, but I think we have to figure out what Therin did and where he placed those eggs. When we understand that, we might be better able to understand more about what he did that allowed the eggs to hatch."

More than that, he started to wonder if that might be what Jessica had already begun doing. Jessica wanted to understand the dragons Therin had created as well. Having seen the power of the dragon misfits, he could easily imagine her trying to do everything in her power to re-create that. It would pose a danger to the dragons of Dragon Haven.

"What are you proposing?" Sarah asked.

"I think we need to keep hunting." The dragons would approve. "Only, now we're hunting for more than Lorach. We're hunting for Lorren. And his dragons."

She spun and looked at Jason. "We need to better understand all of this," she said, "but I'm not convinced wasting our time on the dragon misfits and trying to better understand them is what's going to help us stop Lorach. That's what this is all about, after all."

"I know that it is," Jason said.

"Do you?" She leaned out, motioning toward the ravine below them. "Are you sure you know that, especially given what you've been detecting?"

"What I've detected are the dragons Lorren brought here," he said.

"Exactly. The dragons *Lorren* brought here. That's not the threat."

"He is a threat," Jason said softly. "Until we get him on our side."

She shook her head. "He's always fought Lorach, not work with them."

"Even though he fights Lorach, he still opposes the dragons in a way," Jason said. "He kills the Dragon Soul dragons. That's *his* way of countering Lorach. And he wants to claim my—*our*—misfits. I would have thought you would understand."

She sighed. "I do understand." She looked across the distance—toward Lorach. "When I was captured, everything felt strange. I remember the way that Jessica held me, the fear I felt." She squeezed her eyes shut. "They've wanted to capture my parents and me for years. That it would be my fault she finally succeeded made me angry." She opened her eyes, looking over at Jason. "How would we even start tracking him?"

"Follow his misfits," Jason said. "Track earth. Mist." Maybe even smoke, but there had been no sign of that.

Sarah glanced over at William, who said nothing. He simply stared down into the valley toward the river rushing beneath them.

"I can feel something," William whispered.

Jason stepped over to him and followed the direction of his gaze. "What can you feel?"

William didn't have a connection to the dragons, and other than his training, Jason doubted William would be able to feel anything the way that he could. Probably not even the way Sarah could. William did claim to be lucky, though. Perhaps that was all this was. Luck.

"I don't know. It's just that I can feel something."

Jason stared for a little bit longer, his thoughts pulled by the memory of the egg in the water, the misfit he hadn't been able to find. That dragon was still out there. The river dragon. Somehow, he was going to have to find the dragon before Jessica and before Lorren, especially if Lorren intended to claim the dragons.

Finally he turned away. "Come on. It's time for us to see if our dragons can find his. We've got to get this over with before Lorach decides to attack. Because that's coming next."

Prior to Lorren coming to Dragon Haven, Jason would have thought that the only thing he needed to do was to head to Lorach, rescue the dragons, and defeat Jessica. Now that he knew of Lorren and the role he had in training Therin, he no longer knew if that was enough. He no longer knew if anything was enough. All Jason understood was the answers he thought he had were far more complicated than he had ever known.

Why shouldn't it be the case, though?

His own personal history was more complicated than

he ever would have known. Because of his parents, he had ended up in the northern mountains, but because of their departure from Lorach, Jason had been the one to connect to the ice dragon and had managed to save him along with the iron dragon.

Were it not for him, who knows what would've happened to the misfits?

He turned to Sarah when a flash of an image came to him, drifting through his connection from the ice dragon. It was a familiar mountainside village, a place where Jason had visited before, but not a place that he had expected the ice dragon to show him.

When a strangely flowing mist drifted through it, he realized why.

"I know where Lorren has gone. I know where we need to go."

"What if we can't get there in time?" Sarah asked.

"That's not an option."

12

The dragons guided them to the north. Jason looked over to the others with him. Sarah was well-equipped with her control over the dragon pearls and had enough magic access within those that she would be safe, but William might not be safe, especially if Lorren decided to use his power against them. He had no idea whether or not he would, only that Jason feared he might.

They landed above the city, and he looked down on the city itself. On their journey here, he hadn't seen the mist, which suggested that Lorren had either hidden, or he had already accomplished what he had intended.

The city of Varmin stretched out along the mountainside. It was not a large city, though compared to the village where Jason had grown up, it was enormous. Wooden homes were spaced neatly along the street, almost orderly, as if someone had designed the city intentionally. Several buildings were more substantial, including an inn near the center of the city. An energy existed around the city itself, as if there was some residual power from long ago. It took Jason a moment to realize why he detected that.

"Why would Lorren be here?" Sarah asked.

Jason didn't know. The ice dragon had detected something unusual, a swirl of mist, and had alerted him. Why Varmin, though?

"This is where I found the iron dragon."

"Is he trying to recreate what Therin did with your dragons?" William asked.

"They're not my dragons," Jason said.

William chuckled. "They're something. Do you see any of his misfits?"

"Not misfits," Jason started. There was an energy here that felt familiar, but the question remained: Why Varmin? "I think there's a Dragon Soul here," he whispered to Sarah as they walked toward the city.

He was dressed in his dragonskin, though he had removed the marking for an Auran now that he understood what it meant. Somebody who understood the cut and style might know it didn't belong to him, and might even know who it originally belonged to. It was the reason he had a cloak that covered his shoulders: to conceal the dragonskin. Outside of Varmin, a cloak like that wouldn't have been very comfortable. In Dragon Haven, the cloak was almost too warm.

Sarah wore a similar cloak, though hers had a pale white fur running around the hood. Her dragonskin was a different style, cut as if to fit her exactly, molding to her body. He had to avert his gaze when he found himself watching too long.

William was dressed more simply. He had taken a dragonskin—there were plenty of dragonskins in Dragon Haven, all of it stolen from Dragon Souls defeated over the years and stored to keep others from using it. The dragons didn't seem to mind when they used it. Jason found that interesting, as though the dragons were less concerned about someone taking their skin than they were about someone who didn't deserve power taking it.

"I feel the energy of a dragon pearl here," he said. "But no mist dragon." Whatever the ice dragon had seen was gone.

Sarah looked over at him. "You can feel a dragon pearl?"

Jason nodded. "It's somewhere down there," he said, focusing on Varmin. They had approached from the north, landing the dragons and leaving them situated on the mountainside above the city. At least there, they wouldn't have to worry about anyone stumbling upon them. There weren't many people who traveled up the mountain, and those who did would see nothing, thanks to the illusion Jason had placed around the dragons. Only massive trees.

"I don't feel it," she said. She clutched one of her dragon pearls, squeezing it as she stared into the distance. "Are you sure about it?"

Jason shook his head. "I'm not really sure about

anything." He wouldn't have expected a Dragon Soul to have been within Varmin. They were too far from Lorach, too isolated for the people of Lorach to spend any time here. "Maybe there is nothing more than a pearl here."

"Unless they sent somebody here to investigate the iron dragon," William said. "She will know that he came from here."

He thought he was right. Jessica likely would have known. Not only had Therin known about the iron dragon, but David had come through here, heading back to Lorach, and it was entirely possible that he would have reported to his family. If only he'd had an opportunity to work more with David and understand what he might have done or said, but unfortunately, he'd been lost before Jason had that chance.

"That might be why Lorren came," Sarah said softly.

Jason looked over to her and thought he understood.

It meant dragons were in danger. Not his—not yet—but Dragon Soul dragons.

If Lorren intended to attack…

William was otherwise quiet, staring down into the city. "This place reminds me of home," he whispered. He looked over at Jason. "It's strange. Ever since leaving my home, I haven't been anywhere but Dragon Haven."

"You could return," Jason said.

William shook his head. "I don't really want to. I lost my parents when I was fourteen. Have been on my own since then. When you came across me, I guess… I guess I got lucky." He chuckled. "Didn't I tell you that I was always lucky?"

"I'm not so sure it was luck."

"It was better that I come with you than stay behind and face the same suffering."

"How did you lose your parents?" Sarah asked.

Jason hadn't given much thought to the reason William had been living alone, but he should have. He had been so caught up in himself, in what happened with his sister and his mother, along with what happened to his village, that he hadn't paid any attention to his friend. He had been selfish.

"They were killed in a fire. Much of the village burned, at least along the outer edge of the village, where our home was located. There was a drought that year," he explained, his voice dropping off, "and everything was brittle. Dry. It didn't take long before the fire spread to the forest."

Jason thought about what he remembered about William's village. Not much. At the time, he'd been so focused on trying to survive—and returned to his own village—that he hadn't given it much thought. He could have returned. With his connection to the dragons, it wouldn't be that difficult to do so. It was a place he had considered bringing his sister and mother, though ultimately had not. They were safer in Dragon Haven. At least, they had been. Now that Lorren was proving he had an interest in Dragon Haven, Jason didn't know if that safety would persist.

"I'm sorry," Jason said.

William glanced at him. "It's not your fault."

"I'm sorry I didn't ask about them before."

William watched him for a moment before nodding slowly.

Jason turned his focus back to Varmin. He couldn't shake the feeling of pressure, that of an energy that came from down in the town. He couldn't shake the feeling that he was right, and he detected a Dragon Soul. If that were the case, then there should be an awareness of a dragon, though he didn't feel that.

Sarah took his hand, and he glanced over at her.

Jason guided them into Varmin. He held onto his connection to the iron dragon, though he could feel the ice dragon circling overhead. As they had traveled to Varmin, the ice dragon had guided them toward the mist, but that image had faded the closer they got to Varmin. Having the ice dragon with them in this land was an advantage. Having his connection to the cold, to his home, was a benefit.

Varmin was a trading city. It was situated at the upper edges of what most considered habitable lands. Jason's village was one of the few that existed above Varmin, though there were small clusters of homes along the mountainside, mostly those who had lived there for generations. Within the city, dozens of different merchants catered to traders. Some for furs, some tanners, some blacksmiths, all of them active with their business.

Jason pulled his cloak tight around him, looking everywhere as he headed deeper into the city. He strained toward what he could detect of the Dragon Soul, trying to follow the energy. He needed to find it, counter it, and be prepared for the possibility that they would be attacked. He could feel it calling to him.

"It's so quiet," William said.

"It's late enough that there won't be too many people out," Jason said, looking around. The streets were empty, which was not uncommon in the evenings.

"In my home, there are more people out at night. They like to hit the taverns, and dance and drink and—"

"Gamble?" Jason asked, smiling.

"You say that as if it's a bad thing."

"Only when you lose," Jason said.

Sarah shot them both a dark look. "Can we focus? I don't like this."

"There's a Dragon Soul somewhere," Jason said. "We should find them before Lorren." He could free the dragon, and then they could try to reason with him.

"Which is why I don't like it. You have already said you feel a Dragon Soul, which makes me concerned about *why* you feel that and what it might mean. You spent time here before. Where do you think they might be hiding?"

"I haven't been to Varmin that often. When my father was still alive, we came here a few times, though not so often for me to know the city. Others within my village spent much more time here." Jason looked around. He paused at one of the street corners, smelling a bakery nearby. He was well fed within Dragon Haven, though there was still something to be said about the food from his home. It was familiar. Nearby was a butcher, and the aroma of smoked meats permeated the air, mixing with that of the bakery, a distinctly pleasing combination. "I don't know where they would be. As far as I know, no one in Varmin has a connection to Lorach."

"It wouldn't take much," William said. When Jason looked over at him, William shrugged. "If this place is anything like my home, all it takes is a little bit of coin. That's not so common that anyone could turn it down."

Jason thought he was right. He turned in place, sweeping his gaze around him. The city had a certain normalcy to it, even though there wasn't anyone out in the evening. It made him feel as if he had missed out on what William had experienced his entire life.

Sarah had not had it, either. Her childhood had been as strange as his. In that regard, maybe she was as much of a misfit as he was.

Not that Sarah would view herself in such a way. She saw herself as strong and powerful—which she was. Still, she had gone through something entirely different than most to stay safe, along with keeping the dragons safe.

While trying to feel for the energy of the Dragon Soul, he glanced over at her. There might be a dragon here, as well. He closed his eyes a moment, trying to focus on that power and noticed a distant awareness of it out there. "Did you ever wish for something different?"

William watched them, frowning.

"What different would I have hoped for?" Sarah asked him.

"I don't know. Something different. Not Dragon Haven."

Sarah glanced toward the sky, and then looked off into the distance. "There was a time when I wanted to go to Lorach."

William's eyes widened slightly. "You did?"

She nodded slowly, staring off in the distance. "When I was younger. I wanted to better understand the power I possess. I thought I could learn it better within Lorach. My parents told stories of the Dragon Souls and the way they controlled their power, which left me thinking that perhaps I needed to do the same."

"I didn't know that," Jason said.

"It wasn't until Henry came and started to work with me that I began to accept I wasn't going to. By then, I had started to bond with some of the other dragons and recognize that perhaps it was best that I didn't."

"Would you really have gone to Lorach?" William asked.

Sarah didn't say anything for a moment before finally shaking her head. "I tried once," she said softly. "My parents called for the Dragon Guard, and they came after me."

"Why would you have done that?" William asked.

She looked over at him. "You can't understand what it was like. We were a part of the rebellion my entire life. That's all I ever knew. There was a time when I wanted something more." She closed her eyes, shaking her head softly. "I couldn't help it. I wanted normalcy."

Jason took her hand. "I understand."

She opened her eyes and looked over at him. "I know that you do. That's why it was so frustrating to me when you refused to help us initially. I wanted you to recognize that you weren't the only one who had gone through such strangeness."

"I was concerned about my family," he said.

She squeezed his hand. "That's the only reason I forgave you."

"Even though you didn't get to go to Lorach when you were younger, you did as you got older," Jason said, smiling.

She laughed softly. "Perhaps not quite the way that I intended."

"If you would have gone then, you might have ended up as a Dragon Soul," William said.

Sarah nodded. "It's possible. I like to think that I had known enough about Dragon Haven that I wouldn't have, but..." She offered a sad smile. "We should keep moving."

They continued into the city, and Jason focused on the energy of the dragon pearl to guide him. By following that, he hoped he could get closer and perhaps find the Dragon Soul. They wound through the city, but even as they went, the strange energy didn't change at all. After a while, he paused, looking back up the mountainside, and he probed the city using his connection to the dragons.

"I don't feel anything else," he said.

"What do you think you should feel?"

He shook his head. "I don't really know. The sense of the dragon hasn't changed. I can feel the dragon pearl, though I don't know where it is to be pulling on me."

"Maybe it's not within the city." William looked around. "Didn't you say the dragon came from somewhere beneath the city?"

"The iron mines. Varmin is known for its iron."

He needed to wander through the mines. He might not know his way through them, but the iron dragon would, and he should be able to help guide them. Perhaps it was something he should have done long ago. Jason had long understood his connection to the ice dragon, but only because he had come from the same place. By not coming back here and fully understanding the iron dragon, he felt as if he had missed an opportunity to better know the dragon he had bonded to.

They continued onward, passing a few other shops. In one of them, the sound of hammering rang out, that of a blacksmith. It was the only sound of activity that they heard. He turned a corner, and for the first time saw several people making their way along the street, heading in the opposite direction and away from them. They moved along the street, farther down the slope of the mountain.

As they went, he noticed that the strange pulling sensation from the dragon pearl started to shift. It seemed to guide him.

"You know where you're going?" William asked.

"I can feel something. It's that way," Jason said, pointing.

Sarah frowned at him. "That's not how our connection to the dragons works," she said.

"Maybe I've become sensitized to them." He couldn't help but feel as if he were heading in the right direction. This was leading them somewhere.

It probably guided Lorren to the same place.

The city started to thin out. The buildings became more widely spaced, and trees towered on either side of the road. A building near the outskirts of the city had trees on either side of it. It was a long, low-walled building, and likely a warehouse. For whatever reason, it seemed to be the source of the dragon pearl energy he felt drawn by.

Jason pointed to the building. "I think it's coming from here."

He paused, looking at the door, but it seemed nothing more than solid oak. The building was situated far enough from others in the city that it seemed strange that it would be set here. Closing his eyes, Jason reached for his connection to the iron dragon and could feel the heat radiating to him. If only there was some way to probe through the ground, to use that energy to determine if there was anything they needed to be concerned with.

Sarah reached into her pocket and pulled one of her dragon pearls out, clutching it tightly in her fist before nodding to him.

As he stepped up to the door of the building, he

readied his connection to the ice dragon, adding it to what he detected of the iron dragon. Those were the easiest to connect to, and using that power, he thought he could call upon them to reach across the distance and attack were it needed.

Jason knocked.

William chuckled. "I thought you were going to break in."

"If they come to the door, then we can see if there is anything to be concerned about here."

"I thought you said you detected the dragon pearl here," Sarah said.

"Maybe it's just this place." He motioned all around him. "This is where the iron dragon came from. Perhaps all I detected is the connection I share with the iron dragon." He doubted Varmin was hiding Dragon Souls. The people of Varmin were free. They weren't bound to Lorach.

He waited, holding onto the energy of the iron dragon. The glove glowed faintly on his hand, and he shifted it using his illusion.

"I still can't get over how easy that is for you now," Sarah said. She looked down at his hand. "The way you change things. It's not just your hand, but your eyes too. Did you know that you do that?"

He did it without thinking, using the illusion to change things about himself, and to be honest, he didn't think much of it. The power flowed from the forest dragon through him. It allowed him to maintain a connection to her, maintaining that bond.

"Maybe I should be more careful with it. If someone watched me, and were aware of what I'd changed, they might question how I could do it."

William leaned close to him. He pressed his face up toward Jason's hand, frowning. "How are you able to do it?"

"I don't even know if I could explain it. Not really. When I use the illusion, I call upon power within me, but it's also power of the forest dragon."

William stared for a moment. "She can do it, though."

Sarah shook her head. "Not like Jason."

He waited a little bit longer. There was no answer. Which meant that he was going to have to force his way in, at least to ensure that what he detected wasn't anything they needed to be concerned about. He rested his hand on the door, using the iron dragon glove and letting heat radiate from it, surging into the door. A burst of power exploded, the door coming open as the lock twisted and melted.

"That's one way to do it," William said, chuckling softly.

"They will know we were here," he said. "I had been hoping to avoid that."

"They were always going to know that we were here," Sarah said. She stepped forward into the room. Power radiated from her, the dragon pearl in her hand glowing. Flames danced away from her.

Jason followed her into the room. It was a warehouse. He didn't see or feel anyone else inside, though there still came a sensation of a dragon pearl, only it was faint and almost faded. He swept his gaze around the room. It was a massive, open space. There was a table with papers stacked upon it, and another table with small trunks situated on the table, but otherwise the warehouse was empty.

Jason attempted to open one of the trunks, but it didn't budge. He used a burst of power through his iron dragon glove, forcing it open. Inside was a stack of coins.

"That might be useful," William said, reaching for it.

"We don't need money," Jason said.

William grabbed for the trunk. "Maybe you don't, but some of us still do. Besides, if we are stuck here for the night, don't you think it would be helpful for us to have a way of paying for a room? Food?" He glanced from Jason to Sarah. "Anyway. I'll hold on to this."

"Don't lose it," Sarah chided him.

He frowned at her. "When have I ever been in danger of losing coins?"

"Jason *did* tell me how the two of you met."

"And I seem to recall I didn't lose coins."

"You wanted *me* to lose them."

William held onto the trunk, tucking it up against his side. "I didn't want you to lose them. I wanted you to earn more. If there are others like that, would you be so kind as to let me know so that I can hold onto them?"

Jason chuckled and used a blast of the iron dragon

energy to open the next trunk. It was also filled with coins.

Sarah scooped them up, letting them fall back into the trunk. "Why do you think they need so much money here?"

"A better question is why they left it here."

"The door was locked. Maybe they didn't think anybody was coming in here," William said, closing the other trunk and lifting it. He grunted. "They're a bit heavy."

"Then maybe you should leave them here," Sarah said.

William frowned at her. "What would be the fun in that? Besides, I haven't had a chance to get out of Dragon Haven in quite some time. I could use the coin to get away for a little while."

"And spend time in Varmin?" Jason asked.

"I don't know. They might be more interesting than what I have experienced in Dragon Haven." He glanced over at Sarah, flashing a smile. "No offense."

"You do know you aren't a captive. You can leave at any time."

"Why would I have done that?"

She shook her head. "Sometimes you are more trouble than you are worth. Maybe I will just have my mother exile you from Dragon Haven for good measure."

"Who would train the dragons then?"

Sarah arched a brow at him. "Is that what you call it? I don't know that anyone would have ever believed you were actually training dragons."

"Hey! The dragons enjoy me working with them."

Jason nodded. "They have," he said.

Sarah shook her head. "Don't encourage him."

She wandered over to a bookshelf, pulling books off before setting them back down. She disappeared into a darkened section of the warehouse, though Jason could still feel her. It was as if his connection to the dragons, and the dragon pearls, granted him an ability to know where she was going and what she was doing.

He flipped through some of the books that Sarah had pulled off the shelves, but didn't see much of use. He didn't have much time for books. When he had been in his village, there hadn't been much time to read. His time had been better spent trying to survive.

Sarah returned. "I have been looking for some reason behind the coin and the books and everything here."

"Maybe they were just collectors," William said.

Sarah ignored him. "And there is whatever you detected that drew us here."

Jason frowned. Now that she mentioned it, he realized he didn't detect it quite the same way that he had before. It wasn't so much that it was gone, just that the sensation seemed muted. Not absent. At least, not completely absent. Could the warehouse shield it from him? What purpose would there be in that, though?

"What else do we need to do here?" Sarah asked. "We came to Varmin because of the mist, but it's gone. You detected a Dragon Soul dragon, but now you don't." She swung her gaze around before turning her attention back to Jason. "Why the gold?"

Jason looked through here, and other than the gold, he found a dusty table, with a stack of papers. He began to turn away, when he frowned, turning back.

He sorted through the papers.

They were a ledger.

"What is it?" Sarah asked.

Jason shook his head. "I don't... Oh."

Payments. All of this gold was payments, and it described keeping the dragon here.

The iron dragon.

The more he read, the more understanding began to fill him.

The iron dragon hadn't been held in Varmin because of Therin. Therin wouldn't have even known about it.

It had been Lorren.

That was why he had come back here.

Is that why Lorren was here now? Did he think to place another egg, and to create another misfit?

"We need to go to the caves," he said. "The iron dragon should be able to navigate us through them." If that *was* Lorren's plan, he needed to know.

Sarah nodded, and William pointed to the other trunks on the table. "Should we take those, too?"

Jason shook his head. "Not unless you have some way of carrying all of them." They stepped back out onto the street beyond the warehouse, and the sudden awareness of the dragon pearl surged again. There was something different about it.

"Do you feel anything?" Jason asked Sarah.

She glanced at the warehouse. "I don't. Why do you think you feel it outside, but not inside?"

Jason sighed. "I don't really know. I don't know what it means, either."

They continued toward the lower edge of the city, moving down the mountainside. As they went, the strange sensation of the dragon pearl pressed upon him, and he paused, looking around. He would have to figure out where that sense came from and whether he might learn anything about it. So far, he felt nothing other than the drawing sensation.

Power built within him, stretching between him and the iron dragon, and his hand blazed brightly. He must have released the illusion. He hadn't even known that he had done so. Most of the time, he could see through his own illusion and wasn't aware of which ones he held in place, though maybe he needed to focus on them. He used his connection to the illusion, diminishing the glove's brightness. On a whim, he decided to change his appearance altogether. He shifted his facial features, making them older, and then swept the illusion around his cloak, changing that along with his dragonskin. It was only illusion, nothing else, but for some reason, he felt better having done so.

Turning, he found Sarah watching him, frowning. "What is it?"

"You look different."

"I used my father as inspiration for changing my appearance."

"That might be useful. Can you do it for me?"

Jason used a swirl of illusion and wrapped it around her, using her mother as inspiration. He turned to William and aged him as well.

William glanced down at the trunks he held and chuckled. "It would have been nicer had you made these a bit lighter."

Would that be possible? "I might be able to help with that," he said.

He hadn't given much thought to it, but what was illusion but a frame of mind? Could he do something that would help William with the weight of the trunks? It would be a different use of illusion than what he had attempted before, but in this case, he wondered if perhaps it was the right use.

He called upon the energy of the forest dragon, letting the connection between them build. Power flowed through him from the forest dragon. Using that, he shifted the trunks. It was a simple thing, now that he considered it. It tilted the power within the trunks.

William's arms jerked up, and his eyes widened. "How?"

"I changed it so the trunks weren't as heavy," Jason said.

"I don't even know how you can do that," William said.

Sarah shook her head. "He shouldn't be able to."

He chuckled. "You should be thankful I can do it. It was because of the illusion that we were able to escape from Jessica in Lorach in the first place."

He found Sarah watching him and couldn't read the expression on her face, but he sensed that she was bothered by something.

"Can you make them smaller?" William shifted the trunks on either side of him. "It might be nice if I could tuck them into my pockets."

"Don't press your luck," Sarah said.

Jason wondered whether it would be possible. How much of reality could he truly shift? Maybe the better question was how much of reality did he want to shift. He had no idea whether it would hold. At some point, it was possible the illusion would shatter. If it did, then William would find the trunks were heavy again, and if he were to place them into his pockets, losing the illusion might tear them away. Maybe there were limits to how he could and should use illusion.

"I think she's right. It's probably not a good idea."

They continued along the streets. After a while, Sarah glanced behind her. "It's so different than other places we've visited. Some parts look abandoned." Her voice was a whisper, and she swept her gaze all around. Tension filled her, and were it not for Jason's illusion, he suspected she would have a dragon pearl clutched in her fist, glowing.

"Dragon Souls shouldn't come to Varmin. There's no reason for them to."

Sarah glanced at him. "They did before."

He needed to use his connections now. He focused on the ice dragon circling overhead. "Can you find anything? Do you see the mist?"

He used the connection he shared with the ice dragon, looking through his eyes for a moment. He could make out the city and the ground around him, but nothing else.

The ice dragon rumbled from high overhead, but there came no flicker of the mist through their shared connection. Instead, he saw movement—a bright light that flared in his strange vision. A dragon.

"That's where we have to go," he said.

They headed toward the edge of the city, and from there he paused and looked around. The ice dragon rumbled again, and another rumble came from farther down the slope. This one was farther from the edge of the city. All attempts on Jason's part to try to detect power from the dragon pearl faded.

"Can the two of you slow down?" William panted. "These trunks are still bulky, even if they aren't heavy. I told you it would be easier if you had changed their size."

Jason glanced over. William's face was red, and he gasped for air. "Be thankful I changed anything about them."

He could feel the distant dragon. Now that he could, he thought he might be able to identify where the dragon was located. As they headed forward, he caught sight of it.

It was nestled between trees at the far edge of the city,

moving downslope. Toward the iron mines the city was known for.

Jason held his hand up. "Wait."

He reached for his connection to the ice and iron dragons. He combined that power and swept it away from him, forcing it into the distant dragon. He detected something, but didn't know if it was resistance.

Could this be a trained dragon of the Dragon Souls?

Jason swept that power together again, trying to combine it, and found a bit of resistance from a distant dragon. It was there, just has he suspected.

"I think it's—"

Jason cut off when he saw something else. Mist sweeping out from the trees. His breath caught, and he spun around.

"What is it?" Sarah asked.

Jason glanced over at her. "Lorren. I think he's here."

13

Jason raced downslope toward the dragon. As he ran, he tried to connect to it using a combination of the ice and iron dragons. That might not be enough. At this point, he needed to find a way to bridge a connection between them.

The forest dragon.

By adding power from her, he might be able to shift something to change that distance. He closed his eyes for a moment, halting his running. "I'm not going to harm you," he said. He used the power of the other two dragons to send the words.

Something swirled around him. Jason could feel that power. It pressed in upon him, making his attempt to connect to the forest dragon difficult.

The mist dragons.

He opened his eyes, looking around. As the mist continued to swirl, Jason maintained his connection to the other dragons. He used the ice dragon, trying to freeze the mist. It solidified, and he sent a pulse of ice through it again, slamming into the mist.

"What are you doing?" Sarah snapped.

He jerked his head around and realized that she spoke to William. He was approaching a dragon within the trees, his hand held up, leaning forward as if bowing to the dragon. They were closer than Jason had realized.

"We are here to help," William said. "We can protect you."

"You don't know if this dragon is already trained," Sarah said, running up to William. "If it's with Lorren…" Sarah started.

Jason looked around. The mist hadn't pressed in on him anymore. If he had other dragons with him, he would have used them with his dark and dangerous connection to the dragons. It wasn't quite as awful as what the Dragon Souls did, but that didn't mean that he wasn't dangerous.

Jason forced power through his connection to the iron and ice dragons, testing for anything Lorren might have done. If Sarah was right and this was one of Lorren's dragons, he had to separate Lorren's connection.

William continued forward, holding out his hand.

The dragon lunged. William didn't budge. He remained frozen in place, his hand held out as he stared at the dragon.

"William!"

Sarah reached for him, but she didn't need to.

The dragon withdrew, jerking his head off to the side. William stayed with him, holding his hand out. Jason couldn't help but marvel at William's confidence. He seemed unmindful of his danger.

Of course, Jason had no idea how much danger he was really in.

When William had claimed he was training the dragons, Jason had teased him, doubting that he could have actually been doing anything. Seeing this and how the dragon responded to him, he couldn't help but feel as if William actually had a connection.

William stretched his hand out and touched the dragon on the nose, caressing it. The dragon breathed out a hint of steam that parted around William.

Sarah breathed out. "You *do* have a connection to them."

William didn't look in their direction. "Not so much of a connection as you and Jason, but I've been working with them."

"You have to have some connection to do what you're doing. I've never seen anybody able to approach a dragon like this if they don't have a connection."

Jason joined William, holding onto his connection to the dragons. Distantly, he could still feel the mist dragons trying to press upon him, though they hadn't broken through what he had done with the ice dragon. Did that mean that Lorren wasn't nearly as close as they had feared?

It might mean they had time. Jason hoped they had

enough time.

"We are here to help you," Jason said to the dragon.

The dragon looked at him and breathed out another steamer of smoke from his nostrils. It streamed around him.

"Something has tried to attack you. I don't know what it is, but—"

The dragon roared and spread his wings as he prepared to take flight.

"What do you mean something attacked him?" Sarah whispered.

Jason held his gaze on the dragon. "This might be what I've been feeling. Maybe not even a dragon pearl, but this dragon."

"Why would it be here?" William asked.

The answer came to Jason.

The mist.

There was probably earth.

Maybe smoke.

All of it to draw Lorach here.

"Bait," he whispered.

Sarah looked over, her eyes going wide.

William touched the dragon, patting him on the side of the face in a caress. The dragon settled, lowering his wings and turning to William. His eyes glowed a bright orange, and then he blinked. Something about his expression changed. Jason couldn't detect anything, only that whatever William did had made a difference for this dragon.

There came another rumble in the distance. Jason looked up. It wasn't this dragon.

"Tell him that we won't use him," William said.

"Don't you think you just did that?" Sarah asked.

William shook his head. "I don't know how much the dragon can understand me. I don't know if what Jason does is different enough, but it seems to be."

Jason shook his head. "I doubt I can do anything all that different than what you are doing. Besides, I think the dragon understands you."

"Just do it," William said.

Jason turned to the dragon. "He wants you to know we won't use you. We need to get him away from here. If Lorren intends to use him to draw Dragon Souls…"

The dragon roared.

"I think he understood," William said.

Jason didn't move. "I didn't do anything that differently than what you did."

The dragon roared again, and this time Jason was aware of pressure upon it.

He focused on that pressure and understanding dawned within him. An illusion still held around the dragon. Lorren had warned him that he was the one who had taught Therin how to create illusions. Of course Lorren would be able to do so.

Pressure came from mist swirling around him that Jason hadn't seen. It was an incredible sensation. The more he focused on the mist, the easier it was to realize how Lorren could use it to generate an illusion. The effect was so different than the way Jason created them. He focused on it and tried to push through it, but didn't know if he could overpower it, considering that his connection to illusions was different.

Lorren had shattered his illusion before. Jason would need to do something similar and overwhelm what Lorren did.

"What's going on?" Sarah asked.

"Illusion," Jason said.

"Jessica?"

He shook his head, focusing on the energy he detected. "I don't think so. Jessica uses a similar power as Therin. This is different."

Jason mixed the power of the iron and ice dragon and tried to force it away from him. Sarah suddenly grabbed his arm, and Jason turned. Tendrils of mist emerged from the ground, swirling around them. Jason stared at it, recognizing the energy.

This was Lorren's dragon. He *was* here.

Masked under an illusion the whole time.

Jason tried to use the ice dragon to freeze it, but it failed.

"Be ready," he said to William.

"For what?" William said. He still had his hand on the dragon, who rumbled periodically, though seemed calmer than he had been before.

"I don't know. We may need to get moving quickly."

He was going to need the ice dragon. He could feel the power coming from the ice dragon, and could feel the need to use that power, only… For some reason, the ice dragon felt separated from him in a way he hadn't before.

Was that more of Lorren's illusion?

The iron dragon was there, the power from him still potent and pushing through Jason's awareness, a surging energy that hummed within him. He was going to have to unleash that energy.

As he did, he realized he wasn't the only one attacking. Sarah did as well. She forced a burst of energy through her dragon pearl. Jason noticed a loosening of the connection to the ice dragon and used it as he froze the mist. Sarah burst power outward, as well.

The illusion shattered.

The dragon near William roared, and William took a step toward him, touching him again. William had never had a connection to dragons before. There came a surge of energy and power, and almost a connectivity.

He didn't have time to focus on it.

He could feel the mist dragon sending power around them. The illusion would re-form if he did nothing. Jason radiated the heat of the iron dragon and the cold of the ice dragon and mingled them together. He added what he could of the forest dragon. If Lorren attempted to use illusion on them, then Jason would use the same. He would reject what Lorren had done and form his own illusion. Not only illusion. Jason would form his own reality.

He shifted everything around him, twisting it.

Without looking at William, he said, "Get the dragon out of here."

"Are you sure?"

"I'm sure. You need to get the dragon out—"

Tendrils of mist began to swirl, streaking up and around Jason's feet, working up his legs and around his waist. Somehow they overwhelmed his illusion and reality.

He called upon the ice and heat, shattering them.

The same mist began to swirl around the dragon and William. Jason reacted, shattering that as well.

"Now!"

William scrambled for the dragon. It seemed the dragon lowered his head, giving William an easy way to climb on. "Where should I go?"

Jason shook his head. "Away from here. Not to Dragon Haven. Not yet."

He needed to better understand this dragon before he encouraged William to bring the dragon to Dragon Haven. It was still possible the dragon had been compromised. If so, he didn't want to be the reason the people of Dragon Haven were harmed. Jason and Sarah would have to make sure the dragon William had traveled on to Varmin returned safely.

William climbed slowly onto the dragon's back, and though the trunks didn't look to be as heavy as they probably were, he still struggled with them. He staggered onto the dragon, clutching the trunks, pulling them with him. Once he got situated, he held an arm on either side of him, strapping them down across the trunks, but Jason wondered whether he would be able to hold onto them.

"It might be better if you leave those behind," he said.

William looked at him as if he'd lost his mind. "I'm taking them."

William and the dragon took flight, bursting into the air, and the dragon circled, carrying them higher and higher. He watched for long enough to ensure that the dragon was unharmed and that William would remain unharmed as well. When he was confident that they escaped, he let out a relieved sigh.

Another dragon rumbled.

It was further downslope.

Jason felt for dragons, and vaguely detected another. Several others.

Dragon Souls. They'd already fallen for the bait and had come.

"The Dragon Souls Lorren intends to attack are here," Jason said.

"Then we let him," Sarah said.

"You know what happens when he attacks Dragon Souls," Jason said.

"Jason—let him do what he needs. Isn't that what *we* need?"

"We need to help the dragons."

"And I don't like the idea of helping the Dragon Souls," Sarah said.

Jason shook his head. The mist didn't try to come for them again, as if Lorren had abandoned his attempt to attack them. "I don't either, but not all of them are Therin and Jessica. We need to help the dragons. We need to rescue those dragons. Not destroy them."

Mist started to swirl again.

Jason exploded power out from him again, and the mist shattered.

He had to find Lorren.

It made no sense to hide. If he was here, Lorren should not have been concealing himself. He strode down the mountainside, focusing on what he could of the dragons and straining to detect Dragon Souls. As he made his way along the mountainside, he realized he was heading toward the iron mines.

He closed his eyes for a moment, focusing on the iron dragon. "I'm going to need your help." He used the connection between himself and the iron dragon, pulsing on the power that flowed through the iron dragon, drawing it through to him. There came a reverberation of energy. An acknowledgment. He worried about the iron dragon and Lorren, especially with what they had found. "Bring the others."

He hoped the dragon understood.

Continuing onward, he let the sense of the dragons draw him forward. When he reached a clearing, he suddenly stopped. Not just a dragon. Several.

He reacted. Using iron and ice, he washed power through the nearest dragon. There was resistance that came from the Dragon Soul training that he pushed through. On a whim, Jason added an extra element from the forest dragon. He had no idea whether that would make a difference, but maybe it would augment what he had done. As he pushed power through him, it exploded into the dragon. It freed him from the resistance. He used the same mixture as he swept through the others, one after another, before the dragons had a chance to react.

He didn't see the Dragon Souls who would've commanded them. Instead, he contained his focus on the freed dragons. Now that they were freed, he wanted to send them away.

"Jason?" Sarah's voice was tense. Power radiated from her.

He spun toward her and saw her point. Three dragons came through the trees, the rumbling that he had heard before emanating from them. All three were enormous, though there was something different about these dragons than others that he had seen. They had massive wings and spikes running along their sides. Their scales appeared dappled, almost as if camouflaged. He used the mixture of power he had been drawing, sending it toward these dragons, but even as he did, he could feel resistance.

He tried to take a step toward the dragons but found couldn't. The ground clung to him.

The rumbling persisted. It was the sound he had heard before.

Using the energy of the dragons he had bonded to, he tried to pry his feet out but could not. He was trapped.

With a dawning understanding, he realized what these creatures were.

"The earth dragons," he whispered.

14

The ground squeezed Jason's feet, pulling him under. Everything around him seemed to have changed. He couldn't see the trees nearly as well, and he was sinking deeper into the ground. He had no idea what happened to the other dragons that he had freed from the Dragon Souls—or whether it was even real. The only thing he could think of was the way the earth pulled him under, like an avalanche that would swallow him. Jason had experience with avalanches, but none with the ground itself threatening to consume him. If he couldn't break free, he had no idea what might happen, though he started to have his suspicions. Lorren would trap him.

Lorren wanted to remove Jason. Then he would claim the misfits.

Jason had to fight it. Not just for himself, but for the dragons.

Why wouldn't he work with them? What had Jason

done that had upset him this much? He'd been willing to fight, ready to go to battle against Lorach. Lorren should *want* to work with them, not fight.

Trying to use the ice dragon, he realized that ice might not do anything to counter the power of earth. What would? He searched his mind but couldn't come up with a better solution.

Sarah cried out and anger surged within him.

He shifted his attack. Rather than attacking the dragons, trying to free them from whatever influence Lorren might have over them, he needed to do something different. He needed power.

The iron dragon was nearby. Jason called upon his energy, heating the ground, and found that it merely softened before solidifying around him again. That wasn't going to be effective. He had to try something else.

The only dragon he had remaining was the forest dragon.

He thought about what he had done with William, the way that he had reduced the weight of the trunks. He had to do something similar now.

The forest dragon's power flowed through him. Her energy was there, slow and subtle, the energy of a dragon who remained quiet and mysterious.

What would he do?

Shifting reality. He could solidify the ground and then harden it into stairs, but if he did that, he would have to do it rapidly enough to counter the way the dragons used their control over earth. Then he would have to do something similar for Sarah. All before whatever Lorren intended could take place.

He focused on what he wanted, summoning the power within him, and then burst it outward. It solidified for a moment.

Jason took a step and grabbed for Sarah, pulling her with him.

The illusion shifted, fading.

He swore softly, reaching for the forest dragon's power as he felt it coming through him. This time, Jason shifted everything around him, holding it tightly. As it held, he took another step.

The earth dragon overwhelmed his connection again. This dragon was powerful.

Unless all of the earth dragons had come.

That would be more than what he could withstand.

He had to try another approach.

"Jason!"

He looked over at Sarah and shifted things quickly enough to grab her and pull her into the same pit as him. She wrapped her arms around him.

"What's happening?" Sarah asked.

"This is the earth dragon. Or dragons. There's one more thing I can try, but I don't know if it's going to work." He focused on the iron dragon. "Be ready."

Heat began to build. He had to use it, though he had never tried to use it in the way that he would attempt to now. It was something that he had to try, though.

He forced it beneath him, exploding power from

underneath, out through his feet, all while holding tightly to Sarah and holding her against him.

The explosion shot them up and freed them from the earth. As they streaked into the air, he continued to use the energy of the iron dragon, forcing them higher and higher. Wind whipped around them, cold and biting, threatening to overpower his connection to the iron dragon. Jason ignored it, focusing instead on the way that he held onto the energy of the iron dragon.

Sarah gasped, and they started to descend.

Then the iron dragon was there, swooping beneath them. As they landed, power surged. Jason squeezed his iron glove around the dragon as he gripped his back, settling Sarah onto the dragon's back and holding her there. Only then did he allow himself to breathe out heavily.

"Lorren attacked us?" she whispered.

"He's trying to claim the misfits from me. If he thinks they're his..."

Lorren was capable and had the power of multiple misfit dragons. More than Jason possessed. More than that, Lorren had created those dragons and probably understood the way their power could be used and how to control it. That mattered.

As he tapped on the iron dragon and they started to circle back around, they headed toward the south end of the city and descended. The iron dragon hovered in place, not touching the ground. If he did, Jason didn't know if the earth dragons could trap him. The iron dragon had known the power of the iron mines and had used that to escape, but Jason didn't know if the earth dragons would be able to overwhelm that.

He searched the forest. Where was Lorren?

He wouldn't be able to find him from the air. Which meant that he was going to have to climb back down and risk these earth dragons.

"Stay ready for us," Jason said to the iron dragon.

The dragon roared, and as Jason climbed off, he blasted at the ground to ensure that the earth dragons didn't harm them. Sarah followed, and Jason looked back at her.

"Maybe you should stay with the iron dragon," he said.

"I'm not leaving you alone." She held onto her dragon pearls. "Besides, now I think we know how to escape from them."

"Only if we have a dragon that can reach us."

The iron dragon rumbled.

They moved down the slope, and Jason focused on the energy in the air. He was going to have to hold onto as much power as possible. Thankfully, no pressure on him suggested Lorren attacked again.

In the distance, he could feel the Dragon Soul dragons. That was what Lorren would have to be after. Not necessarily Jason, but the Dragon Souls. And their dragons. He pressed outward, using the connection that had formed when healing them, and realized that connection was missing.

The dragons were still out there. He could feel them,

but they were no longer freed, not the way that Jason had freed them.

They raced down the slope.

Energy filled him. It came from somewhere nearby, though he didn't know if they were going to be able to get close enough to use it. The Dragon Soul dragons were down there, and all he had to do was descend far enough down the slope, and he could get to them.

He had to free them.

Energy built around them. For a moment, he didn't know if it was real, but a rumbling built within that energy.

Beneath him.

That was the earth dragons.

Lorren had claimed they weren't powerful. He had lied. They were incredibly powerful. Knowing they were there, he wondered if he might be able to counter what they were doing. It seemed to him there should be something he could do. He could feel energy and power, and he pushed down, trying to solidify the ground.

Could he freeze it?

In the upper reaches of the mountains, the ground was so hard and frozen that nothing could penetrate it. Given his connection to the ice dragon, he wondered if that would be enough. It would take more than just a connection to the ice dragon, though. It would take a burst of ice lightning.

He hadn't attempted it before.

Rumbling came from deep beneath them, rolling toward them.

Jason nodded to Sarah, and then called to the ice dragon. A burst of ice lightning exploded, shooting toward the ground. The ice lightning held, rolling through the ground and freezing it. The rumbling eased.

Would that be enough?

Jason had no idea. It might be, but he didn't know if there needed to be more power. When he had used the ice lightning against the mist dragons, he had required several strikes. He called the ice dragon again, letting another burst of ice lightning streak to the ground and surge. Power smoothed over the ground, flowing outward. Jason called another burst, then another. With each one, he froze deeper into the ground and farther away from him.

"Will it hold?" Sarah asked.

Jason shook his head. "I don't know. It seems like it is."

Distantly, he felt a rumbling, though not nearly as close as before.

They raced along the ground, hurrying toward what he detected of the Dragon Soul dragons. Something pressed outward, a strange sensation, though he didn't know what it was.

"Why are you hurrying?" Sarah asked.

"It's Lorren. And the dragons need our help."

They reached a clearing along the mountainside where he had first met the iron dragon. He could feel some energy that suggested to him this was probably the exact same place. There was no sign of the tunnel he'd taken to find the dragon, though everything around here struck him as familiar.

"I've been here before. The trail led me here when I came searching with the ice dragon for hatch mates. It brought me to the mines here and the iron dragon."

At the time, Jason had been mostly concerned about the Dragon Souls creating these misfits, but now...

Lorren had been the one. Lorren was responsible for the iron dragon.

How many other dragon misfits had Lorren been responsible for?

Could he have known about the forest dragon? Jason didn't think so, especially considering how Therin had found him, but he didn't even know. What about the storm dragon, the one dragon that Jason struggled to understand and to connect to?

Or the others. The jungle dragon. The missing river dragon. Any of the other powers that he had found.

Had he made a mistake in not trying to work with Lorren?

"I can feel something," he said softly.

"When you see it, let me—"

Sarah didn't have the chance to finish. Power exploded, catching her in the back. She had formed a bubble of energy around her using her dragon pearl, and thankfully it absorbed most of the impact, though not all of it. She was still tossed forward. Jason darted toward her as the ground started rumbling again.

Earth dragons. How many had Lorren said there were?

He called upon the power of the ice dragon. This was going to require more than just ice lightning. He would need the actual ice dragon to help him. "I need your help," he said. There came a burst of energy as a response from the ice dragon. In the meantime, Jason used ice lightning, sending it streaking toward the ground, using his own connection to the ice dragon to freeze everything. If nothing else, he wanted to prevent the earth dragons from harming him. How long would he be able to maintain it?

"Sarah?"

She dusted herself off. "I'm going to be fine." She grabbed for another dragon pearl, and everything about her started to take on heat and energy as she glowed softly. Her face twisted in a snarl, anger surging through her. "He has to be close. Which means that—"

She didn't have the chance to finish. Lorren attacked again, using the earth dragons. The power wasn't nearly as potent as before, but the ground rumbled, nearly throwing him off his feet.

Jason stepped away from Sarah. "Lorren!" Rage filled his voice.

He could feel energy around him, the rumbling of power, and he searched through the trees as he looked for the mist dragons, though there was no sign of them.

If Lorren was here, the mist dragons would be as well. He knew that they would.

Jason braced for another attack. He could feel energy crackling in the air.

"Lorren!" he cried out again.

There was no response.

Jason needed to find some way to meet with him.

"Lorren!"

The ground rumbled. A fog drifted toward him, and a figure stood just outside of the trees. "You shouldn't have come here," Lorren said. His voice was muted by the mist, leaving Jason wondering how much control he had over it.

"You're the reason for the iron dragon."

Lorren took a step toward him, and he glowered at Jason. "You claimed it as your own."

"I didn't claim him. He claimed me. We claimed each other." As much as anyone could claim a dragon. Jason wanted nothing more than to protect the iron dragon, and he had always done so. He had not attempted to use the dragon, not the way that others had, but would Lorren even understand?

"You don't even know what they have done, do you?" Lorren asked.

"Who? Lorach? I can help you. We can help each other."

"Now. You think to use what I perfected."

Jason just stared at him. He recognized the anger at Lorach. It was an anger he felt himself, especially having seen what they were willing to do, the way they were willing to fight. What he needed was some way to harness that anger and find a way to work with him. Perhaps they could even work together.

"You don't have to do this. We can bring down Lorach together, but we can *save* the dragons."

"They are already lost."

"They aren't." Jason took a step toward him, but the ground began to rumble.

He hesitated. He didn't know what the earth dragons might do but had to be careful here. "We can save the dragons. I know we can. I know you want to stop Lorach. It's the same thing I want, but we have to work—"

"Do you think I don't know about the others?" The question was low, dangerous. "I know about all of them. And I will have your so-called misfits."

"They aren't mine. None of the dragons are. And we don't need to do this."

Lorren hesitated. "So ignorant. That is your downfall. Had you only paid attention to what you were doing, what you have revealed them, but no. Now you are the reason I had to come back."

"You said that before. What does that even mean?"

Lorren stared at him and then backed into the mist.

It swallowed him, and he disappeared altogether.

Jason attempt to step forward, but the ground rumbled again.

Where was he going?

"Let them go," Sarah whispered.

"We can't let him go. We need to work together. We need to find some way to fight on the same side. He wants the same thing as us."

"Does he?" Sarah asked. "If he wanted the same thing,

he wouldn't have disappeared for as long as he did. When my family thought he was dead, I remember the relief my mother had. She hated him. And hated what he stood for. He doesn't want to protect the dragons. He doesn't want what you want, Jason."

He sighed. Maybe that was true.

A surge of dragon energy came to him, and there was a strange panic in it.

It was nearby.

He looked over to Sarah, his heart hammering. Distantly, he detected a fluttering of power. It was almost too faint, as if it were muted, but he recognized it. It came from farther down the slope.

"I can feel them," he said.

"Let's get this over with as quickly as we can," Sarah said.

As they started down the slope, Jason could feel something pressing on him. He used ice and iron, finally adding a hint of the forest dragon as well, trying to shift things, but something resisted.

Lorren battled him.

The mist dragons had to be nearby. Jason had to overwhelm them. The forest dragon was more potent. She was a master of camouflage and illusion. The only problem was that she wasn't here like the mist dragons were. More than that, there were more mist dragons than there were forest dragons. That put the forest dragon at a disadvantage.

He knew that he could overwhelm it. He had to believe

that. That was the key to illusions. Belief. It was all about believing in reality. Jason shifted everything again. The pressure around him faded.

In the distance, energy built in unison. It was a blast of power, heading up the slope.

"Dragon Souls," he and Sarah said at the same time.

They had Lorren behind them and Dragon Souls in front of them.

What was Lorren thinking?

The ground started to rumble again. The earth dragons were moving, and moving quickly. They were heading toward the Dragon Souls.

Jason groaned. "I really wish they would stop."

"Can you overpower them?"

"I don't have a way of reaching that deep into the ground," he said.

"Maybe it's not so much a matter of penetrating the ground but using your connections differently."

He had tried, but each of the misfits had a different type of power, and though one his misfits might counter one of Lorren's, there were limits to how much it could do. The ice dragon could freeze the ground long enough to give them a chance to escape, but the earth dragon had proven that it was powerful enough that it could overwhelm what they would do.

He was going to have to find a new strength in his dragons to withstand whatever Lorren intended to throw at them.

The ground rumbled again. When it stopped, he

looked around. Jason probed with the ice dragon's power. The ice dragon was nearby, flying overhead, close enough that his connection could bond them. It allowed them to move as quickly as possible, and hopefully he could use that to escape if it came down to it.

Power built downslope.

The Dragon Souls.

The rumbling headed toward them. Not only to the Dragon Souls. To their dragons.

Jason should have sent those dragons away when he had freed them, and the fact that he hadn't was his mistake. The Dragon Souls must have reconnected to them.

"Come on," Jason said, urging Sarah to follow. They sprinted.

He needed to prevent Lorren from harming the dragons.

When he found them, he could feel the dragons first. There were five of them; at least there should be. The rumbling persisted, but within it came something else.

A shrieking sound. It was horrible and painful, and it tore through Jason.

It was the sound of a dragon dying.

Strangely, he didn't hear it. He *felt* it. It came from all around him, an awareness of power that surged, exploding, and yet started to fade.

He had no idea what had happened to the Dragon Souls, but if their dragons were dying, then he suspected they were as well. He couldn't summon the necessary sadness for them, but he could feel it for the dragons.

"What's happening?" Sarah cried.

"The earth dragons are attacking the Dragon Soul dragons."

There was no sign of them. Only the sense of them.

They were buried alive.

Jason cried out to the iron dragon and focused on him. He summoned him, and it took only a moment for the iron dragon to arrive, streaking through the sky as he raced toward him. Jason embraced the power of the iron dragon and jumped, grabbing for Sarah, and landed atop the iron dragon. As they swooped toward the sense of the fallen dragons, Jason probed at the earth. He had to rescue them, only he didn't know what it was going to take.

"Can you get to them?" Jason asked the iron dragon.

"They repelled me," the iron dragon said.

"Can you do anything?"

"Not against their power," the iron dragon said.

He called upon ice lightning, shooting it from the distant ice dragon, and it exploded into the ground. It sent chunks flying into the sky. Jason summoned ice lightning again, using that but mixing with the power of the iron dragon. The combination was explosive and violent, and it tore the ground apart.

Sarah started to work with him, using her connection to the dragons as she called upon energy and pulled it to the ground the same way that Jason did. With each explosion, nothing changed. "It's not working," she cried out.

Jason could feel that it wasn't. Everything they were doing would still fail.

The dragons stopped fighting. The earth dragons held them in place.

Jason threw every bit of power and energy he had at them, but even as he did, he realized he couldn't do anything. The power beneath him, that of the earth dragons—and Lorren—was too much. He tried again and again, using ice and iron, mixing them, but it wasn't enough. He wasn't enough.

The energy of those dragons faded until there was no life left in them.

The rumbling within the ground finally ceased.

They circled overhead. There was no sign that Lorren remained.

15

Jason jumped from the iron dragon's back. They were in a small clearing in the forest, though it looked as if it had been recently cleared. The charred remains of trees fell around them, and a rocky ground greeted him. He paced, probing with the various energies of the dragons he connected to, calling upon them as he searched for some way to reach the earth dragon energy they'd been following, but he could feel nothing other than the faded dragons.

The iron dragon landed in the clearing, and Sarah climbed off, hurrying over to him.

He stared at the ground. "They're gone," he whispered.

"There wasn't anything you would be able to do," Sarah said.

He had tried. He had failed. The dragons died because he hadn't been able to counter Lorren and his power. He hadn't been enough for them.

"He wasn't even trying to stop the Dragon Souls." Jason could feel how the ground had changed because of the earth dragons. There was something odd about it. Maybe it was only the power here. He looked over at the iron dragon. "I'm sorry I couldn't save them."

The iron dragon pressed his face forward. His entire body glowed with his agitation. "You did what you could."

Jason squeezed his eyes closed, feeling for the trembling that had been here. He had come back to this place thinking he might find a way to better understand the iron dragon and the connection that existed between them so that he could figure out whether there was anything more he might learn about the misfits, and yet he couldn't shake the feeling that somehow he had led Lorren here. Which meant that he was responsible.

"It's not your fault," Sarah said.

He looked up at her. "I don't know if he would have even come here were it not for us."

"You don't know that," she said.

"I don't, but..."

Jason couldn't shake the feeling that these dragons—and perhaps even the Dragon Souls—had died because of him. Which meant that he had to be careful that Lorren wouldn't keep following him.

"We can still see if there's anything we can learn," she said.

Jason's gaze drifted toward the mountainside. Somewhere up there were the caves where he had found the iron dragon. Given how long it had been since they'd come here, this should be a homecoming, regardless of how bittersweet it might be for the iron dragon. Now there was nothing but pain and sadness, sorrow about what they had encountered. Now it was only devastation.

Jason stopped near one of the trees on the outskirts of the clearing. It hadn't changed, despite how the ground had changed, something deep underground shifting. There was only the sign of the scorched ground where the dragons had tried to free themselves.

The iron dragon came up behind him. "Many dragons have been lost," the iron dragon said. He glowed brightly, heat and energy radiating. It pushed back the growing darkness, illuminating everything.

Jason turned to him. "I know many dragons have been lost over time, but these shouldn't have been. There should have been some way to protect them. I tried to free them." And he had. However briefly, he had. If he had only sent them away when he had rescued them, then perhaps they wouldn't have been destroyed.

"You cannot save all," the dragon said.

Jason took in a deep breath. Here he thought the worst thing he was going to have to deal with would be fighting Dragon Souls. At least in that case, he could anticipate what they might do and what he would need to do to protect the dragons. This was something else. This was a slaughter.

Not only of the Dragon Souls but of the dragons. This was cruelty.

"All I wanted was to stop the Dragon Souls," he said.

Sarah joined him, glancing over at the iron dragon. "And you still can."

Jason shook his head. "I don't know how we can stop the Dragon Souls while also dealing with Lorren. I thought we could work together to stop the Dragon Souls." Jason glanced behind him to the clearing. He could still feel the rumbling that had been here, even though it had faded long ago. There was an energy to it, almost a signature, and he wondered, if he were to focus on it for a little while longer, might he be able to track the earth dragons? "If this is how he battles with the Dragon Souls, we *can't* work together. I don't want him to injure any more dragons."

Sarah reached for him, taking his hand. "Someone needs to stop Jessica. Why not him?"

Jason couldn't do it that way. Not if it meant sacrificing so many. And that was what it would be. A sacrifice. A slaughter. Not if he could do anything to stop it. "There would have to be another way," he said.

"Will there? You were there. You were with her inside the palace. You felt her energy and power. You struggled against her. You are connected to the dragons in a way that I have never known, and still you couldn't do it. How do you think we will stop her?"

He shivered, but she was right. Despite everything he'd been able to do, he hadn't managed to stop Jessica. He had halted her attack for a little while, but he hadn't stopped her altogether. To end the fighting, to stop the attacks on dragons, that was what he was going to need to do. Eventually, he was going to need to remove her and her family so they no longer ruled in Lorach.

Turning his attention back to the forest, he let out a long sigh. The iron dragon pressed up behind him. Perhaps Sarah was right, and they needed to use Lorren, regardless of how violent and deadly he might be. The only thing Jason wanted since learning of his connection to the dragons was to ensure they had an opportunity to survive and thrive. They wouldn't be given such an opportunity with the Dragon Souls. Maybe not even with Lorren.

He turned back to the iron dragon. "We should go back."

He had to find that strength. There had to be a reason for the sacrifice so that these dragons had died for a purpose. Heat radiated from the iron dragon, leaving his body glowing with a soft orange light that pushed back the growing darkness. There was an energy that mingled with the heat. It took Jason a moment to realize where that came from. It was an undercurrent of rage and anger that burned within the dragon. Jason held out a hand, and the iron dragon swished his tail from side to side.

"They can't hurt you now," he said.

The dragon pulsed with more heat before starting forward. Jason and Sarah followed.

"What about William?" Sarah asked.

"He's probably safer in the air."

"Should we call him back?"

Jason frowned. Maybe he should.

The iron dragon slowed, and Jason looked up into the sky, focusing on what he felt. There was a faint tracing of energy, and had he not attempted to connect to the dragon before, he wasn't sure if he would've noticed it. He used that and then followed the surge of energy, letting it streak away from him.

"I tried. I don't have a connection with this dragon like I have with others, so I don't know if I can call to him the way that I would these others."

Sarah smiled at him. "The fact that you have some way of connecting at all is impressive enough."

"It would be even more impressive if I could call them all." If that were possible, Jason could imagine how he might be able to save them. They might be able to work together, freeing even more dragons. It was possible that were he to find some way of stretching across the distance, reaching for dragons in general, he might find the Dragon Soul dragons. Perhaps that was something he should practice.

"I can't call to any dragon unless I have spent time with him."

Jason smiled. "Just him?"

"You know there aren't that many female dragons, so I suppose just him."

"We've freed some female dragons," he reminded her.

"Not nearly enough," she said.

They stood off to the side of the small clearing, and Jason stared at the sky. Distantly, he had a sense of the dragon, and gradually that came closer. A dark shadow circled overhead. It began to descend, and as the dragon landed, Jason waited.

William sat astride the dragon, watching them. "Is it over?"

William climbed off the dragon, holding out his hand. The dragon sniffed at him, and then William rubbed his hand along the underside of the dragon's head. William leaned close. "You should go." The dragon snorted, a massive puff of smoke and steam coming from his nostrils. "I can ride back with them. I will find you when I return."

The dragon swung his head around and looked at Jason. His eyes blazed with a certain energy. He seemed to regard Jason for a long time, almost as if trying to decide whether or not he could be trusted. Finally, the dragon took off, circling in the sky before heading away. It seemed as if he were heading for Dragon Haven, though Jason didn't know if the dragon could find it with the illusion over it. Jason focused on the dragon, using the faint connection that he shared with the dragon for a moment, and gave him an image of Dragon Haven, letting it wash over him. The dragon roared quietly before continuing onward.

They reached the entrance to the mine, and Jason was reminded of how he had wandered down it, the ice dragon helping him find this dragon, a fellow hatch mate.

At least, what the ice dragon thought was a fellow hatch mate. Maybe the iron dragon truly was, or perhaps he was something else altogether. It didn't matter. All that mattered was that they had bonded. They had come together. And they had grown as more than just dragons. They had become friends. They had become Jason's family.

"This is where you found the iron dragon?" Sarah asked.

"The ice dragon and I came here trying to find others. He had felt something here," Jason said.

"How long do you think they held the iron dragon captive?" Sarah asked.

Jason looked at the iron dragon. He sniffed at the entrance to the mine but hadn't started toward it. "I don't know. That's something that he hasn't shared with me. I don't even know if he even knows. It's similar to the ice dragon. I tried to see what he might know about what happened to him and how he ended up in the mountains, but he doesn't even know that."

"Lorren must have needed to place the egg deep in the mountain," Sarah said.

"When we were dealing with Therin, I was mostly concerned about trying to keep myself safe, but also protecting the misfits as much as I could. With him gone, I should have spent more time understanding what he had been up to before. Or if he was responsible for all of this. I thought it him, but now..." He looked around the mountainside. "It shouldn't have taken Lorren coming to Dragon Haven for me to try to understand their origin."

"You were more focused on Lorach," Sarah said.

"I don't even know if that was the right thing, though,"

Jason said. "Until we understand the dragons, and until we know that we can protect those with us, I don't know if it makes sense to keep threatening Lorach."

"What are you saying?"

Jason shook his head. "I don't really know."

Which was true. All he did know was that he didn't feel as if they were going to be able to handle Lorren until he fully understood these misfits. He looked at the iron dragon. The dragon turned his attention back to Jason, and the heat radiating off him had shifted a little bit, glowing with a bright light, leaving him squinting into the darkness.

He smiled. It reminded him of when he had come here before. He thought of facing the Dragon Souls, the fear and terror that he had felt at that time. He thought of how the iron dragon had ripped through the forest, his sword-like tail cutting trees down as if they were nothing. He thought of their escape, the way the dragon had slithered down the mountainside, long before he had learned to fly.

They had been through so much together.

"We should go before Lorren finds the others." Jason didn't worry about the ice dragon. He flew high enough that no dragon of Lorren's could reach him. The iron dragon was with Jason. He worried about the storm dragon. Even the forest dragon, though she *should* be able to protect herself with her illusion. Then there was the river dragon. What would Lorren do with that?

The ground suddenly rumbled. It built rapidly—too rapidly. For a moment, the only thing Jason could think of was that it was an avalanche, but given that there would be no avalanche here, he knew exactly what it was.

Jason grabbed for the iron dragon, sending a burst of energy through their connection, but was too slow. The ground swallowed the dragon.

He jumped, reaching Sarah and William, pushing them backward. The rumbling intensified, violently throwing them back and away from the clearing. They managed to get to stable ground, but there was no sign of the iron dragon.

Jason could only stare.

He focused on his connection to the iron dragon, using the iron dragon glove, feeling for energy within it. That energy began to fade.

16

Jason looked around, trying to clear his mind, his vision, and everything else so he could try to find a way to help the iron dragon. The sudden loss of the glowing light coming from the iron dragon left the mountainside plunged in darkness. It took Jason's eyes a moment to adjust, and at that moment, he knew that it was too long. He started forward, holding onto the heat of the iron dragon glove, but it was fading, growing cooler.

"What happened?" William asked.

"The earth dragons attacked," Jason said. "It's Lorren. He's trying to claim the misfits." And here he'd thought he'd left, but he must not have.

He should have known there was a risk. They had been attacked already, and he should have waited. He should have ensured that Lorren had left.

The connection between Jason and the iron dragon continued to fade. He had to find some way to reach through that connection so that he could help. Panic started to set in.

"I need your help," he said to Sarah. "We have to get into the earth and free the iron dragon."

"We weren't able to do that before," Sarah said.

Jason's mind raced. He tried to think about what would work, but there didn't seem to be any answers. When he had dealt with the earth dragons before, he'd had the strength of the iron dragon, and had mixed it with the ice dragon. Without the iron dragon, he didn't know if he could save him. He had to focus. He had to find some way of helping him.

"I don't know how long he can survive under there before Lorren does… whatever he intends!"

The strength within the dragon continued to fade. With each passing moment, he knew they were running out of time. He called upon the ice dragon. He channeled that power, pushing it through him. If nothing else, he would help heal the iron dragon, if only for long enough to give Jason a chance to help.

Something happened.

It came as a shifting of power and an explosion of energy that flowed out from Jason, connecting the iron dragon to the ice dragon. Within that connection, he could use that power. It expanded and then exploded.

A rippling earthquake trembled beneath his feet.

"What was that?" Sarah asked. "Are the earth dragons returning?"

"I think… That was me," Jason whispered.

"Can you do it again?" Sarah asked.

He thought that he could. "It was a combination of ice and iron," he said.

"Steam," William said. "When you add the energy of the ice dragon to the iron dragon, it creates steam. Steam expands. It should be able to press through the space wherever he's trapped. Maybe enough to get him free. Keep doing it."

Jason had done something like that before.

And he would *not* abandon the iron dragon to Lorren.

I will claim him again.

That was what Lorren had said.

Rage filled Jason, and he focused on the dragons, on the energy they possessed, and let that fill him. He was a conduit. He would give the ice dragon the connection to the iron dragon. He let that connection flow through the iron dragon glove, through the iron dragon so he could free himself. Heat and cold mingled. Once again, there came a joining.

As before, it exploded. The ground trembled.

The steam expanded, and it slammed into the space beneath the ground.

A deep roar came with it from the iron dragon. It was distant and muted, almost as if something held onto it.

The earth dragons.

It meant they were there, attempting to constrain the iron dragon. That also meant that Jason had to work harder, and so he mingled the powers of the ice and iron dragons again. As before, there came another explosion.

This time, it burst outward, and Jason and the others went flying. As he got to his feet, he looked over, relieved to see Sarah and William were okay.

He focused on the iron dragon. He had to use the energy within him, and he had to help. He had to grab for power. He continued to pull on energy, using the mixture of the ice and iron dragons, letting it flow through him. It rolled up within him.

He forced it through his connection to the iron dragon. The dragon roared, though it was muted, as before.

He couldn't save the iron dragon this way. He might be able to mix the two powers and give the iron dragon space, but he didn't know if it was going to be enough for him to escape.

What would it take?

The earth dragons were potent. Each time that he mingled the powers, the earth dragons seemed to respond.

"I don't know any way to get to him," he muttered.

"What about the earth dragon?" William asked.

Jason glanced over at him. The ground continued to tremble, and thankfully though he had a sense of the iron dragon, it wasn't nearly as faded as it had been before. "Lorren has control over the earth dragons."

"He might have control over them, but you have a connection to these dragons."

"Not like that," Jason said.

"Why can't it be?" William glanced from Jason to Sarah

before nodding toward the ground. "With your connection, you could connect to the dragons."

Sarah nodded. "Didn't you say that you have a way of connecting to most dragons?"

Jason focused on the ground. He could feel the rumbling, the energy that was there, a signature to it that he recognized. He could feel it. He hadn't tried connecting to the dragon misfits Lorren used. He'd simply tried to stop them. What if he did try to connect to them?

He didn't even know if it would work. He didn't even know how many earth dragons were there. If he could connect to them, even a little, then maybe he could slow the attack.

"I have to try," he said, trying to hide the doubt in his voice.

He moved to the center of the clearing, knowing he put himself at risk if the earth dragons were to try to swallow him, and planted himself in place. He held onto the connection to the iron dragon as he sent a surge of energy through it to alert the iron dragon of what he would try. He had to let the iron dragon know help was coming. The iron dragon needed to know Jason wasn't going to abandon him.

The iron dragon pulsed against him. It was strong. Potent.

He shifted his focus to the trembling beneath him. It was the energy of the earth dragons, their signature. As Jason stood in place, power flowing around him and radiating up through him, he became aware of a rumbling that seemed as if it would force him away. He focused on it.

The energy resisted him.

It was there, though.

He continued to focus on it.

He wasn't trying to abuse or use these dragons. Only connect to them.

He had to know them. It was the same way that he had to know the ice dragon. The iron dragon. Even the forest dragon. It had taken understanding them to gain that knowledge.

Jason strained, continuing to push power out. What if he added a connection to the forest dragon? He might be able to alter something.

It might even help if he could see them. There was a way for that. He could borrow from the iron dragon and might be able to do something different.

Illusion.

He focused on the iron dragon and looked out through his eyes. Everything around him was dark, but the iron dragon pulsed with a hint of light, illuminating his surroundings. Were dragons around him? The strange darkness of those earth dragons surrounded the iron dragon.

He turned his attention to the forest dragon, feeling for the energy of her fluttering through him the way that it often did. It came washing in waves in his mind, the slow breath of the breeze through the trees. Jason used that energy and let it move him, swirling through him.

Power shimmered, and he pushed it out. All he wanted was to shift reality.

Without Lorren opposing him, and without the mist dragons, Jason thought he should be able to overcome this. More than that, there was something he thought he could do that might be more effective. He used his home.

It was something he had taken to doing when needing an illusion. It was the easiest of the illusions he had formed, and it was also one of the more powerful ones because he knew it so well. He could create the illusion, the cold and ice, and the wind.

"Jason?"

He glanced back and saw Sarah and William huddled together.

He shifted the illusion, adding a heavy cloak that would keep them warm. He didn't need to do anything more than give them a different reality.

He held onto the illusion otherwise and could feel it solidifying around him.

He needed the power of that illusion to hold the dragons. He pulled the iron dragon into it.

Suddenly, the iron dragon was there in front of him. Jason held out his hand, and the iron dragon turned to him, a look passing between them. The iron dragon understood this was an illusion, but he also understood that Jason held him there.

"Where are they?" Jason asked the iron dragon.

"Near," the iron dragon said.

"I can't see them," he said.

Wind continued to swirl, and Jason searched through it, looking for signs of the earth dragons. By holding on to the wind and using the way it swirled around him, Jason could make out a change where the landscape was altered. In the distance, he could make out one of the dragons.

He was smaller than Jason had expected. Here he had thought the dragons he'd seen in the forest were massive, but this didn't seem all that large. He could feel something from them, a connection to the ground.

Jason summoned even more power, pulling it into the illusion, solidifying it around him. As it fortified him, the snow and ice and everything coalesced. The wind gusted, powerful and sharp. Jason pulled the earth dragon toward him.

There was another, and though he was distantly aware of it, he didn't see it.

He focused on one only.

Within the illusion, the earth dragon might be able to harm him, but Jason was in control. The ground rumbled, and the dragon tried to thrash at him, but Jason settled the wind around it, creating a bubble of air. The cold was still there, but now the snow drifted with small flakes that fluttered in the air.

He held out his hand. "You don't have to fight anymore," he said, holding his hand out to the dragon.

The dragon rumbled, and the ground thrashed again.

Jason simply waited.

"What did you do?" the dragon rumbled, his voice a deep sound, almost as if the earth was speaking to him.

"I didn't do anything to you. I wanted a chance to talk. I don't know what Lorren has said to you, but you don't have to fight us. You don't have to kill other dragons."

The dragon thrashed, rumbling, but Jason held the wind around him along with the illusion, giving the dragon only so much space before he was forced to turn back around. It required a considerable pull of power. He didn't know how long he would be able to hold it. This illusion required more energy than he'd used before.

"You don't have to fight anymore," Jason said again.

"You would harm us," the dragon said.

Jason held out his hand and tried to think of whether there was another way to form the illusion to embrace the power of the earth dragon. He didn't know if he could. Instead, he focused on the earth dragon, the power within him, and tried to understand him. If he could understand the dragon, a way of connecting to what made them special, he thought he could help.

The earth dragon was bound to the earth. He had to use that somehow.

There was a deep trembling. For a moment, Jason thought the earth dragon tried to fight him and the illusion, but he realized that it came from the dragon and radiated outward. He focused on that trembling and the energy within it.

"You can work with us," Jason said, attempting to soothe the dragon.

The trembling intensified.

He had to find another approach that would allow the dragon to recognize he wasn't going to harm him.

First, he had to place this dragon inside another illusion.

He had no idea what was happening outside this illusion, whether the earth dragon had harmed the iron dragon. Within the illusion, he could keep them separate. He created another pocket of illusion, putting this earth dragon inside it and everything else outside it. Within this pocket of illusion, Jason created a vast expanse of snow and ice. He focused on the dragon. Then he turned it. The dragon needed a connection to the earth itself, and a familiarity with his surroundings.

He created a series of tunnels. Within one, the walls of the tunnels surrounded the earth dragon, and Jason stood in front of it. It was dark, but he created a hint of pale yellow light around him that was enough for him to see.

The trembling within the earth dragon shifted again.

Pressure pushed against the illusion, as if the earth dragon tried to test whether he could overpower Jason, but he maintained his hold.

"You don't have to fight," Jason said.

"What are you doing to me?" There was more anger in the earth dragon's voice, and rage filled him.

This wasn't the right illusion.

Jason shifted it quickly, creating a meadow. There was a forest in the background, and he thought of the forest dragon and the power that existed there. Flowers filled the meadow, and he could practically smell them growing.

There was an energy and vibrancy here. Jason embraced that power and the way that it filled him. He turned to the earth dragon and waited, testing whether the earth dragon might fight.

The trembling began to ease.

Jason shifted the illusion slightly. He added a bright sun shining down, warm and comforting. The earth dragon trembled, though it was less of a trembling and more of a shiver.

"That's what you want, isn't it?" Jason thought he understood. Lorren forced the earth dragons to move through the earth, but they wanted the sunlight. They wanted the warmth. They wanted to be out in the open.

He looked at the dragon. In addition to his grayish sides, long, slender body, and big, chunky legs, he had strange-looking wings.

"I can help you," Jason said.

"You would use me," the dragon rumbled. "You would do the same as the others. He is the only one who has kept us safe."

Jason shook his head. "You've seen what I've done with the other dragons."

He shifted the illusion again, this time adding the iron dragon. He held his hand up, hoping it wasn't necessary. The iron dragon recognized what Jason did, and could feel the connection between them, and seemed to know just what Jason wanted.

"This is another dragon like yourself. He is powerful, much like you are powerful."

"He tells me I'm not powerful."

Jason smiled, holding his hand out. "But you are. I can feel it. The energy within you is incredibly powerful."

Everything started to tremble. Jason thought it came from the earth dragon attempting to break free of the illusion, but that wasn't it. He shifted his attention outside the pocket of the illusion and realized where it came from. It was the other earth dragon. It was trying to break through what Jason did, attempting to penetrate this illusion. Were it to do so, the two dragons together might be impossible to slow. He needed to keep them separate to allow himself to communicate with this dragon and stop its attack. He doubted he had much time remaining, as he could feel the energy building.

If he lost his illusion, if it faded, Jason would fail.

He had to hold the meadow, the warm sun, the comfort of everything around him.

He turned his attention back to the earth dragon and smiled. "You are incredibly powerful. Think about what he has asked of you. He has asked you to control dragons he can't."

"He says that is the price we must pay," the earth dragon said.

"The price for what?"

"For our existence."

Jason frowned, watching him. "Why would he say that?"

"Because we are abominations."

Jason's breath caught. More than ever, he hated Lorren and what he did to the dragons. "You are not."

"We aren't like the others. That is why he gathers us."

Jason started toward the dragon, ignoring the trembling rolling through him that came up from the earth. The longer he waited, the more danger he was in. He tried to maintain his connection to this dragon, to find energy within him to hold onto this communication. He could feel his illusion starting to shimmer. It started on the outskirts of the image, enough that he knew he couldn't maintain it much longer.

He turned the iron dragon and pulled power through him. It was a gamble. The iron dragon was still underground, trapped by these earth dragons. Despite everything he had created within the illusion, the dragon remained held, trapped and possibly suffering. By borrowing power from him, Jason ran the risk of pulling on too much of his energy. Still, the iron dragon pressed back, giving Jason permission. He used that energy to solidify the illusion around them.

"You aren't an abomination," Jason said. It was terrible that he even had to say that. "You are different, but so is the iron dragon. So am I. All dragons are different."

"Not all dragons are different," the earth dragon said. Power pressed against him, and Jason could feel the illusion slipping. He borrowed even more power, but it was beginning to fail him altogether. He didn't know how much longer he could hold onto it.

A different thought came to him, one he hadn't considered before. What if Lorren wasn't commanding them? He thought Lorren was involved, but perhaps there was something more.

"How much do you do on his behalf?"

"He tells us what we need to do."

"Why?"

"Because we are different. We must remove the others."

"But why?" Jason asked.

The ground trembled even more. The illusion shimmered, and Jason solidified it. He could feel that he didn't have much time.

"You don't have to fight the other dragons. They are not the enemy," he said.

"Enemy?"

Jason nodded. "The other dragons aren't your enemy. They have been used and controlled. All they want is to be free. Why would you need to fight them?"

The dragon trembled. This time, Jason felt the energy within it differently. It wasn't pushing against the illusion. He held his hand out, resting it on the dragon's side, feeling the energy within him. The dragon continued to tremble, and Jason smiled at him.

"You could help," Jason said.

"Why would I help?"

"Because you're different. You could help those that are different. You could help those who need to be protected like you."

"The other dragons don't need to be protected. They're powerful."

"And you are powerful," Jason said. "You destroyed the others. You're trapping the iron dragon. That is power."

"He tells us that we—"

The trembling rumbled more powerfully than before. It was enough that Jason lost control over his illusion for a moment. It flickered, and when it did, the earth dragon inside the illusion raged. Power trembled from within it.

Jason turned to the earth dragon. "Please. You don't have to harm the other dragons." The effect of the illusion continued to fade. "Just release the iron dragon. He isn't like the others. He's different. Much like you."

Jason didn't know if it would even work, but he could feel the sense of hesitation within the dragon. He took a chance and used a connection to the iron and ice dragons and created a washing of the two that worked through the earth dragon. As he did, he tried to strip off any influence, but didn't feel anything there. There was only the sense of the earth dragon's emotions. Jason twisted the connection he held, trying to add something more so that he could wrap around that energy and tie it to him, but he then started to feel resistance.

Trembling within the earth dragon forced Jason back.

He staggered, the illusion fading.

"Please. Don't harm the iron dragon. He's my friend."

They were the last words Jason said before the illusion shattered.

He stood once more in the clearing. William and Sarah

were there, both grabbing for his arms and bracing themselves.

Jason turned to them. “I don’t know if it was enough.”

“What did you do to the dragons?” William asked. “All I saw was snow.”

“I tried to trap one of the earth dragons inside the illusion to give me a chance to talk with him, but…”

It wasn’t enough. Jason hadn’t been able to reach that dragon.

He took a deep breath and focused on the iron dragon. He was there, and the sense of him continued to fade. Jason had borrowed power from him, taking what the iron dragon may have needed, which meant that he might not be able to do anything.

He didn’t know if he had enough strength to shift reality again.

He called to the forest dragon, trying to get more power from her, but she didn’t answer. He tried to call to the ice dragon, but he wouldn’t be able to help, either. Both had lent him as much as they could, and their strength faded. Not only theirs, but his had faded too. It had taken everything within him to form the illusion around the earth dragon and trap him. Now that the illusion had shattered, he couldn’t create any more power.

He would lose the iron dragon.

17

Jason sank to his knees, slamming his fist into the ground. Sarah was there, wrapping her arms around his shoulders, her hand on his back.

"It'll be okay," she whispered.

He could only shake his head. The energy within the iron dragon glove continued to fade, leaving him with an emptiness. In time, the power would fade completely, and the iron dragon would suffocate. He couldn't believe the earth dragons would do that.

A memory of the illusion came back to him. Of course he could believe it. He'd seen it already. He'd recognized the anger within the earth dragons, anger that had been stirred up by Lorren. If only there were some way to grant those dragons the same peace he had given the storm dragon.

He realized he might need the power of the storm dragon to combat Lorren. Perhaps he should have gone after that dragon before chasing information about the other misfits. Then he wouldn't have lost the iron dragon.

He held his hands against the ground, focusing on the iron dragon. "I'm sorry," he whispered.

There came a faint stirring of energy, as if the iron dragon was there and trying to reach him, but Jason couldn't hear anything. He borrowed from the ice dragon, wanting to send a healing wave through to him, but he couldn't. The connection was faded and faint. He couldn't reach his dragon friend.

Jason cried out as anger filled him. The ground started to tremble.

He had failed. Not only had he failed to rescue the Dragon Soul dragons, but he'd failed to rescue the iron dragon. He wasn't enough.

He pressed his face up against the ground. Tears streamed down his face. He hadn't lost one of his misfits before. The iron dragon was the second of the misfits, and in many ways was the one Jason was most connected to. He stared at the iron dragon glove, and though it still seemed to glow softly, it wasn't with nearly as much power.

He cried out again. The flickering energy of the iron dragon glove faded even more. His hand started to go cold.

"Jason?" Sarah whispered.

He couldn't look up. He pounded on the ground, his hand throbbing uncomfortably. "He's gone," he whispered.

He held up the iron dragon glove. The ground trembled faintly. Gradually, he was aware of the earth dragons drifting away. At least they hadn't tried to attack him, Sarah, and William.

Only, why would they need to? None of them were a threat to the dragons. Only the dragons were a threat. He lingered, resting on the ground, the sense of the iron dragon faded and absent. He didn't want to move. All he wanted was to break through the ground, to get to the iron dragon to see his remains, to move him.

He had no strength. No power.

Only…

Maybe there was something he could do. Jason glanced at Sarah. "Let me borrow your pearl. There might be something I can still do."

She reached into her pocket immediately, pulling out a handful of dragon pearls. He knew she had several, but hadn't realized she had so many. How many dragons was she connected to back in Dragon Haven?

He cupped one of them in his iron dragon glove. He took two more, squeezing them as he held onto them, focusing on the energy of the dragons, letting that flow through him, through the pearls, and into the iron dragon glove. That power filled him. Jason embraced it, letting energy wash through him and through the glove. It began to glow.

"What are you doing?" William whispered.

Jason didn't look up. "I'm trying to see if I might help the iron dragon still."

"I thought you said he was gone."

"The iron dragon is metal. If he can be heated again…"

That was his hope. He had no idea whether or not it would work, but holding on to these pearls, he had to think there was something he could do. He let energy flow through him, building. It filled his hand, and heat washed through him. Jason focused on it and let it flow outward through the iron dragon glove and toward the dragon. He borrowed from the ice dragon flying overhead. There wasn't much that the ice dragon could offer, as he was exhausted after using as much power as Jason had already drawn from him, but he had some. Jason let it flow through him. He even added a hint of himself. To save the iron dragon, Jason would do whatever it took. Even if that involved forcing as much of himself as he could into the dragon.

He had no idea how far beneath the ground the iron dragon had been dragged, but he tried. Power snaked away from him. Jason continued to force more out, and it slipped into the ground and then deeper and farther down.

There was heat and energy. It connected. For a moment, he felt a flicker.

Jason focused on that, on the iron dragon glove, and pushed more power into it, borrowing as much from the distant dragons within Dragon Haven as he could. He needed to reawaken the iron dragon.

Heat exploded. A connection formed. There was a surge of energy that flowed between them, a drifting of power from one to the other. Jason maintained that connection, embracing it. He borrowed from the dragon pearls, flowing through the dragon glove and outward into the iron dragon. He added the ice dragon again and used that explosion of heat and ice to expand outward as steam. The ground started to tremble. Something began shifting.

Then he felt an awakening.

The iron dragon was there.

Jason pushed through his connection to the iron dragon. "You're going to have to fight your way out."

There came a deep rumble. It wasn't muted this time. Power exploded from the dragon, rolling through the ground. The iron dragon raged, power blasting out of him.

Then he streaked free of his prison, shooting upward before crashing back to the ground. His body glowed a molten metal, and the heat that radiated from him borrowed energy from the dragon pearls, from the other dragons, leaving it slipping along his tired body. There was something else within it. Power, but more than just power.

Something had shifted within the dragon.

Jason hurried to him, resting his hand on the dragon's side. "You're free," he said. He rubbed at his eyes, drying them off. He couldn't believe the iron dragon was free. He couldn't believe the iron dragon was here. He had felt him fading, dying. He had felt that connection slipping away.

"Thanks to you," the dragon said. The timbre of his

voice had changed, as if his capture underground had altered him.

Jason didn't care. All he cared about was that the dragon was free.

He held onto energy, pushing more through the dragon pearls and into the dragon. Each time he did, the dragon released a little more heat. It pulsed, washing along the length of his body, and he continued to build with energy and heat.

He turned to the others. "We need to return."

"We came to understand how Lorren and Therin created the misfits," Sarah reminded him.

Jason squeezed his eyes shut. The dragon was safe. As far as he knew, the earth dragons had disappeared. They did need to know more, but he thought there was something more important that they do now. He didn't want to get in the middle of a battle between Jessica and Lorren, but having felt the effect of the earth dragons and knowing what Lorren had done to them, he thought he needed to help them as well.

The answers Jason needed would be with them. Not looking to the past, trying to piece together how Therin and Lorren had created the misfits, but understanding the misfits that lived.

He climbed on top of the iron dragon's back, settling himself.

"Jason?" Sarah asked. Her voice was tinged with concern.

He looked over at her. "What is it?"

"How… How are you sitting on him?"

Jason glanced down at the iron dragon. His body glowed with a molten heat, radiating the energy that built from deep within him. It slipped along the length of his side. "I've never struggled with his heat before."

"I understand, but this is…" She shook her head. "We aren't going to be able to ride with you."

He focused on the ice dragon. "We need your help."

It didn't take long, but the ice dragon streaked toward the ground and dropped down next to him. He stayed a distance from the iron dragon, though he looked over at him, and something passed between them. Could the ice dragon be pleased that the iron dragon had survived? He was never sure how the two dragons felt about each other. They were different, and sometimes that difference created difficulties between them. This time, it seemed as if the iron dragon and the ice dragon were pleased to see each other.

"The ice dragon will take you," he said.

"Great. I think I might have preferred to ride on the iron dragon," William said.

Jason grinned and tapped on the iron dragon's side as they surged into the air. The other two climbed onto the ice dragon and took flight, joining him in the sky.

Jason pushed on the power of the dragon pearls he clutched. He connected to them, sending a communication to the other dragons and Dragon Haven so they would know what they were doing and where they were going. Holding on to that power, he could feel it flowing and radiating from him.

"Where do you have us going now?" Sarah yelled across the distance.

Lorren was after the misfits, but the iron dragon needed to rest. He would protect him, then find Lorren. "Back to Dragon Haven." Jason stared into the distance before looking down at the iron dragon. "I didn't do what I needed to, though we survived. That has to be enough."

As they flew, he had a different sensation.

It was a flutter, a stirring of the wind, and a faint shimmering.

He blinked for a moment and realized what he detected.

The forest dragon.

Lorren must have known about her.

He leaned toward the iron dragon. "She needs us," he whispered.

They turned, veering toward the distant forest, the others following. It was unusual for the forest dragon to call to him. Usually, Jason summoned her, begging for her help. That she asked for his help now was surprising.

Had he drawn too much power from her?

He didn't know. The connection that formed between them didn't reveal that.

It was dark, late in the evening, though with the heat radiating off the iron dragon, there was plenty of light. He had no idea what they must look like from a distance.

Maybe a shooting star in the sky, though a massive one at that.

When they landed, Sarah and William climbed off the ice dragon's back and joined him at the forest edge.

"I thought we were going back to Dragon Haven," William said.

"We were, but I felt something while we were flying. I think the forest dragon needs our help."

"Do you think Lorren came here?" Sarah asked.

Jason closed his eyes, thinking about the forest dragon. "I would have said that Lorren doesn't know how to find this dragon, but maybe he does."

"Are you sure? Therin knew."

"Given the forest dragon's ability to hide herself, I don't know that he would be able to reach her." At least, he hoped not. He didn't think that the mist dragons would be able to overwhelm her power, not when it came directly from her. If they did, or if they tried, Jason would need to intervene. She was the least likely to fight. "I don't know if she will allow you to see her."

"And if she doesn't allow you to see her?" William asked.

Jason chuckled, glancing at the other two misfits before shaking his head. "Then we go back."

Staying here any longer might not be the right thing, anyway. He was exhausted, not only physically but emotionally. It might make sense to return to Dragon Haven to understand what would be needed to reach Lorren's dragons. He needed to find out more about him, to know what else might be needed to prevent him from harming other dragons.

First, he wanted to check on the third dragon misfit. He headed into the trees, following the energy within the forest, using that to help him reach her. He didn't feel her quite as acutely as he normally did within the forest. He expected that given his proximity to her, he would've felt something more directly, but there was nothing. Power flowed through him, but he couldn't embrace it.

He glanced over at the others with him, but they said nothing.

Jason followed the awareness he had of the forest dragon, meandering through the trees, though he couldn't see her. That didn't surprise him. When it came to the forest dragon, he rarely could see anything unless she chose it.

The farther he went, the more he recognized something else within the forest.

She was nearby, only she was masking herself for some reason. Did she know he had brought others with him and didn't want to reveal herself?

He held his hand up. "I need to go by myself from here."

"Jason," Sarah started, grabbing for his arm. "It's not safe to be here by ourselves."

Jason looked around the forest and could feel the emptiness, other than the forest dragon. "You're safe here."

"I don't like this place," William whispered. "I feel… Uneasy. I don't know how to explain it."

Sarah nodded. "There's something off here. It's different. Are you sure that she is here? She brought the storm dragon away. Maybe she didn't return."

Jason frowned. He didn't have the same sense that they did. The only thing he felt was the density of the forest around him, the trees and the canopy and the leaves. That… And the forest dragon in the distance. She was somewhere up ahead, close enough to reach her, but hidden from him.

Why would she be hidden in that way?

He focused on what he could detect of her. There came a fluttering, a faint stirring, and everything about the forest shifted.

There was an illusion around it. It didn't affect him the same way it did the others. At least he understood why they would be unsettled.

Mixed within that was something else. He frowned. "There's something else here," he whispered.

Sarah stepped toward him. "Lorren?"

"Not Lorren. Something." He frowned. "Stay here." He followed the draw of the forest dragon, but the sense of something else nearby was close to the forest dragon. He had no idea what it was, only that there was a vague tracing of energy from within it, a pulsing of power and something that suggested there was something else here.

He didn't think it was Lorren and his misfits. If they were here, he would have detected something from them by now.

He moved carefully forward, holding on to what he

could of the iron and the ice dragons. He wouldn't draw from them—or from the forest dragon—unless needed, but even then, he'd borrowed enough from her recently that he didn't know if she had much strength remaining. She might have been as spent as he felt.

There was power still available to him. He reached into his pocket and grabbed the dragon pearls that he still had from Sarah. Holding on to them, he drew power through them and embraced it, letting it fill him.

The energy coming from those dragons was different than what he was accustomed to using. Maybe he should use dragon pearls more than he did. It did grant a different sort of strength. Having faced Lorren within Dragon Haven, he had seen how that power could be utilized. He had become so dependent upon the ice and the iron dragon, along with the forest dragon, that he rarely even contemplated using other dragons.

He moved forward and heard a stirring behind him.

Jason spun, and Sarah and William were there.

"I thought I said—"

"I heard what you said," Sarah said. "But we aren't letting you go off by yourself if there is something here."

Jason would have to ask the forest dragon for forgiveness. There was something else here. He pushed the power out from the dragon pearls, letting it flow into the forest as he probed gently.

Only, it must not have been so gentle. Something reacted to him.

It took a moment to realize it was the forest dragon. She reacted strongly—almost too strongly.

"Something's wrong," he whispered.

"What is it?" Sarah asked.

He hurried forward. "I don't know. All I can tell is that something isn't right." He focused on the power of the dragon as he ran, knowing that he needed to understand her reaction. Could she have been attacked by Lorren? He didn't know if that were the case, but the energy he felt was off.

It was near now.

He moved carefully, holding his hand up as he approached, feeling for the power out there. He pushed, this time adding a hint of the ice and the iron dragon, avoiding using the dragon pearls, as that had caused her initial reaction. There was no pressure against him this time.

Jason pushed again, letting energy build within him, the combination of the two dragon misfits mingled as they swept through the forest. He could feel the forest dragon in the distance.

He called upon her power, using just a hint of it, little more than that, and could feel the way that energy swirled around him. He borrowed from it, using it to sweep outward.

Something was going on.

He started forward again. This time, he noticed a rippling. A shimmering.

It was illusion.

He hesitated, motioning to the other two.

"She is using an illusion here. I don't know what we will find when we go through it, but you need to be ready for anything."

"What sort of illusion?" William asked.

Jason shook his head. "I don't know, but if the forest dragon made it, then it will be incredibly powerful. It is likely going to be nothing that you have ever known and will feel impossibly real."

It was surprising to Jason, though. Why would she hold onto an illusion within the forest? *Could* she be in danger?

He called upon even more power from the two other dragon misfits. Thankfully, they had continued to recover, and the energy they lent to him was far more considerable than it would have been earlier. He let that power flow through him, heat building and mixing with the energy of the ice dragon. Steam radiated from him. He tried not to think what that meant.

He headed forward and toward the illusion. The other two stayed with him. When they stepped through the illusion, the forest shifted around him.

It was still a dense forest with trees rising all around, vines growing from them, but there was an opening that Jason didn't remember having been here before. Moonlight streamed down, and he didn't know if that was illusion or not. It created shadows that seemed to ripple, shimmering everywhere. The power here was different than anything he'd ever felt before. All of this was an illusion.

At the center of the clearing was the forest dragon. She curled around the ground, raising her head and looking at him as he approached. Jason tested the connection he shared with her, wanting to ensure that she was real and not merely more illusion. In the faint moonlight, her scales fluttered, catching shimmers of light, mixing with the shadows. The deep greens and blues that were on her scales usually seemed to shift and shimmer. There was something that felt wrong.

"Are you injured?" he whispered as he approached.

She breathed out a streamer of mist. Maybe she was connected to the mist in a way that he hadn't known. Energy radiated from her, flowing outward, creating pressure—and the illusion.

"If you're not hurt, then what is this?" Jason approached, holding on to the energy within him of the other two dragons.

"It is something," she murmured as she turned her attention down toward her belly.

Jason approached carefully, and could feel Sarah and William alongside him. He maintained his hold on the other misfits, that power, unable to shake the feeling that something unusual was taking place and wanting to be ready for whatever it might be. As he neared the forest dragon, he realized what she was doing. She curled around the shape lying on the ground near her. At first,

Jason thought she curled around a stone, but that wasn't it at all.

An egg.

Sarah gasped. "Is that—"

"A dragon egg," Jason said. He looked over at the forest dragon, meeting her gaze. "She has a dragon egg."

18

Jason could scarcely move. All this time, he had believed the strange energy he'd felt had detected had come from Lorach, but that wasn't it at all. It was the forest dragon. Her reluctance to give power over the last few days to weeks made a bit more sense. She was here with this egg. Not only that, but when she'd laid the egg, Jason thought he'd somehow felt it. He had no idea how he had, other than the fact that he was connected to her. Maybe that was why he had felt it.

Unless…

He might not have been the only one to have felt it.

Could Lorren have known? What if that was the real reason he'd come to Dragon Haven and not because of Lorach or what Jason had done? It fit with what Lorren had said. His reasoning for coming now.

This had to be what he wanted Jason for.

This was why he wanted the misfits.

Jason crouched on the ground and took a seat near the forest dragon, crossing his legs as he held onto the energy coming from the other dragon misfits. He hadn't come any closer to the forest dragon, though he could feel the power of illusion all around her and suspected that what she had placed around her was significant—and had a significant meaning. Likely it was to protect this egg.

"Why didn't you tell me?" Jason asked.

"There was no need," the forest dragon said.

Jason stared at it. The egg was different. He didn't know how to describe it any other way, only that it looked like an oblong stone. Shadows swirled around it, the darkness or illusion making it seem impossibly black. "Is it a dragon misfit?"

The forest dragon breathed out, and again a streamer of mist went with it. "Yes."

Jason focused on his connection to her and could feel something between them. Their bond had always been unusual, different than it was with the ice dragon or the iron dragon. In reality, each of the dragons shared a different sort of connection with him. With the ice dragon, it was a connection to his homeland, a familiarity with the cold and the ice and everything that he had experienced while growing up. With the iron dragon, it was the rage and anger they both shared knowing they had suffered. With the forest dragon, it had been tentative at first but had built, allowing a greater connection between them.

She had always been tentative with him. Even when

she'd been used by Therin, there had been a hesitation. He thought he understood that now. Still, he could feel power flowing from her. It formed the illusion, but it drifted outward, beyond her, and surrounded the entire clearing but concentrated upon the egg.

There was energy here. Significant energy. Much of it came from the egg itself.

"The storm dragon," Jason said. He turned to Sarah, then to William. "I think this is the forest and the storm dragon's egg. If so, it was a union of two powerful dragon misfits. An egg like this, and the dragon that would emerge, would be incredibly powerful."

"I have done everything to protect it," the forest dragon said. "That is why I wasn't able to help any more than I did." An image of the iron dragon buried beneath the ground formed in his mind. Here he had feared that he had tapped out all of her strength, but that wasn't what he had done at all. She had limited him, preventing him from reaching more power.

"What do you mean that you protected it?" Jason asked.

"There have been attempts to find me," she said, turning her expression once again to the egg. "I have prevented it."

Jason frowned. "Dragon Souls?" He didn't know whether the forest dragon would understand the Dragon Souls, so he used the connection they shared and reminded her of what they had been through within Lorach.

An image formed, one of mist, strangely rumbling earth, and a hint of what looked to be smoke.

Lorren.

"Lorren came for it."

"Came and failed. I have protected this egg."

She snorted, and another streamer of fog drifted from her nostrils, and once again, the illusion around him solidified. There was incredible power within that illusion. Jason could feel that power—and the way it formed—as it surged around him. It wasn't just an illusion, though. There was something more.

Power. Jason could feel that power. He could feel the egg. He could feel everything.

This was what had drawn Lorren.

He was aware of a misfit.

He knew far too much about the dragon misfits. It wouldn't surprise him that he would recognize when one had been laid. He probably had some way of following it.

By sitting here and controlling everything around her, the forest dragon had shifted reality. She had done what she needed to create the reality necessary to protect this egg.

Of course she would have. Jason wouldn't have expected anything else. She was powerful enough that he could easily imagine she could hold onto that power in a way that gave her the ability to ensure the safety of the egg.

"What can we do to help you?"

"Nothing," she said. "The egg is safe."

"If others are trying to find you, then it's not safe."

"Others have been trying to find me ever since I hatched," she said.

Jason sat there, thinking about the power here, everything around him. Could Lorren break through this illusion? He had control over illusions, but despite everything that he'd already demonstrated, Jason didn't know if Lorren could shatter this one. If so, he would come for this egg. He knew that Lorren would do anything to reach a dragon like this upon its hatching.

"Do you remember anything about what was required for you to hatch?" Jason asked.

The dragon turned toward him. "There was nothing," she started, "and then there was something."

He looked over at the egg. "That doesn't help."

The forest dragon turned her attention to the egg. "Much like now. There was nothing. And now there is something."

Jason held his hand out toward the egg, waiting for her to give permission. When she did, he crawled forward, resting his hand on it. Unsurprisingly, the egg was warm. It had an irregular surface, but there was something about it that seemed almost grooved. As he twisted from side to side, he noticed a faint glowing from within the egg. For a moment, he thought it might be his imagination, but as he continued to swivel in place, he became increasingly certain of that glow coming from the egg. There was power from within it, as well.

This was what he had detected when he'd chased

Lorach. This was the power he had recognized within the forest. The egg was the source of it.

"How long have you had it?"

"A few weeks," she said.

Jason shook his head. How could she have had the egg for that long? "I shouldn't have borrowed your power."

"I only permitted what I could. Had I been able to give you more…"

Jason shook his head. "I'm sorry. Had I known you were protecting the egg, I wouldn't have borrowed from you at all."

Of course, had he not, the iron dragon would have died. The forest dragon must have been aware of what she had done and the gift she had given him. It was because of her power that he'd gained a connection—however slight—to the earth dragon. Had she not lent him what she had, one of the misfits—one of her hatch mates—would have died.

"How long do eggs take to hatch?" Jason asked.

The question was directed partially toward the forest dragon, but Sarah had an understanding of dragon eggs as well. She had worked around the dragons long enough that she should have some understanding of what it would take.

"Usually many months," Sarah said as she scooted up alongside him. She held her hand out, watching the forest dragon the entire time. She waited, as if concerned about getting too close. She wanted permission.

Sarah was skilled at working with dragons. This was

the right strategy with the forest dragon. She was skittish, but at the same time, this was her egg. It reminded him of the sense he had from her when she had been willing to come and work with the storm dragon in the first place. She had taken a risk that she normally wouldn't. She might be skittish, but she was strong, too.

Not that he had ever doubted her strength. It was just the kind of strength she possessed, the energy within her, that was different.

The power coming out of the egg radiated toward him, practically palpable. It was easy to know the misfit that would emerge from this egg would be impressive. It would take on qualities of the forest dragon, the storm dragon, and perhaps whatever environment the forest dragon had provided for the egg.

"How long do you think this egg has left before it hatches?" Jason asked Sarah.

Sarah leaned closer. "This is different than others I've known," she said. "I would have thought this egg was five or six months along, but if it's only a few weeks…" She looked up at the forest dragon and frowned. "With these dragons, perhaps everything is all a bit different."

He had been looking to understand what it would take to have the misfits hatch, and here he had a misfit egg in front of him. He could learn firsthand. All he knew about misfit dragons was that they took on elements of their environment. There had been the ice dragon, the iron dragon, the forest dragon, the jungle dragon, and the storm dragon. All of those dragons had been created by

Therin based on where he had placed eggs. The river dragon was still out there, and Jason had not yet come across it, and the jungle dragon had died.

Then there were the dragons who had been created by what Lorren had done. The earth dragon. The mist dragon. He could only imagine what other dragons Lorren may have attempted. He had talked about smoke dragons, but what other dragons could there be?

As he looked around the inside of the darkened clearing, the shadows swirling around, the moonlight shining down, Jason couldn't help but wonder what sort of power this dragon was taking on. What would this environment do? It would have to have some aspect of the forest dragon and the storm dragon.

"Why here?" Jason asked, looking up at the forest dragon. "You could have created a place for this dragon anywhere. Why here?"

"Because this is where I needed to be," she said.

"How did you know?"

"I could feel it. I could feel the way the egg needed to be placed here, and the energy within it."

Jason held his hand over the egg, doing nothing other than attempting to probe for power. There was a faint trembling within it, but nothing more.

Jason closed his eyes, focusing on the egg itself. He couldn't discern anything more from it. Just power.

When he opened his eyes, leaning back and looking up at the forest dragon, he frowned. "How long do you think it will take for your egg to hatch?"

The forest dragon watched him, and there was energy coming from her. Nothing more than that, just power.

"You don't know," he said.

The forest dragon breathed out a streamer of mist, and the energy of the illusion formed again, solidifying around him.

"I don't know," she said.

"Do you fear the egg?"

"I fear for my hatchling," she said. "It is why I have taken the precautions I have to protect it."

Jason looked around, feeling the illusion she had created. There had to be something more he could offer. Could he summon other dragons to offer protection? Even if he did, would it be enough? Maybe the forest dragon and her illusion was all that was necessary to protect this egg.

Strangely, he could feel the egg pulling on him. He focused on the other dragon misfits, and there came a surge of power. It called on him, coming from the egg. Almost as if…

"It's feeding," he whispered.

It was as if the egg were calling to him, pulling power from the ice and the iron dragon.

He leaned back, releasing his connection to the other dragons.

"Did you feel that?" Jason asked the forest dragon.

She breathed out slowly. "He stirs," she said.

"He?"

She curled around the egg. "He stirs."

Jason glanced over at William and Sarah, feeling power flowing outward. The egg was trying to draw from him, pulling on the iron dragon and the ice dragon. It had required strength on his part to separate from it. He didn't want to diminish them too much, but he wondered if he could help the dragon egg.

"What is it?" Sarah asked.

Jason held his hand out across from the egg, and could still feel energy radiating. "There's something within the egg calling upon the power I'm holding. It's almost as if the egg itself is trying to borrow from that energy."

"What do you mean borrow it?" Sarah asked.

He stared at the egg. Was it glowing more brightly than it had been? "The egg was drawing power off me."

"An egg shouldn't be able to do that. The dragon within wouldn't be developed enough."

"Even if it is farther along than it seems like it should be?"

Jason could feel the energy within the egg, the way it was stirring. There was a fluttering sensation, something that reminded him of the forest dragon, though stronger, if possible. There was something about the egg that he thought he needed to better understand. He wanted to test it, pushing power into it, but at the same time, he didn't want to run the risk of it overwhelming what he could do.

"Even if it's further along than you know, we've never seen an egg draw power off another dragon. We've tried.

We use the energy of the dragon pearls, but nothing has happened when we did."

Jason couldn't help but wonder if it was because of him or whether it was something within the egg. Either way, the strangeness of it tugged at him, an awareness of the egg and the power that came to him, building within him. He needed to know.

He reached for the ice dragon first. He had the most power remaining, and more that he could draw upon. By holding onto that energy, Jason could push a little bit of power outward, and it flowed toward the egg. It was an ongoing sense building within him as it rolled forward, radiating to the egg.

Gradually he pushed it into the egg.

He barely released much. The egg suddenly latched onto that power and began to take it from him.

Power flowed through Jason, funneled through the ice dragon, drawn into the egg.

It was strange, but it reminded Jason of what had happened with the iron dragon when he had pushed power from the dragon pearls into him. Now he could feel power flowing, the way that energy radiated toward the egg. He shifted, adding a hint of energy from the iron dragon, and let that flow into the egg.

A sense of the iron dragon flared within him, heat coming off his glove. More and more power was siphoned through him, going into the egg and coursing outward. The powers mingled within the egg.

Jason started to withdraw but struggled. It was similar

to when he had tried to separate initially. He had to force himself back, ripping the power away before he could cut it off. When he did, he leaned back, sagging as the heat and energy that flowed within him began building again.

There came a rustling through the trees, and he looked up to see the iron dragon slithering toward them. The iron dragon circled before coming to lie next to the forest dragon. Heat built from him, radiating toward the egg. There came another stirring, and a shadow dropped from the sky. The ice dragon approached, landing and taking a place near the egg as well. Power radiated from him as well.

"What are you doing?" Jason asked the two dragons.

"The egg needs to feed," the ice dragon said.

"You will allow it?"

"It must be done," the ice dragon said.

Jason couldn't tell whether the egg would draw too much power from them, though he had a sense that both the ice dragon and the iron dragon were willing to allow it. Both dragons pulled upon energy, buried deep, and it flowed from them and into the egg. That power flowed through Jason, filling him, and he knew what he needed to do. Both of the dragons pushed upon him.

He had no choice but to start forward and hold his hands above the egg. Power flooded through him, coming through the iron dragon and the ice dragon, even distantly through the forest dragon, spreading into the egg.

"Jason?"

He looked over to see Sarah watching him, her eyes wide.

"What are you doing?"

Jason shook his head. "I don't know. The dragons compelled me to do this. I don't know if it's something I'm supposed to do or not, but I feel the egg trying to draw this power off me."

"You need to be careful. I can see you glowing with power."

"I can't help it. It feels as if…"

Jason didn't have a chance to finish. The energy built within him and the egg seemed to stir, the power within it building and swirling, drawing through him. Jason wanted to try to separate, but even as he attempted to cut back on that power and withdraw, pressure built again, squeezing on him to force more through him. There was no point in resisting. It radiated out of him, rising with intensity. He couldn't back away even if he were to want to.

The egg was drawing on him.

This time, he could feel it drawing on him as well as the other dragons.

Somewhere distantly, he felt a rumbling.

For a moment, he thought it came from the earth dragons, but there came a crackling of energy all around. He glanced up, and although the sky was still a bright shining moon, a burst of lightning came down and added to the egg. The storm dragon had come.

"What's happening?" Sarah asked. There was panic in

her voice. Jason understood. He had no idea what was happening to him, only that he couldn't move. Energy flowed through him, coming from all of the dragons as it built around him. It came from everywhere.

The egg started to take on a faint glowing, and it seemed as if the darkness swirled around, night swallowing the egg. Or perhaps the egg was swallowing the night. It pulled all of it in.

It started to tremble, the energy within the egg building to an intensity that Jason could scarcely stand. The other dragons remained near him, power pressing from them, mingling, the four misfits all binding together through Jason.

Still, Jason was aware of something more.

More power.

There was another misfit out there. Several others, actually. If he could call upon the earth dragons, maybe he could use their power, though he didn't know if he could summon them and use the rumbling power that he knew existed.

He had to try. He focused on what he remembered from within the illusion, the power that he had felt from the earth dragon. Stored energy started to summon through him, drifting in a way that called upon even more power. Jason fought the urge to cry out. It came with a vibrant intensity, building within him. He couldn't do anything other than let it build. It swirled through him.

He braced himself.

Strangely, the rumbling in the earth continued to build

as if he had formed a connection between the earth dragon and this egg. Everything crackled around him. It seemed as if energy writhed within the air.

Heat built in his hand. He looked down to see that he was still holding onto dragon pearls.

"Jason!"

He glanced over at Sarah only to see her trying to get close to him, but the dragons had blocked her out, holding her back. William was back there somewhere as well, though Jason couldn't see him.

He turned his attention to the egg, focusing on the power within it. The more he focused on the egg, the more he thought he could feel something rising within it, mixing with the energy that built within him. He had to push it out from him, feeding the egg. Power flowed in a torrent into the egg.

Then it stopped.

Everything felt suspended.

The crackling energy of the storm dragon. The illusion of the forest dragon shimmering around him. The heat of the iron dragon, a furnace of fire that blasted him. The cold ice dragon energy. Even the deep-seated rumbling coming from the earth dragon. All of that filled him, swirling around.

Jason could finally pull his hand off the egg. He backed away, watching it. There wasn't anything different about it, only that shadows swirled around it. Energy still radiated from it.

He stopped near the iron dragon. Heat radiated from

him but started to retreat, receding back to a soft glowing. Finally, the iron dragon slipped away into the trees. The ice dragon launched himself into the air, shooting higher and higher, calling cold to him. Jason could feel the energy of the ice dragon as it replenished, summoning it from the sky, his power restored again. He glanced over to see the forest dragon now asleep, the illusion still around her, though not as potent as it had been. Only the storm dragon remained distant. Jason recognized his power, but nothing else about him. He was out there, even if Jason couldn't see it or see how the dragon held onto his power.

He watched the egg as he backed up. Power glowed from it.

"What happened?" Sarah whispered as she grabbed for his arm.

Jason couldn't tear his gaze away from the egg. "I don't really know. I can't tell what happened. It was feeding, but..."

"You were glowing," William said.

"I was channeling power from each of the dragons," he said.

"From all of them?" William asked. "How?"

He watched Jason with a strange look in his eyes.

Jason stared. "I don't really know. All I can tell is that I felt the energy coming from each of the dragons. Even from the earth dragon, though I don't even know how that was possible."

"What about the river dragon you saw?"

"I never had a chance to connect to that dragon. I don't know if I would have been able to do so."

He slowed his breathing, calming himself. The energy of each of the dragons lingered within his mind, little more than a memory. He could feel it and could feel that power. Jason wondered if he might be able to reach for the river dragon, but he would need to know more about her to do so.

There came a shimmering, a shifting of the illusion.

The forest dragon was changing it.

As he looked over at her, he realized that wasn't the case at all. She slept, barely moving. Which meant that the shifting of the illusion came from somewhere else. It had to be an external force, pressure building on the illusion she formed.

Gradually, he recognized rumbling from beneath them. Earth dragons.

Which meant Lorren had learned of this egg.

And now he was coming.

19

Jason raced over to the forest dragon, touching her on the side, feeling her velvety scales. There came a surge of a connection between them, though she didn't stir. "You need to wake up. The egg is in danger."

She moved slightly, mostly her tail swirling around her, but there was nothing other than a lethargy to her. She had used considerable force to feed the dragon, on top of what she had used to help him with the iron dragon. Now she faded.

All of the other misfits had used considerable power.

Which meant they had to find another way to protect the egg—and the forest dragon. Jason wasn't entirely sure what it was going to take, only that he refused to allow Lorren to get to the egg and the forest dragon.

The iron dragon slithered away as he disappeared into the forest. The ice dragon was high overhead, feeding on the cold and ice to recharge himself. Jason didn't know where the storm dragon had gone, though considering he had little connection to the storm dragon, he wasn't sure if he could even ask him for help.

He had to find some other way.

A rumbling continued around him, building with more and more power. The illusion crackled, and with more time, the illusion would fade, and then Jason had no idea what Lorren might do.

If he learned about the egg, Lorren would try to claim it. He would use it, the same way he had used the other misfits that he had with him. *That* was why he'd come. Jason could not allow it. He had to protect the egg before Lorren claimed it—or destroyed it.

Turning to Sarah and William, he motioned to the egg. "You need to help me. We have to protect the egg. I can feel Lorren coming, which means we need to get moving so that he cannot get it."

William looked around, his gaze darting throughout the clearing. "Lorren is coming? You can feel him?"

Jason approached the egg, crouching down next to it. "I can feel the illusion starting to bend. The earth dragon is here, as well."

They were distant, but getting closer. He could feel their presence and worried that if he waited too much longer, he wouldn't have an opportunity to escape.

How heavy would the egg be? He lifted it, testing to see how heavy it might be, and was surprised by how light it was.

Sarah joined him. "How are you lifting that?"

Jason wrapped his arms around the egg, clutching it to his chest. It was massive, nearly as tall as him, but he could keep his arms wrapped around it. The surface of it was warm, and dimples within it pressed up against his face. "I don't know. It feels light."

"When they get to that size, we are no longer able to carry them. How are you able to do so?"

Several questions entered his mind. It surprised him that the eggs would grow in size. That was different than other animals that laid eggs. Why would dragon eggs be so different?

The air crackled with energy again.

"We need to go." The energy shimmering around him persisted, growing with a vibrant intensity. It seemed to build even more, and if they did nothing, Lorren would get here before they had an opportunity to escape. The illusion around them faded, the air crackling as it did.

"I can call the other dragons," Sarah suggested.

Jason looked around. They stood in a clearing, and he hoped it was a real clearing and not simply part of the illusion.

Sarah clutched her dragon pearls and power built within her before radiating outward. Gradually, there came the distant sense of dragons. Jason was aware of them and could feel their energy coming, sweeping toward them. It felt as if he were connected to them, and he realized that the dragon pearls he held in his hand represented those dragons.

The forest dragon started to stir, and when she opened her deep green eyes, she looked at Jason, meeting his. He reached toward her, holding a hand up, trying to reassure her.

"I'm going to protect the egg," he said.

She breathed out, and the mist drifting from her nostrils billowed into the clearing. For a moment, the illusion solidified once again. It didn't hold quite as profoundly as it had before, though Jason hoped that it would hold back Lorren for another moment.

"You won't need to protect it for much longer. You did what you needed to do, Jason Dreshen."

She stared again, and the illusion formed around her, her entire body shimmering. When it faded, she disappeared, blending into the forest. He lost sight of her.

That might be for the best. He wouldn't have to protect her, not while also protecting the egg.

A shadowed form loomed overhead, and for a moment Jason worried it was Lorren, but then a second one appeared, and they spiraled down, joining them in the clearing. The illusion of shadows and moonlight, started to fade, but not so much that he could see past it. Moonlight still streamed down, though it was fading, dawn beginning to come. The opening in the canopy was real, and the clearing was exactly what he had seen. That much had been real.

The rumbling from the earth dragons continued to approach. He didn't know how much longer he had before the dragons got here, but he would be ready. He focused on the iron and the ice dragon and whispered a caution to them. "Be ready."

There came a faint murmuring in response, but nothing more. He didn't know if the dragons could even respond or if they were too tired. If fatigue claimed them, Jason understood. They had fought, and then they had fed the egg. It was all too much.

The dragons landed in a flutter of wind. William scrambled up onto the back of a dark green one, and Sarah hurried onto a black one. Jason tried to hand the egg to Sarah, but she shook her head.

"I won't be able to hold that," she said.

"You haven't even tried," he said.

She shook her head again. "I think you have to do this, Jason."

He could feel energy through the egg, some stirring of the dragon within it, but nothing more. The forest dragon claimed he wouldn't have to protect the egg for much longer, but he wondered what more he might need to do for it. He could feel the power within it, the energy radiating outward. He hoped it wouldn't hatch before they could escape. It would be even more difficult to hold onto a newborn dragon.

He squeezed the egg as he tried to maintain his grip, climbing up the black dragon's back and settling onto him. He looked over at Sarah. "I'm ready," he said.

The dragon took to the air with a lurch that forced

Jason to squeeze the egg tightly, clutching it up against him. As the dragon gained altitude, Jason leaned forward, holding the egg up tightly. Every so often, he detected a rumbling in the distance, the earth dragon coming toward them. He looked down at the forest and made out a faint shimmering along the edge of it. It looked as if the illusion formed around the forest was faint, little more than a blur, as if to try to mask the presence of the forest. Had the forest dragon attempted to conceal the entirety of the forest? As he watched, that shimmering began to flicker and then faded completely. He felt a surge of power as it disappeared altogether.

Jason strained, looking for any sign of Lorren, but found nothing. He should be thankful, but it worried him. The forest dragon was down there.

"She will be fine," Sarah said, turning back to him.

"I don't know if she will. Lorren can break through her illusion."

"She's the most powerful of the dragons with illusion."

Jason knew she was and that she could call upon even more energy and control than even the mist dragons, but that didn't change his concern. She had spent considerable strength to feed the egg, expending herself, and risking danger. Perhaps he needed to stay behind in the forest to protect her.

A stirring in his mind fluttered through him, a reminder of the forest dragon. It was faint, though when it came to her, he rarely felt much strength when it came to their connection. Within that stirring, he recognized her urging him away.

He turned, clutching the dragon egg as they flew. Wind whipped around, the power of the dragon surging beneath him, and nothing more. There was no pressure, nothing to suggest he needed to be afraid of anyone chasing them.

He squeezed the egg and could feel it shifting. It was almost as if the egg itself trembled, but it seemed filled with power as well. The eggshell trembled. Every so often, a gust of wind fluttered at them, and he worried that it might pull the egg out of his grip, but then the egg settled, the wind died down to the roar around the dragon, and Jason held on.

They veered toward Dragon Haven.

While flying, he focused on the ice dragon and the iron dragon and recognized how tired they still were. They flew alongside, but he wondered if they could survive much longer if it came down to another attack. He doubted that they would. The sense of those two dragons was distant, and he knew he needed to try to get closer, but the dragons passed through the illusion surrounding Dragon Haven and made their way toward the clearing.

Jason sent a connection to the other dragon misfits to invite them into Dragon Haven, not only for their safety but also to protect the egg. Within the clearing, there were several other young dragons. A navy dragon, along with a pale yellow, the color of early morning sunlight, slammed into each other on the far side of the clearing while a deep maroon dragon curled up far enough away so as not to be trampled. A narrow wall surrounded the clearing, dividing this section off from the rest of Dragon Haven. The ground was trampled grass, from boots and dragons and the occasional wagon.

Jason climbed off the dragon's back. One of the Dragon Guard was nearby, dressed in black dragonskin leathers, a slender, pale white dragon bone blade sheathed at his side. Jason didn't know him, but as he watched, the Dragon Guard glared at him for a long moment.

Jason held onto the egg, and Sarah nodded to him. "You can bring it over here. When we have eggs, we keep them by the other dragons to ensure that they are protected."

He looked down at the egg. "Did they feed the eggs while they were protecting them?"

Sarah studied the egg for a moment, her brow furrowing. "I don't know. To be honest, I never noticed anything quite like that. The dragons couldn't tell us, either. They just protected them."

Jason thought about what he knew of dragon eggs and about what it would take to hatch them, to provide power within them, and to feed them the energy of their environment. That seemed to be the key, didn't it? The ice dragon had fed upon the cold and ice of the northern mountain. The iron dragon had fed upon the heat of the mines. The forest dragon had fed upon the energy within the forest itself. Each of the misfits had done the same.

What could he offer this egg?

Maybe it was not about him offering this egg anything. The egg might have already fed on what it needed. Still, he considered what the forest dragon had done, the way that she had protected the egg by placing it within the clearing in the forest. That might have been what he needed to do.

"I think I need to bring it into the forest near the city," he said, turning to the trees. When Sarah frowned at him, he nodded to the egg. "Think about where we found it. It was protected by the illusion, but it was also within the shadows of the forest."

William, who had climbed off his dragon, joined him. "Why do you think that was?" He held out his hand, reaching for the egg, but didn't touch it. It seemed as if the trembling within the egg started to shake a little bit more as William did that, though maybe that was only Jason's imagination.

"It might be because the forest dragon tried to protect the egg, or it might be something more." As far as he knew, it was only to nurture the egg, to feed it upon the forest itself. Maybe when this egg hatched, there would be another forest dragon.

He remembered the way the forest had felt to him, the energy within it that had come off the forest dragon. He might be able to create something similar, but even if he could, he didn't know if that would be drawing upon his energy or on the energy of the forest dragon. Given how tired the forest dragon was, Jason didn't know if such a thing would even be safe to do, or if it would drain too much from her. It might be necessary to wait longer and give her a chance to replenish her energy before he summoned the illusion. Only, if he did that, he worried that he would deplete the dragon egg of what it needed.

Turning to Sarah, an idea came to him. "Do you have other dragon pearls I might use?"

"Of course. Why?"

Jason turned his attention back to the egg. "I think I need to see if there's a way to borrow energy in them to create an illusion. We need to protect this from Lorren. By taking it to Dragon Haven, we can use the Dragon Guard to help us defend it."

"Your illusion is connected to the forest dragon," Sarah said.

"It is, but I still think I can use the energy of the other dragons to help create it." Maybe not just create it, but solidify it. Though he was connected to the forest dragon, along with the ice and iron dragon, he could still use power from the other dragon pearls. He thought it would allow him to use that power to solidify the illusion rather than drawing upon the forest dragon. If so, then he could do what was needed without straining her. At least until her strength returned. Then he would use what she might be able to offer.

They headed into the forest, and the others followed. He found the egg seemed to grow increasingly heavy the longer that he carried it, though it might be simply the bulk that made it difficult. He paused in a clearing not far from where they had landed. As he looked around, glancing at the sky and seeing the rising sunlight coming up that still left the forest floor cast in shadows, he set the egg down.

"Why here?" Sarah asked.

Jason shook his head. "I don't know. This just feels right."

William wrapped his arms around himself, as if hugging himself. "It feels dark."

Jason frowned. That wasn't his sense of it at all. Of course, maybe it wouldn't be. His connection to the dragon was different. His connection to everything around him was different. Maybe even his connection to the egg was different. He could feel power around him, the connection that was here, and it felt right.

He stepped away from the egg, holding on to the dragon pearls Sarah had given him, and began to pull upon power. As he did, it flowed up through him, filling him. It came slowly at first, but as he pulled upon more and more energy, he found the illusion growing and building. He re-created what he had seen within the forest with the forest dragon, summoning as much of that familiarity as he could. It wouldn't be perfect. He didn't know everything that the forest dragon had done, but he had a feeling about what she had created. He even added moonlight overhead, swirling shadows around the center of the forest.

Something trembled within the egg, and Jason realized it wasn't quite right. The egg needed something more. It wasn't just the illusion the egg needed. He needed it to be solidified so that this was more like reality that had shifted and now existed here.

That was a different use of power, a more complicated one. Jason could do it, but could he do it without the forest dragon? Normally when he used that kind of power, it was borrowed energy from the forest dragon herself. Now he refused to borrow from her, which meant he was going to have to use the power of these dragon pearls along with what existed within him.

He focused, thinking about the illusion, and then thinking about how he needed to shift it as well.

Gradually, it solidified. Within that shifting, he felt the egg starting to ease. Still, there was something not quite right.

He set the dragon pearls around the clearing, creating a triangle around the dragon.

"What are you doing?" Sarah asked.

Jason looked up. He had been arranging one of the dragon pearls near a tree. "It feels like I need to leave these here," he said. "The illusion is feeding off them."

"Feeding?" Sarah arched a brow.

Jason shook his head. "Not quite the same as what happened with the dragons, but similar." It was similar enough that he thought he needed to be careful. It could be possible that the dragons would have enough energy drawn through these pearls to overwhelm them, weakening them. "We can ask the dragons."

"The dragons have control over the pearls," Sarah said.

"If they're getting too weakened, they could just separate their strength from it."

Jason wasn't sure if that would even work. He had felt the way the egg had pulled on power from him, through the other dragons, and wondered if the egg might be able to overwhelm the dragons associated with the pearls.

Stranger still was that the comment revealed to him just how little he knew about the dragon pearls. His connection to the dragons was so different than the way that Sarah reached for power, different enough that he didn't really understand it or how that magic was used.

As he got to his feet, looking at the egg, he couldn't shake the feeling that there remained some trembling within it, as if the egg reacted to him.

He settled on the ground across from it, studying it, and felt power within it. Sarah took a seat next to him, and William joined them too. They sat for a long moment, all of them looking at the egg. Energy radiated from it to Jason. Moonlight shone down from the illusion overhead, and shadows swirled around the clearing, as if to attempt to wrap the egg itself in them.

After a while, Sarah took his hand. "What are you going to do?"

"Maybe sit here for a little while and ensure that the egg is settled."

The longer he sat there, the more that he began to worry about the egg. There had been an incredible amount of energy poured into it, given to the egg and the dragon inside from each of the misfits. What would that mean?

He let out a heavy sigh as he twisted in place and looked at the others with him. He could feel the ice and the iron dragon, both of them near enough that their power flowed from them and radiated to him. Their strength gradually returned, though it was coming to them slowly. Even the forest dragon was there in the back of his mind, safe.

Jason wondered about the storm dragon. He had been summoned by the forest dragon to feed the egg, which told him something. It suggested the storm dragon was responsive to these other misfits and recognized the connection to them. He should have known that.

Would they even be able to keep the egg safe?

Lorren would come for them. If he had learned about the egg—and given that he had gone to the forest, Jason suspected that he had—he would try to reach this egg. He probably had felt the power coming off the other misfits as they had fed the dragon.

Jason wanted and needed to keep the egg safe. This was his misfit. This was his responsibility.

Only it wasn't just Lorren they had to worry about. He worried about the Dragon Souls. He worried about Jessica and what she might do. He worried about Lorach and whether they would pose a real danger to Dragon Haven.

The illusion protected them, but how long would it last? Lorren had shown him that there were limits to how well any illusion would hold, and limits to what Jason could do with it.

Eventually, he would need to take more action.

As he stared at the egg, he wondered if that action was on behalf of the people of Dragon Haven or on behalf of the dragons. Maybe it didn't even matter. All that mattered was that he would do whatever necessary to protect both. He had to. It seemed to him that was the reason he had come to Dragon Haven.

20

Jason was tired. He had spent the better part of the last day making preparations, his own unique protection for the dragon egg, and one he didn't even know if it would be fully effective. He had traveled far beyond the borders of dragon haven, placing illusions, shifting reality as much as he could, all to convince Lorren to chase another egg. He needed to buy time until he could find Lorren, figure out how to stop him, and then Jason could make sure that the misfit egg was safe.

Only then.

Until that time, he would keep placing illusions. Let Lorren chase those illusions. Jason could do it as long as the forest dragon provided him the strength. The mist dragons might give Lorren the ability to look past those illusions, but there were limitations to it, as well. Jason intended to overpower them, and intended to continue placing illusions until he was satisfied that Lorren would not find the egg.

He'd already begun to feel one of the illusions crack, Lorren uncovering it as he searched for the egg. It brought a dark satisfaction to Jason.

Now it was time for him to head back to Dragon Haven.

Jason ran into Kayla as he made his way through Dragon Haven. The city streets were mostly empty, though there were a few people out, strolling leisurely along. Most people within Dragon Haven had no idea that Lorach posed much of a threat. To them here in the city, he supposed that was true. Fewer people would even know anything about Lorren, and would not know they needed to fear anything. Perhaps that was for the best.

He passed a massive dragon sculpture, finally catching up to his sister. She glanced over at him, smiling.

"Mother says you spoke to her," Kayla said.

Jason slowed for a moment. His sister had always been helpful with their mother while she was sick. Now that she was no longer sick, what would Kayla do? Her entire life had been wrapped up in that, and without it, Jason worried that she would not have a sense of purpose.

"I spoke to her. Did you?"

Kayla shrugged. "She doesn't want to talk to me about it. She says that whatever she said to you was between the two of you."

"I suppose that's true," Jason said.

"She says that whatever she did was to protect us."

Jason breathed out. "They had tried to protect us, but it feels like the way they did it was impossibly difficult." Why force them to the mountains? Why that life? And when his father had died, why stay?

He had to forgive.

Not that there was all that much to forgive, other than her silence over the years about what he could and should be—and what he needed to know about himself.

"You can let Mother know that I would appreciate having further conversations."

Kayla arched a brow at him. "You don't think you can tell her yourself?"

"I have a feeling that she would hear it best from you."

They headed a little farther along the hall before she spoke again. "I hear you have been out dragon hunting again."

Jason looked along the street. Even now, he could still feel the hint of power from the dragon egg, though it was faint. "Not hunting dragons. I've been trying to find more misfits."

Kayla leaned toward him. "I hear there's somebody else who does the same thing." Her voice was soft, and she flicked her gaze in either direction, as if someone else along the street might suddenly hear her and say something.

"Lorren," Jason said. "That's his name. He is powerful, and it seems he knows how to create misfits."

Her face wrinkled as she frowned. "Why would he want to do something like that?"

They reached the entrance to the building where his family made his home, and stepped into the halls. "Several reasons, though I suspect he did it to attack the Dragon Souls."

Her expression hardened. "If he's willing to attack Dragon Souls, then we should work with him."

"He's also willing to... attack dragons," Jason said.

Not just attacking. Killing. Murdering.

That was what Lorren had been willing to do.

All for power.

For the misfits.

"What?"

He continued through the halls, moving past a series of dragon artifacts. Some were sculptures, some were paintings, and one was even a carpet with the form of a dragon worked into the weave.

"He doesn't seem to care. He thinks he's freeing them."

"I'm sure that angers you," Kayla said.

Jason glanced over at his sister. "You have no idea."

She sniffed. "I have some idea."

They stopped in front of a door, and Jason pressed his hand up against it. He could feel energy radiating through it as he borrowed from the iron dragon. It was more potent than what he had felt from the dragon before, as if ever since the iron dragon had nearly died, he'd become greater. It was a strange thing to be aware of, though he was certain of it. As he surged power through the door, he could count the number of people inside. He wondered if he might be able to determine even more if he pushed even more power. It seemed strange that he would be so attuned to it.

"What are you doing?" Kayla asked.

"Trying to see how many people are on the other side of the door."

Her breath caught. "You can do that?"

"I didn't know if I could, but it's strange. I can feel them on the other side. It's…" He shook his head. "I wish I could help you understand."

Kayla nodded to him. "That's actually something that I wanted to talk to you about."

Jason withdrew his hand and turned to his sister. She was biting her lip, and a nervous energy caused her to shift her weight from one foot to the other. "What is it?"

She took a deep breath and met his eyes. "Ever since we've been here around the dragons, and with everything that happened to you, I can't help but wonder if I might have the same ability."

"Which ability is that?"

"I want to know if I can connect to the dragons," she said hurriedly. "I don't even know if I can, but the more I see you doing with them, and the more I have learned about dragons, the more I realize they aren't what I grew up thinking they are."

"You know why that was," Jason said.

A cloud crossed over her face. "I know why we think that it was, but…" She shook her head. "It doesn't matter. All that matters is that I wondered if you might help me find a connection to the dragons the same way that you formed one."

It was a reasonable question, and given what he had gone through—and what he knew of his family now—he suspected he should have asked that question before now. There were many things he should have done before now.

He reached into his pocket, pulling out one of the dragon pearls that Sarah had given him. This one had a faint greenish shimmering to it. "Have you seen one of these before?"

"Is that a dragon pearl?"

Jason nodded. "It is. It is from a Dragon Haven dragon, a smaller green one, and I suspect friendly enough for you to work with." He squeezed the pearl for a moment, sending a pulse of energy through it as he connected to the dragon. He could feel energy radiating through the pearl and then back to him. Through that connection, Jason sent a desire to the dragon, wanting the dragon to work with his sister. He couldn't tell whether or not the dragon would respond, but it seemed as if he got an answer in return. "If you find the dragon, you can see if you might be able to learn anything from him. The first step is testing whether there is any sort of connection. You will feel it deep within you." He remembered when he had first learned about his connection to the dragon pearl and the way that it had triggered power within him. He wouldn't have been that much older than Kayla was now. "If you feel that, you will be able to start on the path to understanding dragons."

"And if I can't?"

"It doesn't mean that you won't have the ability," Jason said. "It just means that might not be the dragon for you."

He debated whether or not to tell his sister that she was descended from Dragon Souls. Knowing that she was, just like Jason, it was entirely possible that she could learn to work with dragons. Here he had worried that she wouldn't have a purpose, but perhaps that was misguided on his part. Kayla absolutely had a purpose. She needed to understand whether or not she had a connection to the dragons the same way Jason did. He suspected that she would.

She took the pearl from him, staring at it. "Thank you," she whispered. After a moment, she looked up. "What about the dragons you call the misfits? Can I try to connect to one of them?"

Jason started to smile but realized she was asking a serious question. "Why would you want to do that?"

"I don't know. There's something about them. They seem so much more… More, I guess. Interesting."

Jason chuckled. "Don't let the other dragons know that you said that about the misfits."

"What did I say?"

"That they aren't interesting," he said.

She turned her attention back to the dragon pearl, cupping it in her hand. "I didn't mean it like that," she said quickly.

He smiled. "I know you didn't."

"Do you think one of your dragons would let me try to work with them?"

Jason shrugged. "I could ask them."

"You would do that for me?"

"You're my sister. Of course I would."

She smiled, holding on to the dragon pearl, and tipped it up to the lantern set into one of the nearby walls. "I'll see if I can't find this dragon and talk with him. If you would talk to the other dragons…"

Jason smiled again, nodding. "I will do so. I can't make any promises, but if you can, it would benefit us here."

As soon as he said it, he hated that was the way that his mind started to work these days. Was everything about a benefit? Unfortunately, it might be. How could it not be when they needed any edge they had to defeat Lorach, along with Lorren?

Kayla held tightly onto the dragon pearl and hurried away down the hall. It was strange to think of her actually trying to reach the dragons, let alone one of the misfits, but she had changed considerably in her time within Dragon Haven. She might even be successful with it. Knowing what he did of the dragons, and knowing of his own connection, maybe she was meant to share the same connection he had.

Jason turned his attention back to the door, resting his hand on it, and felt for the energy inside. If he was right, there were several Dragon Guards inside. A few others, as well. He held his hand in place, focusing on what he could feel.

Finally, he pushed the door open and stepped into the room, unsurprised by what he found. There were five Dragon Guards here. Henry as well, though he stood along the side and watched.

Jason joined Henry. "What is it?"

Henry tipped his head as he nodded to the Dragon Guard. "They found something."

"Lorren?"

Henry glanced over, shaking his head. "Not Lorren, though I understand you came across him."

Jason chuckled. "Did Sarah or William tell you?"

Henry shrugged. "Sarah. Are you surprised?"

Jason shook his head. Sarah rarely kept anything from Henry, not that Jason wanted to conceal anything from him anyway. She had known him a long time, and he had trained her. It made her closer to Henry than to almost anyone else within Dragon Haven.

"Is it true?" Henry asked.

"Is what true?"

"That you nearly lost one of your dragons."

"I nearly lost him." Jason let out a slow breath.

Sarah had told him that, but thankfully she hadn't told him the rest. He hadn't been sure whether Sarah would reveal the presence of the dragon egg. There was an illusion around it, and he hoped that keeping that illusion in place would protect the egg, though he didn't know if it would. He wanted to protect the egg, which meant keeping it from those within Dragon Haven as well. Still, with the power he felt coming off the egg, he suspected others also recognized it and might be able to detect something more within it. If so, there was only so much that Jason could do to keep it safe.

As he stood talking to Henry, he felt another illusion shattered.

He placed almost two dozen of them, all throughout the surrounding land, and all using the speed of the ice dragon to do so. Somehow, Jason would have to use those illusions to force Lorren to go where he wanted so he could stop him. Jason had no idea what that was going to take, though.

How long would he need to protect it, though? If it was anything like a traditional dragon egg, it might take months, though considering how it had fed and the power Jason detected in it, he didn't think there was anything traditional about it. Which meant that the egg might hatch far sooner. Especially given what the forest dragon had said to him.

"He used the earth dragons to trap the iron dragon beneath the ground. They softened the ground and surrounded him."

"I heard he did the same with Dragon Souls."

Jason nodded. "Five dragons. I don't know if the Dragon Souls were captured as well, but the dragons were lost."

"Bastard," Henry whispered.

Jason glanced at him, but he didn't get a chance to ask anything more because one of the Dragon Guard turned to him. Jason recognized Max. He was broad-shouldered and had a thick gray beard, and was dressed in a combination of dragonskin and heavy furs, as if he'd come from the northern mountains. It was as if he had taken aspects of the Dragon Souls and mixed it with aspects of how Jason had lived.

"I have been waiting for Olar and Cherise to arrive, but seeing as how they have not, perhaps it is time for us to proceed."

"Where are they?" Henry asked. "I was supposed to meet with them yesterday."

Max frowned. "I don't know. I thought that you would have known."

That was strange. In the time Jason had been within Dragon Haven, Olar and Cherise had never left. They ruled within Dragon Haven and served as something of the leaders of the rebellion, even though the Dragon Guard truly served that role. Why would they have gone? And where?

He glanced over at Henry and saw no expression on his face.

Maybe it was nothing.

"What did you find?" Jason asked Max.

He flicked his gaze to Henry before turning back to Jason. "We followed Lorren as well as we could until we found a sense of his dragons and trailed after them."

Jason frowned. "How far did you trail after them?"

"To the edge of the forest."

"Which forest?" Henry asked, not looking in Jason's direction.

Could the Dragon Guard have known about the forest dragon and her forest? Jason didn't think so, and given her ability to cast an illusion around it, he thought she was protected, though there remained the possibility that they could have learned something about it anyway.

"To the edge of this forest," he said.

Jason breathed out slowly. "I found him near Varmin."

Max frowned at him. "Why so far?"

"I think he was trying to draw me. Or Dragon Souls. I don't even know any longer." It could even be that he'd been looking for evidence of the egg.

Max's gaze darted to Jason's hand. "That's where you found that dragon?"

Jason nodded. "Buried beneath the ground in the mines. He was in a cell that they used to trap him and keep him from escaping."

Max glanced behind him at the other Dragon Guard before turning his attention back to Jason. "Interesting."

"Why?"

Max shook his head. "Because he's been moving along our border, at least as much as we can call it our border. There's a periodicity to it."

"He's searching," Jason said.

"Either that or it means he's doing something with the Dragon Souls," Henry answered. He watched the Dragon Guard, and Max nodded.

"That is our thought as well. We don't know exactly what it is, only that it seems he is tracking Dragon Souls. Presumably, to attack them."

Jason had seen it. He knew what would happen were Lorren to attack more of the Dragon Souls. It wasn't so much about them as it was their dragons.

Max nodded. "This is a good thing," he said. "We've been concerned about the buildup of the Dragon Soul presence along our borders, trying to decide what to do as we struggle with how to confront Jessica, but we might not need to do anything, anyway. If Lorren is taking care of it, then we don't have to worry."

"He's killing their dragons," Jason said.

Henry looked over, shaking his head slightly.

Jason frowned. "We can't let him continue to harm the dragons. Even if they are Dragon Soul dragons, we can't allow Lorren to destroy them. They don't deserve that."

"I know you think you can save them, but can you save all of them?" Max asked. "As far as I can be concerned, those dragons are lost."

Jason stiffened. He could feel power flowing from the iron dragon. "They're lost until I free them," he said.

"And how many have you freed?" Max asked, turning to him, crossing his arms over his chest.

"A hundred. Maybe more," Henry said.

Max glanced over at Henry before turning back to Jason. His stance shifted as he uncrossed his arms and reached for the sword sheathed at his side. "A hundred, and yet there are still more than that. Nearly four times as many. Do you really think you can free all of those dragons?"

Jason knew more than four hundred dragons

remained. There were probably a thousand in all of Lorach, and to defeat the Dragon Souls, he would have to free their dragons first. "I don't really know, but we owe it to the dragons to try. If we allow Lorren to destroy them, then what have we become?" He swept his gaze around the room, looking at the others. "The entire purpose of Dragon Haven is to rescue dragons and allow them to live openly. If we destroy them, then we become them."

"We have an opportunity to finally defeat Lorach. We aren't going to abandon that out of fear of what could have been. We called you here to see if you would help, but I can see that it will not be the case."

Jason looked at them both, frustration filling him. This wasn't about Lorach. Not entirely. He needed to stop Lorren. He was the real threat now. Only after they dealt with Lorren could they stop Lorach. Couldn't they see that?

It was a strange thing for him to think, especially as when he had first met Lorren, Jason had wanted nothing more than to work with him so that they could defeat Lorach.

Now he could think of nothing more than stopping Lorren for him to save additional dragons.

"Have you even talked to the dragons about this?"

"The dragons don't have any input on this," Max said.

That surprised Jason more than anything, especially given his experience in Dragon Haven. The dragons were practically worshipped here. Why would they change that now?

"They will if you ask them. They should. Take the time."

"It is decided."

"By who? Cherise? Olar?" Jason hadn't seen them in a while and wondered where they'd gone. It wasn't like them to be gone this long.

Without them, the Dragon Guard had a plan. They were going to use Lorren for his violence, and despite what Jason might say and object to, there wasn't anything more that he would be able to do to convince the Dragon Guard otherwise.

Lorren would continue to attack the Dragon Souls.

He would take the fight to Lorach.

There was a part of Jason that still questioned whether or not Max was even right. Given everything Jason had experienced with Lorach and everything they had done, he couldn't help but question whether Max and the Dragon Guard were pursuing the best path.

Knowing what he had felt when the dragons had died hurt Jason. He had felt their pain and agony. More than that, connected as he was to the iron dragon now, he recognized how the misfits wanted to protect the other dragons.

"No," Jason said.

Max glared at him. "You don't have any input in this."

"Don't I? I'm the one who's freed dragons. I'm the one who's actually been into Lorach. I'm the one who has—"

"Revealed the presence of Dragon Haven. To an Auran, I might add."

"And then bound him to me." The words hung in the air a moment. "Do what you need to do, but I'm going after the Dragon Soul dragons to rescue as many as I can and to stop Lorren." As much as he hated it, Lorren *had* to be stopped. He posed too great a danger to the dragons they worked with.

Max sneered at him. "You won't be able to do anything to rescue them. If they're moving in the forest where we have seen them—"

Jason took a step toward him. "What forest have you seen them moving through?"

Max frowned. "You haven't heard?"

Jason shook his head. "I haven't heard anything about Lorach forces moving. Or seen them."

"As I said, they were moving along our border. They are coming this way, sweeping steadily toward us. If we do nothing, Lorach will eventually reach Dragon Haven."

Jason glanced over at Henry, who rubbed his hand across his scraggly beard. "I didn't have the opportunity to tell you that hundreds are moving this way."

How had he not seen the Dragon Souls in his travels? They had been there, which meant that he should have seen them.

Hundreds meant that it was a significant portion of the Dragon Soul dragons. Enough that it would be too hard to rescue them all. He'd faced hundreds of dragons when he had been in Lorach, though that was when he had been distracted, trying to protect the storm dragon. If he didn't have his focus diverted, maybe he could save more.

Knowing what he did about Lorach, he suspected they were approaching methodically. He could imagine the way they were sweeping through the forest, making their way toward them.

Maybe he *didn't* have time to stop Lorren. They might have to deal with Lorach first.

Which was what Lorren wanted.

"Looking for Dragon Haven," he murmured. Or the egg. He couldn't tell the others that. Maybe Henry, but certainly not Max.

Maybe Jason *was* responsible for bringing Dragon Haven into danger.

Max nodded. "That is our thought as well," he said. "The Dragon Guard has run interference, slowing them, but as you can see, having Lorren and his dragons attack would be beneficial to us."

Jason squeezed his eyes shut, his mind racing. He focused on the ice dragon, wondering if he might be able to see anything. He circled, flying high overhead, and he borrowed his eyesight. When he did, there came a surge of color.

Jason looked for movement, focusing on energy, on anything the ice dragon could see. There were shades of energy in the distance. Dragons. Dozens of them. Dozens upon dozens of them.

Thankfully, none of them were close. Not yet. Still, as he looked through the ice dragon's eyes, he could see them and the way they swept toward them, moving ever closer. There was energy within them, and before long, they would reach Dragon Haven. When they did, the illusion would no longer be effective.

The egg would be in danger.

He had to stop them. Stop Lorren.

Protect the egg and the misfits.

"They're coming," he whispered.

"You can see them?" Max asked.

Jason opened his eyes and looked at Max. "I can connect to the dragons I bond to and use their eyesight to see."

Max pressed his lips together in a tight frown, glancing at Henry, who nodded. "How long have you been able to do this?"

"For a while," Jason said.

"If you can do this, then you'd be beneficial to us as we try to protect Dragon Haven. You could alert us of their movements."

"I'm not going to help you harm other dragons," Jason said.

Max clenched his jaw. "Even if it means sacrificing others?"

"There won't be any dragons sacrificed. They are things we can do to protect the Dragon Soul dragons. I know it can be done. If you give me an opportunity, we can help those dragons, saving as many as possible."

Jason had no idea how many could be saved, but he had a sense that if it came down to it, he could use his connection to the ice and iron dragons to protect more of them. The key was getting there and rescuing them before

Jessica or other powerful Dragon Souls could intervene. Along with Lorren.

There were ways he could move unseen. The ice dragon could fly high enough that they wouldn't even know. He could streak along like ice lightning, and Jason could borrow that power. The problem was that he might be the only one who could travel with him.

He had a sense from the iron dragon of understanding and a willingness for Jason to work with the dragon.

"Do what you need to do. I'm going to stop Lorren and then save the dragons." Jason turned. When he did, Henry grabbed his wrist.

"What do you think you're doing?" Henry whispered.

"I've got to stop him before he hurts more." Misfits, he didn't add.

"All by yourself?"

Jason glanced at the Dragon Guard. "I won't be by myself. I will have the other misfits with me."

"That's too dangerous."

Jason shook his head. "If I don't do it, then no one will. The dragons will be attacked by the Dragon Guards, or by Lorren."

Henry pulled him closer. "Why? Why help them?"

"This isn't about Lorach, if that's your concern. It's about Lorren now. All I'm trying to do is help the dragons. They've been used in this. I need to stop him first, and the Dragon Guard can deal with Lorach" He frowned at Henry. "Remember what you experienced working with dragons in Lorach? Remember how you felt about them?

Think about how little you would've cared were the dragons to attack. Would you have protected yourself or the dragons when Lorren attacks?"

Henry shook his head. "You know the answer as well as I do."

Jason nodded. "That's why I have to do this. No one else is going to."

"That's not the whole reason."

Jason squeezed his eyes shut. "Lorren is who I might become, Henry. I need to stop him to prove it can be done *my* way, not his."

"You'd never become him, Jason. You care too much." Henry looked Max, then nodded to the other Dragon Guards. "Keep them away from the border. I'm going with him," he said, nodding at Jason.

Max frowned. "You would risk yourself for him?"

"I would risk myself for what he represents. He is doing what we claim we do for the dragons. We claim that Dragon Haven is about the dragons. If we don't offer them any protection, then how can we make that claim?"

Jason nodded to Max before turning and leaving.

Once outside, he glanced at Henry. "There something else you need to know about," he said.

"What?"

"Something else we found when we were gone. The other reason that we have to save those dragons and keep Lorach—along with Lorren—from coming through here."

Henry cocked his head to the side.

Jason just nodded. "I will show you."

21

Jason stood in the middle of the clearing with the egg, power drawn through the dragon pearls creating the moonlight and the swirl of shadows while masking the presence of the trees nearby. Strangely, he could feel the pressure of the trees and recognized the energy within them, though he was not aware of anything more than that.

The dragon pearls still held power, maintaining the illusion. Jason worried about how much longer it would last and whether there would come a time when it began to fade, knowing that he might need to replace the dragon pearls if it did.

Standing here, he could feel the energy of the illusion and attacked the contours of it. He didn't need to add anything to it, but he solidified it, focusing its power.

He nodded to Henry.

"Here?" Henry whispered.

"Don't you see it?" Jason asked, turning to the egg.

Henry stepped forward. He must have parted through an aspect of the illusion, for his breath caught. "What is that?"

Jason approached the egg. It was larger than it had been when he had been here before, and it seemed to pulsate softly. It hadn't done that before. As he approached, he could feel the energy within it. There was something strange about the way it pulsated. Darkness swirled around it, flexing, almost as if it were causing the shell of the egg to move. Was that part of the illusion? Jason probed at the illusion and realized that he wasn't entirely in control of it anymore. He could feel energy from within the egg, and it seemed almost as if it were breathing.

He tore his gaze away. "We came across this in the forest after we were attacked by Lorren. I don't know if Lorren is aware that this is here. I think he might be, though."

"How would he have been aware of it?"

"I don't know. I don't know if he simply has female dragons or if he has some way of detecting eggs."

"All of Dragon Haven is in danger," Henry said.

"Not all of Dragon Haven is in danger. Besides, the city can protect the egg. I couldn't leave it where I had found it before. Lorren isn't coming after this egg. I've made sure of it."

"How exactly have you made sure of it?" Henry asked.

"I've placed other illusions. He has removed three of

them so far." Three of the nearly two dozen. It bought them time, but not nearly enough. "And I can keep placing more. It's how I can protect the egg."

"You have proven yourself to us, Jason. If you believe that this is necessary, then it's necessary."

"You will help protect it?"

"It is a dragon."

"It is. A misfit." Jason could feel something coming off the egg and knew that it was potent. "Possibly a powerful misfit, though I won't know that until the dragon hatches."

"How many people know of this?"

"William and Sarah. That's it."

"The illusion is strong enough to hold it?"

"As far as I can tell. It seemed strong enough, and I used these dragon pearls to solidify it. Now that I am recovered, and the forest dragon has recovered"—Jason could feel her energy distantly and could tell that she was strong enough, though she didn't push out too much of the illusion—"the illusion holds."

"It's hers, isn't it?" he asked softly. Henry crouched down near one of the dragon pearls before reaching into his pocket and pulling out two more, which he handed to Jason.

Jason took a deep breath. "Yes."

"Use the pearls as you need to protect this."

"Sarah claims there is something different than other dragon eggs," he said.

Henry nodded. "There is. At the same time, there's

something almost deadly beautiful about it. I can feel it, and I'm not exactly sure what it is."

Jason had the same sense. He made a circle around it, watching as it pulsated. It was more than just the egg itself. It was pressure that pulsated as well. It swirled around him. Had the egg matured? Given the size increase, he suspected the egg would be too large for him to carry. Perhaps the way that it had fed upon the other misfits had changed it that much.

"I don't know how much longer it will be until it hatches," he said.

"You want to keep it from Lorren."

Jason nodded. "He can bond to misfits. He uses them. But he won't have this one. I don't know how he forges a connection to them or convinces them, but I refuse to allow him to do the same thing with this dragon."

If Lorren were to connect to this dragon, Jason didn't know if he could free it.

Jason probed, touching upon the energy within the egg. He could feel power working through it. Maybe he could use that power to understand it, and possibly even bond to the dragon before it hatched. Maybe he could attach to the dragon and prevent Lorren from doing so.

"The illusion is impressive," Henry said, making a circle around the inside of the clearing. "It was bright and sunny, at least within Dragon Haven. Within the outskirts of the forest, it was a little bit darker, but this looks like deepest night."

"I don't know why they created that illusion. I suspect it

matters for the egg, though I don't know why." Jason sighed, looking around the illusion. "I can hold on to this, and if the forest dragon helps, she can help hold it as well, but I worry about Lorren. He can break through illusions. The mist dragons give him that ability somehow. If he does, I don't know what he might accomplish with this dragon."

"And the dragon pearls?"

"They give me the power to shift reality."

"What do you mean by that?" Henry asked. He had been crouching in front of the egg, holding his hands out in front of him, but he pulled them back and stood, turning his attention to Jason.

Jason realized that he hadn't shared aspects of his control over illusions with Henry before. "I mean I can turn an illusion and manifest it as reality. I take that power and turn it so that it feels as if it is real."

Henry frowned. "Such a thing shouldn't be possible."

"It is power from the forest dragon."

"Are you sure it is nothing more than an illusion, then? I've seen that dragon and the way that she draws power. She can camouflage herself unlike any other creature."

"I don't know. She asked what an illusion is other than believing something that is not."

Henry crouched down near one of the dragon pearls. "You think that by altering reality, you can protect the egg and prevent Lorren from breaking through the illusion."

"For a time. Eventually, I fear that he might be able to overpower it. When I was with the forest dragon, and she was holding onto the illusion, Lorren managed to break through it. That is why we need to do what we can to protect this egg."

Henry stepped over to the egg, holding his hands up. He could get within a step of it, but no closer. "May I?"

Jason nodded. "It's not my egg."

Henry glanced over at him. "Strangely, I have a sense that it is. Something about it keeps me away." He pushed on his hands and couldn't get any closer. "There's a pressure coming from the egg. I don't know how to explain it, only as if I feel as if it's trying to prevent me from getting too close."

Jason remembered what William had said about the forest being unpleasant. Could he add to it? Maybe that aspect of the illusion would keep others from finding the egg and approaching it.

He focused on the illusion, thinking about the power worked within it, and tried to add to it. He used the power of the dragon pearls, adding those that Henry had given him, trying to build up pressure that would force anyone else away.

He'd never attempted to repel someone from getting close to another within an illusion, and he wondered if it would work. He held onto more and more power, sweeping through the illusion, pressing through the dragon pearls.

Henry cried out.

"What is it?" Jason asked.

"Something is pushing on me. It's unpleasant and painful. Is it the egg?"

Jason smiled to himself. "Not the egg. I think that was me. I wanted to know if I could augment the resistance and push people away."

Henry grunted. "I would say that it's working."

Jason solidified that connection and locked it in place.

"I'm not going to be able to stay here much longer," Henry said. "I feel as if I have to move. We should go."

Jason took a step toward the egg, finding that the resistance didn't push him back, though as he was responsible for the illusion, he wasn't surprised by that. He hoped it would be strong enough to hold and protect the egg, but there wouldn't be any way of testing it.

He probed with power, stretching into the egg, and didn't feel any latching of the power, and no attempt to feed. Perhaps the egg didn't need it anymore.

Henry started away from the clearing, and Jason lingered for a moment before following him. As they passed through the boundary of the illusion, Henry glanced behind him. He shook his head. "That was interesting. I've been around you when you've created illusions before. This is different."

"I think I added more layers to it," Jason said.

Henry frowned. "I'm not even sure that it's a matter of adding layers to the illusion. It's what you are adding to it. There's elements that I can feel and smell and even experience emotion within it." Henry shook his head. "I have been around others who have created illusions, but those were nothing like this. When Thomas does them, it is quite different."

Jason chuckled, thinking about the illusion master. It had been a while since he had worked with him. "The way I create illusions is different than Thomas."

"The way you create them is much more dangerous than Thomas."

They reached the edge of the forest. In the distance, the clearing with the dragons was nearby, and a sense of the iron dragon was more prominent. Jason probed, focusing on that energy to summon the iron dragon. With a swirl of power, the iron dragon slithered through the outskirts of the forest, joining him. Heat radiated from him, leaving his body glowing.

Henry pulled a dragon pearl from his pocket and squeezed it. With a surge of energy, Jason detected what Henry did, the way he connected to his dragon. A dark shadow formed as the dragon began to descend.

"I don't know if you intend to go now, but knowing you, you weren't going to wait."

"I wouldn't rush off quite yet. Besides, I am waiting for help. I doubt Sarah would be thrilled if I departed without her."

Sarah was indeed along the street, making her way toward them. She was dressed in her dragonskin cloak, prepared for travel.

"How did she know to meet us here?"

"I connected to her through the dragon pearl," Jason said.

Henry grunted. "I think your connection to dragon pearls and mine are radically different. Perhaps you will teach me someday."

Jason snorted. "I'm happy to teach you anything that I can."

"Unfortunately, I wonder if there's anything you can teach."

When Sarah joined them, she looked at Jason, then Henry. "What's going on?"

Jason told her about the Dragon Guard, about Lorren and the Dragon Souls' movement.

"That's what they were doing near the forest," she said.

"Who?" Henry asked.

"I suspect it was mostly Lorren and his dragons. They must have detected the egg again." Even knowing it was likely didn't make that easier for Jason to hear. Jason had no idea if he would be able to prevent him from reaching it. If he started to attack…

"That doesn't change the fact that Lorach has been moving our way," Henry said.

Jason closed his eyes. He could practically visualize the movement again, even though he didn't use his dragon sight. "They were moving south. Sweeping toward us. I don't know if they can find Dragon Haven, but they will try." With Jessica, he feared she would succeed.

"Lorren's presence there makes sense," Henry said. "He has already shown you what his purposes are."

"That's not what he's after. He's after the egg, and I have to stop him before he finds it." He looked over.

"That's not all, though, and you know it. I can't let Lorren destroy dragons, and we have to keep Lorach from reaching Lorren and his misfits." Jason didn't want to even consider what might happen if Jessica discovered enough power to control those dragon misfits.

"Then we go," Henry said.

"What about my parents?" Sarah asked. "I haven't seen them in a while. I don't know where they've gone, but I know they are concerned about Lorren. And Lorach."

"We haven't spoken to them," Henry said.

Sarah turned, glancing behind her but bit her lip, a troubled look on her face. "Maybe that's for the best, too. I doubt they would be pleased. Just the three of us, then?"

"It might be easier to stay hidden that way," Jason said.

She nodded. "You're probably right. Well?"

"Just like that?" Jason asked.

"I don't want you to sneak off without me again. Not like you did with the storm dragon. At least this time, you are getting the help you need."

"With hundreds of dragons coming toward us, I think we need to go."

"Let's see if we can't diminish those numbers a bit," she said.

Jason climbed onto the iron dragon and waited as Henry climbed onto his dragon. It took only a moment before Sarah summoned hers, and then they departed.

22

The dragons circled high in the sky, staying as high as was safe. Jason could feel the ice dragon over him, circling. Every so often, he would pause, borrowing from the ice dragon's eyesight, and use that to know more about where they were and whether there were Dragon Souls nearby. So far, he hadn't determined anything.

This was where he'd seen evidence of Lorren moving. Which of the illusions had he gone after?

"How close are we?" Sarah called.

Jason shook his head. "We still have to go a little way."

They were searching, and unfortunately, he didn't know if he could stay with Sarah and Henry. Ultimately, he suspected he might need to join the ice dragon to hunt. For now, he would stay to learn what they might find.

There was something out in the distance, though, as he focused on it, Jason couldn't tell exactly what it was. Not the illusion of an egg, though. He borrowed from the other dragons, using their power, but still could not understand. Sarah watched him, and he could see a question in her eyes, though it was a question he did not have an answer to. How could he when it would explain what he was doing?

Distantly, he could see the dragons moving above the forest, though it was from the ice dragon and his borrowed vision. There was only a day or two, no more than that, before Lorach and the Dragon Souls would reach them. The moment those dragons reached the border of the forest, the people of Dragon Haven would no longer be safe.

"You see something," Sarah said, guiding her dragon closer.

Jason nodded. He glanced over at Henry, who rode astride his dragon, keeping his body bent low as he looked out over the distance. "They aren't far from here," he said. "But I feel something." Could it be another misfit? It wasn't Lorren, but he don't know quite what it was.

He closed his eyes, focusing on what he detected. There was power. Potent power.

A misfit.

"I think we need to see what this is before we deal with Lorach and Lorren."

"Why?" Sarah asked.

"It seems like this is closer than anything else. And it might be another dragon. If we don't get to it first..."

Jason didn't know how to finish. He didn't know what this was, only that the longer they flew, the more certain he was that he detected something here. It was within the boundaries of what he considered to be Dragon Haven.

He tapped on the iron dragon and the dragon veered off, barely needing any guidance. He seemed to know what Jason could feel, a shared sense between them tracking what Jason detected. They streaked toward the ground, flying above the forest, the strange sense guiding him. A glistening blue lake called to him. That was what he detected.

Jason didn't recall ever having visited here before, though there was something familiar about it. They landed along the shoreline, rocks dropping off a cliffside until it reached the water's edge. The day was calm, and the water was flat. Sun shone overhead, reflecting back at them, revealing the image of the two dragons along with the iron dragon's glowing heat.

Jason approached the rocky edge overlooking the water. The air was cool and crisp, though there was something more within it. As he stood there, he recognized power and familiarity.

"Have you ever been here before?" Jason asked Sarah as she approached him.

She shook her head. "We are careful about how far we venture from Dragon Haven. This is far enough away that we haven't been willing to spend time out here."

"I have," Henry said.

Jason glanced over at him. "What lake is this?"

"There was a time when this was a part of Lorach,

though it was long ago. They called it Rostal Lake. I don't really know much more about it than that."

"This was a part of Lorach?" Sarah asked.

Henry swept his gaze around him. "All this was a part of Lorach at one time. Before there was a rebellion, most of this was claimed by them. Even if they didn't live here, Lorach claimed it."

Sarah stood at the rocky overlook, hands pressed on her hips. "I didn't realize that."

There was something strangely familiar about this place. Jason had no idea why he should feel that distinct sense, but he closed his eyes, searching for what he detected and why he should feel something.

It came from within the water.

He took a seat, dangling his legs off the rocky ledge, and began to pull his boots off.

"What are you doing?" Sarah asked.

Jason nodded to the water. "There's something here."

"You think you need to go into the water to detect it?"

Jason glanced over his shoulder at Henry. "We found an egg in a river. I need to see if that is what I'm detecting."

He had no idea whether that river even connected to this lake, but if it did, then that would explain what he detected. He hoped the dragon lived and that it hadn't been influenced by Lorren. Once his boots were off, he pulled off his cloak, setting it alongside them. He remained in his dragonskin.

He glanced back at the iron dragon. "I won't be long."

He jumped.

When he pierced the water, it was cold, and it swirled around him. He ignored it. He had known cold his whole life, and there was no challenge from it now. Less so than it once had been, especially with his connection to the iron dragon and the heat that flowed through him. He took a deep breath while bobbing in the water, focusing on the energy here. He thought about the shell and what he had felt.

Jason plunged beneath the water.

For a moment, he panicked. He wasn't a swimmer. In the mountains, there was very little freestanding water other than the stream that was almost too cold for anyone to touch. Jason had never had an opportunity to swim.

He knew there was something here. It was power. He could feel it.

He had to reach for it.

He stayed beneath the water. He didn't attempt to swim. His lungs burned, and he didn't know how much longer he could stay. Probably not much longer before he would have to surface, gasping for air. He could use the iron dragon to blast out, but if he did so, he might lose his opportunity to gain a connection to whatever dragon was here. Now that he was underwater, he felt increasingly certain there was a dragon.

He tried calling the dragon from his mind. He had been near the egg. He had seen where the dragon came from. He had touched the shell. He should know that dragon.

There was something else he thought he should be able to understand. It was more than just helping the dragon. It was a matter of reassuring it that he wasn't going to harm it.

He probed outward, using a hint more power that flowed into the lake. As that power swept away from him, he could feel a shifting. It reminded him somewhat of the shifting of an illusion, though this one slipped past him. He didn't hold back and used everything in his power to probe outward.

Energy was here. He had to find it.

His lungs burned.

Distantly, he could feel power. He recognized a connection. Using that, he propelled himself forward, gliding through the water. He wouldn't be able to stay underneath the surface for much longer. He would need to take a breath.

An idea came to him.

He could use the forest dragon. Though he didn't want to draw too much power off her and weaken her, now that she was no longer directly guarding the egg, it might not be a problem. He used her power and created an illusion of a pocket of air around him, then shifted it and created that reality.

He took a breath.

There was a part of him that questioned whether it would work, but as he breathed in and relaxed, the illusion held.

Now he swam through the water, gliding and

propelled by the power of his dragons toward the energy that he detected. The water around him was dark, making it difficult to see anything. He probed, using the power of the dragons he had bonded to, and tried to feel for something else. The iron dragon pushed power through him and helped illuminate the darkness.

There was something here.

A darkened shape in the water moved quickly near him.

Jason thrust with the iron dragon energy, using it to try to propel himself toward it. It wasn't enough. Adding that of the ice dragon, he blasted forward.

As he neared, he realized the translucent shape in front of him was a dragon. It was almost translucent, and different than any other dragon he had seen before. The energy he had detected here radiated from this dragon. He created a spiral of water around him, using a hint of illusion mixed with it, wanting to keep the river dragon—lake dragon?—from escaping before Jason had an opportunity to connect to him.

The swirling power held.

The dragon stopped fighting. It turned toward him, and deep blue eyes that seemed to swallow the water looked at Jason.

"You are the river dragon," Jason said. "I found your egg."

The dragon blinked.

Jason tried to focus on the dragon, wondering if he could communicate with the dragon, but he didn't know whether the dragon could speak underwater. He could feel power, though.

"My name is Jason Dreshen. There are others like you." He created an image of the iron dragon in front of him, then shifted it to the ice dragon, then the forest dragon, and finally to the storm dragon. All were misfits that he knew. He held off on using the mist dragon or the earth dragons; he didn't know them as well. "I want to help you."

He had no idea whether the dragon even needed his help. Water swirled around him, flowing from his connection to the other dragons.

"Have you been approached by any others?"

The dragon swirled, increasingly agitated.

"That was what I thought. I won't hurt you. I want to help."

Could the Dragon Souls have tried to come here? Worse, what about Lorren? Jason held onto his connection to the other misfits, flowing toward the water dragon.

It came out slowly, flowing outward. Pressure began to build, and Jason pushed harder, straining. It was almost as if the dragon were fighting.

He tried something else.

He held onto the energy of the forest dragon. He used that connection, that power, and thought about whether he might be able to draw on a new connection. He let power flow from him for a moment before releasing it.

Maybe the water dragon hadn't been influenced. The

dragon seemed capable of resisting Jason's attempt to probe, which meant that it should have been able to have resisted Dragon Souls. The dragon should have been safe.

What about Lorren?

"I was testing whether you have been influenced," Jason said.

The dragon watched him, and he had no sense that the dragon understood. He took a breath, frustration filling him. There had to be some way to communicate with the dragon, though what was it going to take? It had to come naturally. He knew that. When he spoke to the other dragons, he had done so in their environment.

Which meant that he had to release his illusion.

As soon as he did, he heard the dragon rumbling. There was a strangeness to it and energy that flowed within it, and something almost like a wave that washed over him. As it did, its energy built within Jason. Power flowed with it, and he embraced it. The dragon started to swim, swirling around him. Within that swimming was a stirring. The sound that built allowed Jason to hear the dragon.

"I can protect you," he said.

He didn't know how he could even speak underwater, but his words came out, and he heard them.

"There is no protection. Only danger."

"Who came after you?"

The water dragon did the same as Jason and created an image. The image formed, building, and a figure took form. The dragon reacted, water flowing around him with more violence. The dragon had been assaulted by Lorren.

"You were able to fight him," Jason said.

"They were not going to use me," the dragon said.

"No, they're not. I'm glad you held out. If you like, I can help you. I help others."

He had no idea if the dragon would accept any help from him, but he held on to the power of the other dragons, though his lungs started to burn. He didn't know how much longer he could stay beneath the water. He was going to have to take a breath, but if he called upon another illusion, he ran the risk of alienating the dragon. He needed the dragon. If this dragon could keep Lorren from attacking, having a connection like that would be beneficial.

"Let me show you the others. Friends. You can follow me and I'll make sure you're safe. Please."

Jason started to swim. He propelled himself, feeling for the energy of the dragon, though he wasn't sure at first if it was going to follow.

The dragon followed.

Jason surfaced and took a gasping breath of air. A burst of energy carried him all the way to the shore, and he propelled himself out, resting on the rocky ledge. He borrowed heat from the iron dragon and water washed away from him, turning to steam.

Sarah looked down at him. "What happened?"

"The river dragon is in the water."

"River?" Henry asked.

Jason nodded. "I think it's the same. I spoke to the dragon, but I don't even know if he's going to follow me. I think Lorren intended to use him. He was strong enough to fight. He's different. Lorren tried to get to this dragon, but couldn't." He certainly had moved away from here, which meant that the dragon was safe. He couldn't control this one, which gave Jason some hope that Lorren wouldn't be able to control the egg if it were to hatch.

When. Not if.

All of a sudden, a dragonlike face appeared above the water. It seemed to be made of water, trailing toward the surface, glistening in the sunlight.

Henry gasped and Sarah only stood there. Jason could feel the power coming off this dragon. The water dragon. That was probably the best way to regard it. It might've been born of the river, but it was made of water. Maybe that was what gave it the energy to defend against Lorren.

Jason reached for the power of the misfits, probing toward the water dragon. He needed to understand the water dragon, much like he understood all of the misfits. As he probed, he realized that might have been a mistake. The dragon resisted.

He attempted to push a message through. He wanted the dragon to know that he was working with the others, and he felt a stirring within him of the ice, iron, and forest dragons that surged, as if trying to reassure the water dragon.

"I pushed too hard." And Jason knew better, but knowing Lorren was out there, and Lachen, had him acting in ways that he wouldn't have otherwise. Having a dragon like that which could deal with Lorren, and which wouldn't fear what he might do, would be a benefit, but he didn't have a sense this dragon was willing to do that.

Power burst from the dragon and washed over Jason.

He didn't fight.

There was no purpose in doing so, but more than that, he thought he needed to allow it. As it did, he embraced the energy the dragon swept through him. It worked over him. There came a cold chill that faded, slipping through him and then was gone. The dragon disappeared with it, slipping beneath the surface of the water and then away.

"I guess that is it," he said. He stared at the water, noticing rippling waves across the surface. He could see where the dragon moved, the way that he undulated through the water. He could feel power, even though he didn't think he could use it. He had done everything that he needed to. "With as few misfits as there are out here, I keep thinking that I can gather them, but maybe I've gathered all I can," he said.

The water dragon wouldn't be the last of the misfits, but he might be the last of them created the way Lorren used. At least, until Jason found a way to create more. Then again, he wasn't sure he even wanted to. He didn't know if creating misfits was good for the dragon or whether it only created a different kind of power. If he were to do so, if he were to create that kind of power, modifying the dragons to change them, he didn't know if it turned them into something they were not meant to be.

For a moment, there came another rippling, and within that echoing sense, Jason wondered if the dragon were responding to him, attempting to communicate, but then there was nothing. Just an emptiness. Not the violence of the storm dragon, but almost as bad. The water dragon didn't want to work with him. Not that Jason could even blame him. He had already done enough. He had fought enough.

Jason pushed power out to see if he might detect anything more, but there was nothing.

Instead, he squeezed energy from himself, letting it radiate out. Jason couldn't help but wonder if he could find a way to ensure Lorren—and Lorach—wasn't able to harm the misfits. There might not be anything he could do. It might even be too late. The power sweeping toward Dragon Haven might be more than they could withstand. With as many dragon as were coming toward them, and the danger Lorren posed, he couldn't help but worry that they were already outmaneuvered. Dragon Haven would no longer be safe.

Where would they go? There were plenty of free dragons that could carry the people of Dragon Haven away, but he wanted the dragons of Dragon Haven and of Lorach to live freely and to survive, not hide. Only, by running, they would be doing just that.

Using the dragon sight, he looked through the iron dragon's eyes as he circled high above them. He couldn't see everything the dragon saw, but there was movement. Lots of it.

And Jason knew where they needed to go.

He breathed out, feeling power flowing through him. He climbed onto the dragon's back, and they took to the air, heading toward the border, toward Lorach, and toward Lorren.

23

As they neared the Lachen dragons, Jason had a distinct awareness of energy building in front of him. It came from dragons, but it was something else as well—the strange misfit energy that came from Lorren's dragons. There were hundreds of dragons. That was only part of the power he felt. The rest came from Lorren's misfits. He somehow had to save both.

He braced himself by holding onto the ice dragon power along with that of the iron dragon. He mixed the connection as he soared above the forest, the colors blurring past him.

He found Sarah watching him.

"We aren't far," he said.

"Are you sure about this?"

Jason nodded. "We need to—"

He cut off. There came a surge of power. He didn't know what it was, only that he could feel the buildup of a kind of dragon power that he had never felt before. An explosion of energy, though he didn't have a sense it was directed at them.

Henry twisted, leaning off the side of his dragon, looking down at the ground.

"Can you see anything?" Sarah asked.

Henry sat back upright. "I can't. Whatever it was had incredible power, but I don't know what they're using it for."

Jason tried to determine what was out there, though the power and pressure continued to build. Whatever was happening would come again. As he looked over the side of the iron dragon, he could feel it rising. The suddenness of that buildup left him uncomfortable. It was Dragon Soul power, but not the kind that he had known before, and he didn't think it came from the misfits.

Jason headed toward it.

Another energy rumbled alongside them as Lorren headed toward the Dragon Souls.

"That fool," Jason muttered.

Henry looked over at him, frowning. "What is it?"

"I think he intends to attack the Dragon Souls."

"That many dragons?"

There were several hundred. Far too many. Jason knew Lorren was powerful, but against this many dragons, the misfits would be overpowered. Even with what he'd experienced, he had a hard time thinking that the earth dragons and the mist dragons could withstand this kind of onslaught. They would be overwhelmed.

He wasn't willing to allow any dragon to die. They to had intervene now.

"If I don't do anything now, Lorren is going to destroy these dragons. We have to free them."

But why here?

That was the real question he had. Why would Lorren have come here?

Not only that, but why would Jessica and Lorach have come here?

Could it be only that Jason had placed the egg illusion here?

That wouldn't have drawn Lorach.

There was still that strange energy he detected. He had no idea what it meant, only that there was something about it that left him worried.

The ice dragon circled overhead. He could feel the power and energy of him, the cold coming from him, and he thought about the heat of the iron dragon, even the illusion of the forest dragon. If something were to happen to him, the dragons would still be safe. He had a shared bond to the dragons, not one that forced them to serve them.

"If something happens to me, be ready to act. Otherwise…"

Henry frowned, shaking his head. "I'm not going to wait here while you do something stupid." He started to pull off.

"Where are you going?" Sarah called after him.

"He can't do this alone. Neither can Lorren. If these

fools think to take on Lorach, then I'm going to see if the Dragon Guard will join us, but I need to be closer to Dragon Haven to summon them."

These fools.

Jason didn't want to be a fool. He didn't want to be like Lorren, either.

How could he be something different?

That was the answer he had to discover before Lorren started destroying more dragons and before Jason felt more death around him.

Energy rumbled in the distance with a buildup of power from the Dragon Souls.

The dense fog in the distance caught his attention, and Jason raced toward it. That was Lorren.

Tendrils of the mist streaked toward him. Lorren strode upward, somehow walking on those tendrils the same way as Jason would ride upon a dragon.

"You would use illusion against me? I will find that egg."

"No," Jason said. "I'm going to keep you chasing illusions—"

Lorren blasted him with another tendril of mist, and it came streaking toward Jason, forcing him to react, to press power out from him that froze the fog. He dropped for a moment.

Lorren reacted, catching himself, came streaking toward Jason.

Using the ice and the iron dragons, Jason sent another burst of power toward Lorren. The combination crackled together, streaking through him, ripping him with power.

Lorren disappeared.

Then Jason felt a strange shriek.

Dragons under attack.

He couldn't wait.

Even if they waited, there was no guarantee that they would be able to act in time. No guarantee that the Dragon Guard would reach them. And if he waited, dragons would die. He had felt it before, and had almost felt it with one of the dragon misfits.

Jason turned to Sarah. "Stay up here. If dragons get directed off, I need you to help them."

"And what about you? What happens if you get turned away?"

He smiled at her. "Then I'm going to need you to find a way to get to me." Jason patted the iron dragon on the side. "This one isn't your fight. Not yet."

The dragon rumbled.

He climbed to his feet and used a burst of energy that carried him up to the ice dragon. He landed on the ice dragon's back, immediately leaning down, whispering to him. Then they dove.

It happened quickly, shooting on a burst of ice lightning, carrying them to the ground as quickly as possible. Jason added to it, using what he could of the iron dragon to give them a burst of power. He pushed it out, blasting at the nearest of the dragons. It was a surge of power and a combination that allowed it to swirl, flowing over the dragons.

He felt resistance, but with as much force as he utilized, it fluttered only a moment before fading. There came a roar. Dragons scattered, and five of them took flight. There came other shrieks from the dragons. He couldn't see it, only that there was something more taking place, the energy that Lorren was using. And he was targeting the dragons, harming them.

Jason had the distant sense of dragons tossing their Dragon Soul riders, and he hoped they acted quickly enough to keep them from restoring their hold over the dragons. If they didn't…

The dragons took off.

Sarah was there, guiding them.

She headed toward the dragons, joining with them, sweeping them off and toward Dragon Haven.

Jason used a hint of ice and iron together, pushing through those five dragons again to ensure they were protected, and found that they were.

He turned his attention to the dragons in front of him. The ice dragon roared, power coming from him, energy building. That sense filled him. There wasn't anything else that he could do. The ice dragon's power exploded.

More dragons were down there. Jason had started to push when a flock came toward him. Dozens of them.

He braced himself.

Sitting astride the ice dragon, Jason started to call upon as much power as he could. He sent ice and iron energy through them, picking them off one at a time and healing them. The resistance swept away. Dragons were freed, one by one, and they tossed their riders.

Jason wasn't fast enough. Dragons streaked toward him. They moved quickly, with Dragon Souls on top of them, guiding them. Several of the dragons had more than one rider.

Dragons of every color came toward him. Black, blue, green, yellow, red. All of them streaking, all of them building power. All of them filled with the energy of the Dragon Souls. Jason couldn't see Lorren, but as he heard the shrieking agony of Dragon Soul dragons around him, he knew that Lorren continued his attack. It wouldn't be much longer before he finished it. Then those dragons would destroy the Dragon Soul dragons.

Jason needed to save them.

First, he needed to protect himself.

Jason had to try a different approach. He shifted reality. He created a barrier around him, thickening the air and preventing the dragons from penetrating it.

The ice dragon roared. "How long will that hold?"

"I don't know. I might be pulling on too much power. I worry she won't have the strength to replenish her egg."

More than that, if he didn't act quickly enough, the illusion he needed to hide the egg would fade. Then Lorren would know how to find the *real* egg.

He had to move quickly. With the barrier around him, he could form the healing and swept power toward each of the dragons. It gave him a little bit more time, but they continued to come in an onslaught of dragon power.

There was an explosion beneath him. He needed to be here. Whatever he detected was the reason Lorach was here, and maybe even why Lorren had come.

"Be ready," Jason said. "I'm going to need you to call power from above."

The dragon roared, understanding filling him.

The ice dragon could use a different kind of attack than others, and maybe with the ice lightning, he could slow things. Jason pushed out a blast of power, and it exploded toward the ground. They descended, dropping quickly. He clung to the ice dragon's back. Dragons followed them, circling. Jason tried to heal more of the dragons as they descended, and each time he did, they tossed a Dragon Soul rider. He still didn't worry about the rider. All he cared about was the dragon.

Distantly, he had a sense of Sarah directing dragons away. He hoped she could work fast enough. He hoped that he could continue sending the dragons toward her. He hoped they could be enough.

When he had done this around Jessica, she'd managed to fight him. At that time, Jason hadn't used the same technique that he used now. He had barely been able to withstand the storm dragon and hadn't been able to mix the power as well as he could now. This time, he added all of the misfits together. He formed that barrier around him as he healed other dragons.

They neared the ground, sweeping just above the tree-tops. Power came from below, assaulting them. Jason could feel that power building, the energy in the air, slamming into them. He couldn't do anything differently.

He held onto the barrier as much as he could. Power came toward him.

Another explosion of power built near him.

A fog in the distance caught his attention, and a faint, vague rumbling. Lorren was out there. His power targeted the Dragon Soul dragons, though Jason couldn't get to them. He had to focus on what was in front of him.

Jason directed the ice dragon toward that power. Something burst near him.

They reached the ground. There were dozens of dragons near him, all of them turning toward him, but they didn't move. Power flowed through the dragons. Jason could feel that energy, was aware of it, and realized there was something about it that he could use. There was more power within him.

Strangely, he'd felt something like that before.

It was a drawing sensation. The only time he had felt that before had been with the dragon egg and the dragon misfits. This time, there were only these dragons.

They circled a rocky plain with trees all around. The burst of energy he detected was focused downward, toward the ground. As he noticed it, Jason thought he understood.

There was an egg. The size of it was distinct, and had Jason not carried an egg from the forest to Dragon Haven, he might not have truly understood what it was, but he recognized it. More than that, he realized there was a strange power here.

He studied the ground. Why here?

Could this be one that Lorren had placed?

Doubtful. This was still in Lorach. Which meant this would be somewhere Therin had placed an egg.

It was a unique location. A chasm dropped off nearby, and heat and steam drifted up, combining with a faint mist around it. The combination would likely create a powerful dragon. Heat. Water. Mist. Earth. A combination egg.

Jessica and Lorach intended to create a misfit.

Not just any misfit, though. A *powerful* misfit.

And from what he could tell by the way that they were pushing power into the egg, they knew how to feed it the same way as the misfit egg in the forest had been fed.

Jason could feel energy building. Dozens upon dozens of dragons were pushing power out from them, the drawing sensation growing increasingly intense. All of it was feeding Jessica's egg.

Jason didn't need to get close to the dragon egg to know what was happening. He could feel it. Energy came from what they were doing, squeezing power out from them, which meant he was going to have to do something different.

He might have to interrupt what was taking place, but how could he do so?

Energy burst again. This time, something changed. There came a soft rumbling.

For a moment, Jason thought that it came from the earth dragons, but that didn't seem to be what it was. It was gentle, softer than what he had detected before. It was coming from where they stood, power they were summoning into the egg.

The dragons turned toward him.

Jason pushed, sweeping ice and iron dragon energy through them. The first layer of dragons scattered as the power swept through them, freeing them and letting them race into the sky. Dragon Souls turned toward him, holding dragon pearls. The Dragon Souls were no longer bound to the dragons, but they still had the power that came from the pearls.

Dragon magic assaulted Jason. Had he not created the barrier around himself using the power of illusion, he might've been overwhelmed.

They streaked toward the ground, and Jason jumped off of the dragon, heading toward the egg. This was what the blue dragon had warned him about.

Where was that dragon?

He'd been searching. Had he been caught by Lorach?

Jason thought he would have known, but with Jessica attacking, it was possible he wouldn't have known. Now he had to get to the egg and keep it from Jessica before Lorren did. He could hide it. Maybe even with the other egg.

He couldn't get to the egg. The Dragon Souls prevented him. Jason landed nearby, at the edge of a clearing, and tendrils of mist began to streak toward him again.

Jason crackled power from the ice dragon and shot it toward the mist dragon.

Lorren strode toward him. He was dressed in green and black, and the mist swirled around him, making Jason question how much of it was real or illusion.

"There it is," Lorren said. "This is the egg you've been trying to keep from me."

"We need to help this dragon, not harm it," Jason said.

Lorren shot him a look. "We? You're the reason they're even here. Had it not been for you revealing these dragons, Lorach would never have known. They never would have attempted this sort of power. They would have been content. Instead, you showed them the power of these dragons."

"I didn't show them anything. I wanted to free the dragons."

"Because you are ignorant."

Could that be the reason that he attacked? He blamed Jason?

A roar erupted, and a dozen dragons dove from the sky, all darting toward Lorren.

He swirled back, enveloped by the mist.

Jason moved forward, getting out of the way, letting the Dragon Souls take on Lorren.

He would protect their dragons later.

For now, he had to deal with the egg.

He hurried forward, trying to reach the chasm, trying to find the egg itself, when he realized he wasn't alone.

A darkened figure strode toward him, dressed all in

black dragonskin, rage flowing from her. Jessica. Her hair flowed with the wind, power exploding from her. She was terrifying.

"You would dare interrupt me?"

"You aren't going to control this misfit," he said.

"Misfit?" She sneered at him. "There is nothing misfit about what I have created." There came another soft rumbling, and she glanced over her shoulder. "And perhaps you can stay here and watch as I gain control over him. Do you realize how hard I've looked for a record of where Therin left the eggs?" She sneered at him. "This one finally has potential. The others… Not so much."

Jason realized what she was saying. She had destroyed other eggs.

All this time and that was what Lorach had been searching for.

Not Dragon Haven. At least, not yet.

She had wanted the eggs.

She had wanted misfits.

She had wanted the power that they could offer her.

"I'm not leaving this dragon I'm not allowing you to harm any more of them. Not any longer." He flicked his gaze to the sky and the swarm of dragons that flew within it. "This is going to be the end. I'm going to stop you. I'm going to stop Lorach. Whatever it takes." Rage filled him at how she intended to harm another dragon, to control a misfit.

As that rage hit him, he forced it away.

It was that rage that drove Lorren.

He could not be like him. Jason had to be better.

Lorren had been twisted by anger. He had allowed that to influence how he treated the dragons, and he had allowed that to turn him into something else, someone willing to harm dragons rather than to protect them.

"What do you mean?"

"I know what Lorren did."

At the mention of his name, her brow darkened.

"He is killing your dragons. He is killing your Dragon Souls. I would—"

Power exploded from her, causing the ground to erupt and flames to streak toward him. He had to hurriedly create a barrier of power around him, and nearly didn't do it in time. His connection to the ice and iron dragons, along with a hint of the forest dragon, solidified that connection so he could prevent her from harming him any more than she had just done. Even then, he barely withstood what she did.

There was considerable power within her. Energy built up, slamming into him. He needed to separate her from her dragon, but he had no idea if he could. Other dragons started to surround him.

Jason focused on the ice dragon. "Be ready to call lightning," he whispered.

The ice dragon roared gently.

Jessica turned her attention to him and pressed toward his barrier. "An interesting trick. Do you really think it will hold if I wanted to come through?"

"It will hold long enough."

"Long enough for what?"

"Long enough for me to continue to free your dragons. And help this one."

Jason swept power away, using it against all the dragons around him. He forced it everywhere, sweeping as far as he could, more power building. The more he pushed, the more he could feel it striking through the resistance of those dragons, overwhelming it.

Jason struggled, holding onto power. Dragons took flight, erupting into the sky, the energy around them shifting and fading. Still there were more. Each time he freed another five or six dragons, more pressed forward. He knew there were hundreds of dragons here, but this seemed impossible.

An illusion.

Jason could feel the illusion around him, and he shifted it. What he thought he'd been doing had not been that at all. The dragons he'd freed in the sky had been freed, but once he had landed, Jessica had protected them.

She laughed a dark laugh. "Very good. You see, once you demonstrated what you could do to free them, I needed to find an alternative strategy to ensure they remained under my control."

Power built around him, more than he thought he could withstand. Jason felt it slamming into him, almost overwhelming the barrier he had placed. There was too much power. It hammered at him. It would eventually overwhelm him.

It was in the way Jessica created her illusion. She could

pick at the barrier, drawing upon the dragons. There were too many dragons.

Jason was trapped. He reached for the ice dragon, feeling for power within him, but it wasn't going to be enough. He could already tell that he didn't have enough strength, and it took everything within him to withstand the power that was slamming upon him now.

"I might make you watch as I take this dragon," Jessica said, grinning at him.

He closed his eyes, focusing on the ice dragon. "Call on the lightning," he said.

The dragon roared, and power built. Energy crackled, and a massive bolt of ice lightning streaked toward him and then outward. When it cleared, Jason expected that some of the dragons would have been scattered, but nothing had changed.

Jessica had used her power to protect not only herself, but the other dragons around her. "Do you really think I would have been unprepared a second time?"

She started toward him and stepped through his barrier. Jason couldn't stop her.

Suddenly, the ground rumbled.

"You will get to see my new dragon soon."

The rumbling came again, deeper in timber. Earth dragons, but not the one she had just hatched. Somewhere distantly, one of the dragons shrieked. Then another. Then another.

Lorren hadn't been close. He'd been battling with the Dragon Souls.

And he must have succeeded.

Now he came. His dragons came. Death came.

Jessica turned, frowning.

"Send them away," Jason said.

She turned to him. "Why would I do that? I have you held captive here. I'm not going to release—"

"Because Lorren is here. He's coming for the dragon you just hatched."

She pressed her mouth into a tight frown. "If he's here, then he will—"

Another dragon shrieked. This one was louder than before, filling his ears with a painful sound. People—Dragon Souls—began to scream. More and more dragons started to shriek.

Jessica turned away from Jason. Her power over him was gone.

Something was wrong. Jason could feel it, not only from the strange energy in the air, but in the ground beneath them, from the dragons that were out there, shrieking in agony. He could feel it in the dragon magic that flowed, even from his connection to the ice dragon. The strangeness that he detected was terrifying, and it was something he needed to stop.

He reached for the ice dragon, jumping onto his back, and they quickly took flight. They circled over the dragons. He could feel something changing. The air swirled with the strange mist of Lorren's dragons.

"We have to stop it."

The ice dragon shot a bolt of ice lightning, solidifying

the air. Energy crackled around him, and he froze everything. Something shifted again.

Each time Jason solidified the air, he could feel the trembling of the ground, the way the mist swirled, the mist dragons using that energy to assault the Dragon Soul dragons.

Jessica raged with power. The dragon had disappeared. He could feel her influence, the way she attempted to try to call that dragon, and Jason strained for it, but she intervened.

She was powerful.

And she had connected to the dragon misfit that she had hatched.

It was an incredible display. He could feel energy radiating away from her, drawn from dozens upon dozens, possibly hundreds of dragons. Each time it did, energy exploded but still wasn't enough. There was something more taking place. Lorren called upon power, a considerable amount of it, and sent it toward her.

Jason didn't know what he needed to do.

Somehow, he had to help, though who should he help?

Jessica shrieked, and dragons around her screamed.

That answered it.

He tapped the ice dragon on the side. They streaked toward the ground, toward the assault. When he landed, he found Jessica with power flowing from her and swirling around her. The mist shimmered around her as well. The other dragons she had controlled had all disappeared. The Dragon Souls had scrambled, and now the air was filled with dragons. Jason didn't think it was an illusion. They were retreating.

Jason had heard that sound before. He had felt the agony of dragons shrieking in the throes of death, and he had known the torment those dragons had encountered. Hearing it now, feeling it now, left him trembling with that power, knowing that he needed to do something —anything.

He had to stop this.

Jessica would attack Lorren, trying to claim his dragon misfits, and if she succeeded, she would turn that power upon Jason's dragon misfits, and even upon Dragon Haven.

If Lorren were to succeed, he would destroy Lorach's dragons.

Neither option was one he was willing to accept.

Which meant he had to act. Quickly.

It left him with Jessica and Lorren.

This was his opportunity.

Jessica watched him. "Is this your doing?"

"I wouldn't harm the dragons," he said.

"To stop Lorach, you would," she said. Power swirled from her, heading toward him.

The mist interrupted it. Jason added a hint of power, freezing the mist again. Jessica glared at him. The ground rumbled.

She looked down. "You're with him, aren't you?"

"I'm not with him. I wouldn't be with someone like him."

Not even if it meant stopping her.

With the realization, he knew what he had to do.

He would have to *help* Jessica if he wanted to stop Lorren.

She flicked her gaze over to the ice dragon. "You are. That's how you know how to control these dragons. This is not over."

The dragon hatchling crawled toward her. It was not anything like a dragon he had ever seen. Brown, with heat that radiated from it, and swirls of steam that flew around it. Jason hurriedly pushed power toward the dragon, trying to connect to it, but Jessica was there, intervening.

She glared at him.

"You don't have to go with her," Jason said to the dragon, not even sure if it understood him. "You can stay with others like you."

"You will not keep this dragon," Jessica said.

She used a swirl of power and grabbed the dragon.

With that, she jumped, bringing the dragon with her. She used incredible power with her jump, heat and energy exploding her into the air. Jason had once done something similar.

With it, she disappeared, joining the Dragon Souls as they retreated.

He could go after her.

She had a misfit, a dragon that would become powerful.

And he had the upper hand here. She was running. She was afraid.

If he stopped Lorach now, all of this would be over.

But it wouldn't. Not with Lorren still willing to attack.

None of this would be over until he defeated Lorren.

That was what Jason had to do first.

To save the dragons, he would have to stop Lorren for good.

The ground rumbled again.

Jason turned. Lorren was coming.

24

Pressure built all around him and Jason focused on the energy and power that was out there, focusing on the mist swirling near him. He controlled the power coming from the ice dragon, sending it streaking out to solidify the mist. He had to use as much power as he could, trying to interrupt whatever Lorren might do. He had to stop him.

A layer of mist hung around the forest. He borrowed from the power of the ice dragon and solidified the mist. As soon as they did, he exploded it, trying to create steam and clear the air. It did so momentarily, but then the mist solidified again.

"You must do that again," the ice dragon said.

Jason focused on the ice again, solidifying it, and then added a hint of power to explode it. Distantly, there came a rumbling from the earth dragons.

The ice dragon could neutralize some aspect of the

earth dragon magic, but if there were many of them, it might not be enough. He didn't want to risk the ice dragon the way he had with the iron dragon, when he had nearly died, but there might be something that Jason could try.

"It's going to be risky," he said to the ice dragon.

"I am ready," the ice dragon said.

The mist streamed toward them, but this close to them, the ice dragon radiated cold, and the mist froze. The ground beneath the ice dragon started to crackle, ice rippling across its surface. The ice dragon solidified it. What would've happened had the iron dragon done something similar? He might have been able to use his heat in a way to turn the ground to molten rock. They hadn't tried that, but he wondered if he should have.

The ground rumbled as the earth dragon attempted to slam into the ice. The mist seemed to be denser. Power was building around him.

Lorren was *here*.

Jason reached for power again, although this time there was resistance, something pushing on him and on the power of the ice dragon. The ground trembled and the ice crackled. When it did, the air shimmered, shifting.

It was illusion.

Rather than fighting, Jason embraced the illusion, the power that came from Lorren, and added his own power to it. He wouldn't fight it. He would instead call Lorren into it.

"What are you doing?" The ice dragon turned toward him, cold radiating from him.

"I'm trying to summon him here."

"Is that wise?"

Jason grunted. "Probably not."

He had to try to get to Lorren. He had to somehow trap him. He had to defeat him.

Jason twisted the illusion, adding the swirling wind, the snow gusting out of the mountains, the cold. He created everything out of the north, solidifying it. There was a resistance, then the illusion crackled around him. Lorren stepped forward. There was a dark grin on his face.

"This is where you acquired that wonderful dragon," he said, turning to Jason. He held his hands up, and snowflakes danced upon his palms. Lorren had gained control over the illusion already. "The other may be mine, but that one is all Therin's."

It was vastly different than when Jason had faced Therin. At least Therin hadn't been able to overwhelm Jason's ability with the illusion. With Lorren, not only did he have control over the illusion, but he had more strength than Jason. He could use that and control the illusion, twisting it.

"You have interesting control," Lorren said, turning to him.

Snowflakes rippled, turning to a shimmering rain. Jason attempted to regain control over the illusion but could feel Lorren resisting him. He strained as he reached through the forest dragon to summon energy, but failed.

Lorren stepped toward him. The rain shifted with him. "You have potential, but you are inexperienced. I'm surprised you eliminated Therin. Of course, Therin was often too arrogant for his own good."

"You aren't going to hurt the dragons."

"I'm not going to do what?" The rain shifted and now began to spiral around him. There was a strange twisting to it. This time, Jason realized what Lorren did. He turned the rain into a violent mist, accosting Jason and preventing him from doing anything. "As soon as I'm done with you, I'm going after that one. I will have your dragons, and then I will claim the one she created."

At least Lorren didn't know anything about the other egg from the forest. At least he didn't know about the one in Dragon Haven.

Lorren grinned at him. "And when all of that is done, I will go to Dragon Haven, and I will find the other. The one you have been trying to hide from me." He sneered at Jason. "Did you think I wouldn't know? Did you think the dragons wouldn't tell me?"

Jason's heart hammered.

Unless he stopped Lorren, that dragon, and that egg, were in danger.

Not only that, but Dragon Haven was in danger.

He would have to stop him.

This was not a man he could work with. This was not a man he wanted to be like.

He tried to grab for more energy and power, but couldn't do anything other than what he had already done. Lorren assaulted him, power building and hammering at him, swirling mist and energy twisting around him. Jason tried to hold his hands out and brace himself against that power, but there was too much.

He held his hands away from him, bracing, but couldn't.

There had to be another way.

It wasn't going to be illusion. Lorren used his mist dragons in the illusion primarily. That was his connection to power. That was the way he overwhelmed Jason, who had to find a different way to overpower him.

Maybe heat would work.

He added heat, then ice, mixing the two. Given the way Lorren had control over the illusion, the moment Jason shifted one thing, Lorren shifted it to something else. It wasn't going to work that way. Jason needed to try something more. There might be another way of reaching through the illusion and overpowering Lorren.

Heat, then ice, then the forest dragon.

He called on each of them, but none were enough. The moment he pushed out with one power, Lorren tried something else. Lorren took a step toward him, and everything shifted. He changed reality. The suddenness was jarring, but Jason barely reacted, pulling himself back into the icy landscape. He held onto it, forcing the ground to be solid, for snow and ice to swirl around him, and for the ice dragon to be here.

The power was significant. Jason struggled against it, straining, but Lorren used power in a way Jason couldn't counter.

He had to call upon the forest dragon. She relied on a different technique for illusion than that of the mist dragons. It was similar enough that Lorren could overwhelm it, but this was the forest dragon. She was the master of illusion. Jason could borrow her power, fumbling through himself. He embraced that power as it built. He had to find the core of that energy.

He added hints of ice and iron, mingling them together.

There was another sense buried within him that he hadn't detected before. The energy of it was there, one that he was familiar with, having recognized it when the dragon egg fed. It was electric. It left him crackling with energy, rumbling along his skin, deep within him.

Jason thought he understood. When he had been helping feed the dragon egg, he had pulled upon power from each of the dragons. That included the storm dragon. He called that power to him.

It crackled, bursting through the air.

Of all the dragons, the storm dragon was one of the most potent and difficult to overwhelm. It was the reason Jason had been concerned about the storm dragon and how he would interact with the others. Now that he could feel it and was aware of his power, he had to think there was some strength that he could use that he had not before.

Jason called that power to him. A bolt of lightning struck.

Lorren glared at him. "Nice trick."

"It's no trick," Jason said.

He called another bolt of lightning, and it nearly blasted Lorren before he blocked and deflected the power. "You will provide me with that dragon. You could even be a part of it. You could help. Together we could destroy Lorach. I've seen the look in your eye. I have seen that you want to do it." He flicked his gaze to the sky. "We can ensure the dragons are saved."

Jason took a deep breath. Had Lorren propose that when they had first met, Jason might've been convinced. Even now, there was a part of him that wanted nothing more than to defeat Lorach that considered it. As much as he hated it, he thought that maybe they could work together.

But not like Lorren intended.

"I can't do it like you. The dragons can be saved. Truly saved."

"Not when they've already been tainted," Lorren said.

That told Jason all he needed to know about Lorren. As if there were any question, Lorren answered it.

Tension built within Jason, a rumbling sort of energy. He had to add to it. He needed the power of the storm dragon, but also that of the ice dragon and his ice lightning, that of the iron dragon, and even the forest dragon. All of that energy was here, and it filled him.

Deep within him came another sense.

Power, but different than he'd ever felt.

A rumbling of energy. It took a moment, but he detected the pull of earth.

That dragon was there. Gifting some of his magic to Jason.

Lorren may have connected to the dragon misfits and forced them to serve him, but Jason had a different connection to them. He was a conduit for their power. He mixed them, including earth, and let that power explode.

It streaked toward Lorren. He held his hands up, blocking, as if it were nothing more than an illusion.

It was not.

When the ice lightning struck, followed by storm dragon lightning, the surge of power continued to build, heat, and illusion slamming into him, one after another. It crashed through him, a cascade of energy. Finally Jason relented.

He had to stop Lorren. That was the thought that stayed with him.

He called lightning down. A bolt of electricity. Ice lightning. Fire streaking from the sky. All of it mixed together, swirling within the power of reality and illusion coming together.

Then the ice dragon struck.

He used the powerful spikes of his body and shot ice outward. It pierced Lorren.

For a moment, he feared it might be nothing more than an illusion.

Lorren didn't get up. Blood pooled around the spikes.

The dragons pressed power through Jason. He didn't have a chance to control it. It came as a bolt of lightning, mixed with ice and fire, all of that melding together. Earth joined in, much as it had before, a true betrayal of Lorren.

All that power struck Lorren.

Jason was surprised that the dragons would use such violence, but realized why.

There was a layer of illusion over him.

They shattered the illusion, shredding it.

Then Lorren was truly down.

He continued holding his hand up as the mist swirled around him. The power he commanded from the mist dragons worked around him, but the onslaught of power coming from Jason's dragon misfits continued to strike him.

Jason reached for the ice dragon, grabbing hold of one of the icy spikes on his back and pulling it free. He strode over to Lorren and jammed the icicle into Lorren's belly.

Lorren stared at him, holding his gaze, his eyes wide before narrowing.

"Perhaps I had you wrong," Lorren said.

With that, he faded, falling back and crashing to the ground.

The mist swirled around him for a moment before it began to solidify.

Jason held out the icicle, clutching it tightly. He had no interest in battling the mist dragons, but rather than that, he watched as the mist dragons solidified around him, forming a layer, and then the remaining earth dragons rumbled, pulling Lorren's body underground. It left nothing behind.

The mist dragons started to dissipate, but before they did, they watched Jason for a moment before disappearing altogether from view.

Jason let out a heavy sigh and turned to the ice dragon. "It's time to go back."

25

When Jason reached Dragon Haven, he was relieved to find it still intact. With everything he'd encountered, and with how powerful Jessica had been, he wasn't sure what would've become of the city. Thankfully, it was still there.

Sarah rode alongside him, looking down upon the illusion, and as they pierced through it, tension within her returned. "I still can't believe you allowed Jessica to go."

"It meant saving the dragons," Jason said.

"Did it?" Jessica asked, turning her head and frowning at him. "Even after everything you've seen? Everything that she has done to you? To us?"

Jason took a deep breath, looking away. He understood the anger Sarah felt, but at the same time, he had chosen.

"Stopping Lorren meant saving the dragons. Jessica won't kill them."

"Only use them."

Jason nodded. “She will. And we still have to stop her, but at least this way, we have something to save.” Had he not stopped Lorren, there would have been nothing left for them to save. Lorren would have hunted, killing, and slaughtering dragons until he had what he wanted.

Misfits.

That would have been all that survived.

The other dragons deserved to live, as well. Jason had seen they could be saved. Sarah knew they could be saved, as well, even if she refused to acknowledge it.

Jason had done what was necessary.

Now he would protect the egg.

Then he would have to find some way to reach the misfit Jessica had created. He would have to see if he could call to him, and perhaps even rescue him.

Now they had something else they could do. Dozens upon dozens of dragons were saved.

“You did well,” he said. “You protected those dragons as they were saved. What happened to them?”

Sarah frowned at him, and he sensed her frustration, but she shook her head, looking out upon Dragon Haven. “The others are elsewhere. I’ve tried to encourage them to stay here, but I don’t know if they will.”

The other dragons that they had freed had not remained nearby. It was part of the reason Lorren had grown so powerful.

They had passed the Dragon Guard on the way back and given word to Henry that the battle was over, but he had remained with the Dragon Guard, trying to ensure that any Dragon Soul that might remain was eliminated.

The illusion overhead remained intact, but that wasn't the only illusion he was concerned about. He probed and felt that it remained unbroken.

As he climbed off the dragon's back, Sarah nodded. Jason followed the direction of her gaze and saw William racing toward them, his eyes wide, his hair standing on end.

"Jason. Sarah. I'm glad you're both back. I need you to come with me."

They shared a look. "Why? What happened? Is the egg—"

William shook his head. "I don't think there's anything wrong with the egg, but…"

He grabbed Jason's arm and pulled him. He had no choice to go along. Sarah followed him.

As they headed into the forest, William glanced over. "I wasn't sure at first. When I came through here, I wasn't able to detect anything. I couldn't get that close. Then some sort of strange pressure built against me. All of a sudden, it was gone."

Jason stopped, glancing at the sky. Lorren was gone, wasn't he? "What do you mean that it was gone?"

"That's just it. Had I not known what was here, and understood that it prevented anybody from getting close, I wouldn't have even tried. That sense disappeared. I don't know what it was, only that something changed."

Jason frowned. There was no reason anything would

have changed. No reason unless Lorren had somehow attacked.

Jason focused on the illusion and could feel the effect of it out there, faint but still present. Within the illusion was some other sense of power.

He followed William, Sarah chasing after them.

When they reached the illusion, Jason noticed it as a shimmering veil in front of them. He could see the illusion and was aware of it, but there was something else that was different.

He stepped forward. "It's gone," Jason whispered.

"What is?" Sarah asked.

He glanced over at her. "The power I placed here. It was meant to prevent anybody else from getting here."

"That's what I was saying. Something repelled me, and I assumed it was something you did." William glanced over at him, and Jason nodded. "I could feel it. There was a circle of it as if it created a barrier within the forest. Then it disappeared. I don't know what happened, only that I could get much closer than I could before. There's still a pressure against me, but it's different than before. Not nearly as unpleasant."

Jason focused on that. If there was something here…

Power. Only what kind of power?

He probed with his connection to the dragons, now adding the connection to the storm dragon since he knew that he could. He probed outward.

"Come," he said, murmuring to the other dragons.

He hoped they would respond. Distantly, he had an

awareness of them coming toward him. The ice dragon dropped from overhead, and the iron dragon slithered through the trees. More power was coming as well. The forest dragon.

He frowned. That was unusual. She never came.

Thunder rumbled distantly.

That wasn't the forest dragon.

The storm dragon was coming. He could feel the energy crackling from it as he streaked toward them.

When they all appeared, they came to rest in the clearing nearby. All of those dragons were filled with power. There was something more, a new energy that swept toward him. There was something… incredible… to it.

Power built from the dragons, radiating out from them, mingling as it swirled between them.

"What are they doing?" Sarah asked.

Jason had no idea. He could feel the power that they were using and mingling, but he didn't know if the other power that he felt was coming from them—or from the egg.

That was it.

He turned to William and Sarah. "I'm not so sure that you should be here for this," he said.

"Why not?" Sarah asked.

"Because I don't know what exactly is going to take place. I can feel something, but it is dangerous."

Enough that it made him nervous. He could feel power building, trembling.

He looked over at the other dragons, and they watched him.

"I'll find you when I'm certain," he said to Sarah.

She held his gaze for a moment, then tapped on William's arm. The two of them backed away.

"If you see any of the Dragon Guard, warn them that they should stay away from here."

As they disappeared back into the trees, Jason turned his attention to the clearing. There was a building sense of energy that mingled within the dragons. That sense filled him, though it came from everywhere around him. There was a singular source emanating from it, a darkness that swirled around.

For a moment, Jason thought that was simply the illusion he'd formed, but as he headed forward, he realized the illusion had shattered. There was no more remaining. Whatever he saw now was not his illusion. It came from something else.

He moved forward slowly, holding his hands up. He could feel the power coming from the egg. It was different than before, but also the same.

The iron dragon nudged him gently, and he moved forward.

In the distance, on the far side of the clearing, the storm dragon remained a nebulous dark cloud, almost impossible to connect to, though he felt the energy radiating from him. It was similar to what he felt coming off the ice dragon and the iron dragon. Even the forest dragon radiated considerable power, pressing toward him.

All of them wanted him to move closer.

As he did, nearing the center of the clearing, Jason was aware of the egg. He could feel it, but with the darkness swirling around it, he couldn't see it quite as well.

Jason reached for it.

A thunderous crack echoed.

Jason watched the egg. Darkness emanated from it, followed by a loud roar. Something slithered past him, slipping around him, and then the shadows twisted and twirled, brushing up against him.

With a sudden understanding, Jason realized what this was.

The dragon.

He held his hand out. Darkness as black as night worked around him, slipping around his arm, through him, before disappearing altogether. He glanced up, but the illusion of the moonlit sky was gone.

He thought he understood. The forest dragon had helped create her misfit. Darkness and night. With the thought, he knew it fit.

Jason smiled. "A night dragon."

The other dragons roared.

The Dragon Misfits concludes with Night Dragon!

A true misfit may be the key to finally defeating Lorach, but only if Jason learns its powers in time.

Having stopped Lorren and saving the egg, Jason now faces his most dangerous threat as Lorach moves on Dragon Haven.

With the city under attack from a strange new power, only with an understanding of the misfit dragons will Jason—and the dragons—finally be free. When even Dragon Haven seeks to use their power, Jason is forced to make a choice between the people who took him in and the dragons he pledged to protect.

For Jason, long a misfit himself, the choice is more difficult than he ever imagined. One choice means Lorach will extend their influence beyond their borders and continue their reign of devastation, but the other means the misfits will be sacrificed.

SERIES BY D.K. HOLMBERG

The Dragonwalkers Series

The Dragonwalker

The Dragon Misfits

Elemental Warrior Series:

Elemental Academy

The Elemental Warrior

The Cloud Warrior Saga

The Endless War

The Dark Ability Series

The Shadow Accords

The Collector Chronicles

The Dark Ability

The Sighted Assassin

The Elder Stones Saga

The Lost Prophecy Series

The Teralin Sword

The Lost Prophecy

The Book of Maladies Series

The Book of Maladies

The Lost Garden Series

The Lost Garden

Printed in Great Britain
by Amazon

59479684R00225

W… …or

Wildlife in Glamorgan

Edited by Nigel Ajax Lewis

Glamorgan Wildlife Trust

YMDDIRIEDOLAETH BYWYD GWYLLT MORGANNWG

First published by Pisces Publications 1991

ISBN 0-9508245-7-7

Design and Camera-ready copy by the Nature Conservation Bureau Limited
36 Kingfisher Court, Hambridge Road, Newbury, RG14 5SJ

Printed by Information Press, Oxford.

Cover illustration by Adrian Lascomb of Blackpool and the Fylde College

Dedicated to the memory of
Neville Douglas Jones (1915-1989)
Solicitor and Naturalist

In recognition of almost 30 years of work with Glamorgan's wildlife and the Trust. The sites listed in this volume are a living memorial to Neville's work.

ACKNOWLEDGEMENTS

I would like to thank the following people for their help in producing this book:

Alex Coxhead, for the bird information
Peter Creed, for his patience
Gwyn Davis, Chairman of the Trust
Mary Gillham, for her invaluable help
Rosemary Mason, Chairman West Area
Vincent Rey for producing the maps for this Handbook
Derek Thomas, former Chairman of the Trust
Mel Watkins of the NCC
John Zehetmayr OBE, South Area

All the voluntary reserve wardens.

And finally, to all the medical staff at the Princess of Wales Hospital, Bridgend, without whose assistance I would not be here today.

Nigel Ajax Lewis
August 1991

CONTENTS

WHERE TO GO FOR WILDLIFE IN GLAMORGAN

The Glamorgan Wildlife Trust is the leading Glamorgan voluntary organisation for the conservation of all forms of wildlife and their habitats. Through its network of County Committees and local groups, the Trust promotes the enjoyment and protection of wildlife throughout Mid, South, and West Glamorgan. A very important part of this work involves setting aside wild places to establish as nature reserves, where the enjoyment and protection of wild plants and animals can be made a priority. The creation and management of these nature reserves includes the care and consideration of our needs as visitors, as well as the need to give special protection to sensitive or rare wildlife.

Not all of these reserves contain rarities but each one has something special about it. Some are large, some very small; some can cope with large numbers of visitors, while others are more fragile and can only tolerate a small amount of human disturbance.

Given that the over-riding priority must always be the conservation of the plants and animals for which the reserve has been acquired, the Trust's policy is to encourage visitors to come and enjoy Glamorgan's marvellous heritage of wildlife on as many of your Trust's Nature Reserves as possible.

This handbook provides the visitor with information on the Glamorgan Wildlife Trust's Nature Reserves: their location, wildlife interest and land-use history, together with the facilities available for those visiting them.

The Reserves, are grouped by the present County, in alphabetical order. Each page includes a location map and a site map showing habitats, access points, paths and other details. As well as describing the Reserve and its wildlife, the text gives information on good times to visit, any special precautions that may be necessary when visiting, and the distances to neighbouring Trust Reserves. Also included in the entry is information on the status of the site, whether Trust owned, leased or held by agreement, and which Trust County Committee is responsible for the site management.

The primary purpose in establishing a Nature Reserve is to conserve the habitats and wildlife that the site supports. Active management is generally necessary, and for each of its Reserves the Trust prepares a management plan setting out both the scientific aims for the site and the means by which it is intended to achieve them. A brief summary of the conservation aims and projects is given for each reserve, to help the visitor understand the reasons for any work they may see in progress. Much of the work of managing Trust Reserves is carried out by Trust members voluntarily, under the guidance of the Trust's Scientific Committee, and Reserves Officer.

When visiting nature reserves, or any wild places, please respect the wildlife by leaving things undisturbed and observing the country code - remember that most animals and people enjoy these places for their quietness.

Please note that it is Trust policy for admission to all Glamorgan Wildlife Trust public access sites to be completely free of charge; if you would like further information; and wish us to maintain this service, please join the Trust.

All enquiries to the Trust Office:

Glamorgan Wildlife Trust
Glamorgan Nature Centre
Fountain Road
Tondu
Bridgend
Mid Glamorgan
CF32 0EH

Tel. (0656) 724100

Glamorgan Wildlife Trust Nature Reserves 1991

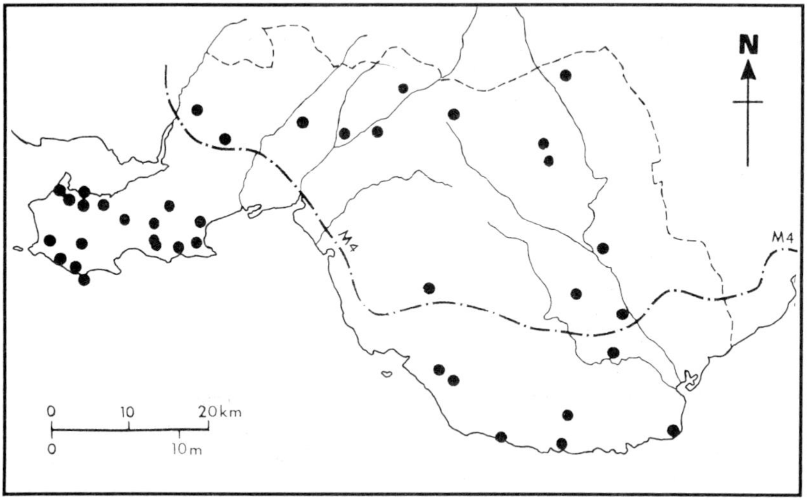

WHEN TO GO FOR WILDLIFE IN GLAMORGAN

A month by month guide to the reserves and their main features of interest

JANUARY

MID GLAMORGAN
Park Pond Wintering Birds

SOUTH GLAMORGAN
Aberthaw Saltmarsh Wintering Birds

WEST GLAMORGAN
Blaenant y gwyddyl Waterfall (after a period of rain)
Broad Pool and Bog Passage migrant birds and wintering birds of prey
Long Hole Cliff Sea watching
Melincwrt Waterfalls Waterfalls, especially after rain
Port Eynon Birdwatching for wintering divers
Sedger's Bank Wintering migratory shore birds and Grey Seals

FEBRUARY

MID GLAMORGAN
Coed y bwl Spring flowers
Park Pond Wintering Birds

WEST GLAMORGAN
Blaenant y gwyddyl Waterfall (after a period of rain)
Broad Pool and Bog Passage migrant birds and wintering birds of prey
Long Hole Cliff Sea watching
Melincwrt Waterfalls Waterfalls, especially after rain
Port Eynon Birdwatching for wintering divers
Sedger's Bank Wintering migratory shore birds and Grey Seals

MARCH

MID GLAMORGAN
Coed y bwl Spring flowers

WEST GLAMORGAN
Blaenant y gwyddyl Waterfall (after a period of rain)
Broad Pool and Bog Passage migrant birds and wintering birds of prey
Cwm Ivy Woods Woodland flowers
Long Hole Cliff Spring coastal flowers and sea watching
Lucas Reserve Spring flowers
Melincwrt Waterfalls Waterfalls, especially after rain
Overton Mere Spring coastal flowers

Port Eynon Spring coastal flowers
Priors Wood and Meadow Spring woodland flowers
Redley Cliff Spring coastal flowers
Sedger's Bank Wintering migratory shore birds and Grey Seals

APRIL

MID GLAMORGAN
Aberdare Canal Aquatic flowers and birds
Coed y bedw Woodland flowers
Coed y bwl Woodland flowers and birds
Nant Myddlin Woodland flowers and birds
Nightingale's Bush Aquatic flowers and insects
Ogmore Down Limestone grassland flowers and insects
Park Pond Aquatic flowers and insects
Taff Fechan Woodland, limestone grassland, birds and insects

SOUTH GLAMORGAN
Aberthaw Saltmarsh Spring migrant birds
Coed Garnllwyd Woodland flowers
Cwm Colhuw Spring migrant birds
Lavernock Point Spring migrant birds

WEST GLAMORGAN
Berry Wood Woodland flowers and birds
Betty Church Reserve Woodland flowers and birds
Blaenant y gwyddyl Woodland flowers
Bolgoed Quarry Woodland flowers
Broad Pool and Bog Aquatic flowers, insects and passage migrant birds
Bunker's Hill Spring flowers
Coed Gawdir Woodland and aquatic flowers
Craig Cilhendre Woodland flowers
Cwm Ivy Woods Woodland flowers
Deborah's Hole Spring coastal flowers
Elizabeth and Rowe Harding Reserve Spring flowers
Gelli Hir Wood Woodland flowers, butterflies and birds
Hambury Wood woodlland flowers and birds
Kilvrough Manor Woods Spring woodland flowers
Llanrhidian Hill Spring flowers
Long Hole Cliff Spring coastal flowers
Lucas Reserve Spring flowers
Melincwrt Waterfalls Spring woodland flowers
Overton Cliff Spring coastal flowers
Overton Mere Spring coastal flowers
Peel Wood Spring woodland flowers
Port Eynon Spring coastal flowers
Redden Hill Wood Spring woodland flowers
Redley Cliff Spring coastal flowers
Ridgewood Park Spring woodland flowers
Sedger's Bank Spring shore flowers

MAY

MID GLAMORGAN
Aberdare Canal Aquatic flowers and birds
Coed y bedw Woodland flowers and birds
Coed y bwl Woodland flowers, birds and insects
Nant Myddlin Woodland flowers and birds
Nightingale's Bush Aquatic flowers and insects
Ogmore Down Limestone grassland flowers and insects
Park Pond Aquatic flowers, birds and insects
Taf Fechan Woodland, limestone grassland, birds and insects

SOUTH GLAMORGAN
Aberthaw Saltmarsh Spring migrant birds
Coed Garnllwyd Woodland and meadow flowers, birds and insects
Cwm Colhuw Coastal and limestone flowers and insects
Lavernock Point Migrant birds, limestone grassland flowers and insects

WEST GLAMORGAN
Berry Wood Woodland flowers and birds
Betty Church Reserve Woodland and meadow flowers and birds
Blaenant y gwyddyl Woodland flowers and birds
Bolgoed Quarry Woodland flowers and birds
Broad Pool and Bog Aquatic flowers birds and insects
Bunker's Hill Spring flowers and birds
Coed Gawdir Woodland and aquatic flowers, birds and insects
Craig Cilhendre Woodland flowers, birds and insects
Cwm Ivy Woods Woodland flowers, birds and insects
Deborah's Hole Spring coastal flowers and coastal breeding birds
Elizabeth and Rowe Harding Reserve Spring flowers and breeding birds
Gelli Hir Wood Woodland flowers, butterflies and birds
Hambury Wood Woodland flowers and birds
Kilvrough Manor Woods Spring woodland flowers and breeding birds
Llanrhidian Hill Spring flowers and summer breeding birds
Llyn Fach Summer breeding birds
Long Hole Cliff Spring coastal flowers and summer breeding birds
Lucas Reserve Spring flowers and breeding birds
Melincwrt Waterfalls Spring woodland flowers and woodland birds
Overton Cliff Spring coastal flowers and breeding birds
Overton Mere Spring coastal flowers and coastal breeding birds
Peel Wood Spring woodland flowers and summer woodland birds
Port Eynon Spring coastal flowers and coastal breeding birds
Priors Wood and Meadow Spring woodland flowers and breeding birds
Redden Hill Wood Woodland flowers, birds and butterflies
Redley Cliff Spring coastal flowers and coastal breeding birds
Ridgewood Park Spring woodland flowers and suburban breeding birds
Sedger's Bank Spring shore flowers and shore breeding birds

JUNE

MID GLAMORGAN
Aberdare Canal Aquatic flowers and birds
Coed y bedw Woodland flowers and birds
Coed y bwl Woodland flowers, birds and insects
Nant Myddlin Woodland flowers and birds
Nightingale's Bush Aquatic flowers and insects
Ogmore Down Limestone grassland flowers and insects
Park Pond Aquatic flowers, birds and insects
Taf Fechan Woodland, limestone grassland, birds and insects

SOUTH GLAMORGAN
Aberthaw Saltmarsh Saltmarsh and sand dune flowers and insects
Coed Garnllwyd Woodland and meadow flowers, birds and insects
Cwm Colhuw Coastal and limestone flowers and insects
Lavernock Point Limestone grassland flowers and insects

WEST GLAMORGAN
Berry Wood Woodland flowers and birds
Betty Church Reserve Woodland and meadow flowers and birds
Blaenant y gwyddyl Woodland flowers and birds
Bolgoed Quarry Woodland flowers and birds
Bunker's Hill Spring flowers and birds
Coed Gawdir Woodland and aquatic flowers, birds and insects
Craig Cilhendre Woodland flowers, birds and insects
Cwm Ivy Woods Woodland flowers, birds and insects
Deborah's Hole Spring coastal flowers and coastal breeding birds
Elizabeth and Rowe Harding Reserve Spring flowers and breeding birds
Gelli Hir Wood Woodland flowers, butterflies and birds
Hambury Wood Woodland flowers and birds
Kilvrough Manor Spring woodland flowers and breeding birds
Llanrhidian Hill Summer breeding birds
Llyn Fach Upland flowers and breeding birds
Long Hole Cliff Spring coastal flowers and summer breeding birds
Lucas Reserve Spring flowers and breeding birds
Melincwrt Waterfalls Spring woodland flowers and woodland birds
Overton Cliff Spring coastal flowers and breeding birds
Overton Mere Spring coastal flowers and coastal breeding birds
Peel Wood Spring woodland flowers and summer woodland birds
Port Eynon Spring coastal flowers and coastal breeding birds
Priors Wood and Meadow Spring woodland flowers and breeding birds
Redden Hill Wood Woodland flowers, birds and butterflies
Redley Cliff Spring coastal flowers and coastal breeding birds
Ridgewood Park Spring woodland flowers and suburban breeding birds
Sedger's Bank Spring shore flowers and shore breeding birds

JULY

MID GLAMORGAN

Aberdare Canal Aquatic flowers and birds
Coed y bedw Woodland flowers and birds
Coed y bwl Woodland flowers, birds and insects
Nant Myddlin Woodland flowers and birds
Nightingale's Bush Aquatic flowers and insects
Ogmore Down Limestone grassland flowers and insects
Park Pond Aquatic flowers, birds and insects
Taf Fechan Woodland, limestone grassland, birds and insects

SOUTH GLAMORGAN

Aberthaw Saltmarsh Saltmarsh and sand dune flowers and insects
Coed Garnllwyd Woodland and meadow flowers, birds and insects
Cwm Colhuw Coastal and limestone flowers and insects
Lavernock Point Limestone grassland flowers and insects

WEST GLAMORGAN

Berry Wood Woodland flowers and birds
Betty Church Reserve Woodland and meadow flowers and birds
Blaenant y gwyddyl Woodland flowers and birds
Bolgoed Quarry Woodland flowers and birds
Broad Pool and Bog Aquatic flowers birds and insects
Bunker's Hill Wild flowers and birds
Coed Gawdir Woodland and aquatic flowers, birds and insects
Craig Cilhendre Woodland flowers, birds and insects
Cwm Ivy Woods Woodland flowers, birds and insects
Deborah's Hole Spring coastal flowers and coastal breeding birds
Elizabeth and Rowe Harding Reserve Breeding birds
Gelli Hir Wood Woodland flowers, butterflies and birds
Hambury Wood Woodland flowers and birds
Kilvrough Manor Woods Summer breeding birds
Llanrhidian Hill Summer breeding birds
Llyn Fach Upland flowers and breeding birds
Long Hole Cliff Summer breeding birds
Lucas Reserve Summer breeding birds
Melincwrt Waterfalls Summer woodland birds
Overton Cliff Coastal breeding birds
Overton Mere Spring coastal flowers and coastal breeding birds
Peel Wood Summer woodland birds
Port Eynon Summer coastal breeding birds and sea watching
Priors Wood and Meadow Summer breeding birds
Redden Hill Wood Summer woodland birds and butterflies
Redley Cliff Spring coastal flowers and coastal breeding birds
Ridgewood Park Suburban breeding birds
Sedger's Bank Summer shore breeding birds

AUGUST

MID GLAMORGAN
Nightingale's Bush Aquatic flowers and insects
Ogmore Down Limestone grassland flowers and insects
Park Pond Aquatic flowers, birds and insects
Taf Fechan Woodland, limestone grassland, bird s and insects

SOUTH GLAMORGAN
Aberthaw Saltmarsh Saltmarsh and sand dune flowers and migrant birds
Coed Garnllwyd Woodland/meadow birds and insects
Cwm Colhuw Coastal and limestone flowers and insects
Lavernock Point Migrant birds, limestone grassland flowers and insects

WEST GLAMORGAN
Broad Pool and Bog Aquatic flowers birds and insects
Coed Gawdir Woodland and aquatic flowers, birds and insects
Llyn Fach Upland flowers
Port Eynon Sea watching for large scale seabird movements (it is essential to be on site at day break for this activity)

SEPTEMBER

MID GLAMORGAN
Coed y bedw Woodland Fungi
Coed y bwl Woodland Fungi
Nightingale's Bush Aquatic flowers and insects
Ogmore Down Heathland flowers
Park Pond Aquatic flowers, birds and insects
Taf Fechan Autumn colours, Woodland Fungi and lower plants

SOUTH GLAMORGAN
Aberthaw Saltmarsh Autumn migrant birds and butterfly
Coed Garnllwyd Woodland fungi
Cwm Colhuw Autumn migrant birds and woodland fungi

WEST GLAMORGAN
Berry Wood Woodland Fungi
Betty Church Reserve Woodland fungi
Blaenant y gwyddyl Woodland fungi
Bolgoed Quarry Woodland fungi and lower plants
Broad Pool and Bog Passage migrant birds and wintering birds of prey
Bunker's Hill Fungi
Coed Gawdir Woodland fungi
Craig Cilhendre Woodland fungi
Cwm Ivy Woods Woodland fungi
Gelli Hir Wood Fungi
Hambury Wood Fungi
Kilvrough Manor Woods Fungi
Melincwrt Waterfalls Fungi
Peel Wood Fungi

Priors Wood and Meadow Fungi
Redden Hill Wood Fungi
Ridgewood Park Fungi
Sedger's Bank Wintering migratory shore birds and Grey Seals

OCTOBER

MID GLAMORGAN
Coed y bedw Woodland Fungi
Coed y bwl Woodland Fungi
Taf Fechan Autumn colours, Woodland Fungi and lower plants

SOUTH GLAMORGAN
Aberthaw Saltmarsh Autumn migrant birds and butterfly
Cwm Colhuw Autumn migrant birds and woodland fungi

WEST GLAMORGAN
Berry Wood Woodland Fungi
Betty Church Reserve Woodland fungi
Blaenant y gwyddyl Woodland fungi
Bolgoed Quarry Woodland fungi and lower plants
Broad Pool and Bog Passage migrant birds and wintering birds of prey
Bunker's Hill Fungi
Coed Gawdir Woodland fungi
Craig Cilhendre Woodland fungi
Cwm Ivy Woods Woodland fungi
Gelli Hir Wood Fungi
Hambury Wood Fungi
Kilvrough Manor Woods Fungi
Melincwrt Waterfalls Fungi and waterfalls, after rain
Peel Wood Fungi
Priors Wood and Meadow Fungi
Redden Hill Wood Fungi
Ridgewood Park Fungi
Sedger's Bank Wintering migratory shore birds and Grey Seals

NOVEMBER

MID GLAMORGAN
Park Pond Wintering Birds

SOUTH GLAMORGAN
Aberthaw Saltmarsh Wintering Birds
Coed Garnllwyd Woodland fungi

WEST GLAMORGAN
Betty Church Reserve Woodland fungi
Blaenant y gwyddyl Woodland fungi and waterfall (after a period of rain)
Broad Pool and Bog Passage migrant birds and wintering birds of prey
Bunker's Hill Fungi

Cwm Ivy Woods Woodland fungi
Hambury Wood Fungi
Kilvrough Manor Woods Fungi
Melincwrt Waterfalls Fungi and waterfalls after rain
Peel Wood Fungi
Priors Wood and Meadow Fungi
Redden Hill Wood Fungi
Ridgewood Park Fungi
Long Hole Cliff Sea watching
Sedger's Bank Wintering migratory shore birds and Grey seals

DECEMBER

MID GLAMORGAN
Park Pond Wintering Birds

SOUTH GLAMORGAN
Aberthaw Saltmarsh Wintering Birds

WEST GLAMORGAN
Blaenant y gwyddyl Waterfall (after a period of rain)
Broad Pool and Bog Passage migrant birds and wintering birds of prey
Long Hole Cliff Sea watching
Melincwrt Waterfalls Waterfalls, especially after rain
Sedger's Bank Wintering migratory shore birds and Grey seals

USING THIS BOOK

This book has been carefully planned for easy use; the reserves are listed alphabetically under each county. At the end of each county section there are a few blank pages for notes and information about new reserves. The text and the map for each site are arranged for ease of reference.

Each reserve is described by its area, nearest towns, location and access, description and management. Months when wildflowers can be expected to be in bloom are indicated by the month numbers in brackets, e.g. Ragged-Robin (5-7). Reserve maps show boundaries, where to enter the reserves, the main footpaths and habitats.

Grid references

The locations of the reserves are given as grid references on the relevant Ordnance Survey 1: 50,000 scale Landranger Series maps. The reserves can be located by using the six figure grid reference number given for each site; in case you are unfamiliar with this reference system it is explained below:

E.g. ST 068 856

1. The first two numbers represent the vertical lines on the map within the square indicated by the letters.
2. The 4th and 5th numbers represent the horizontal position on your map.
3. Each vertical and horizontal line is numbered at the edge of the map. To use the reference, find the intersection of the lines in (1) and (2). Imagine a letter 'L'; the reserve will be in the square bounded by the L.
4. The 3rd and 6th numbers represent 1/10 marks between the whole numbers of each line and can be used to pinpoint a precise location within the square. E.g. for ST 068 865 the point is 8/10 between 06 and 07 and 6/10 between 85 and 86.

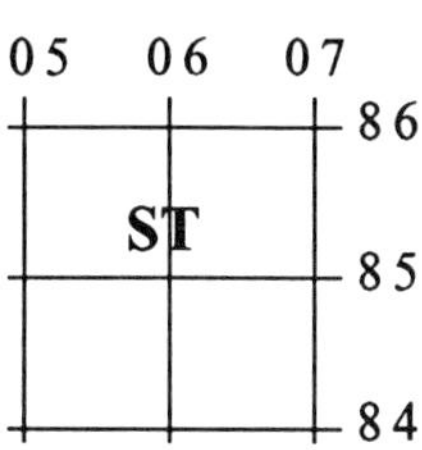

Abbreviations and Name Changes

FC	Forestry Commission
MGCC	Mid Glamorgan County Council
NCC	Nature Conservancy Council, now the Countryside Council for Wales
OS	Ordnance Survey
RSNC	Royal Society for Nature Conservation, formerly the Society for the Promotion of Nature Reserves (SPNR)
SGCC	South Glamorgan County Council
SSSI	Site of Special Scientific Interest
WWF	World Wide Fund for Nature, formerly the World Wildlife Fund

MID GLAMORGAN NATURE RESERVES

Aberdare Canal

Coed y Bedw

Coed y Bwl

Nant Myddlin

Nightingale's Bush

Ogmore Down

Parc Slip Nature Park

Park Pond Nature Reserve

Pwll waun Cynon

Taf Fechan

ABERDARE CANAL

Cwmbach, Aberdare

OS Sheet 170; SO 013024

Disused canal and wet woodland. Area 2.96 ha (7.3 acres). Acquired July 1979; under leasehold for 5 years from 1989. Managed by Mid Area Committee.

Location

1 km south-east of Aberdare town centre, and 1 km north-west of Cwmbach. Access is via the A4059 (Canal Road) and by turning onto a Public Footpath 50 m north of the Aberdare filling station. This footpath runs alongside the old towpath of the Canal.

Description

The reserve forms the end of the old Aberdare Canal, which is a side branch of the Glamorgan Canal which runs from Merthyr to Cardiff. The reserve can be divided into two sections, the northern and southern ends.

At the northern end there is about 150 m of canal, which was re-excavated in 1973. This involved the walls being built up to form a rectangular section of open water, 10 m wide and approximately 3 m deep. A variety of aquatic plants are present, including an area of Great Reedmace (6-7) and a large quantity of Curled Pondweed (5-10). Alongside this is a water-logged grass sward in which several Sycamores have been planted. Grey Heron and Moorhen have been sighted.

At the southern end there is a concrete dam and culvert leading to the unrenovated part of the canal, which stretches a further 350 m. Here a channel has been cleared and a bank thrown up in the old Canal on which a number of large willows grow. The water is approximately 1 m across and 0.2 - 0.7 m deep, is fairly stagnant and contains a typical community of aquatic plants. Beyond the old canal bank is a strip of woodland running the length of the unrenovated section, with four inlets of apparently fresh water. Willows grow in the water in some parts of the canal, and from the towpath wall. Japanese Knotweed (8-9) is present in a few clumps. Alongside the towpath is a hedge containing standard trees.

The invertebrate population in the reserve is varied, and includes a large number of wandering snails. Fish include sticklebacks. There are several items of industrial archaeological interest including, adjacent to the renovated northern section, the remains of a derrick used for the loading and unloading of barges, and at the southern end of the reserve, a fine old bridge supporting a disused railway line.

Management Objectives

To maintain the area of open water within the canal and the wooded areas along the bank. Also to maintain the features of industrial archaeological interest and to cut back obstructing vegetation, particularly the Japanese Knotweed, from the immediate vicinity.

ABERDARE CANAL

OS Sheet 170; SO 013024

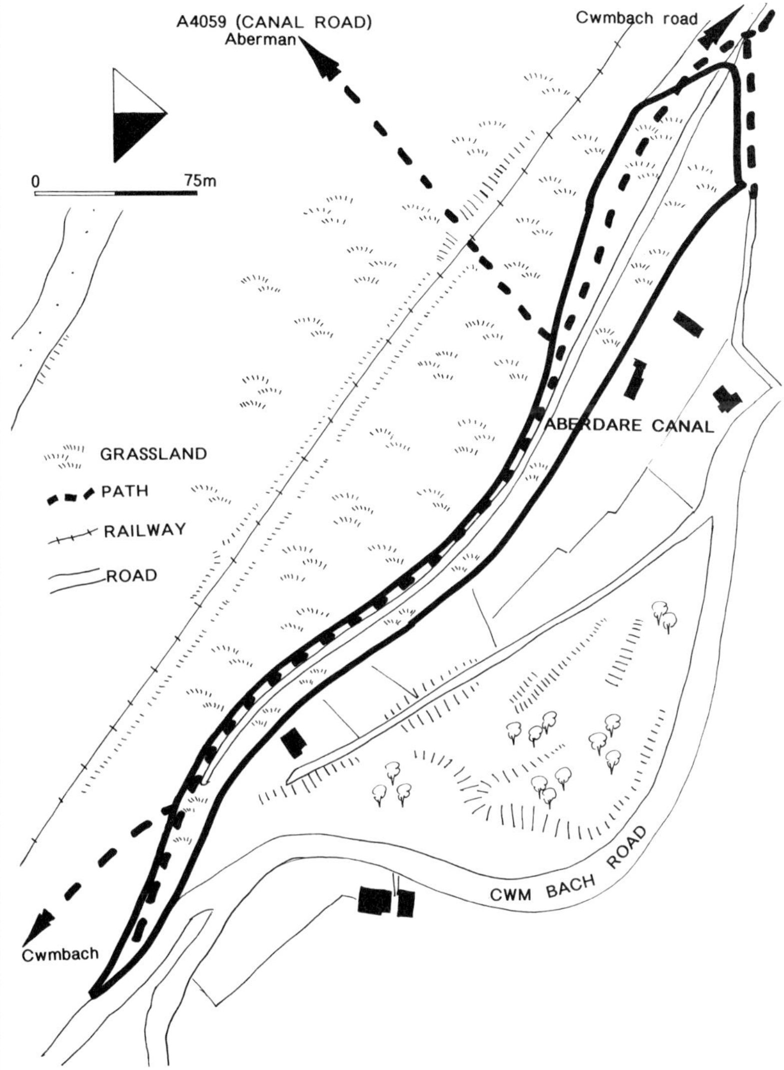

Good times to visit
April - July Aquatic flowers and birds

Nearest Reserves
Llyn Fach, West Glamorgan 11 km; *Nightingale's Bush, Mid Glamorgan* 14 km; *Pwll waun Cynon, Mid Glamorgan* 3 km; *Taf Fechan, Mid Glamorgan* 6.5 km

COED Y BEDW

Pentyrch

OS Sheet 171; ST 111827

Ancient wet broadleaved woodland, on the boundary between acidic and lime-rich soils, notified as an SSSI. Area 16.6 ha (41 acres). This reserve was acquired by leasehold for sixteen years in October 1968 and was then purchased from the Forestry Commission in 1984, with the help of grant aid and donations from the Countryside Commission, the Joseph Frazier Memorial Fund, Dr Mary Gillham, the Glamorgan Watch Club, the National Heritage Memorial Fund, NCC, Pentyrch Community Council, WWF and the Welsh Water Authority. Part of the site is under agreement with private owners. Managed by South Area Committee.

Location
3 km north-west of Cardiff. The reserve can be reached from the west via the Llantrisant road (A4119) and minor roads to Pentyrch, or from the east via the Taff's Well junction of the A470T Cardiff to Merthyr Tydfil trunk road, north of the M4. Take the Pentyrch Road over Ynys Bridge and turn right at the roundabout to Heol Berri Green, Gwaelod-y-Garth.

Description
Coed y bedw consists of a fine broadleaved woodland grading from wet oak/birch in the east to drier Beechwood in the west, with Ash locally dominant on the Carboniferous Limestone areas to the south. Much of the site occupies a steep north-facing slope, following the Garth Hill Coal Measures and the Carboniferous Limestone of Little Garth.

Two lime-rich springs arise in the south-west of the site and join an acidic stream, Nant Cwmllwydrew, flowing eastward along the valley floor. This mixture of acidic and lime-rich waters in the drainage system supports an interesting assemblage of aquatic invertebrates, including a number of rare species.

In the wet valley bottom, stands of Great Horsetail (4) are found in three areas, amongst the best to be found in the district. The herb layer is dominated in spring by Ramsons (4-6) on the lime-rich soils, and by Bluebell (4-6) on the acidic soils.

There is a great diversity of resident woodland birds including Tawny Owl, Nuthatch, Great Spotted Woodpecker and Treecreeper, which are augmented in summer by Pied Flycatcher, Redstart, Willow Warbler and Blackcap.

Management Objectives
The management objective is to conserve the character and diversity of the woodland and streams. This has been helped by major management projects including the renewal of fencing along the north and western boundaries to prevent sheep grazing in the woodland. A circular pathway has been created for visitors.

COED Y BEDW

OS Sheet 171; ST 111827

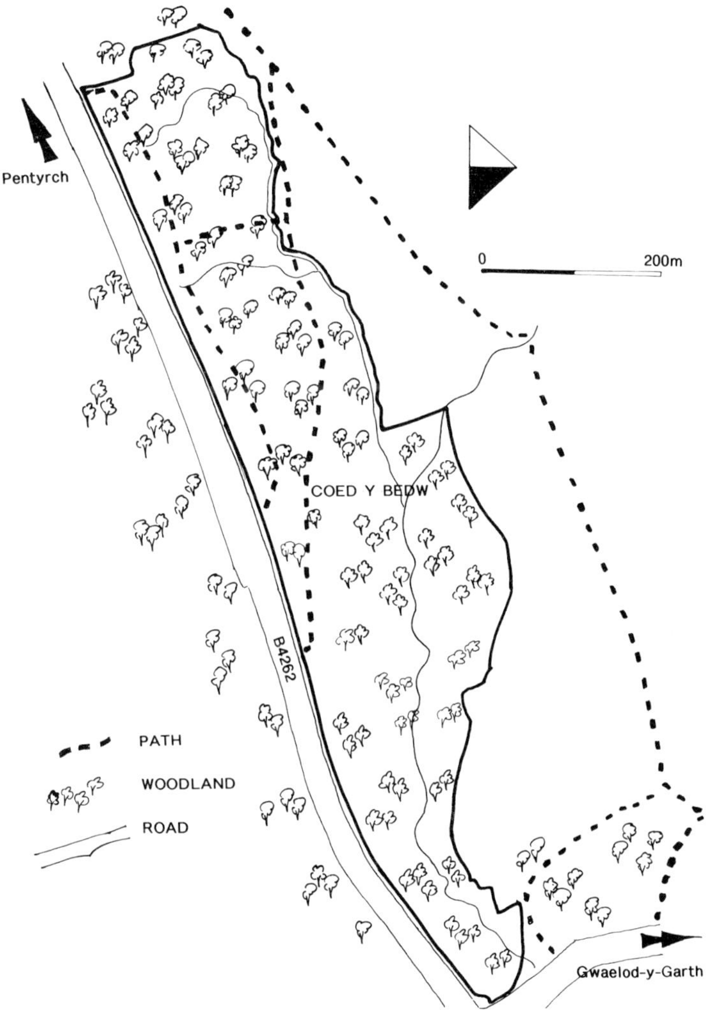

Good times to visit

April - June Woodland flowers; *May - July* Woodland birds; *September - October* Fungi

Nearest Reserves

Gwern Rhyd, South Glamorgan 6 km; *Coed Garnllwyd, South Glamorgan* 13 km; *Nightingale's Bush, Mid Glamorgan* 8 km; *Nant Myddlin, Mid Glamorgan* 5 km

COED Y BWL

Castle upon Alun

OS Sheet 170; SS 909751

Ancient broadleaved woodland on limestone soils, forming part of the Alun Valley SSSI. Area 2.4 ha (5.9 acres). The reserve was acquired in December 1970 by leasehold for 21 years. Managed by the Mid Area Committee.

Location

1 km east of St. Brides Major, 3 km south of Bridgend. The reserve can be reached by minor roads leading north into the Alun Valley via the B4265 from St. Brides Major to Wick.

Description

Coed y Bwl is an ancient deciduous woodland situated on the north-west side of the Alun Valley and overlies the Carboniferous Limestone. The wood is dominated by Elm at the southern end, grading into Ash towards the north, with an understorey of Field Maple. Since the decline in Elm due to Dutch Elm disease, the south end of the reserve has been opened up and replanted with Ash and Field Maple.

The reserve is best known as a Wild Daffodil (2-4) wood, with these flowers dominating the field layer of the southern part of the wood in early spring, whilst Bluebells (4-6) predominate on the northern slopes.

The reserve supports a range of common woodland birds including Nuthatch, Treecreeper, Blue Tit and Great Tit, Willow Warbler and Chiffchaff.

Management Objectives

To replant and maintain the woodland as high forest and conserve the Wild Daffodil population.

Wild Daffodil

COED Y BWL

OS Sheet 170; SS 909751

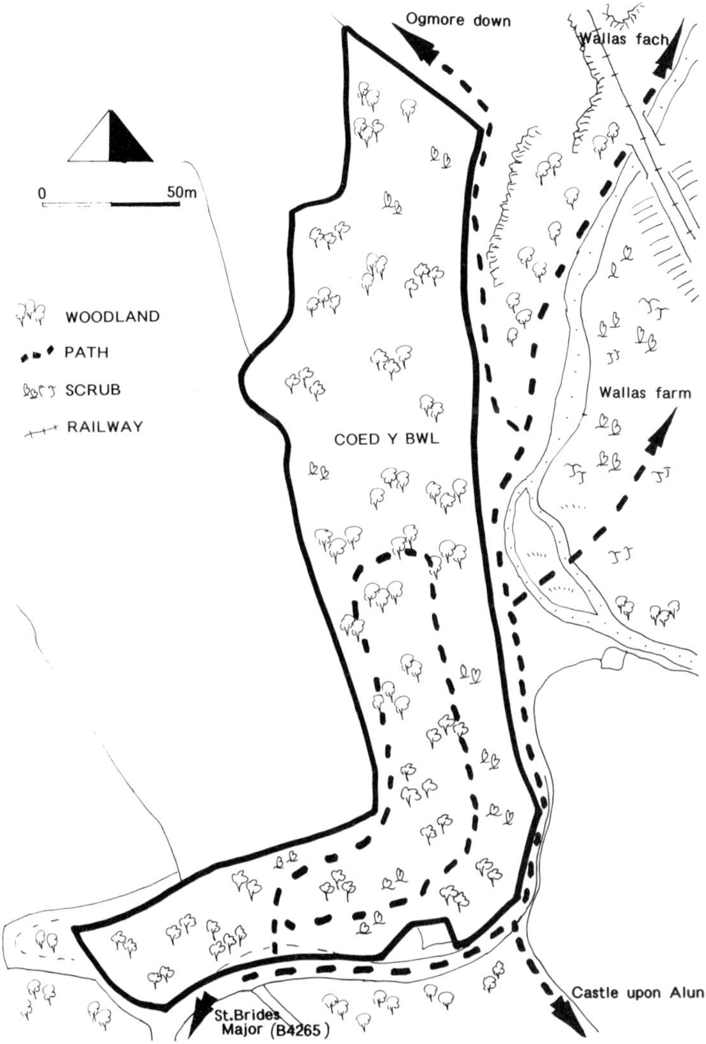

Good times to visit
February - March Wild Daffodils; *April - July* Woodland flowers and butterflies; *September - October* Fungi

Nearest Reserves
Cwm Colhuw, South Glamorgan 9.5 km; *Ogmore Down, South Glamorgan* 2 km; *Park Pond, Mid Glamorgan* 9.5 km; *Parc Slip Nature Park, Mid Glamorgan* 9.5 km

NANT MYDDLIN

Llantwit Fardre

OS Sheet 170; ST 068850

Secondary acidic woodland and stream. Area 4.9 ha (12 acres). Acquired February 1980 by annual Agreement. Management by Mid Area Committee.

Location
2.5 km north-east of Llantrisant, between Beddau and Llantwit Fardre. The reserve's southern boundary borders the A4058 on the western outskirts of Llantwit Fardre, the eastern boundary is the B4595, signposted to Beddau.

Description
Nant Myddlin consists of broadleaved semi-natural woodland, part of which has been cleared for coal mining and allowed to regenerate naturally on either side of the Nant Myddlin. The reserve also includes part of a disused railway line. The canopy is made up of Oak, Ash, Birch and Rowan, with Alder and Willows occurring on the wetter soils close to the stream. There is an understorey of Hazel, Holly, Dogwood and Hawthorn with Honeysuckle (6-9), Ivy and Dog Rose (6-7).

The streamside herb layer is characterised by Marsh-marigold (3-5) and Water Mint (7-10), with some areas of rushes and Common Reed (8-9).

The reserve is visited by a range of woodland birds such as Tawny Owl, Jay, Nuthatch and Coal Tit, with Woodcock in winter.

Management Objectives
To maintain as woodland high forest.

Woodcock

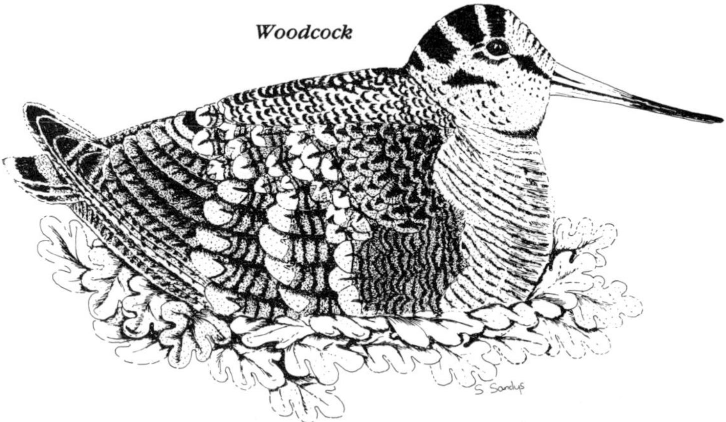

NANT MYDDLIN

OS Sheet 170; ST 068850

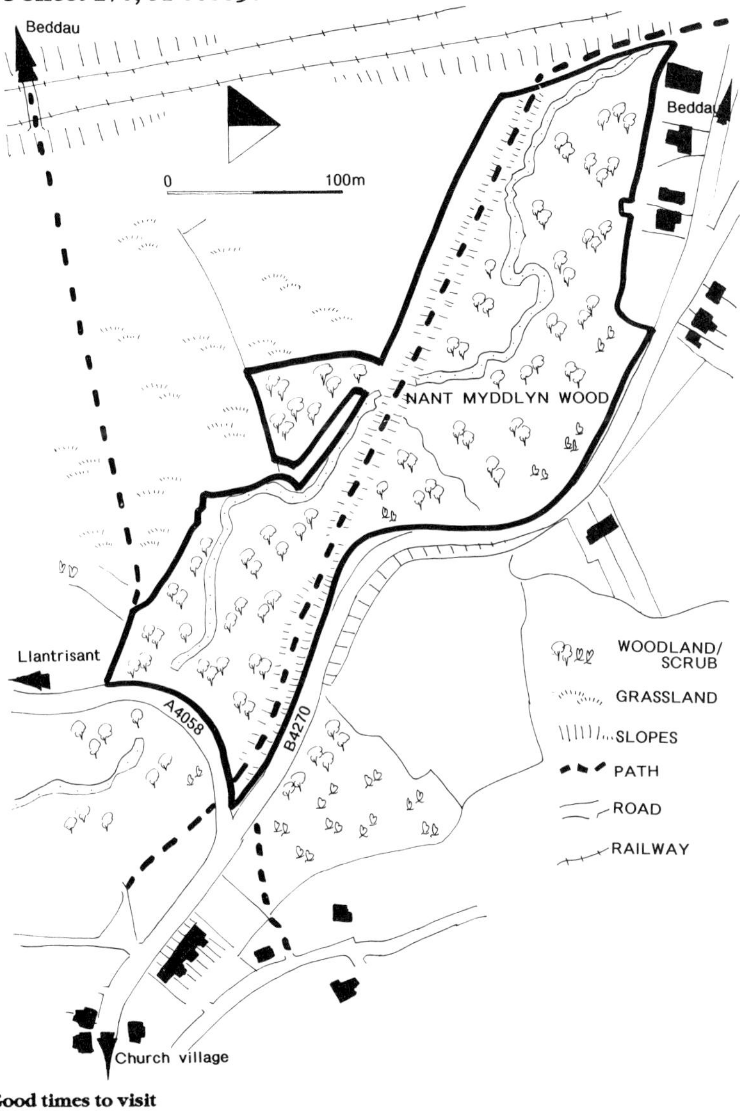

Good times to visit
April - July Woodland flowers and birds

Nearest Reserves
Coed Garnllwyd, South Glamorgan 13.5 km; *Coed y Bedw, Mid Glamorgan* 4.5 km; *Gwern Rhyd, Mid Glamorgan* 8.5 km; *Nightingale's Bush, Mid Glamorgan* 5.5 km

NIGHTINGALE'S BUSH

Pontypridd

OS Sheet 170; ST 081899

Disused canal. Area 0.3 ha (0.65 acres). Acquired April 1974. Owned by the Glamorgan Wildlife Trust. Managed by Mid Area Committee.

Location
Nightingale's Bush consists of a 200 m stretch of disused canal, towpath and bank, lying between Abercynon and Tongwynlais. This section of the canal is the only part which escaped destruction when the A470 trunk road was constructed in the early 1970s.

Description
The canal is about 3 m wide and 0.5 m deep, containing slow-moving water. On its western side is the towpath, and on the eastern bank occupying a steep slope, is a narrow strip of willow scrub, with Grey Willow, Osier, Sycamore and Guelder-rose (6-7). The water supports an assemblage of aquatic plants with stands of Arrowhead (7-8), a rare species in Wales.

Management Objectives
To maintain the canal as an open water aquatic habitat.

Arrowhead

NIGHTINGALE'S BUSH

OS Sheet 170; ST 081899

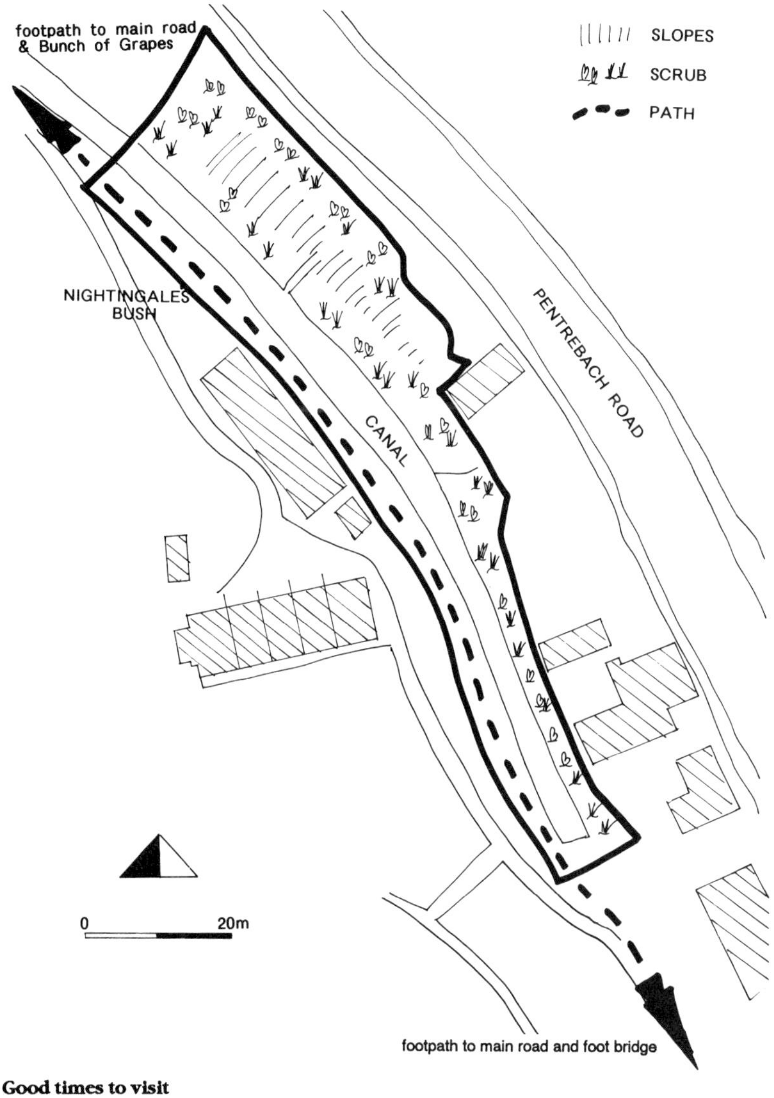

Good times to visit

April - September Aquatic flowers and insects

Nearest Reserves

Coed y Bedw, Mid Glamorgan 8 km; *Gwern Rhyd, South Glamorgan* 13 km; *Nant Myddlin, Mid Glamorgan* 5.5 km; *Pwll waun Cynon, Mid Glamorgan* 13 km

OGMORE DOWN

Ewenny

OS Sheet 170; SS 894763

Limestone grassland, heath and gorse scrub, forming part of Old Castle Down SSSI. Area 26.5 ha (65.5 acres). The reserve was acquired in September 1975, and since 1989 has been under a 5 year licence. Registered Common Land. Managed by Mid Area Committee.

Location
On the west side of the B4265 between Ewenny and St. Brides Major, between two limestone quarries.

Description
Ogmore Down occupies part of a plateau and steep east-facing slope of Carboniferous Limestone. A limestone heath occupies the thinner soils of the upper slopes whilst the deeper more acidic plateau soils bear Gorse/Heather heath. Limestone heath is uncommon, being composed of a mixture of lime-loving plants such as the Common Rock-rose (5-9) and Lady's Bedstraw (7-8) together with lime-hating plants such as Cross-leaved Heath (6-9) and Tormentil (6-9). This site forms part of a complex which represents one of the largest remaining areas of this vegetation in western Britain. Mountain Everlasting (6-7) is present on the reserve and the rare Soft-leaved Sedge (5) occurs close by.

The Gorse and grass-heath provide nesting sites for Stonechat, Skylark and Yellowhammer. Kestrels hunt along the dry valley frequently.

The reserve is one of the last few sites in Glamorgan where Glow-worms are found.

Management Objectives
To maintain the limestone pasture and heath.

Stonechat

OGMORE DOWN

OS Sheet 170; SS 894763

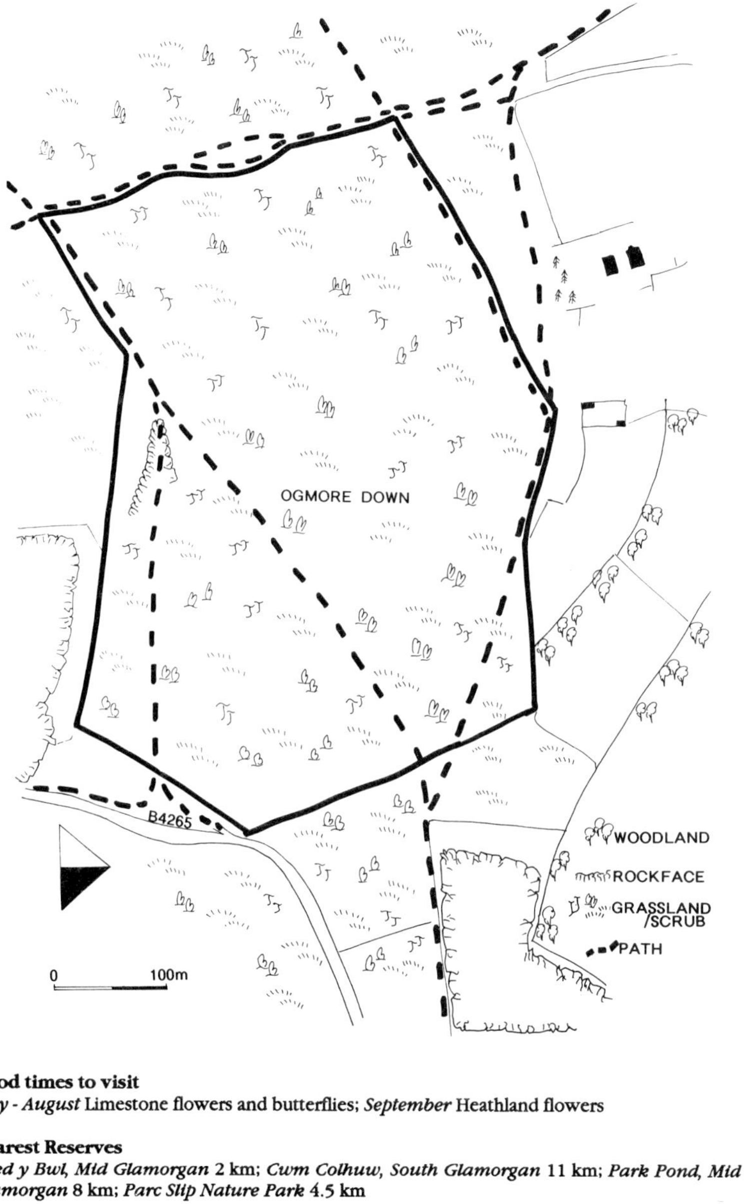

Good times to visit
May - August Limestone flowers and butterflies; *September* Heathland flowers

Nearest Reserves
Coed y Bwl, Mid Glamorgan 2 km; *Cwm Colhuw, South Glamorgan* 11 km; *Park Pond, Mid Glamorgan* 8 km; *Parc Slip Nature Park* 4.5 km

PARC SLIP NATURE PARK

Aberkenfig

OS Sheet 170; SS 880840

Parc Slip Colliery and Opencast Mine under restoration. Area 100 ha (247 acres). Acquired January 1990 under agreement with British Coal Opencast. Managed by British Coal Opencast South Wales Region and Glamorgan Wildlife Trust.

Location
1 km west of Aberkenfig, adjacent to the south of the Glamorgan Wildlife Trust's headquarters at the Glamorgan Nature Centre.

Description
Parc Slip Nature Park is a valley bottom area on the watershed between the Ogmore and Afon Kenfig catchment, which has had a history of mining from the Nineteenth century to the present day. Restoration of the landform from colliery coal tips and recent opencast coal mining had been completed by the late 1980s and a five year plan is presently being undertaken to enhance natural succession and recreate semi-natural habitats, such as wildflower grassland, ponds, marshes and a scrape, and broadleaved woodland.

The Park is made up of young planted broadleaved and coniferous woodland, improved grassland, and four flower rich fields which are being managed as pasture and as hay meadows. The grassland areas provide feeding for snipe in winter, and nesting ground for lapwing in summer.

There are three bird hides, with access for disabled people, overlooking two wetland sites: one a wader scrape and the Northern Wetland, a small lake with an island. A further three wetland and open water areas add further interest.

An illustrated leaflet for the Nature Park is available from the Glamorgan Wildlife Trust headquarters on request.

Management Objectives
To continue to undertake restoration and re-creation management techniques to conserve and enhance the habitats present within the nature park.

PARC SLIP NATURE PARK

OS Sheet 170; SS 880840

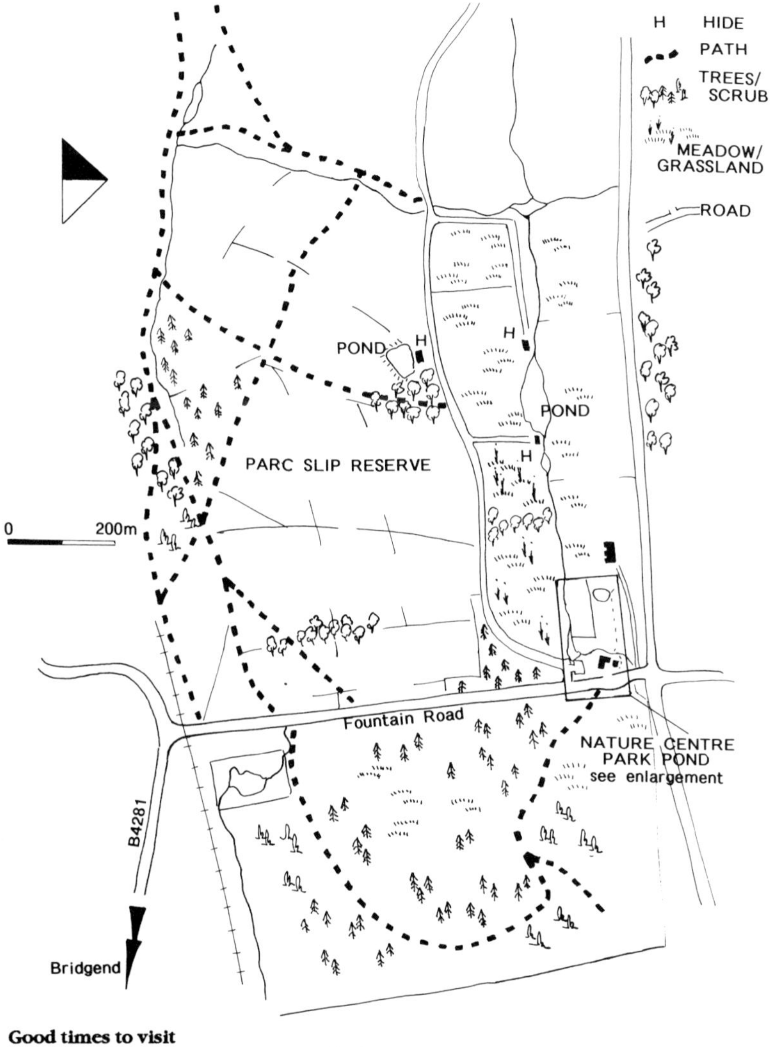

Good times to visit

February - April Spring passage migrant birds; *April - September* Aquatic and marsh flowers and dragonflies; *May - July* Meadow flowers and butterflies; *August - October* Autumn passage migrant birds; *November - February* Wintering birds

Nearest Reserves

Coed y Bwl, Mid Glamorgan 9 km; *Ogmore Down, Mid Glamorgan* 8 km; *Park Pond, Mid Glamorgan* 100 m

PARK POND NATURE RESERVE

Tondu

OS Sheet 170; SS 880844

Small acidic woodland, pond and freshwater marsh. Area 0.631 ha (1.6 acres). The reserve was purchased by the Trust from British Coal Opencast in 1977. Managed by Mid Area Committee.

Location

Adjacent to the Glamorgan Nature Centre which lies 3 km north-east of Cefn Cribbwr and 1.5 km west of Tondu. Cars may be parked at the Glamorgan Nature Centre car park. The reserve is reached from either of the paths from the north-west side of the car park to the bridge, where the left hand route provides access to the bird hide and the right to the boardwalk which provides easy access across the marsh to the open water.

Description

Park Pond is thought to have been built as a brickworks millpond in the 1920s. At the time the Trust acquired the reserve, succession had turned the pond into marsh. With the help of Shand Ltd coal contractors, a pond was dug out in the south-west corner of the reserve. Others habitats include a stream, willow carr, a small area of coppice-with-standards woodland and overgrown hedgebank.

The reserve's varied habitats support a diverse flora ranging from Water Plantain (6-8), Creeping Willow (4-5), Common Fleabane (8-9) and Marsh-Orchids (6-8) in the wetland, to Bluebell (4-6), Honeysuckle (6-9), Zig-zag Clover (6-9) and Meadow Vetchling (5-8) to be found in the woodland and damp grassland.

Trees and shrubs include Oak, Ash, Alder, Willows, Hawthorn and Elder which provide cover, food and breeding places for birds such as Wren, Long-tailed Tit, Willow Tit, Bullfinch, Green Woodpecker and Nuthatch. On the marsh and pond, Moorhen, Reed Bunting and Mallard may be seen, all of which breed amongst the sedges and willows. Water Rail, Snipe and the occasional Grey Heron are regular winter visitors.

The wetland provides a locally important amphibian breeding site for Common Frog, Smooth Newt and Great Crested Newt.

Numerous invertebrates have been recorded on the reserve including ten species of dragonflies and damselflies such as the Broad-bodied Chaser and Emerald Damsel and twenty species of butterfly including Brimstone, Orange Tip, Grayling and Meadow Brown.

Management Objectives

Management mainly involves the control of marsh succession by removing encroaching willows and sedges, and clearing silt and invasive aquatic plants from the pond. The diversity of the ground flora is encouraged by annual clearance of scrub and coarse grasses. Water levels of the marsh and pond are maintained by a sluice outlet.

PARK POND NATURE RESERVE

OS Sheet 170; SS 880844

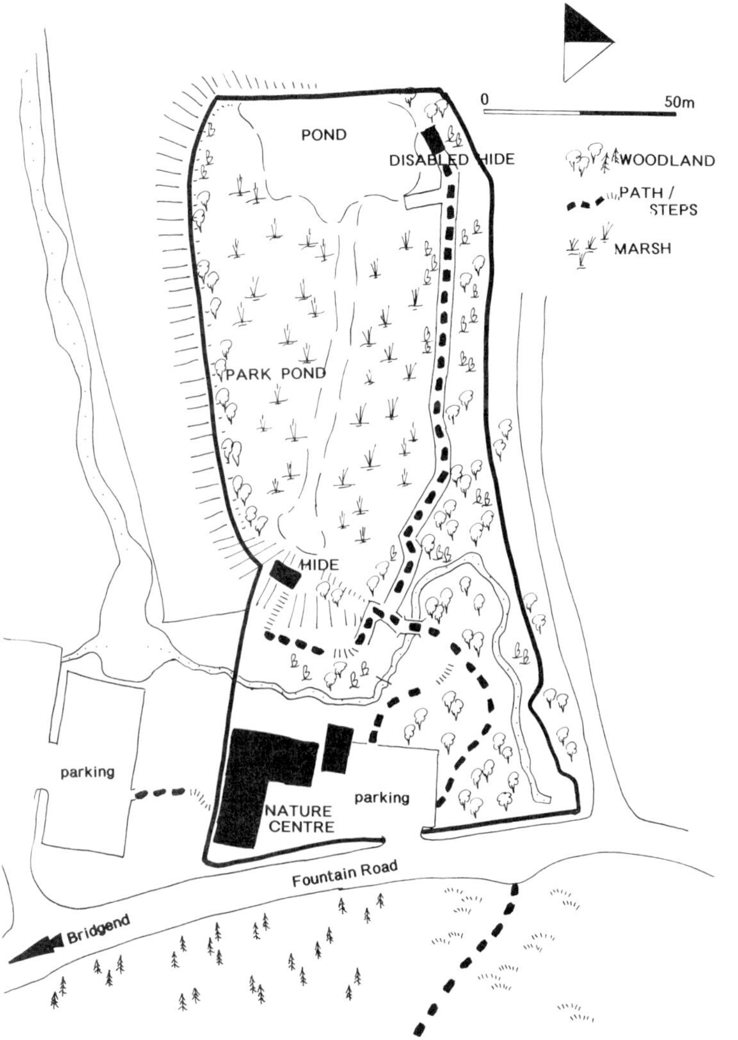

Good times to visit

April - September Aquatic and marsh flowers and dragonflies; *May - July* Woodland and wetland birds; *November - February* Wintering birds

Nearest Reserves

Coed-y-Bwl, Mid Glamorgan 9 km; *Ogmore Down, Mid Glamorgan* 8 km; *Parc Slip Nature Park, Mid Glamorgan* 100 m

PWLL WAUN CYNON

Mountain Ash

OS Sheet 170; ST 034997

Pond, meadow, scrub and acidic woodland. Area 7.2 ha (17.8 acres). Pwll waun Cynon was generously given to the Trust by Lord Aberdare in November 1986. Managed by Mid Area Committee.

Location
1 km north-west of Mountain Ash. The reserve is situated between the A4059 Aberdare to Mountain Ash road and the A4224 Aberaman to Mountain Ash road, south of the River Cynon, and is bisected by a railway line. Access can be obtained from a public footpath which crosses the reserve from the A4059 opposite the school to the A4224.

Description
The site has a selection of habitats including a large pond, marsh, flood meadow, Oak and Ash woodland and scrub.

The reserve is situated in an area that had previously been known as one of the most polluted parts of the UK in the days of the infamous Phurnacite plant. After the plant finally closed in the late 1980s the pond and surrounding area completely recovered and now support an impressive selection of water birds including breeding Little Grebe and Moorhen with a Sand Martin colony close by. Regular visitors include Kingfisher, Grey Heron, Common Sandpiper and many other species.

The pond also has several regionally rare flowering plants, including Fat Duckweed (6-7), Water Chickweed (7-8), Marsh Yellow-cress (6-9), Greater Pond-sedge (5-6) and Common Club-rush (6-7).

Management Objectives
To maintain the aquatic variety of the pond and surrounding area. To restore the flood meadow by winter grazing.

Moorhen

PWLL WAUN CYNON

OS Sheet 170; ST 034997

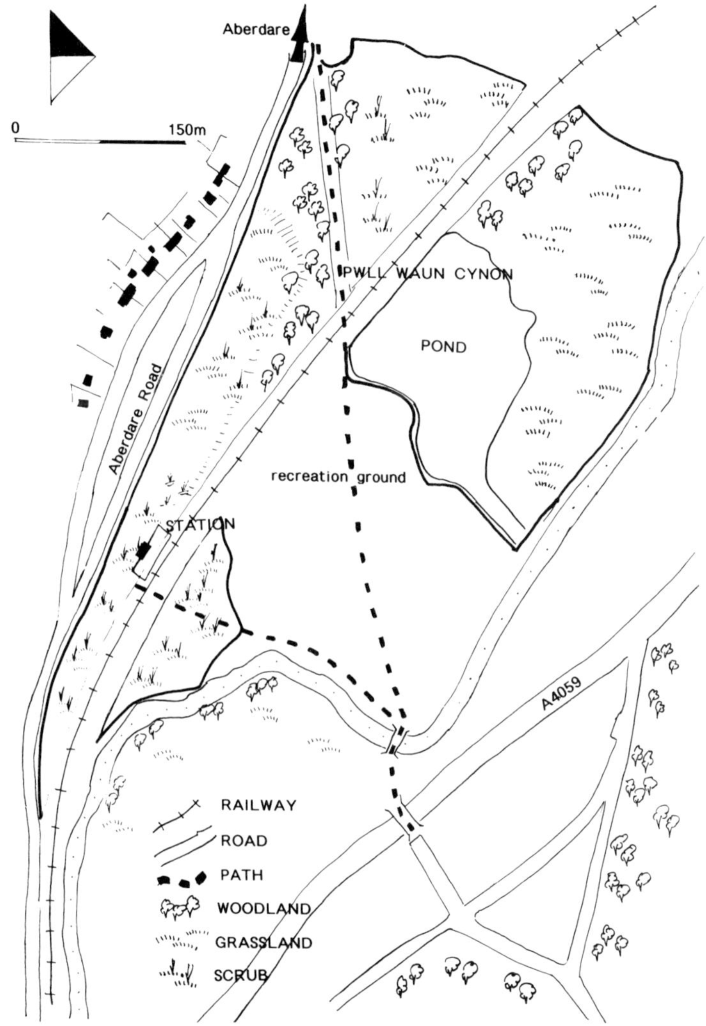

Good times to visit
May - August Meadow flowers and butterflies

Nearest Reserves
Aberdare Canal, Mid Glamorgan 3 km; *Llyn Fach, West Glamorgan* 14 km; *Nightingale's Bush, Mid Glamorgan* 11 km; *Taf Fechan, Mid Glamorgan* 10 km

TAF FECHAN

Merthyr Tydfil

OS Sheet 160; SO 035085

Ancient limestone broadleaved woodland, grassland and river. Area 42 ha (102.5 acres). The reserve is designated as an SSSI and a Local Nature Reserve and was acquired in February 1975 under leasehold for 99 years. Managed by Mid Area Committee and Merthyr Tydfil Borough Council.

Location
Situated in the Taf Fechan Valley, between the Old River Bridge at Cefn Coed y Cymmer and the river bridge at Pontsarn, about 2.5 km north-west of Merthyr Tydfil. Access can be gained from two places, at the southern end of the reserve at Cefn Coed bridge (SO 037076) and at the northern end by Pontsarn bridge at the new car park and picnic site near the Blue Pool (SO 045097).

Description
The Taf Fechan nature reserve comprises about 2.5 km of winding river with steep valley sides of Carboniferous Limestone. In some places, the limestone shows interesting potholing features. It comprises a mosaic of deciduous woodland on the slopes with a canopy made up of Beech, Birch and Ash, giving way to Alder and Grey Willow closer to the river, together with Hawthorn scrub, limestone grassland and heath, cliff and wet flushes. The valley is one of the richest sites for mosses and liverworts in Glamorgan.

The area of limestone grassland to the south on the eastern bank of the river is particularly rich in lime-loving flowers such as Wild Thyme (5-8), Rough Hawkbit (6-9) and Mouse-ear Hawkweed (5-8). On the western bank, the limestone is overlain by acidic soils where Birch, Bracken, Heather (7-9) and Small Scabious (7-9) occur.

The woodland attracts a variety of birds such as Tawny Owl, Buzzard, Jay, Great Spotted Woodpecker and Nuthatch, while Dipper and Yellow Wagtail are frequently seen on the river.

Of archaeological interest are an old tramway to Cyfarthfa Ironworks on the eastern side of the river, a feeder canal to Cyfarthfa Lake and the remains of disused fulling and corn mills.

Management Objectives
To conserve the area in as natural a state as possible, to allow natural development to take place whilst maintaining specific habitats for flora and fauna, and to extend the recreational and educational use as far as this is compatible with conservation.

TAF FECHAN

OS Sheet 160; SO 035085

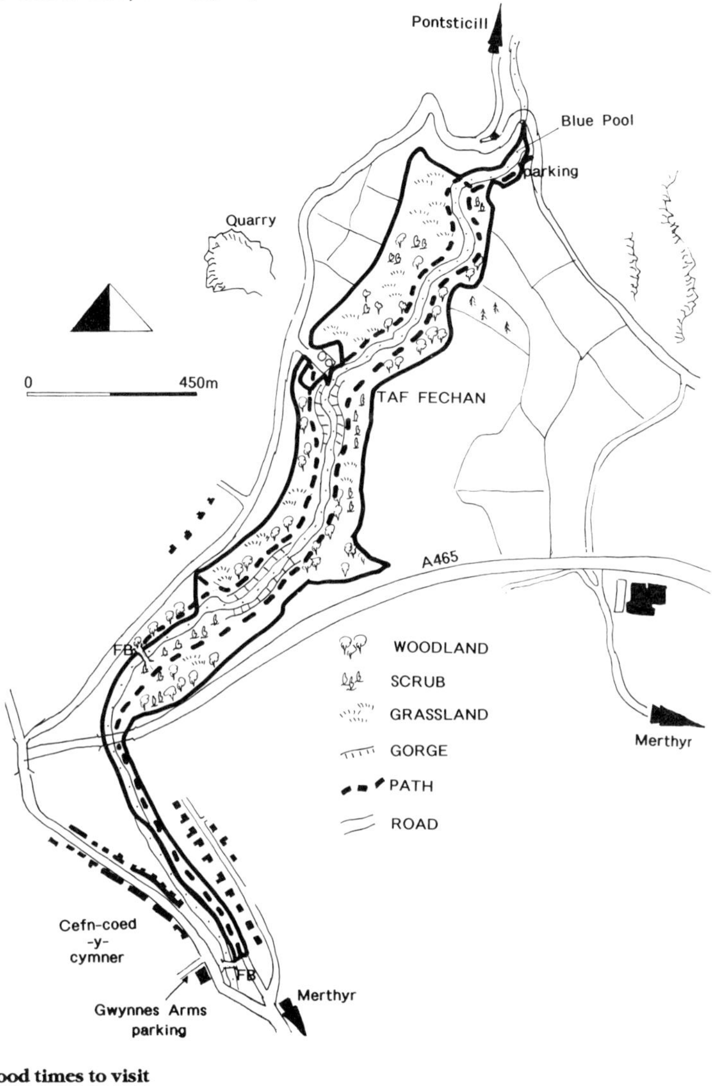

Good times to visit

April - August Woodland and limestone grassland flowers birds and insects; *September - October* Autumn colours, woodland fungi and lower plants

Nearest Reserves

Aberdare Canal, Mid Glamorgan 6.5 km; *Llyn Fach, West Glamorgan* 14.5 km; *Blaenant y Gwyddyl, West Glamorgan* 16 km; *Pwll waun Cynon, Mid Glamorgan* 9 km

SOUTH GLAMORGAN NATURE RESERVES

Aberthaw Saltmarsh

Coed Garnllwyd

Cwm Colhuw

Lavernock Point

PERMIT ONLY

Coed Llwyn Rhyddid

Gwern Rhyd Reserve

ABERTHAW SALTMARSH

Rhoose

OS Sheet 170; ST 043659

Cliffs, saltmarsh, sand dune and pebble beach, forming part of the East Aberthaw Coast SSSI. Area 36.3 ha (89.7 acres). The reserve was acquired in November 1980 and is presently under annual Licence from National Power. Managed by South Area Committee.

Location
0.5 km south-east of East Aberthaw and 0.5 km east of the Aberthaw A and B power stations. Access is from the B4265 road between Rhoose and East Aberthaw. There is a lay-by (ST 038663) for parking on the seaward side of the road. The reserve can be reached on foot over the railway bridge and down a hill, turning left along a footpath past a disused lime works to the sea wall. Some steps over the sea wall provide immediate access to the reserve.

Description
The seaward edge of the reserve is bounded by a storm beach of pebbles and shingle which protects it from the sea. At the eastern end of the reserve this storm beach converges with an inner pebble beach, on which some common shingle plants can be found, such as Yellow Horned-poppy (6-9). In the lee of the storm beach, a small saltmarsh has developed, which supports many species of salt-tolerant plants, including various coastal grasses.

Where the two pebble beaches converge, there is a small relict sand dune system, which contains Sea Holly (7-9). The 20 m high cliffs to the rear and towards the western end of the reserve support extensive scrub vegetation grading into maritime grassland at the base. Species present include Stinking Iris (5-7) and the occasional Teasel (7-8). On certain very steep parts of the cliff, Maidenhair Fern (5-8) and Water Figwort (6-9) can be found.

The reserve is one of the premier bird sites in Glamorgan, especially for spring and autumn passage. Large numbers of Whimbrel pass through in late April and early May. Little-ringed Plover and Turtle Dove have been recorded together with the usual movements of migrating passerines. Autumn is good for waders on passage, and Redshank, Turnstone and Ringed Plover are normally present all year. Regular wintering birds include Merlin, Peregrine and Grey Plover. The adjacent brackish pools, outside the reserve, but overlooked by the public footpath, are an important wintering site for wildfowl and Little Grebe.

The reserve supports a large population of Slow-worms and Adders, and has a rich and varied invertebrate community.

Management Objectives
To maintain the diversity of wildlife habitats and their associated flora and fauna.

ABERTHAW SALTMARSH

OS Sheet 170; ST 043659

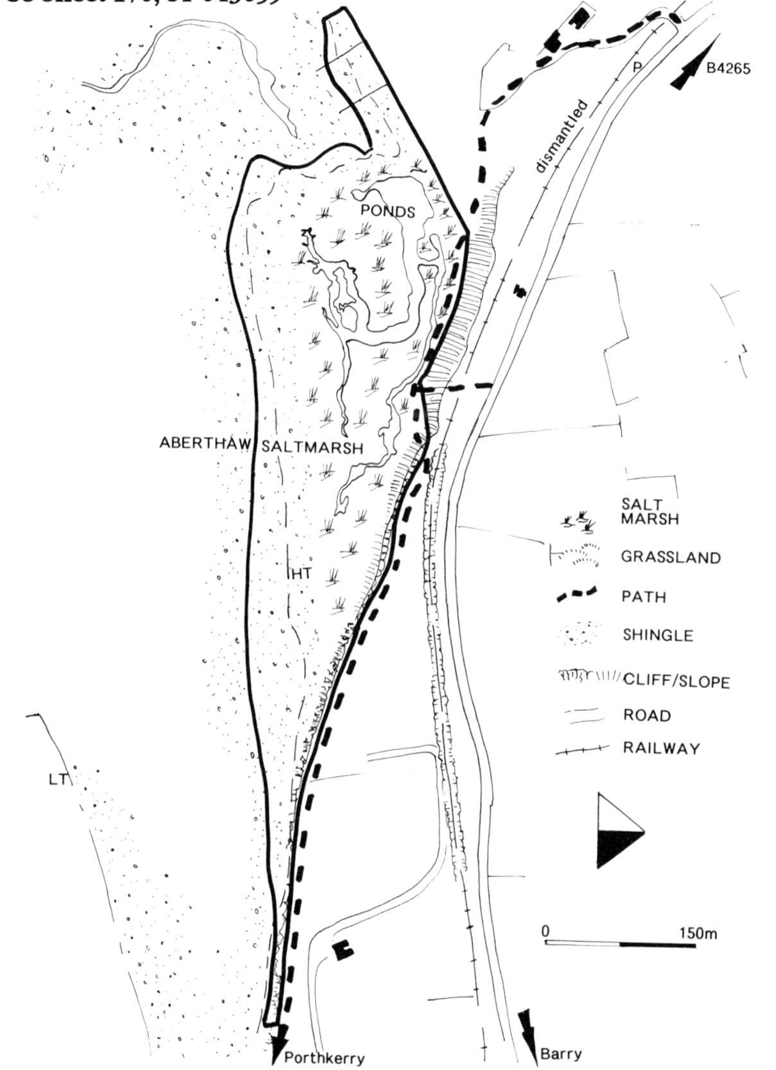

Good times to visit
April - May Spring migrant birds; *June - July* Saltmarsh and sand dune flowers; *August - October* Autumn migrant birds and butterflies; *December - January* Wintering wildfowl

Nearest Reserves
Cwm Colhuw, South Glamorgan 8 km; *Coed Garnllwyd, South Glamorgan* 5 km; *Gwern Rhyd, South Glamorgan* 13 km; *Lavernock Point, South Glamorgan* 14 km

COED GARNLLWYD

Llancarfon

OS Sheet 170; ST 058713

Ancient broadleaved woodland and meadow on calcareous soils, forming part of the Nant Whitton Woods SSSI. Area 13 ha (32 acres). Purchased from the Forestry Commission in March 1983, with grant aid from NCC, the National Heritage Memorial Fund and WWF. Managed by South Area Committee.

Location
0.75 km north-east of Llancarfan, approximately 5 km west of Barry. Access is by a public footpath either from the Llancarfan to Bonvilston road to the south of Garnllwyd Farm, or through the livery stables on the Walterston to Llancarfan road. Car parking is very limited close to the reserve, so parking space should be found in Llancarfan village.

Description
Coed Garnllwyd forms part of a woodland complex which occupies the southern and eastern sides of the small Nant Whitton and Nant Llancarfan valleys. The whole of the reserve is underlain with Lias Limestone. A spring-line runs through the reserve producing wet flushes within the wood.

The woodland is primarily an Ash/Oak coppice-with-standards, with Hazel, Field Maple, Holly, Crab Apple, Hawthorn, Spindle and Wayfaring-tree (7-9) making up a rich shrub layer. Clear felling in 1921 would appear to have been the last major management undertaken, as many of the standard trees are of medium size with multiple stems, although some of the standard oaks are larger and appear to pre-date this operation.

The ground flora is particularly rich, and contains species typical of lime-rich ancient woodlands. Herb-Paris (5-8), Broad-leaved Helleborine (7-9), Early-purple Orchid (4-5) occur, together with Bluebell (4-6), Wood Anemone (3-5) and Goldilocks Buttercup (4-6).

There is a varied bird fauna including Buzzard, Tawny Owl, Treecreeper and Nuthatch. Within the woodland, dead timber (predominantly Elm) supports invertebrates and fungi.

The reserve has a small meadow which has been undergrazed in recent years. It supports plants typical of basic soils such as Quaking-grass and Salad Burnet (5-8). On the border of the meadow, an area of bramble attracts many butterflies and moths and supports many woodland edge and hedgerow birds, such as Bullfinch and Whitethroat.

Management Objectives
To manage as a varied woodland by coppicing and some replanting of oak to provide future standard trees. This management has increased the structural diversity of the wood and has created glades. If continued for 10-15 years, about one third of the wood will consist of young coppice-with-standards. The woodland has now been completely fenced to stop grazing by livestock. It is intended to graze the meadow with cattle.

COED GARNLLWYD

OS Sheet 170; ST 058713

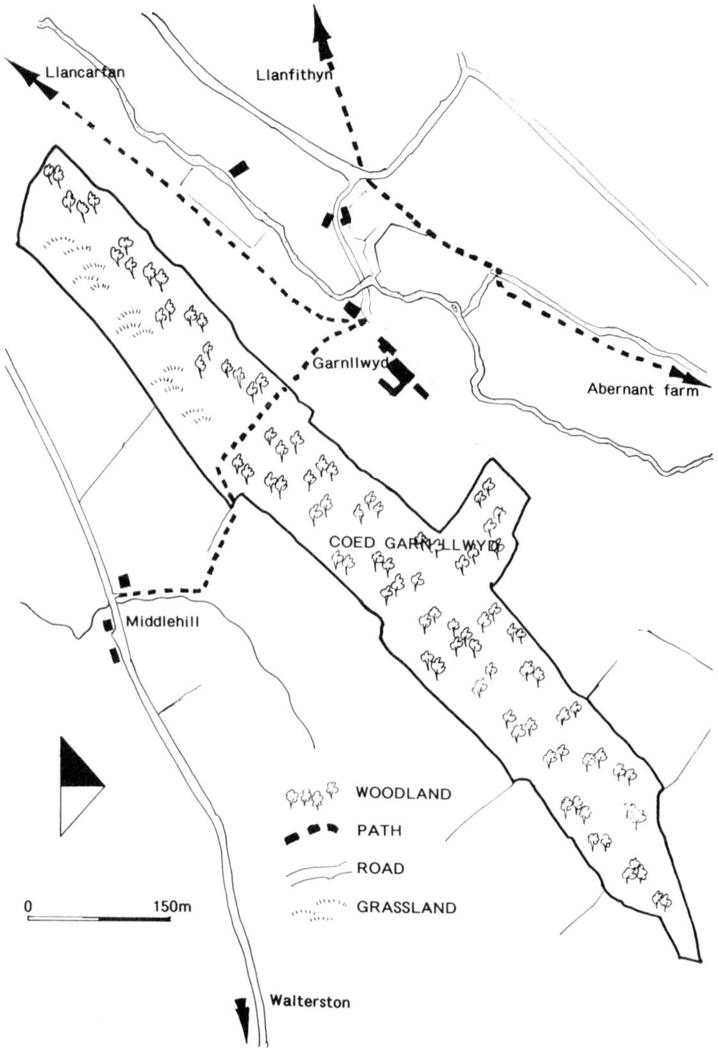

Good times to visit

April - July Woodland flowers; *May - July* Woodland flowers, birds and meadow flowers; *September - October* Fungi

Nearest Reserves

Aberthaw Saltmarsh, South Glamorgan 5 km; *Cwm Colhuw, South Glamorgan* 9.5 km; *Gwern Rhyd, South Glamorgan* 6.5 km; *Lavernock Point, South Glamorgan* 13 km

CWM COLHUW

Llantwit Major

OS Sheet 170; SS 960674

Coastal Jurassic limestone grassland and scrub. Area 11.5 ha (28.4 acres). The reserve was acquired in February 1989 under a 99 year lease from SGCC and lies within the South Glamorgan Heritage Coast. Managed by South Area Committee.

Location
1 km south-west of Llantwit Major. The reserve is situated on the east side of the beach road from Llantwit Major. Access can be obtained on foot either from a stile at the head of the valley (SS 968678), or by way of the steps from the east side of the beach car park. A public footpath runs the length of the reserve.

Description
The reserve is situated on the southern slope of the Afon Colhuw valley and comprises a mosaic of limestone scrub and open limestone grassland glades.

A postcard photograph of the Colhuw valley taken in the 1930s shows the reserve as open grazed pasture with isolated scrub. The cessation of grazing during the Second World War and after, has allowed Hawthorn, Blackthorn, Gorse and Bramble to take over the majority of the slope, with Ash taking hold at the inland end.

The scrub provides nesting sites for a number of passerine birds such as Bullfinch, Goldfinch and Yellowhammer, Willow Warbler and Whitethroat.

Two areas of under-grazed grassland are still open on the summit of the slope dominated by Oat Grass and Colt's-foot (3-4). Clumps of Bird's-foot Trefoil (6-9), Wild Thyme (5-7) and Salad Burnet (5-8) survive on the short turf of the pathways, ant-hills and archaeological remains.

The grassland provides a habitat for butterflies such as Meadow Brown, Small Heath and Common Blue.

The reserve contains the part of the bank and ditches of an Iron Age Promontory Fort. The majority of the Fort, including the impressive ramparts, known locally as "Castle Ditches" are just outside the reserve boundary to the east.

Management Objectives
To manage and extend the limestone grassland, by introducing grazing to the existing grassland areas and creating a system of clearings and glade through the scrub.

CWM COLHUW

OS Sheet 170; SS 960674

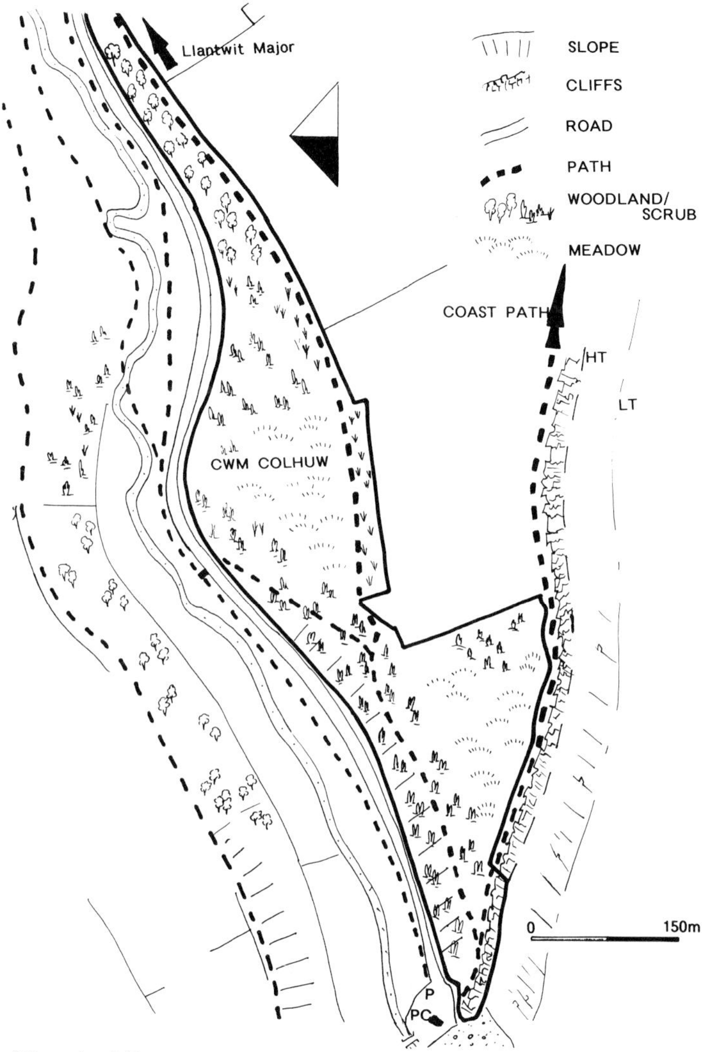

Good times to visit
April Spring migrant birds; *May - August* Limestone flowers and insects ; *September - October* Fungi and autumn migrant birds

Nearest Reserves
Aberthaw Saltmarsh, South Glamorgan 8 km; *Coed y Bwl, Mid Glamorgan* 9 km; *Coed Garnllwyd, South Glamorgan* 9.5 km; *Ogmore Down, Mid Glamorgan* 11 km

LAVERNOCK POINT

Penarth

OS Sheet 171; ST 182680

Coastal Jurassic limestone grassland and scrub, forming part of the Lavernock Point SSSI. Area 5.8 ha (14.5 acres). The reserve was acquired in January 1966 under annual licence. Managed by South Area Committee.

Location
8 km south of Cardiff and 6 km east of Barry. Access is obtained from the B4267 via a minor road signposted Lavernock Point. Vehicles can be parked before the entrance to the Marconi Club, and access on foot can be obtained by way of a public footpath through a kissing gate into the adjacent field and over a stile, through a gap in the hedge on the left. The public footpath runs through the reserve. Three stiles allow access into the fenced paddock area.

Description
Lavernock Point is made up of two fields, an inland unimproved meadow and a cliff-top field bearing a mosaic of fine unimproved limestone grassland and scrub. The grassland supports a rich assemblage of plants with numerous uncommon species such as Yellow-wort (6-10), Dyer's Greenweed (7-9), Adder's-tongue Fern (5-8), and Cowslip (4-5). Common Twayblade (5-8), Early-purple Orchid (4-6), Common Spotted-orchid (6-8), Bee Orchid (6-7) and Greater Butterfly-orchid (5-7) occur in glades in the scrub.

There is a large resident population of butterflies and moths, including Meadow Brown, Common Blue, Large, and Small Skipper, as well as regular migrants such as Painted Lady and Red Admiral.

The reserve is an important site for the observation of bird migration. Large numbers of Yellow Wagtails pass through in late summer , with many of the more unusual migrants such as Firecrest, Brambling, and large parties of Redpolls using the scrub as a resting station.

The Point is a good place from which to sea-watch for unusual vagrant sea birds, especially after summer storms,when there is a good chance of seeing considerable numbers of Manx Shearwaters, Skuas, or one of the less common terns.

Winter brings Peregrine, and the occasional Common Scoter offshore, and large numbers of waders on tidal passage between Cardiff Bay and Sully Island. There are a number of Second World War concrete gun emplacements , and associated buildings to the seaward side of the reserve, which are what remains of part of the Bristol Channel coastal defences.

Management Objectives
To manage and extend the limestone grassland, with particular attention to the less common flowering plants by creating and maintaining a system of clearings and glades through the scrub. Part of the reserve was fenced into the farm by Trust members in 1982 to allow it to be grazed.

LAVERNOCK POINT

OS Sheet 171; ST 182680

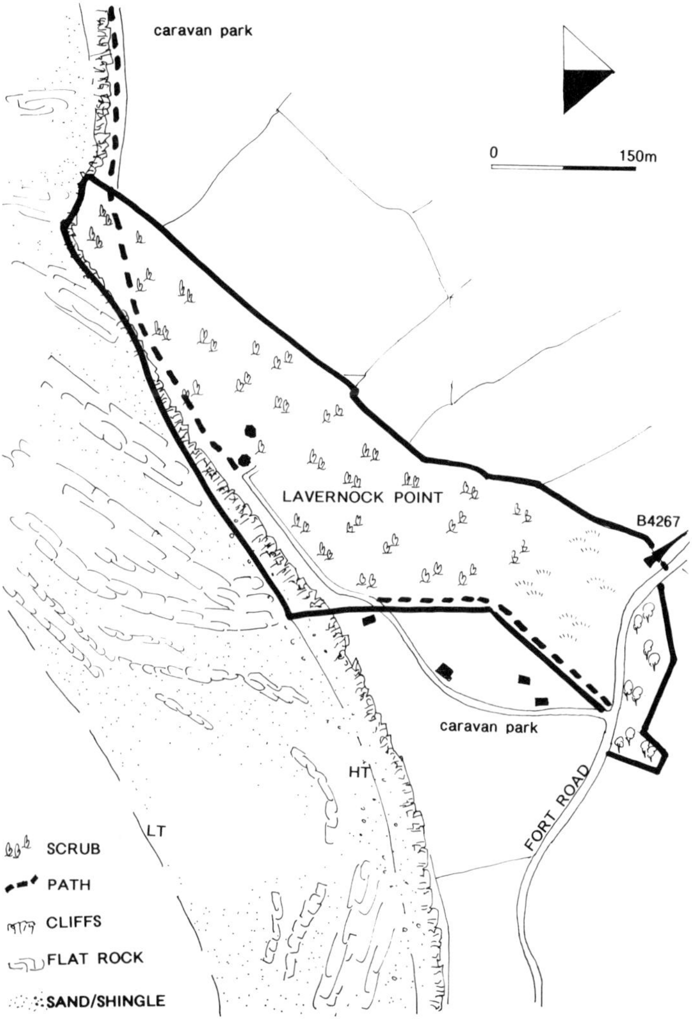

Good times to visit
April-May Spring migrant birds; *May-August* Limestone flowers and butterflies; *August-October* Autumn migrant birds; *September - October* Fungi

Nearest Reserves
Aberthaw Saltmarsh, South Glamorgan 13.5 km; *Coed Garnllwyd, South Glamorgan* 13.5 km; *Coed y Bedw, Mid Glamorgan* 16 km; *Gwern Rhyd, South Glamorgan* 12 km

COED LLWYN RHYDDID

Hensol

Ancient broadleaved woodland, partly planted with conifer. Area 4.9 ha (12.2 acres). Purchased by the Trust in July 1989. Managed by Mid Area Committee.

Access
Please contact the Trust's headquarters for details of organised Heron viewing days.

Description
Coed Llwyn Rhyddid is a small broadleaved woodland whose canopy is made up of Oak, Ash and Beech with an understorey of Yew and Rhododendron, into which a mixture of conifers has been planted. There is a poor herb layer, but the drainage ditches support Opposite-leaved Golden-saxifrage (4-7).

The conservation value of the wood is that it is, at present, the only permanent Heronry in the county of South Glamorgan, and one of only three in the Glamorgan counties. Grey Herons have been recorded in the immediate area of this wood for the last 150 years.

The Herons arrive at the wood in January and February, and the breeding cycle lasts until July for the year's young to fledge and September for Herons to leave the wood. Because Herons are easily disturbed, this nature reserve is managed as a closed access site, with the intention of organising group viewing days during the period of time that the Herons are present.

Good times to visit
February - July Nesting Grey Herons

Grey Heron

GWERN RHYD RESERVE

St. Georges

Wet riparian woodland, with rich flora. Area of Section A 0.3 ha (0.76 acres) and Section B 0.6 ha (1.53 acres). Section A was acquired in 1979 under leasehold for 21 years; Section B under leasehold for 7 years from 1981 (this was renewed in 1989). Managed by South Area Committee and the owner.

Access
Access to Glamorgan Wildlife Trust members only, please contact the Trust office.

Description
There are two sections to this reserve, A and B. Section A consists mainly of coppiced Alder on damp peaty and sandy soils, which is where Monkshood (5-6), Giant Bellflower (7-8), Orange Balsam (6-8) and the False Oxlip (4-5) occur. Other parts of this section represent a secondary succession from old pasture and include blackthorn scrub, Bramble, Bracken, coarse grassland and Common Reed (8-9).

Section B consists of more mature woodland with Oak, Ash and a few Larch trees as well as Alder. The underwood contains Spindle, Elder, Dogwood, Hazel, Hawthorn, Holly and Red Currant. There is an ox-bow lake which is gradually being colonised by marsh plants.

Management Objectives
To create conditions for the continued healthy development of populations of Monkshood, Giant Bellflower and Orange Balsam where they are found. Also to manage those areas where these plants are not found to create the maximum ecological diversity.

Good times to visit
April - July Riparian flowers

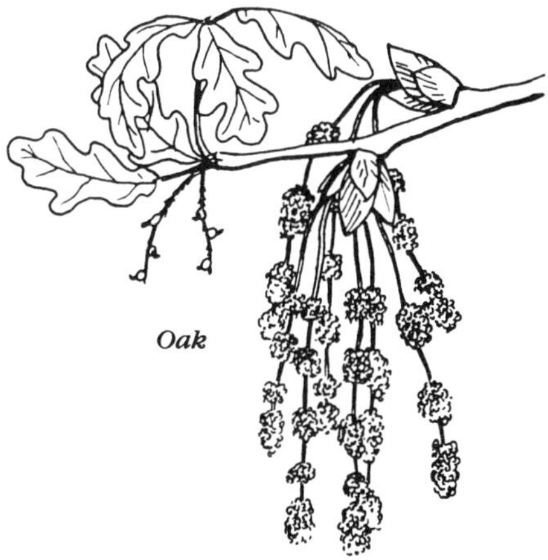

Oak

WEST GLAMORGAN NATURE RESERVES

Berry Wood

Betty Church Reserve

Blaenant y Gwyddyl

Bolgoed Quarry

Broad Pool and Bog

Bunker's Hill

Castle Wood Field

Coed Gawdir

Craig Cilhendre Woods

Cwm Ivy Woods

The Elizabeth and Rowe Harding Nature Reserve

Gelli-hir Wood

Hambury Wood

Kilvrough Manor Woods

Llanrhidian Hill

Llyn Fach

The Lucas Reserve

Melincwrt Waterfalls

Peel Wood

Prior's Wood and Meadow

Redden Hill Wood

Redley Cliff

Ridgewood Park

South Gower Coast – Deborah's Hole

South Gower Coast – Long Hole Cliff

South Gower Coast – Overton Cliff

South Gower Coast – Overton Mere

South Gower Coast – Port Eynon Point

South Gower Coast – Sedger's Bank

BERRY WOOD

Knelston, Gower

OS Sheet 159; SS 474884

Ancient broadleaved woodland, notified as an SSSI. Area 6.8 ha (16.9 acres). Purchased by the Trust in December 1969. Managed by West Glamorgan Committee.

Location
500 m south-east of Knelston, Gower. Access can be obtained by following the public footpath, starting opposite the entrance to Stouthall, south for 1.7 km, or from the a track which runs north from Berry Farm (keeping to the right of the farmhouse). A public footpath passes through the woodland. There are no car parking facilities close to the reserve.

Description
Berry Wood is an example of an ancient Oak dominated coppice-with-standards woodland, rare in this part of Gower, situated on poorly drained glacial drift over Millstone Grit. Both Pedunculate and Sessile Oak are present with Birch, Ash, Hazel, Grey Willow, Rowan and Aspen. The oldest Oaks (up to 200 years in age) are to be found on the western side of the reserve. The remainder of the wood is much younger and is made up of even-aged stands of Oak, Birch and Ash. This suggests that much of the wood may have been clear felled at some stage and allowed to regenerate naturally, although there is some evidence that Oaks were planted in the north-western corner.

The south-western corner of the wood is open and grassy, due to past incursions by cattle. Towards the centre of the wood and in the north-west the ground is very poorly drained. The remainder of the field layer of the reserve is covered in dense Bramble, with patches of Bracken. Hazel coppice, Hawthorn, Crab Apple and Holly make up the shrub layer, with Honeysuckle (6-9) and Ivy. Narrow Buckler-fern, Wood Millet (6) and Opposite-leaved Golden-saxifrage (4-7) are amongst the less common plants found. There is an abundance of epiphytes on the Oak and Willows, with bryophytes, ferns and lichens all well represented.

The native Common Dormouse is recorded as having inhabited the wood in the past, but has not been detected since 1969. Wood Mouse, Bank Vole, Grey Squirrel, Fox and Rabbit have all been recorded on the reserve, together with Buzzard, Goldcrest, Willow Warbler and Blackcap. Mixed finch flocks which occur in winter.

Management Objectives
To maintain as high forest and institute coppicing.

BERRY WOOD

OS Sheet 159; SS 474884

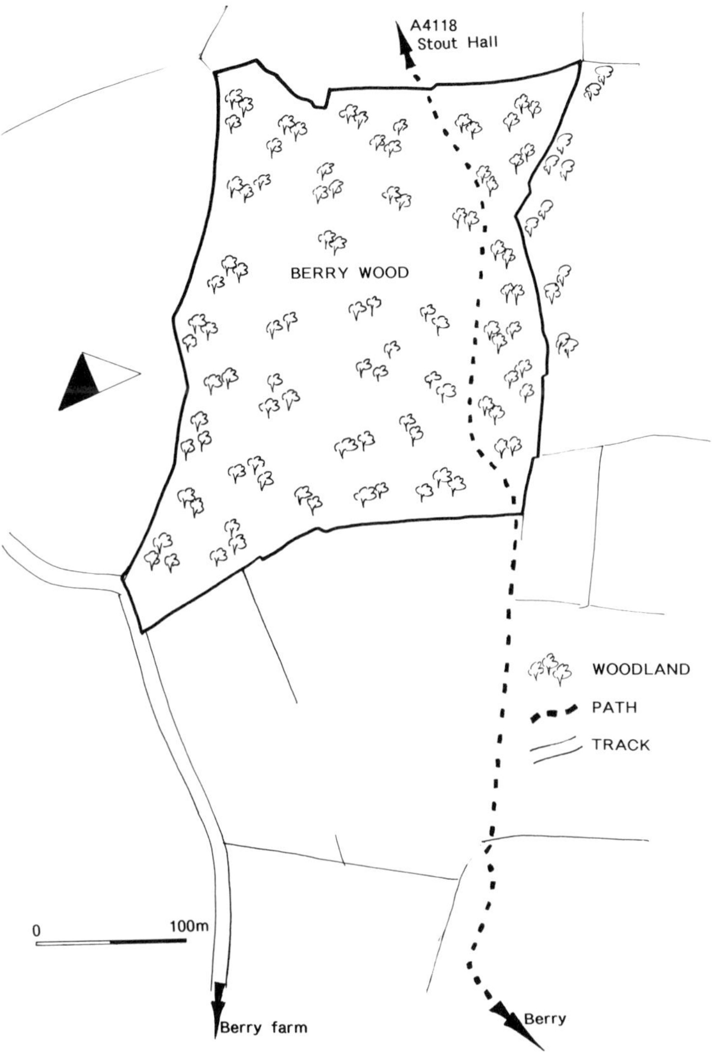

Good times to visit
April - July Woodland flowers and birds; *September - October* Fungi

Nearest Reserves
Broad Pool, West Glamorgan 4.5 km; *Hambury Wood, West Glamorgan* 4.5 km; *Llanrhidian Hill, West Glamorgan* 4 km; *South Gower Coast - Port Eynon Point* West Glamorgan 3 km

BETTY CHURCH RESERVE

Cwm Ivy, Gower

OS Sheet 159; SS 440937

Limestone woodland, plantation and pasture. Area 2.2 ha (5.5 acres). The Betty Church Reserve was given to the Trust in 1983 as a bequest by Betty Church, in whose memory it is named. Managed by West Glamorgan Committee.

Location
Adjacent to the village of Cwm Ivy.

Description
The nature reserve is made up of three small fields which abut the Trust's Cwm Ivy nature reserve.

The largest field is maintained as grassland with wide hedges where planted Snowdrops (1-3) and Daffodils (2-4) flourish in spring, and Ox-eye Daisy (6-8), Common Knapweed (6-9) and Crosswort (4-7) can been seen is summer. This field also provides good views of Cwm Ivy Marsh and the Whiteford National Nature Reserve, when the leaves are off the trees in winter. The two smaller fields have been planted up with deciduous native trees such as Ash, Field Maple and Hazel to provide an extension to Cwm Ivy Woods and additional cover for birds.

Management Objectives
To maintain the grassland through cutting or grazing in late summer, and to continue to weed and replace any failures of the recently planted trees.

Ox-eye Daisy

BETTY CHURCH RESERVE

OS Sheet 159; SS 440937

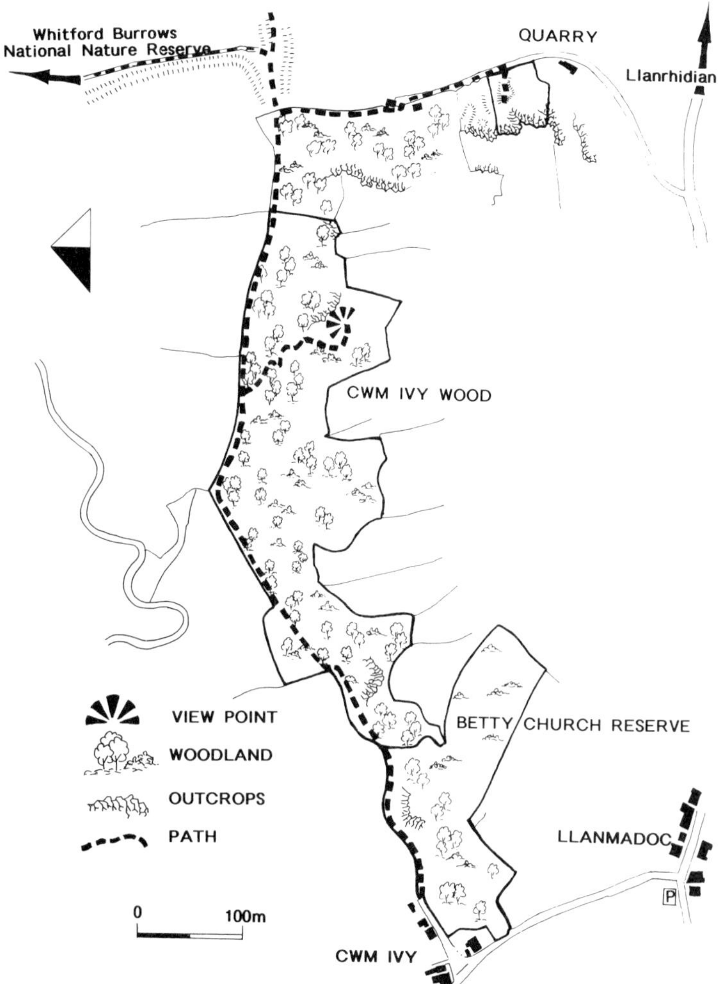

Good times to visit

April - July Woodland flowers and birds; *May - July* Meadow; *September - November* Fungi

Nearest Reserves

Castle Wood Field, West Glamorgan 2.5 km; *Cwm Ivy Woods, West Glamorgan* adjacent; *Frog Lane, West Glamorgan* 1 km; *Hambury Wood, West Glamorgan* 2.5 km

BLAENANT Y GWYDDYL

Glyneath

OS Sheet 160; SN 885076

An upland area of ancient broadleaved woodland, stream and waterfalls. Area 10.1 ha (24.9 acres). The reserve was acquired in October 1988 under leasehold for 999 years. The lease was purchased by the Trust with financial support by sponsorship funding by British Coal Opencast under the Government's conservation and business sponsorship initiative, administered by the World Wide Fund for Nature's Corporate Fundraising Department. Managed by West Glamorgan Committee.

Location
0.5 km north of Glyneath.

Description
Blaenant y Gwyddyl is an area of ancient semi-natural broadleaved woodland on thin Coal Measures soils, on the north side of the steeply sloping valley of the Blaenant Gwyddyl. There are several non-woodland habitats including the rocky river bed fed by streams flowing down the valley side, several large glades and bare rock exposures near two attractive waterfalls.

The reserve is made up of upland Birch/Sessile Oak woodland, with areas containing Ash, Alder, Small-leaved Lime, Sycamore and Wych Elm. The understorey is not well developed because of past sheep grazing, giving the reserve an open character. It consists chiefly of Hazel with some Field Maple, Hawthorn, Holly and Blackthorn. There are several areas dominated by large stands of Bracken. The ground flora is largely dominated by grasses, particularly Common Bent (6-8) and Tufted Hair-grass (6-8). Herbs include Tutsan (6-8). A richer flora can be found in the wet flushes throughout the wood.

Management Objectives
The major concerns for work to be carried out will be to exclude grazing stock from the woodland, to retain a system of glades by scrub control and the provision of basic facilities for visitors, including stiles, pathways, steps.

BLAENANT Y GWYDDYL

OS Sheet 160; SN 885076

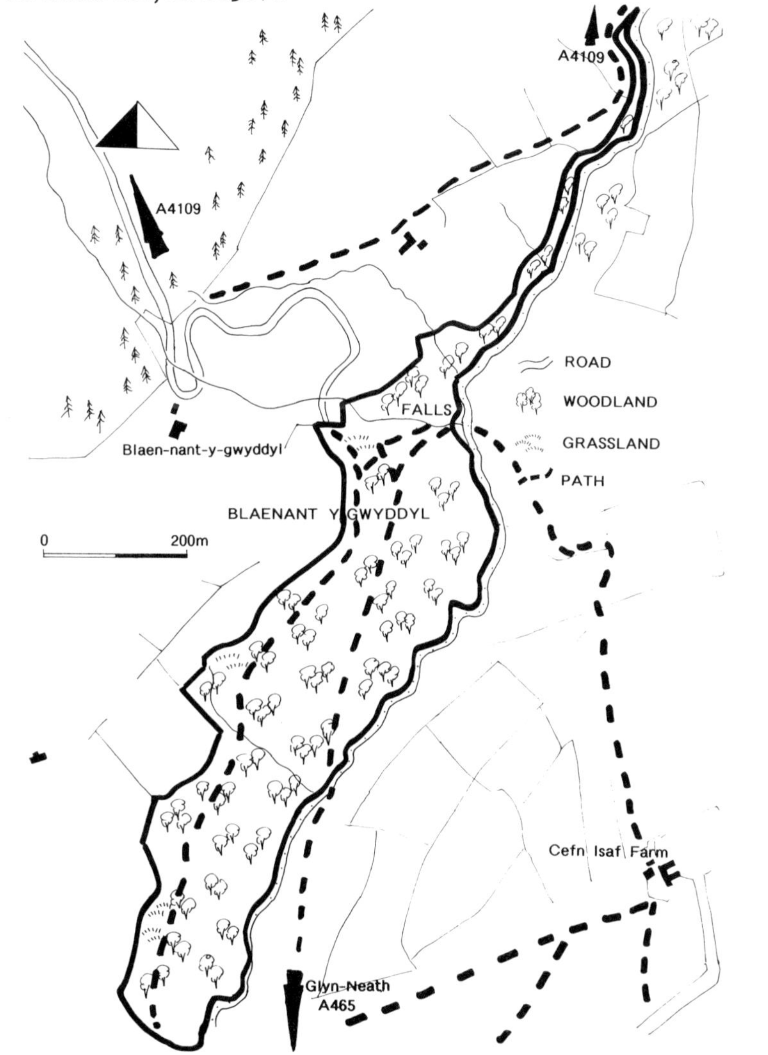

Good times to visit

April - June Spring woodland flowers; *May - July* Summer woodland birds; *September - November* Fungi; *November - March* waterfalls (after a period of rain)

Nearest Reserves

Aberdare Canal, Mid Glamorgan 14 km; *Coed Gawdir, West Glamorgan* 12 km; *Llyn Fach, West Glamorgan* 4 km; *Melincwrt Waterfalls, West Glamorgan* 8 km

BOLGOED QUARRY

Pontardulais

OS Sheet 159; SN 603027

Disused sandstone quarry. Area 0.81 ha (2 acres). The reserve was purchased by the Trust in March 1968. Managed by West Glamorgan Committee.

Location
Lies on the north side of the A48T between Pontlliw and Pontardulais.

Description
Bolgoed Quarry, is an old sandstone quarry and consists mostly of open-canopied, deciduous woodland of Ash and Birch, with a ground layer dominated by Ivy and Bramble. The remainder is dominated by dense gorse scrub.

The major quarry faces, which are irrigated with groundwater seeping from the cracks in the sandstone strata are locally important for lower plants such as mosses and liverworts.

The reserve encourages a range of woodland birds such as Great Tit, Tawny Owl, Nuthatch and Treecreeper and the wet nature of the quarry floor makes it an ideal wintering site for Woodcock.

Management Objectives
To manage the woodland as high forest and maintain the quarry faces for lower plants.

European Gorse

BOLGOED QUARRY

OS Sheet 159; SN 603027

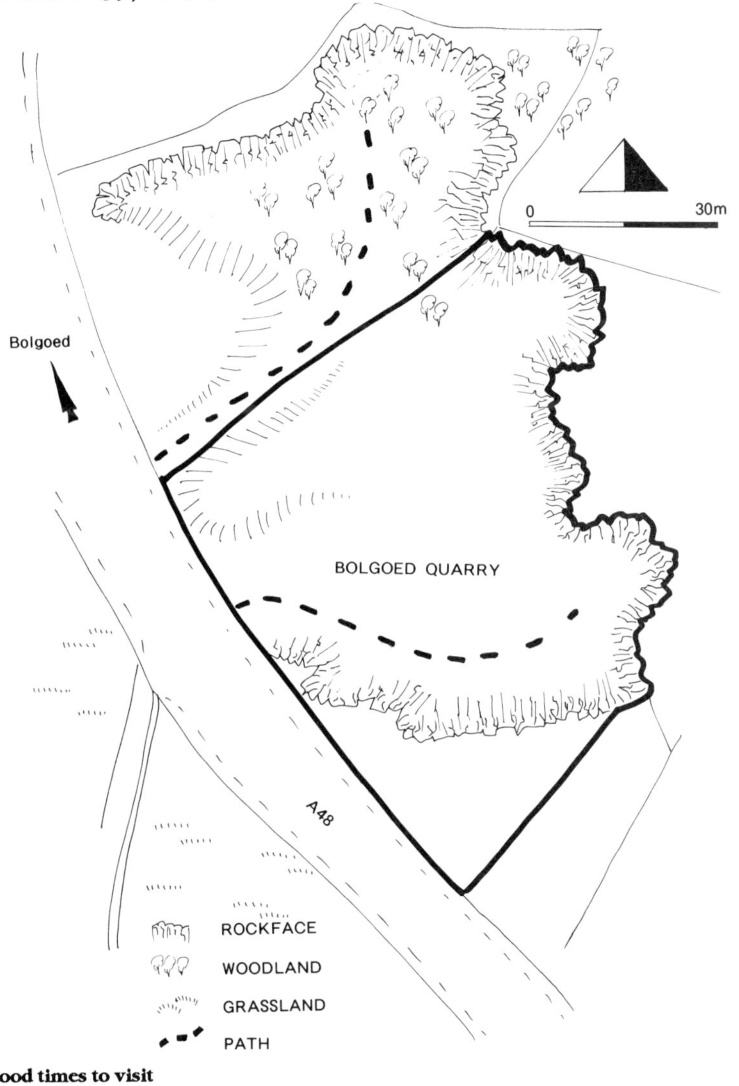

Good times to visit

April - June Spring woodland flowers.; *May - July* Summer woodland birds; *September - October* Fungi

Nearest Reserves

Craig Cilhendre, West Glamorgan 12 km; *Gelli-hir Wood, West Glamorgan* 10.5 km; *Llanrhidian Hill, West Glamorgan* 15 km; *Prior's Wood and meadow, West Glamorgan* 9.5 km

BROAD POOL AND BOG

Cilibion, Gower

OS Sheet 159; SS 510910

Acidic pond, heath and bog. Area Broad Pool 1.71 ha (4.2 acres); Bog 9.31 ha (23 acres). Broad Pool was given to the Trust in May 1962 by the Duke of Beaufort, as the Trust's first nature reserve. The Bog was acquired in September 1974 and is under leasehold for 25 years. The reserve now forms part of the Cefn Bryn and Broad Pool SSSI and is Registered Common Land. Managed by West Glamorgan Committee.

Location

3 km north-east of Reynoldston, Gower. The reserve may be approached from the north Gower road (B4271) via Cilibion, or from the south Gower road (A4118) via Reynoldston. The reserve lies on both sides of the road between Reynoldston and Cilibion and is in two parts.

Description

Broad Pool lies in a shallow basin on the limestone plateau beneath Cefn Bryn. It is one of the most conspicuous and best known features of central Gower. The Pool is known to be have been in existence in 1645. Its origin appears to have been natural, although there is evidence that the pool was modified by scouring (removal of sediment and vegetation) from the late Eighteenth century. The Pool contains a rich assemblage of aquatic plants, including Lesser Marshwort (6-8) and Alternate Water-milfoil (5-8), both rare in South Wales. Fringed Water-lily (6-9) is present and has dominated the aquatic vegetation in the past. This attractive and uncommon plant is only native in a small area of south-east England and was introduced to Broad Pool in around 1952.

The pool is visited by a wide range of waterfowl and wetland birds, including Grey Heron and Little Grebe, with passage migrants such as Ruff and Spotted Redshank. It is a locally important breeding site for amphibians, and supports a rich aquatic invertebrate fauna, including fourteen species of dragonflies and damselflies.

The adjacent area of bog and moor is dominated by heath plants, such as Cross-leaved Heath (6-9) and Heather (7-9) with Purple Moor-grass (6-8), rushes, Bog-myrtle (4-5) and Round-leaved Sundew (6-8) in the wetter areas.

The heathland and area around Broad Pool is also of ornithological importance, with nesting Snipe and Lapwing in summer, and Hen Harrier, Merlin and Short-eared Owl regularly recorded in the winter months.

Management objectives

To maintain an area of open water in the pool and control the fringed water-lily. The spread of the fringed water-lily during the 1960s and the subsequent encroachment of rushes and *Sphagnum* moss threatened a change from open water to bog. The drought of 1984 provided the opportunity to remove the build-up of silt and restore the Broad Pool to its former condition.

BROAD POOL AND BOG

OS Sheet 159; SS 510910

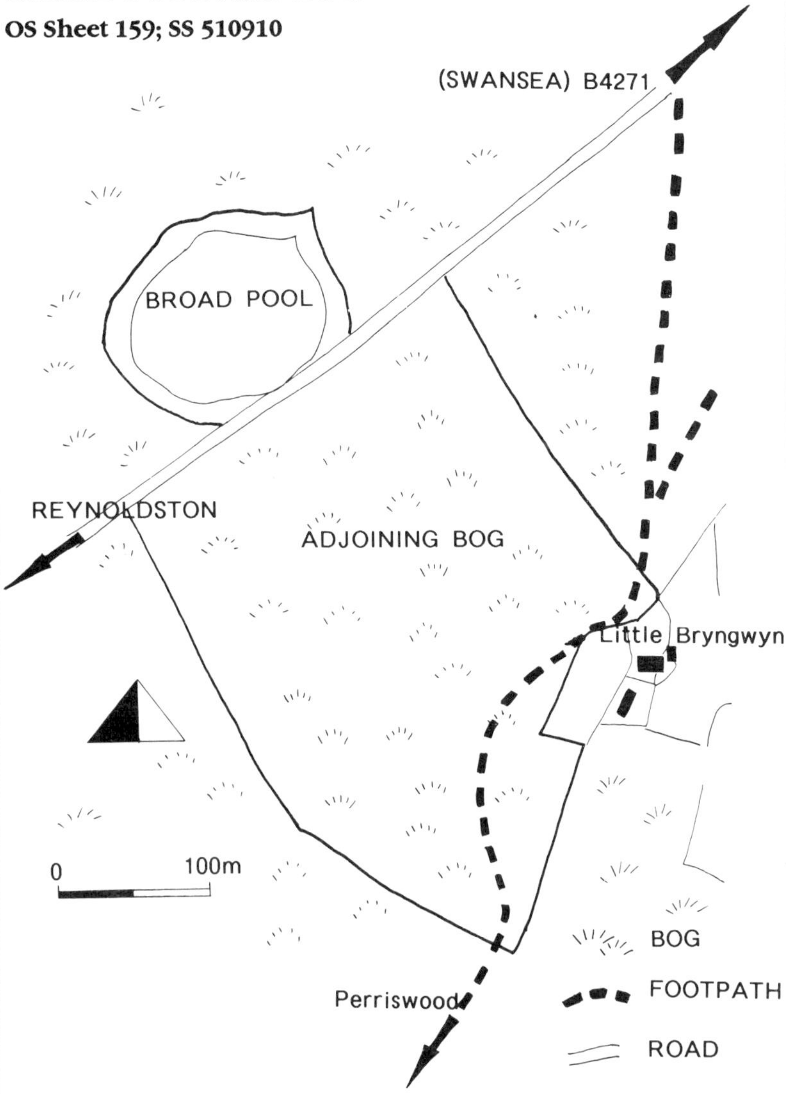

Good times to visit

May - August Aquatic flowers and dragonflies; *September - April* Passage migrants and wintering raptors

Nearest Reserves

Berry Wood, West Glamorgan 4.5 km; *Ilston Quarry, West Glamorgan* 4.5 km; *Llanrhidian Hill, West Glamorgan* 2 km; *Redden Hill Wood, West Glamorgan* 3.5 km

BUNKER'S HILL

Pitton, Gower

OS Sheet 159; SS 428881

Mixed scrub. Area 0.28 ha (0.7 acres). The reserve was given to the Trust by Mr P. Jenkins in August 1970. Managed by West Glamorgan Committee.

Location
1 km west of Rhossili. The reserve is approached by a steep track to the north of the hamlet of Pitton, where cars are best left at the bottom of the slope. Access can be obtained by way of a stile on the eastern side of the reserve.

Description
Bunker's Hill is a small triangle of land occupying a south-facing slope. The reserve is dominated by a mosaic of Bracken, with scrub including Bramble, Blackthorn, Hawthorn, Holly, Sycamore and some Gorse, much of which is moribund. An area of less well drained ground is occupied by willows, with some Ash regenerating.

Although only a small area, more than sixty species of flowering plants have been recorded, including Primrose (1-5), Bluebell (4-6), Wood Sage (7-9) and Tutsan (6-8) in the drier areas, with Wild Angelica (7-9), Water Mint (7-10), Ragged-Robin (5-6) and Marsh Thistle (7-9) colonising the damper ground.

Management objectives
To allow the majority of the reserve to develop to a natural climax vegetation through non-intervention (it is potentially important as an area of scrub woodland, in view of the scarcity of such sites in the immediate vicinity). Smaller areas are managed by cutting, in order to maintain and enhance the diversity of the ground flora.

Ragged-Robin

BUNKER'S HILL

OS Sheet 159; SS 428881

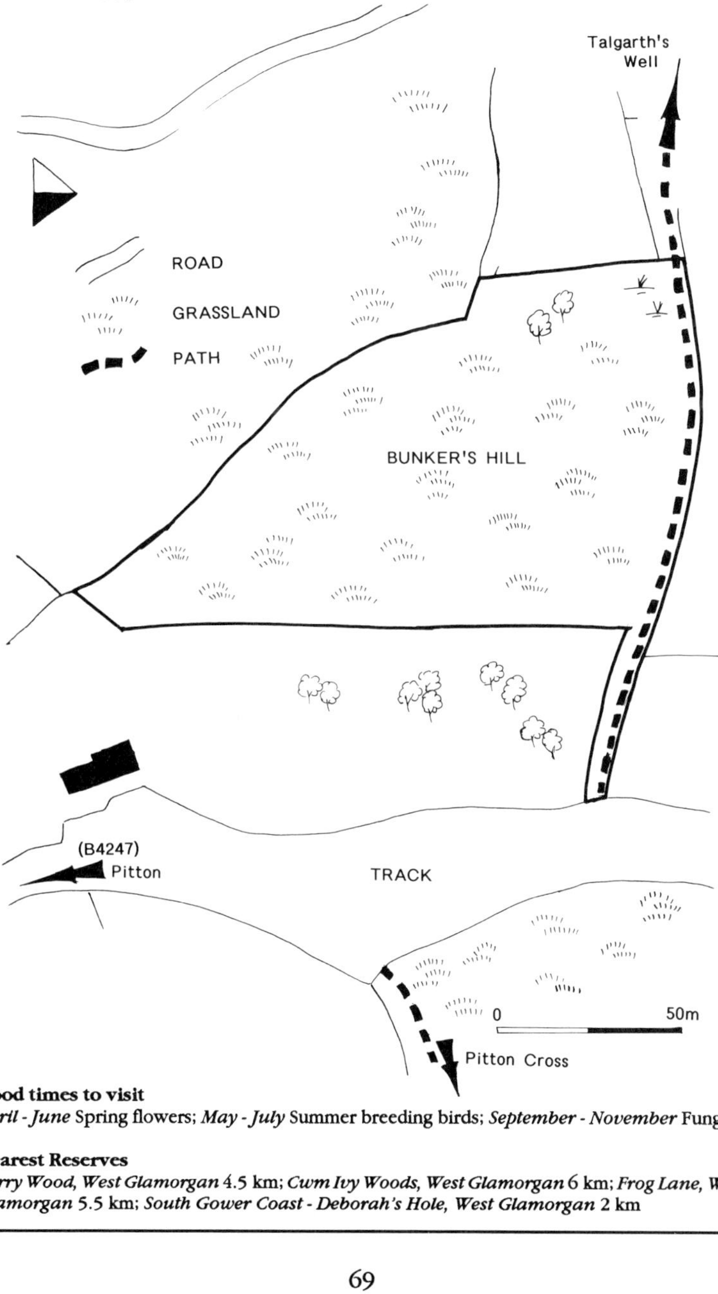

Good times to visit

April - June Spring flowers; *May - July* Summer breeding birds; *September - November* Fungi

Nearest Reserves

Berry Wood, West Glamorgan 4.5 km; *Cwm Ivy Woods, West Glamorgan* 6 km; *Frog Lane, West Glamorgan* 5.5 km; *South Gower Coast - Deborah's Hole, West Glamorgan* 2 km

CASTLE WOOD FIELD

Landimore, Gower

OS Sheet 159; SS 472931

High level saltmarsh. Area 0.34 ha (0.8 acres). The freehold of this reserve was given to the Trust in June 1968 by an anonymous donor. Managed by West Glamorgan Committee.

Location
1.2 km east of Landimore, almost adjacent to Hambury Wood.

Description
Castle Wood Field forms part of the Burry Estuary saltmarsh complex, occupying the uppermost part of the marsh. It is bounded on three sides by drainage ditches which link with the extensive system of drains which intersect the marsh. The reserve lies on estuarine alluvium and sand, overlying Millstone Grit.

The vegetation is typical of a grazed saltmarsh, consisting of a close mat of Red Fescue (6-7), Thrift (4-10) and Buck's-horn Plantain (5-7), interspersed with clumps of rushes.

Management Objectives
To maintain the present level of grazing and monitor any changes in the floral composition of the pasture.

Thrift

CASTLE WOOD FIELD

OS Sheet 159; SS 472931

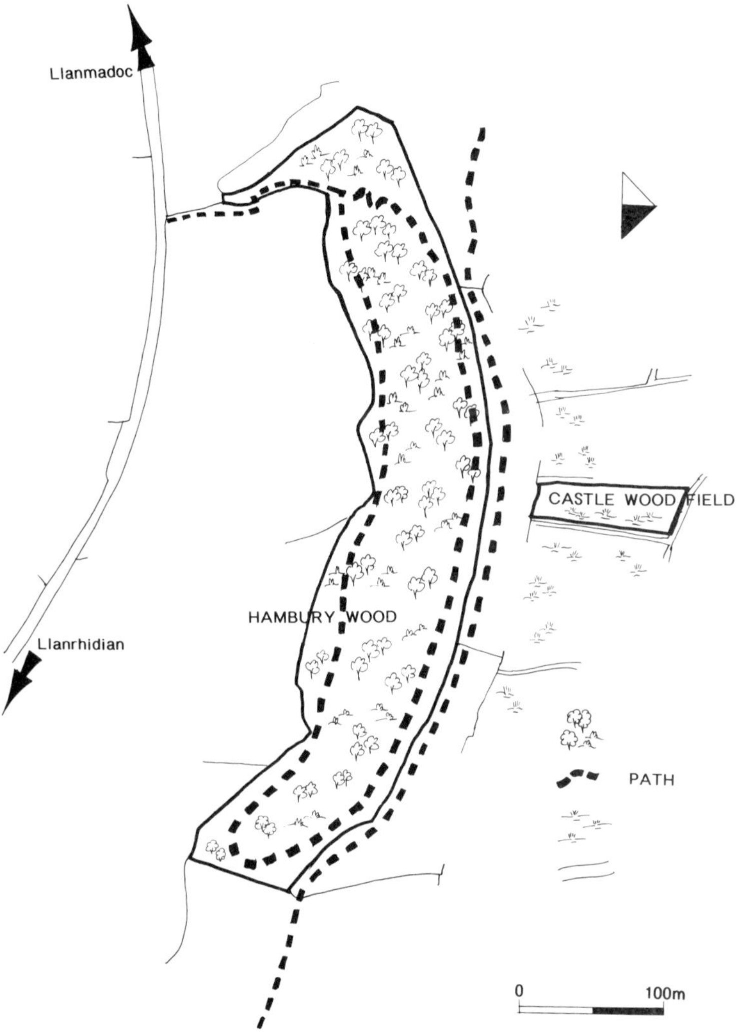

Good times to visit
April - July Spring salt marsh flowers; *May - July* Summer coastal birds

Nearest Reserves
Cwm Ivy Woods, West Glamorgan and the Betty Church Reserve, West Glamorgan 3 km; *Frog Lane, West Glamorgan* 2.5 km; *Hambury Wood, West Glamorgan* 200 m; *Llanrhidian Hill, West Glamorgan* 2.5 km

COED GAWDIR

Aberdulais

OS Sheet 170; SN 783007

A small acidic pond and conifer plantation. Area 0.1 ha (0.25 acres). The reserve was acquired March 1970 under leasehold for 99 years. Managed by West Glamorgan Committee.

Location
1.5 km north-east of Aberdulais.Take a westerly track from the A4109.

Description
The main interest of the reserve is the man-made freshwater pool which occupies about one third of the reserve area. It is fed by a stream which enters the pool on the eastern side and has an outflow on the western bank.

The aquatic vegetation is dominated by Floating Sweet-grass (5-8), whilst rush species line the pool edges. The eastern side of the pool has silted up and supports a small area of Sphagnum bog, with a small developing area of alder/ willow carr.

The pool lies within a mature plantation of Scots Pine and European Larch, interspersed with Oak, Silver Birch and Alder. The shrub layer is dominated by Rhododendron.

The principle interest of the site is its bird life, such as Great Tit, Coal Tit, Siskin and Robin.

Management Objectives
To manage the pool and its surroundings as an undisturbed habitat for wildlife, by maintaining the main body of water in an open condition, together with the area of bog. The Rhododendron is being cleared to encourage the natural regeneration of native trees and shrubs.

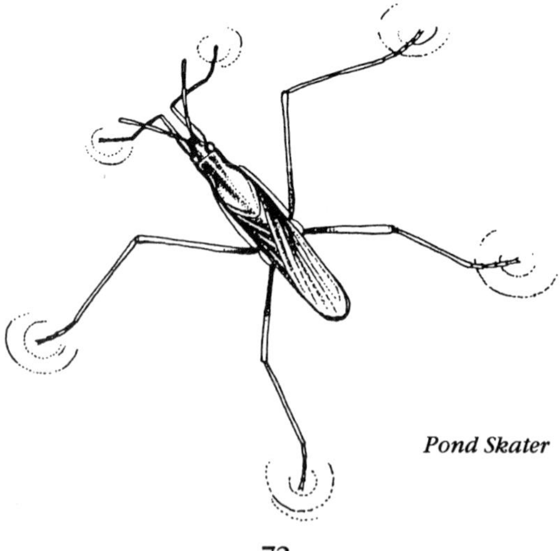

Pond Skater

COED GAWDIR

OS Sheet 170; SN 783007

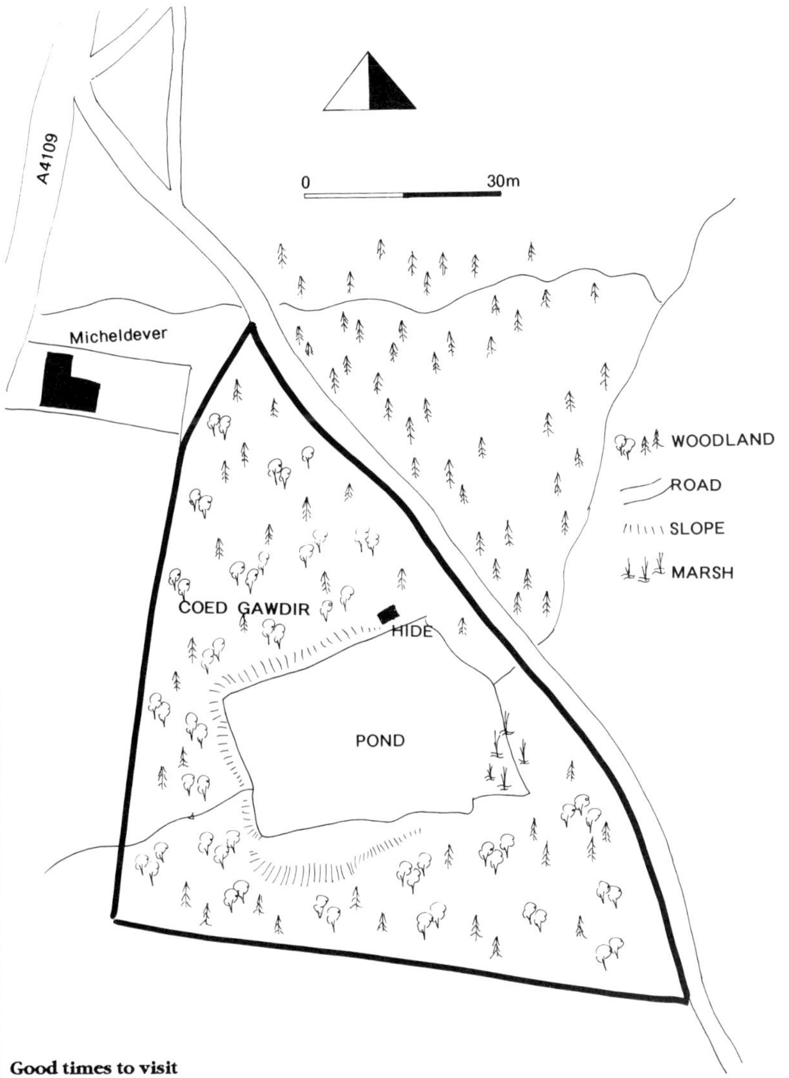

Good times to visit

April - June Spring woodland flowers; *May - July* Summer woodland birds; *September - November* Fungi

Nearest Reserves

Blaenant y Gwyddwyl, West Glamorgan 12 km; *Bolgoed Quarry, West Glamorgan* 12 km; *Craig Cilhendre, West Glamorgan* 6.5 km; *Melincwrt Waterfall, West Glamorgan* 4.5 km

CRAIG CILHENDRE WOODS

Pontardawe

OS Sheet 170; SN 719022

Semi-natural broadleaved woodland, part of which is ancient in origin. Area 16.1 ha (39.8 acres). The freehold of this reserve was purchased in March 1987 with grant aid and financial help from Dr Martin Cahn, the Countryside Commission, WGCC and WWF. Managed by West Glamorgan Committee.

Location

1.5 km south of Pontardawe. Access to the reserve is by way of a made up track to a small car park at the north-west corner of the reserve.

Description

Craig Cilhendre Woods comprises of over 16 ha of ancient semi-natural broadleaved woodland, situated on a steep north facing hillside. Several broad tracks which date from earlier coal extraction, including the route of a former tramway, run through the reserve. A sandstone cliff, about 8 m high and over a kilometre long, runs along the top of the reserve and fine views over Alltwen can be gained from the top.

The woodland has a very diverse age structure, particularly in the western part of the wood. A few dense areas near the entrance reflect where clear felling has occurred in the recent past. The woodland canopy comprises a mosaic made up of Sessile Oak, Beech, Birch, Ash, Sycamore and Alder. Part of the reserve is shown as not wooded in a map dated 1831. Craig Cilhendre is underlain by Pennant Sandstone and a number of small coal seams outcrop on the site.

In most of the western, more ancient, part of the woodland, there is a prominent shrub layer where Hazel and Holly are particularly abundant. Several minor watercourses descend the slope and there are areas of impeded drainage at the base of the slope where large areas of Marsh Violet (4-7) can be found.

The reserve, being rather damp, supports a variety of mosses and liverworts.

Management Objectives

A policy of non-intervention is being followed at present, with the intention of maintaining the reserve as high forest. A car park has been provided and the site enclosed with stock proof fencing. Footpaths will be re-established, and will link up with the existing network of rides.

CRAIG CILHENDRE WOODS

OS Sheet 170; SN 719022

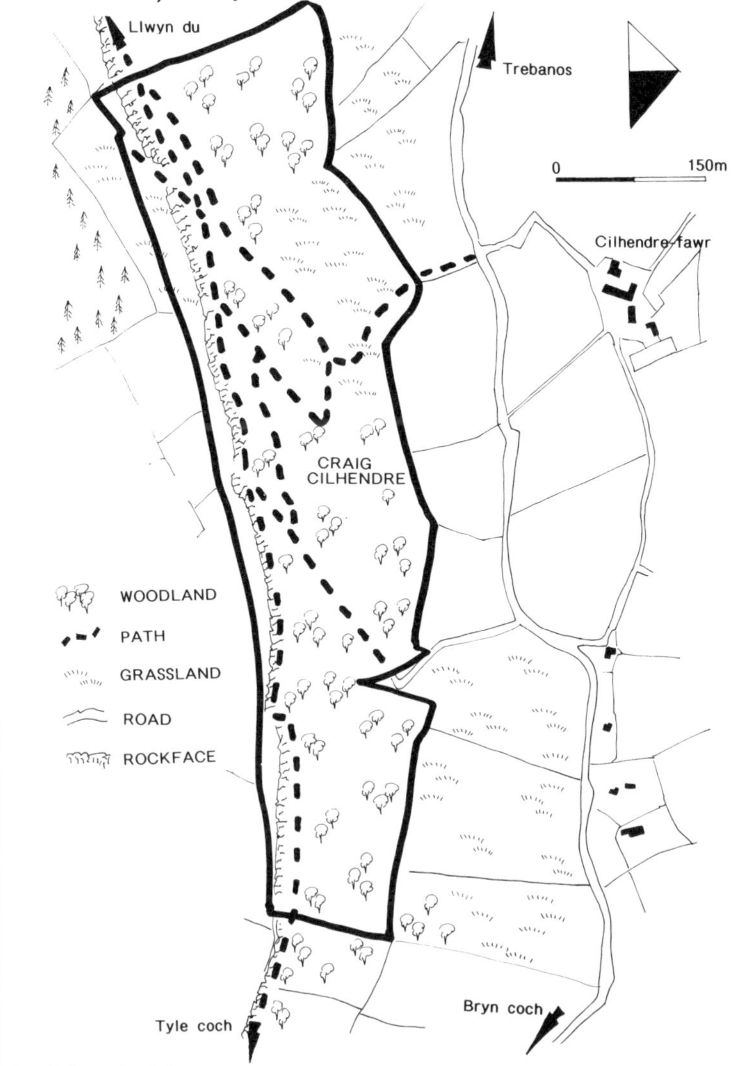

Good times to visit

April-June Spring woodland flowers; *May-July* Summer woodland birds; *September-November* Fungi

Nearest Reserves

Blaenant y Gwyddyl, West Glamorgan 16.5 km; *Bolgoed Quarry, West Glamorgan* 12 km; *Coed Gawdir, West Glamorgan* 6.5 km; *Melincwrt Waterfall, West Glamorgan* 10 km

CWM IVY WOODS

Cwm Ivy, Gower

OS Sheet 159; SS 443939

Ancient limestone woodland and quarry. The reserve forms part of the Cwm Ivy Marsh, Dunes and Tor SSSI. Area 11.08 ha (27.4 acres). Part of the reserve was purchased by the trust in July 1964 and the remainder is under a 99 year lease signed in February 1966. The purchase was made with financial help and grant aid from SPNRs Nuffield Fund, the Pilgrim Trust and WWF. Managed by West Glamorgan Committee.

Location
0.25 km east of the hamlet of Cwm Ivy. Access to both parts of the reserve can be obtained from the public footpath which runs between Cheriton and Cwm Ivy, along the base of the scarp.

Description
Cwm Ivy Woods reserve is situated on the western extremity of the north Gower limestone escarpment and is in two parts - a section of woodland and a limestone quarry - separated by a private woodland and house. The two sections are linked by the public footpath. The larger part of the reserve is a fine example of a limestone Ash wood with strongly calcicole field-layer vegetation, with Oak and Birch occurring throughout. Plants such as Dog's Mercury (2-4), Bluebells (4-6) and Herb-Bennet (6-8) are abundant. Limestone outcrops and fallen timber provide habitats for bryophytes and ferns.

The old limestone quarry displays an advanced stage of colonisation. Its open grazed floor supports an interesting sward of lime-loving plants, such as Milkwort (4-7) and Wild Thyme (5-8).

Management Objectives
Manage as high forest and replant and maintain the small areas of felled trees and the area of windblown trees that were blown down in the great storm of the 25th January 1990.

Wood Mouse

CWM IVY WOODS

OS Sheet 159; SS 443939

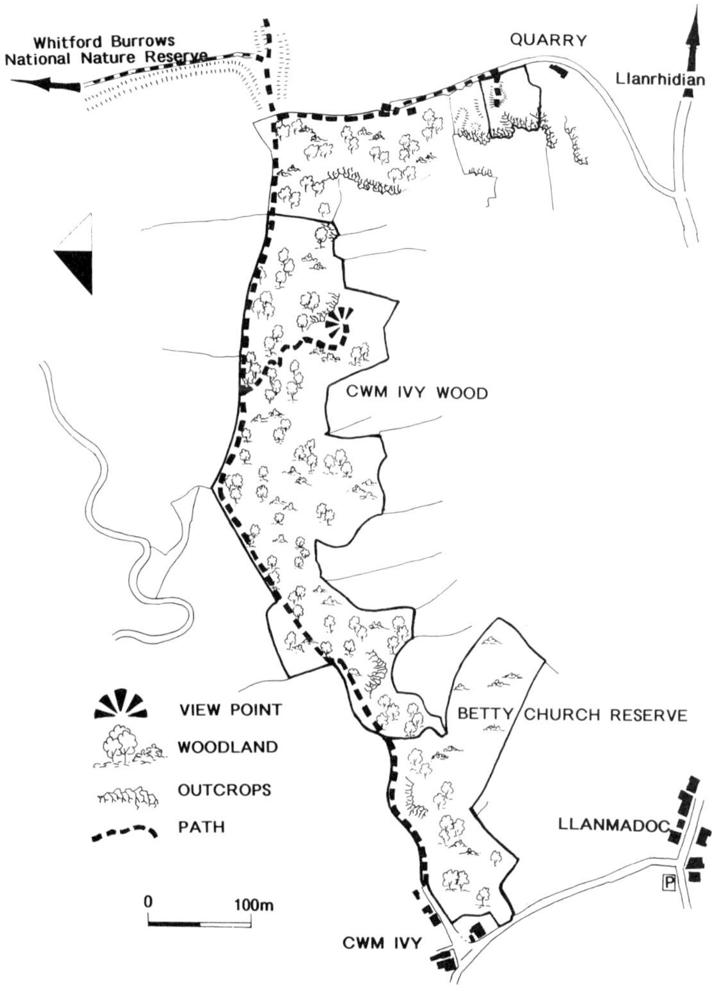

Good times to visit

March - June Spring woodland flowers; *May - July* Summer woodland birds; *September - November* Fungi

Nearest Reserves

Betty Church Reserve, West Glamorgan adjacent; *Bunker's Hill, West Glamorgan* 6.5 km; *The Lucas Reserve, West Glamorgan* 1 km; *Hambury Wood, West Glamorgan* 3 km

THE ELIZABETH AND ROWE HARDING RESERVE

Ilston, Gower

OS Sheet 159; SS 555905

Carboniferous limestone quarry, plantation, scrub and surrounding woodland. The reserve includes Ilston Quarry geological SSSI. Area of quarry 5.7 ha (14.1 acres); woodland 2.0 ha (4.9 acres). The woodland was purchased by the Trust in September 1972. The quarry was acquired by leasehold in 1967 for 21 years and was generously given to the Trust in 1989 by Judge and Mrs Rowe Harding. Managed by West Glamorgan Committee.

Location

0.25 km north of Ilston Village, Gower. The reserve is entered across a shallow ford by way of a stile, from the unclassified road just north of Ilston village. The northern woodland is reached on foot from Bryn-afel Farm.

Description

The quarry was worked until the middle of 1966 and was at a very early stage of natural colonisation, when the Trust first took it over, with plants such as Colt's-foot (3-4) and Wild Strawberry (4-7). Initially, a mixture of trees were planted by the Trust to enhance the naturalisation of the quarry floor and spoil heaps, and a pool was created.

The quarry face is of national geological interest, exposing alternate beds of crinoidal limestone with clays associated with thin seams of coal; a geological exposure unique in Wales.

Kestrels have nested on the quarry face and Kingfisher, Grey Wagtail and Dipper visit the pool.

Management Objectives

To continue to enhance the natural succession of this post-industrial site and maintain the mature woodland as coppice with standards.

Kingfisher

THE ELIZABETH AND ROWE HARDING RESERVE

OS Sheet 159; SS 555905

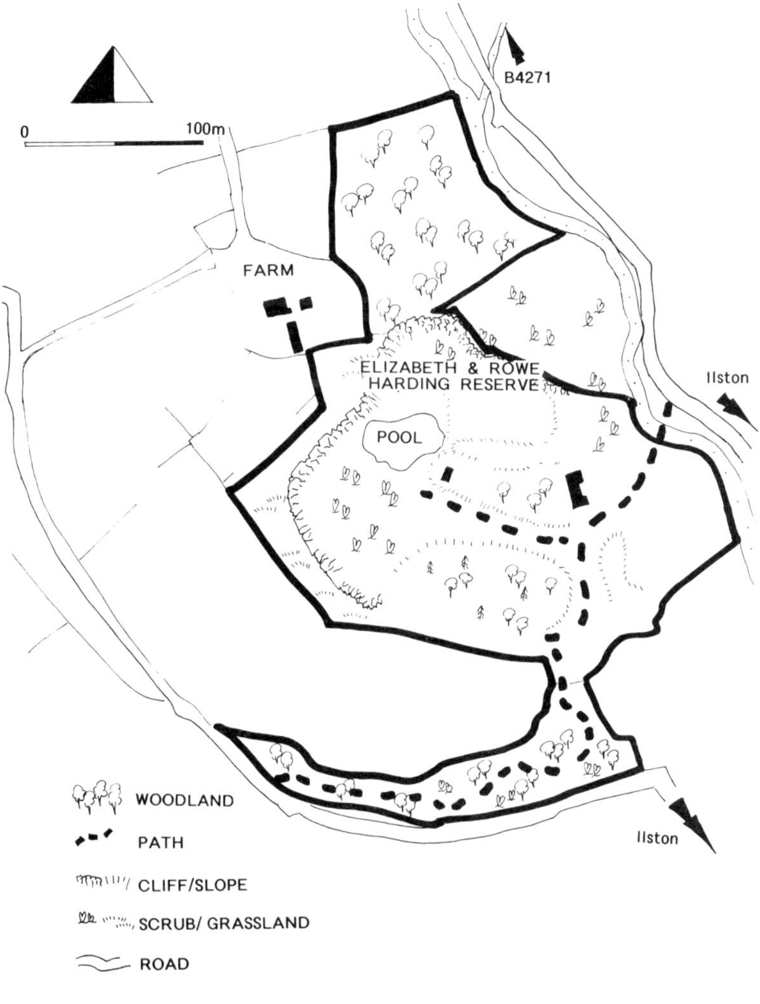

Good times to visit
April - June Spring flowers; *May - July* Summer breeding birds.

Nearest Reserves
Broad Pool, West Glamorgan 4.5 km; *Gelli-hir Wood, West Glamorgan* 2.5 km; *Kilvrough Manor Woods, West Glamorgan* 1.5 km; *Redden Hill Wood, West Glamorgan* 2 km

GELLI-HIR WOOD

Fairwood Common, Gower

OS Sheet 159; SS 562925

Secondary broadleaved wet woodland and pond. Area 28.6 ha (70.8 acres). The reserve was purchased by the Trust in October 1967 with the help of a grant from WWF. Managed by West Glamorgan Committee.

Location
The wood lies on the northern edge of Fairwood Common, Gower. Access is gained over a stile on the unclassified road which runs from the B4271 north to Cil-onen. Car parking adjacent to the reserve is limited.

Description
Gelli-hir Wood is situated on deep glacial drift over Carboniferous grits and shales. The reserve grades from wet Oak/Birch woodland in the south and east to drier Ash/Elm woodland in the north and west. There is a variety of associated habitats including open rides, streams and a pond.

There is a large and varied population of birds, with records of breeding Buzzard, Tawny Owl and Sparrowhawk in the woodland, and Mallard and Teal around the pond. Fallen timber and rotting stumps support an abundance of lower plants and invertebrates.

Moths and Butterflies are well represented, including species such as Comma, Silver-washed Fritillary and Holly Blue.

Management Objectives
To manage the two types of woodland and maintain the diversity of habitat by keeping the rides and glades cleared, coppicing, and periodic pond clearance.

Silver-washed Fritillary

GELLI-HIR WOOD

OS Sheet 159; SS 562925

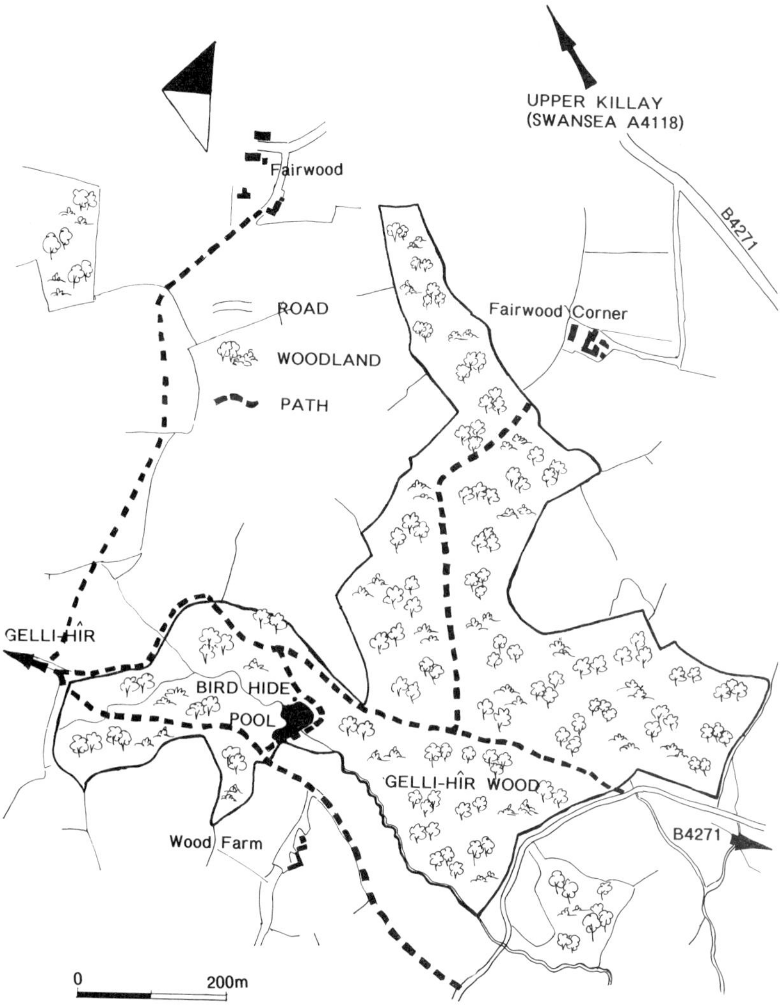

Good times to visit
April - July Woodland flowers, butterflies and birds; *September - October* Fungi

Nearest Reserves
Broad Pool, West Glamorgan 6 km; *Ilston Quarry, West Glamorgan* 2.5 km; *Prior's Wood and meadow, West Glamorgan* 1.5 km; *Redden Hill Wood, West Glamorgan* 4 km

HAMBURY WOOD

Llandimore, Gower

OS Sheet 159; SS 472929

This deciduous limestone woodland reserve was purchased in June 1977 and re-named by the Trust as a memorial to Col H. Hambury, the Trust's founding Chairman (the wood is named "Castle Wood" on OS maps of 1: 250,000 and larger scale). A memorial seat at the centre of the northern boundary of the wood gives fine views of Whiteford Point, the North Gower saltmarsh and Burry Estuary. Area 4.79 ha (11.84 acres). Managed by West Glamorgan Committee.

Location

The reserve is situated just west of Weobley Castle on the steep slopes of the North Gower limestone escarpment, 1.2 km east of Landimore and 1.2 km west of Llanrhidian. Access can be obtained from the unclassified Oldwalls to Llanmadoc road, by way of a stile to the east of a stone wall on the north side of the road. A short walk down the field boundary gives access to the wood through a wicket gate at the western end of the reserve. Car parking on the side of the road close to the reserve is limited.

Description

Hambury Wood is dominated by Oak and Ash with an understorey of neglected (overgrown) Hazel coppice. This, and past grazing by sheep has resulted in a sparse field layer of herbs. The tree canopy is augmented by some fine Field Maples, the occasional Sycamore and a certain amount of dead and dying English Elm. The shrub layer is predominantly Hazel coppice, interspersed with Hawthorn, Elder and Holly. Other species include Ivy, Honeysuckle (6-9) and Blackthorn.

There are an abundance of epiphytes; with mosses, ferns and lichens all well-represented.

Woodland birds such as Treecreeper, Nuthatch and Marsh Tit have been frequently recorded, and good views of Buzzard can be obtained on almost every visit.

Management Objectives

With the help of WGCC, the wood has now been completely fenced to exclude grazing animals, and steps built to allow ease of access up and down the steep slope. It is proposed to introduce coppicing to parts of the woodland, whilst other areas will be allowed to develop into high forest.

HAMBURY WOOD

OS Sheet 159; SS 472929

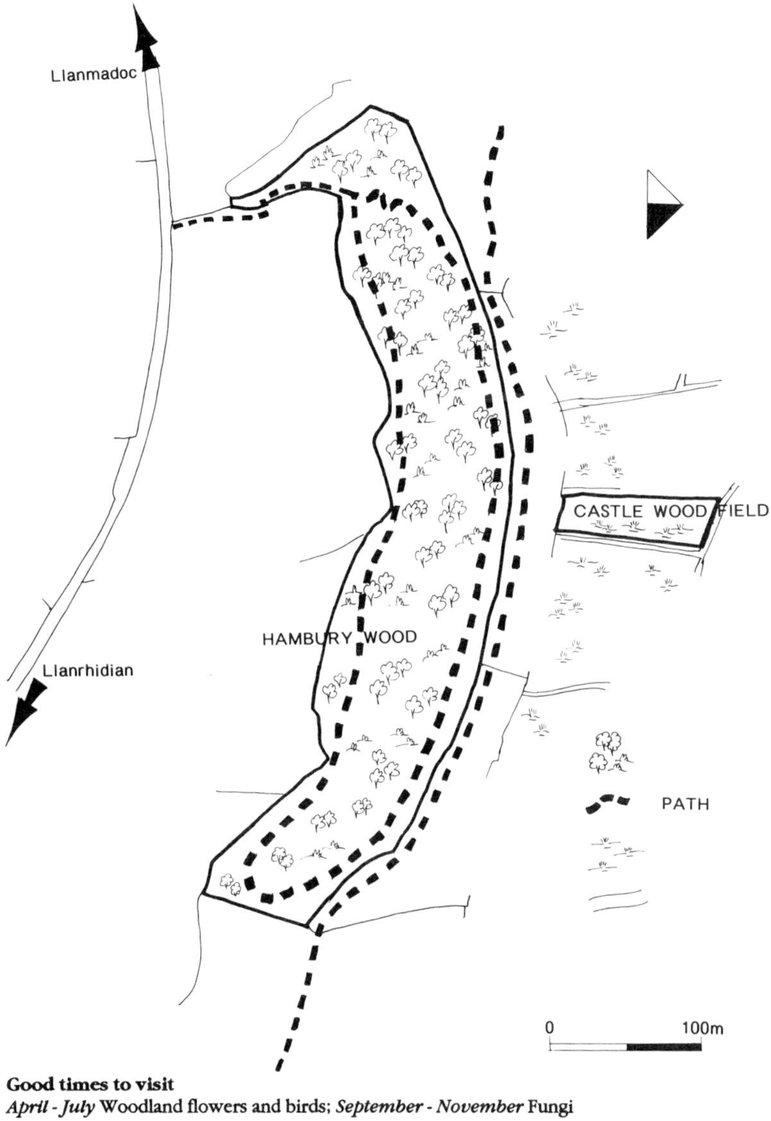

Good times to visit

April - July Woodland flowers and birds; *September - November* Fungi

Nearest Reserves

Castle Wood Field, West Glamorgan 200 m; *Cwm Ivy Woods, West Glamorgan* 3 km; *The Lucas Reserve, West Glamorgan* 2.5 km; *Llanrhidian Hill, West Glamorgan* 2.5 km

KILVROUGH MANOR WOODS

Parkmill, Gower

OS Sheet 159; SS 555892

Ancient limestone broadleaved woodland and plantation. Area 7.5 ha (18.5 acres). A 999 year lease was purchased by the Trust in March 1988 with financial help from the Countryside Commission and sponsorship from Office Cleaning Supplies Ltd through the WWFs Corporate Fundraising Department. Managed by West Glamorgan Committee.

Location
On either side of the A4118, before entering Park Mill, Gower. There is limited parking space at a lay-by on the northern side of the A4118, and further parking can be found in the village of Parkmill. A public footpath crosses the south-western part of the wood, along the line of a water authority sewer, and a second public footpath runs the length of the southern boundary of the reserve. There is a permissive path through the centre of the southern wood, but there are no public rights of way in the northern wood.

Description
The woods are mostly ancient semi-natural and broadleaved, comprising Ash, Oak, Beech and Elm with an understorey of Hazel; and a Beech plantation making up a large part of the southern woodland. There is also a small amount of Larch planted in some areas.

Bramble, Bluebell (4-6), Ramsons (4-6), Twayblade (5-8) and Hart's-tongue Fern occur in abundance. The Woods are one of the last Gower localities for the Greater Butterfly-orchid (5-7).

The woodland provides a suitable habitat for a range of breeding woodland birds such as Chiffchaff, Robin, Great Tit, Treecreeper and Willow Warbler with other species such as Buzzard, Great Spotted Woodpecker and Woodcock regularly seen.

Management Objectives
The woodlands require a degree of thinning, particularly in the Beech plantation and the clearance of some Cherry Laurel. It is hoped to restart the cutting of the long stood over Hazel coppice to benefit the spring-flowering herbs. The provision of information boards and the upgrading of various paths, especially in the southern portion of the wood are essential.

KILVROUGH MANOR WOODS

OS Sheet 159; SS 555892

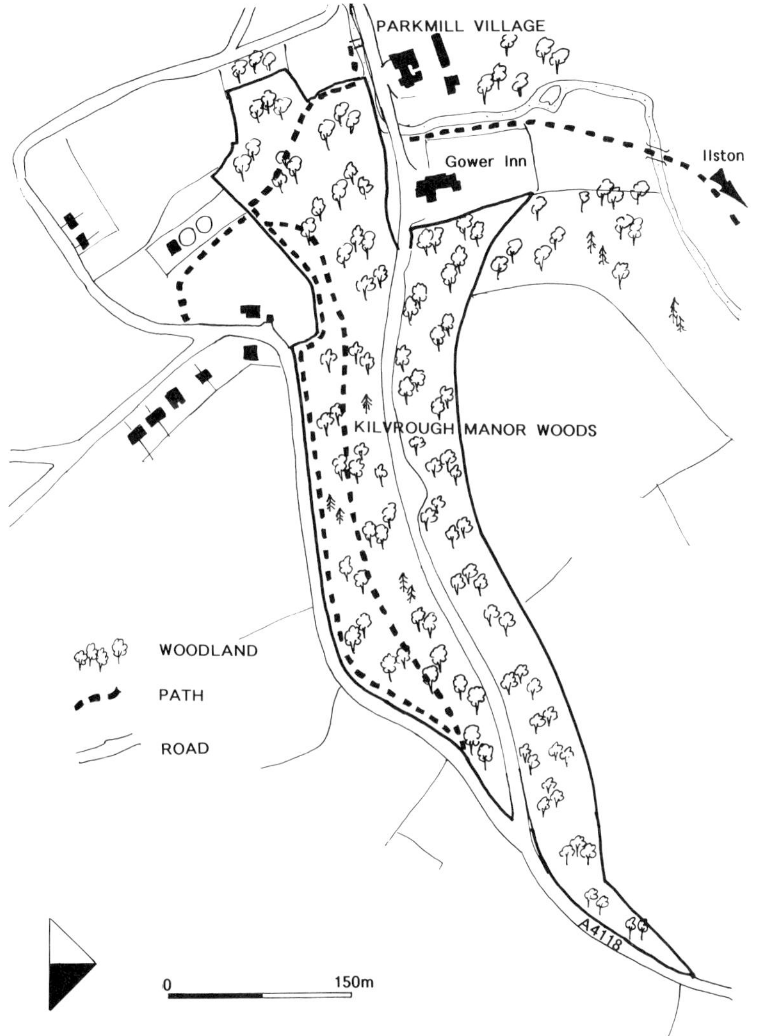

Good times to visit
April - June Spring woodland flowers; *May - July* Summer breeding birds; *September - November* Fungi

Nearest Reserves
Gelli-hir Wood, West Glamorgan 4 km; *E & R Harding Nature Reserve, West Glamorgan* 1.5 km; *Redden Hill Wood, West Glamorgan* 1.5 km; *Redley Cliff, West Glamorgan* 4 km

LLANRHIDIAN HILL

Llanrhidian, Gower

OS Sheet 159; SS 495922

Limestone grassland, scrub and quarry. Area 3.09 ha (7.6 acres). Purchased by the Trust in April 1966. Registered Common Land. Managed by West Area Committee.

Location
Adjacent to Llanrhidian village, 15 km west of Swansea.

Description
Much of the site occupies a steep north-facing slope on Carboniferous Limestone, giving fine views overlooking the Burry Estuary.

It is composed mainly of species-rich limestone grassland with Common Rock-rose (5-9), Wild Thyme (5-8) and Milkwort (4-7) abundant, with patches of Elder, Hawthorn and Ash scrub which grades into mature woodland to the west. At the eastern end there are two limestone quarry sites. The smaller one is scrub-filled. The larger quarry is shallow with a grassland-covered floor, its rocky sides supporting a slightly different assemblage of lime-loving plants.

Management objectives
To maintain an area of limestone grassland whilst allowing the natural progression of part of the site to woodland. To allow natural colonisation of the larger quarry site, preserving the quarry face in an open state.

Common Rock-rose

LLANRHIDIAN HILL

OS Sheet 159; SS 495922

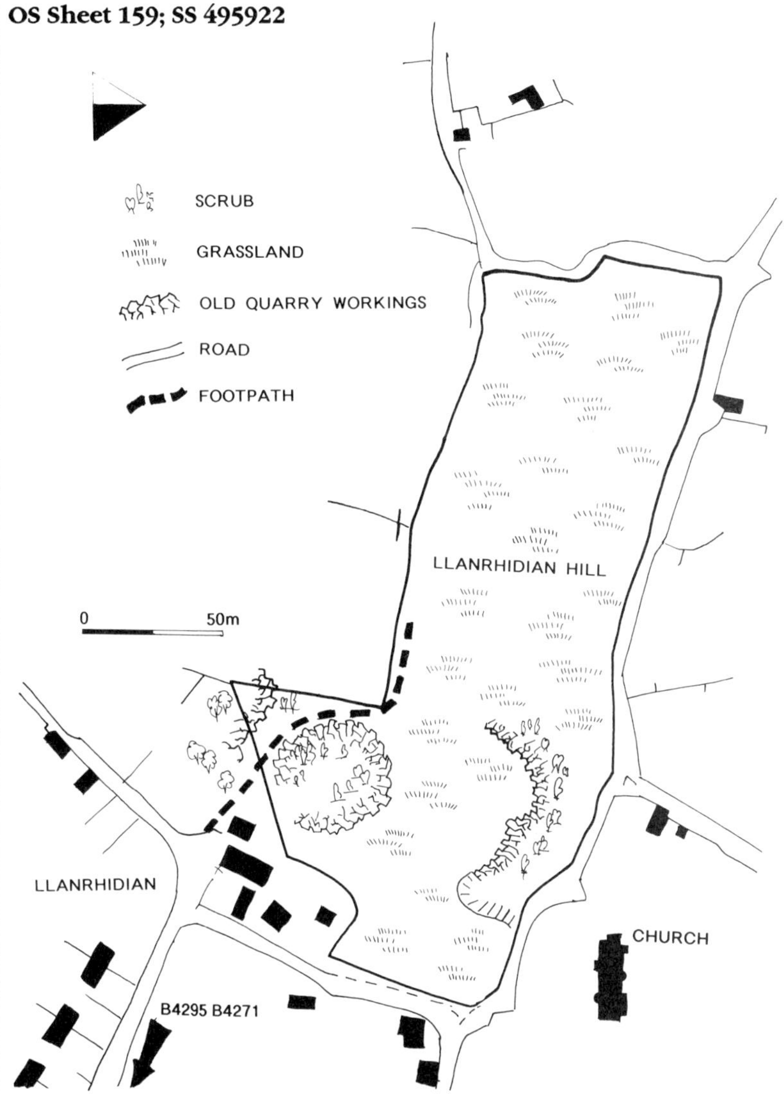

Good times to visit
April - June Spring flowers; *May - July* Summer breeding birds

Nearest Reserves
Berry Wood, West Glamorgan 4.5 km; *Broad Pool, West Glamorgan* 2 km; *The Lucas Reserve, West Glamorgan* 2.5 km; *Hambury Wood, West Glamorgan* 2.5 km

LLYN FACH

North of Treherbert

OS Sheet 170; SN 905033

Cliffs, scree, corrie lake and bog, forming part of the Craig-y-Llyn SSSI. Area 16.2 ha (40 acres). The reserve was acquired in June 1968, and since 1987 has been under a 5-year licence from the Forestry Commission. Managed by Mid Glamorgan Committee.

Location
Access is obtained on foot from the A4061 following the Forestry Commission roads for about 2 km.

Description
Llyn Fach is one of the southernmost corrie lakes in Britain, lying at 435 m in a nivation cirque beneath the Pennant Sandstone escarpment of Craig-y-Llyn. This peak rises to 550 m with a lower cliff brink at 48 m. The highest point in Glamorgan (600 m) lies on the plateau just south of the reserve. The head of the scarp commands fine views north to the Brecon Beacons.

The reserve, surrounded by Forestry Commission plantations, includes the lake, its rocky shore, an area of bog, and a large area of steep cliff and scree. Both the lake and the escarpment bear an assemblage of montane and arctic/alpine plants, some rare, and many at or near the southern limit of their range.

The nutrient-poor waters of the lake carry a typical flora, with a number of less common species such as Water Lobelia (7-8), Floating Bur-reed (6-7), Quillwort (5-7) and Water-purslane (6-10). It has a thriving population of invertebrates and amphibians, including Smooth and Palmate Newts.

The escarpment provides a habitat for Roseroot (5-8), Lesser Meadow-rue (6-8), Parsley Fern (7-8) and Clubmosses.

Kestrel, Raven and Ring Ouzel nest on the crags and Buzzard, Peregrine and Sparrowhawk have all been seen. The surrounding conifer plantations provide a habitat for Crossbills to breed.

Management Objectives
To conserve and maintain the habitats and discourage the increase in public pressure on the area.

Raven

LLYN FACH

OS Sheet 170; SN 905033

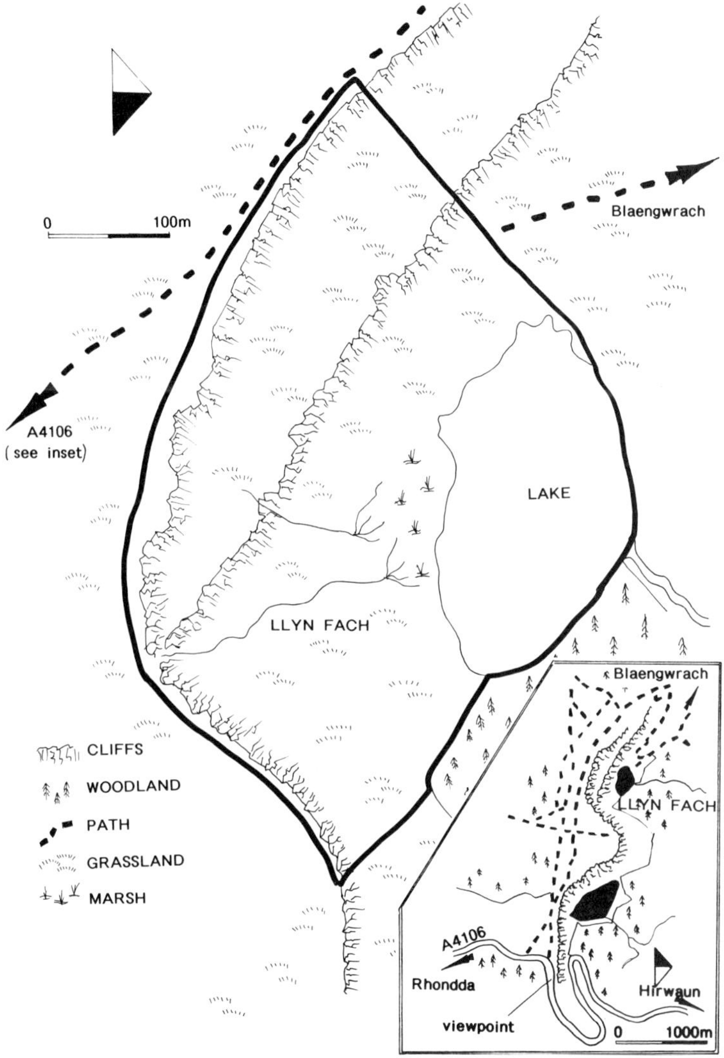

Good times to visit

June - August Upland flowers; *May - July* Summer breeding birds

Nearest Reserves

Aberdare Canal, Mid Glamorgan 11 km; *Blaenant y Gwyddyl, West Glamorgan* 4 km; *Coed Gawdir, West Glamorgan* 12.5 km; *Melincwrt Waterfall, West Glamorgan* 8.5 km

THE LUCAS RESERVE

Frog Lane, Llanmadoc, Gower

OS Sheet 159; SS 447933

Wet grassland and scrub. Area 0.45 ha (1.1 acres). The reserve was acquired in September 1970 under a 99-year lease. Managed by West Glamorgan Committee.

Location
Adjacent to the Britannia Inn, Llanmadoc.

Description
The Lucas Reserve takes the form of a long narrow field sloping northwards down to Burry Pill. Most of the reserve is on a slope made up of boulder clay and is dominated by Bracken/Bramble scrub with Willow, Ash and Oak developing into secondary woodland. The northern part of the reserve, which is the lowest point, is level ground on alluvial sediments and experiences periodic salt-water inundations from Burry Pill at high tides. This area consists of damp meadowland with stands of Yellow Flag (5-7) and Marsh Mallow (8-9), its junction with the scrub and woodland marked by a dense stand of Common Reed (8-9).

Management Objectives
To maintain the diversity of the site through grass cutting and tree planting.

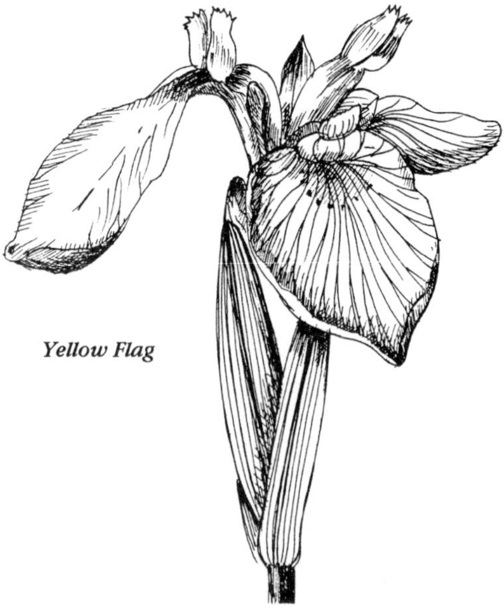

Yellow Flag

THE LUCAS RESERVE

OS Sheet 159; SS 447933

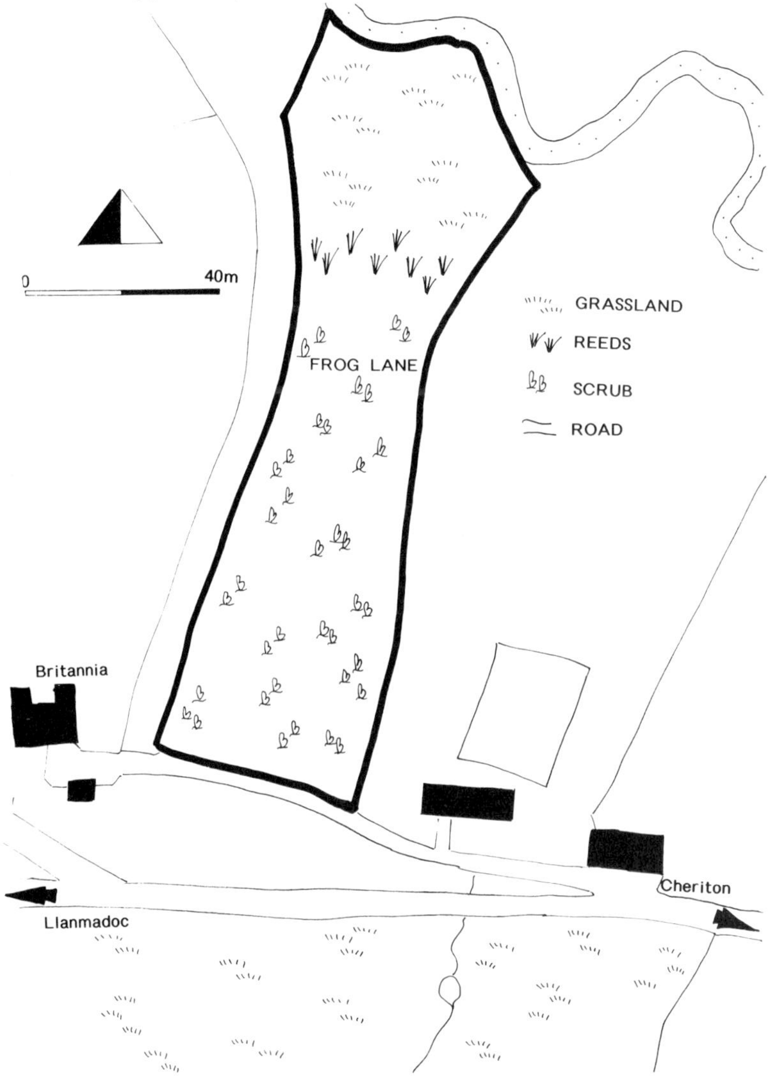

Good times to visit

March - June Spring flowers; *May - July* Summer breeding birds

Nearest Reserves

Betty Church Reserve, West Glamorgan 1 km; *Cwm Ivy Woods, West Glamorgan* 1 km; *Hambury Woods, West Glamorgan* 2.5 km; *Llanrhidian Hill, West Glamorgan* 4.5 km

MELINCWRT WATERFALLS

Resolven

OS Sheet 160; SN 825017

Ancient broadleaved woodland, stream and waterfall. Area 5.2 ha (12.8 acres). The reserve was purchased in September 1986 with grant aid and financial assistance from the Countryside Commission, WWF and from the RSNC Land Fund. Managed by West Glamorgan Committee.

Location
0.5 km south-west of Resolven, 8 km north-east of Neath. Melincwrt Waterfalls is signposted from the A465(T). Neath Borough Council provide a car park on the west side of the road south of Resolven. The reserve can be reached by a public footpath, the entrance being on the opposite side of the road from the public car park.

Description
Melincwrt Waterfalls is made up of a mature sessile oak woodland ascending steeply from the narrow gorge of the Melincwrt Brook. It is interspersed with gnarled Silver birch, Wild Cherry, Rowan and Crab Apple. Alder dominates the stream bank. The spectacular eighty foot high waterfall on a tributary of the Neath River was painted by Turner in 1974.

The woodland floor is carpeted with Bluebells (4-6) in spring, with Enchanter's-nightshade (6-8) taking over later in the year. Alternate-leaved Golden Saxifrage (4-5) and Tutsan (6-8) are confined to the wet flushes. Ferns thrive in the local humid atmosphere in this narrow valley; twenty species been recorded from the reserve, including Green Spleenwort (8-11), Brittle Bladder-fern (6-9), Hay-scented Buckler-fern (8-10) and Wilson's Filmy-fern (6-7).

The birdlife, typical of this type of habitat, includes Redstart, Wood Warbler and Pied Flycatcher in summer, with Dipper and Grey Wagtail being regularly seen along the stream at all times of the year.

On the northern boundary of the reserve the remains of a blast-furnace and iron works can be found. These were built in the Seventeenth century and the works were opened in 1708 for a century of iron production. The great overshot water wheel was powered by a leat leading water from above the Melincwrt Waterfalls.

Management Objectives
To maintain the site as high forest and allow natural regeneration.

MELINCWRT WATERFALLS

OS Sheet 160; SN 825017

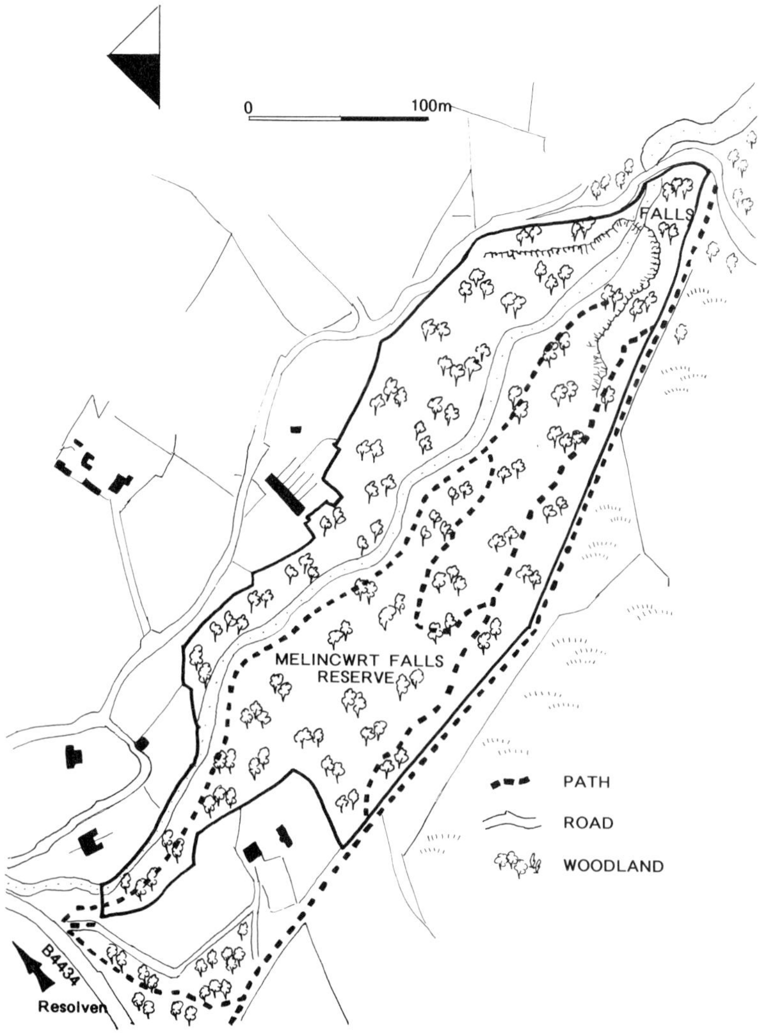

Good times to visit

April - June Spring woodland flowers; *May - July* Summer woodland birds; *September - November* Fungi; *October - March* waterfalls (particularly after a period of rain)

Nearest Reserves

Blaenant y Gwyddyl, West Glamorgan 8 km; *Craig Cilhendre, West Glamorgan* 10 km; *Coed Gawdir, West Glamorgan* 4 km; *Llyn Fach, West Glamorgan* 8.5 km

PEEL WOOD

Oystermouth

OS Sheet 159; SS 607883

Secondary broadleaved woodland and quarry. Area 1.1 ha (2.8 acres). The reserve was acquired in September 1969 and the freehold was bequeathed to the Trust by Mrs S.M. Peel upon her death in 1978. Managed by West Glamorgan Committee.

Location
0.75 km west of Oystermouth. Access is obtained by entering the reserve through the gate from a path which leaves the Newton Road to the south of the "Sunnyside" old people's home.

Description
Peel Wood occupies the site of the former Callencroft limestone quarry. The mature woodland is dominated by Sycamore, with Ash and Oak as lesser components. Ivy is common, with Hart's-tongue Fern and Soft Shield-fern both plentiful. The ground flora has displays of naturalised Daffodils and Solomon's-seal in early spring which later give way to Ramsons (4-6).

The quarry cliffs support a rich bryophyte and fern flora.

There is a good range of woodland birds including breeding Tawny Owl.

Management Objectives
To conserve and maintain the present character of the quarry and woodland and preserve the lime kilns.

Ash

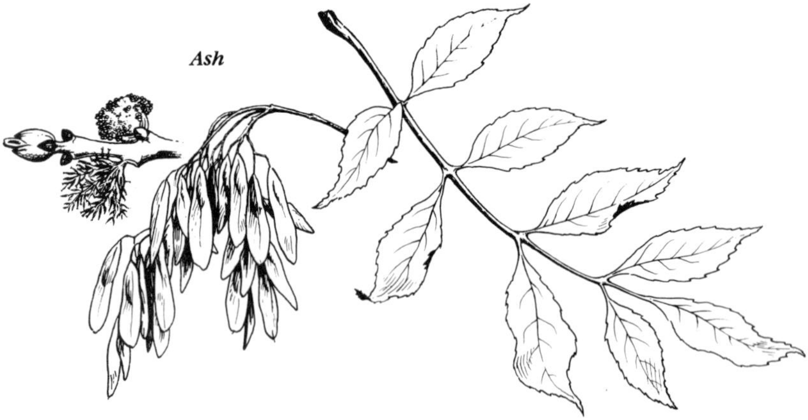

PEEL WOOD

OS Sheet 159; SS 607883

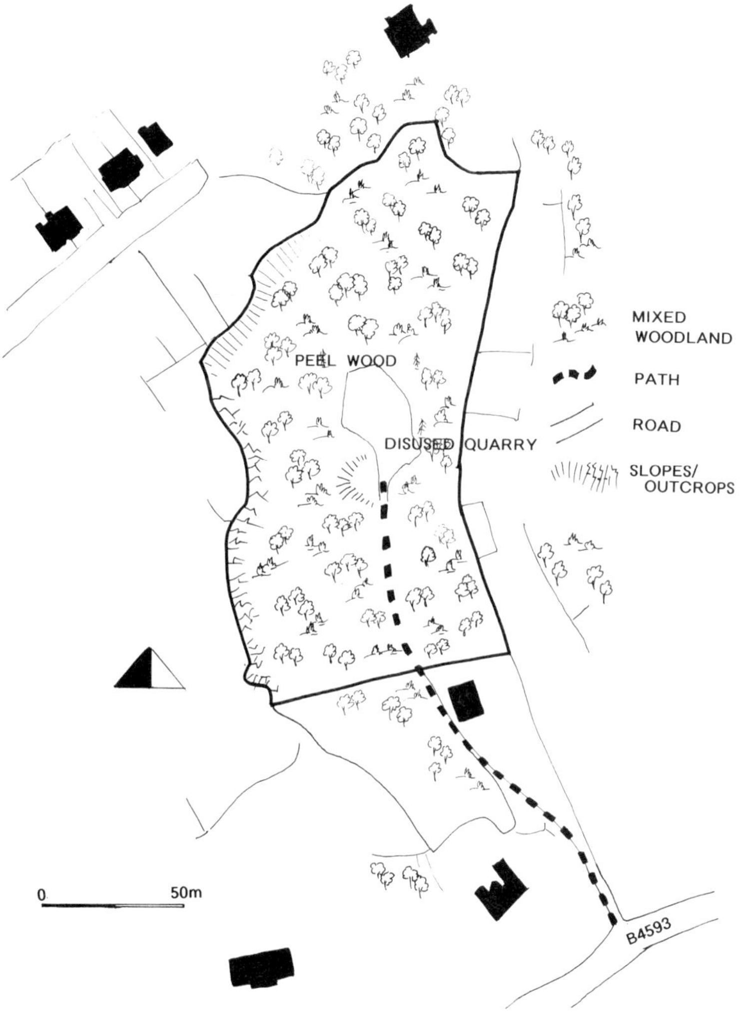

Good times to visit
April - June Spring woodland flowers; *May - July* Summer woodland birds; *September - November* Fungi

Nearest Reserves
E & R Harding Nature Reserve, West Glamorgan 6 km; *Kilvrough Manor Woods, West Glamorgan* 5.5 km; *Redley Cliff, West Glamorgan* 2 km; *Ridgewood Park, West Glamorgan* 2.5 km

PRIOR'S WOOD AND MEADOW

Three Crosses, Gower

OS Sheet 159; SS 577938

Secondary broadleaved wet woodland and meadow. Area 17.4 ha (43 acres). The reserve was purchased in March 1987 with grant aid and financial support from the Countryside Commission, WWF and from the CEGB through RSNCs Welsh Wildlife Appeal. Managed by West Glamorgan Committee.

Location

0.5 km east of Three Crosses and 1 km west of Dunvant. Parking is restricted. One should park on the roadside at Three Crosses and follow the public footpath across Fairwood Common towards Ty Gwyn (Dunvant) until reaching the reserve. There are no public rights of way within the reserve.

Description

The reserve comprises 12.1 ha of semi-natural broadleaved woodland, small spinneys, a considerable length of hedge and 5.3 ha of meadow. There is some evidence of old mine workings.

The woodland canopy is made up of a considerable mixture of species including Sweet Chestnut, Beech, Ash, Alder, birch, Sessile Oak, Yew, Elm and Small-leaved Lime. This diversity, together with cartographic evidence which shows that the site was originally called "Prior's Meadow", suggests that the woods have arisen from natural regeneration, probably aided by Victorian planting.

A variety of interesting shrub species may be found, including Eared Willow, Creeping Willow and Alder Buckthorn. The varied ground flora is complemented by a rich mixture of ferns, mosses, liverworts and lichens, including Royal Fern. Much of the wood is very damp, with two springs arising within the reserve.

The Prior's Meadow slopes gently in a south-easterly direction and is somewhat drier than the woodland. The turf is made up of a wide range of typical meadow plants, such as Yellow-rattle (6-9), Ragged-Robin (5-8) and Devil's-bit Scabious (6-10), together with a number of uncommon species such as Whorled Caraway (6-8). The meadow also contains a great variety of grasses and sedges.

Management Objectives

To maintain the site as high forest with clearings. Manage the meadow with a late summer haycut and aftermath grazing.

PRIOR'S WOOD AND MEADOW

OS Sheet 159; SS 577938

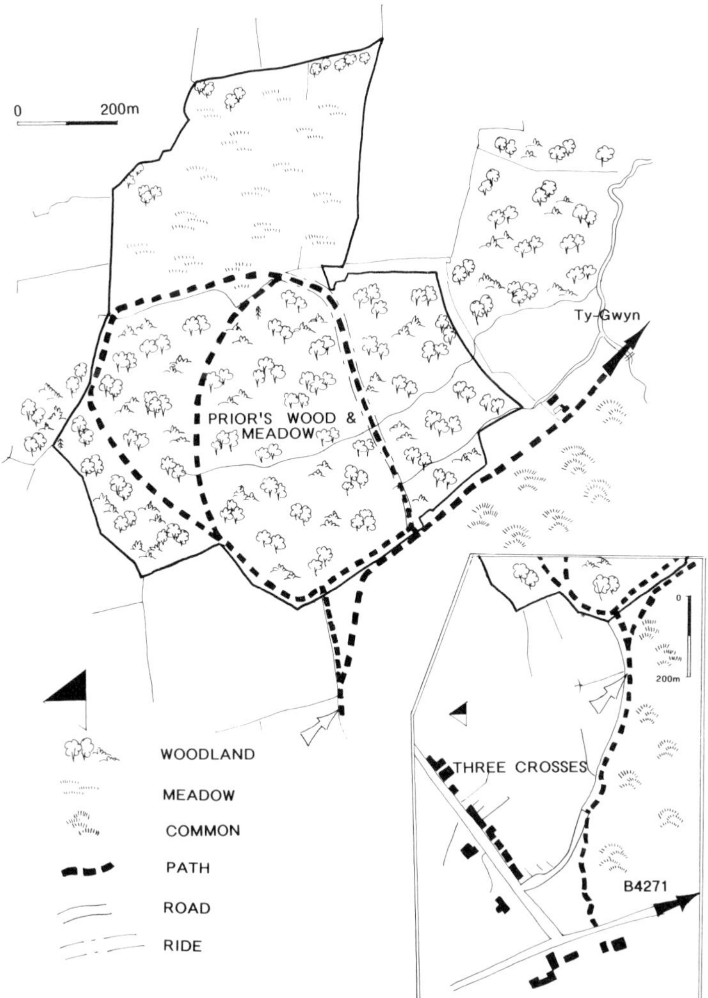

Good times to visit
March - June Spring woodland flowers; *May - July* Summer breeding birds; *September - November* Fungi

Nearest Reserves
E & R Harding Nature Reserve, West Glamorgan 4 km; *Gelli-hir Wood, West Glamorgan* 1.5 km; *Kilvrough Manor Woods, West Glamorgan* 5.5 km; *Ridgewood Park, West Glamorgan* 4.5 km

REDDEN HILL WOOD

Parkmill, Gower

OS Sheet 159; SS 538894

Broadleaved plantation and scrub. Area 1.1 ha (2.8 acres). The freehold of the reserve was given to the Trust by Messrs J.C. and D.W. Isaac of Swansea, in July 1979. Managed by West Glamorgan Committee.

Location
0.5 km north-west of Parkmill. Access is via the A4118 and the Parc-y-Breos Wood.

Description
Redden Hill Wood was originally a small conifer plantation when the Trust first acquired it. The conifers have largely been felled and a deciduous woodland dominated by Ash has been allowed to regenerate naturally. A circular walk has recently been established.

Species to be seen include Speckled Wood butterfly and Redstart, which breed in the vicinity.

Management Objectives
To allow the mixed forest to flourish.Sycamore to be removed.

Speckled Wood

REDDEN HILL WOOD

OS Sheet 159; SS 538894

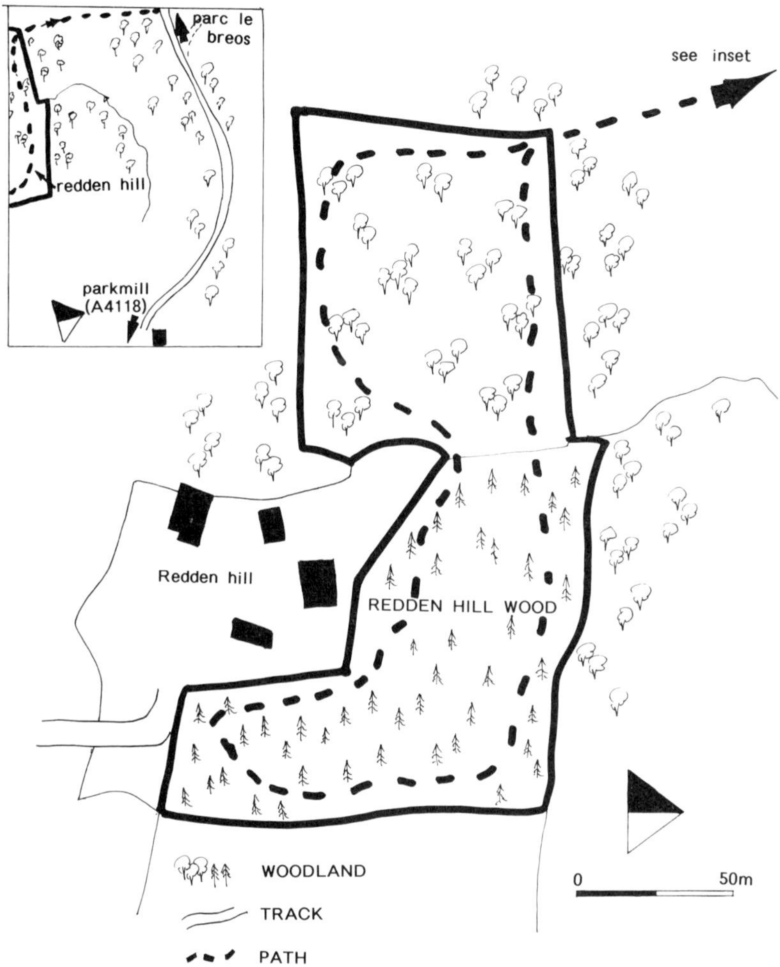

Good times to visit

April - June Spring woodland flowers; *May - July* Summer woodland birds and butterflies; *September - November* Fungi

Nearest Reserves

Broad Pool, West Glamorgan 3.5 km; *Gelli-hir Woods, West Glamorgan* 4 km; *Ilston Quarry, West Glamorgan* 2 km; *Kilvrough Manor Woods, West Glamorgan* 1.5 km

REDLEY CLIFF

Caswell Bay, Gower

OS Sheet 159; SS 589875

Coastal limestone broadleaved woodland, scrub and grassland. Area 3.6 ha (9 acres). The reserve forms part of the Caswell Bay SSSI and includes a Scheduled Ancient Monument. The reserve was purchased by the Trust in August 1979. Managed by West Glamorgan Committee.

Location
2.5 km west of Mumbles.

Description
Redley Cliff lies on the limestone headland at the western end of Caswell Bay, Gower. The northern and eastern parts occupy a steep north-facing slope supporting wind-trimmed scrub woodland of Ash, Hazel, Hawthorn and Blackthorn, and a strongly-calcicole field layer. The remainder of the reserve occupies the steep south-facing slope of the headland, stretching down to and including the sea cliffs. The summit bears limestone grassland and the slope carries a mosaic of bracken, gorse, heath and scree. In the more sheltered eastern parts are patches of scrub with naturalised Holm Oak. Cotoneaster is well-established on the scree. Fox and Rabbit are present. Stonechat and Yellowhammer are among the commoner birds. There are remains of a scheduled Iron Age hill fort at the summit.

Management Objectives
To maintain the mosaic of natural vegetation.

Yellowhammer

REDLEY CLIFF

OS Sheet 159; SS 589875

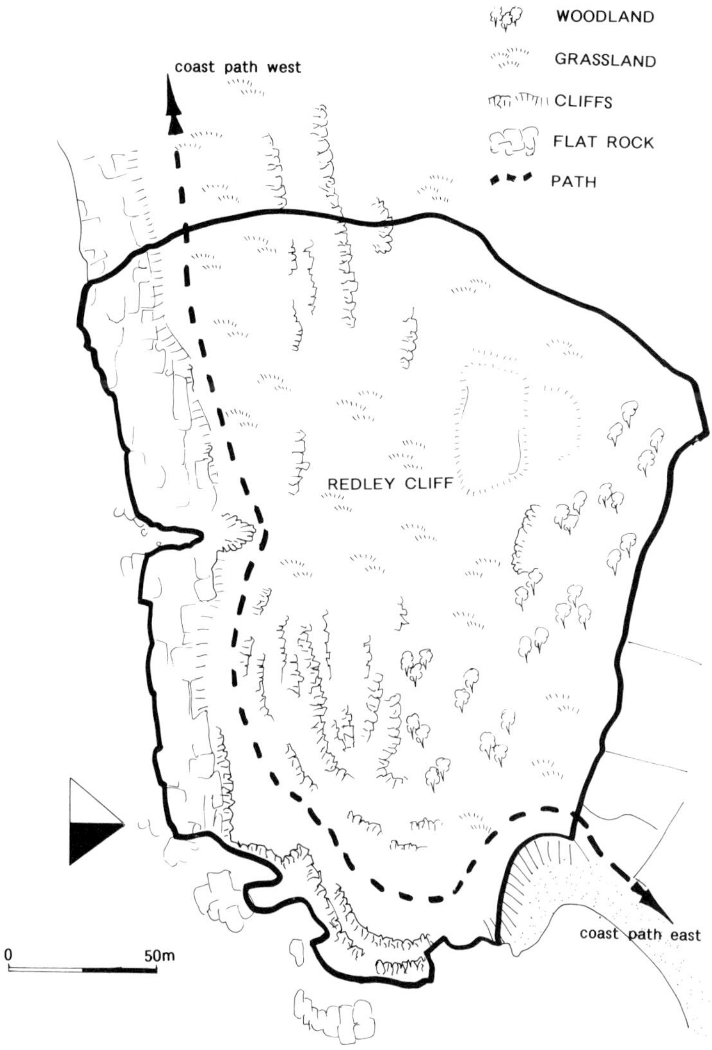

Good times to visit

March - July Spring coastal flowers; *May - July* Summer coastal breeding birds

Nearest Reserves

E & R Harding Nature Reserve, West Glamorgan 4.5 km; *Kilvrough Manor Woods, West Glamorgan* 4 km; *Peel Wood, West Glamorgan* 2 km; *Ridgewood Park, West Glamorgan* 3.5 km

RIDGEWOOD PARK

Mayals

OS Sheet 159; SS 611906

Small urban plantation. Area 0.3 ha (0.75 acres). The reserve was acquired in June 1962 under a 99-year lease. Managed by West Glamorgan Committee.

Location
1.5 km west north-west of Mumbles. Access can be gained from the B4436 Black Pill to Pennard road, turning right past Clyne Gardens in the town of Mayals. The reserve is on the corner of St. Catwag Walk, the next right turn off Westport Avenue.

Description
Ridgewood Park is a small building plot bounded by roads and urban development on three sides and by Clyne Gardens on the other.

The reserve is dominated by a variety of trees and shrubs, such as Ash, Larch, Sycamore, Lime, Holly and Rowan, which was planted by the Trust. The field layer, which is wet in places, gives a display of Bluebells (4-6) in spring, and is dominated by Bramble and Wavy Hair-grass (6-7).

Management Objectives
The principal conservation aim at Ridgewood Park is to create and maintain an undisturbed wildlife habitat in an urban environment. Nestboxes are provided for the urban titmouse population.

Great Tit

RIDGEWOOD PARK

OS Sheet 159; SS 611906

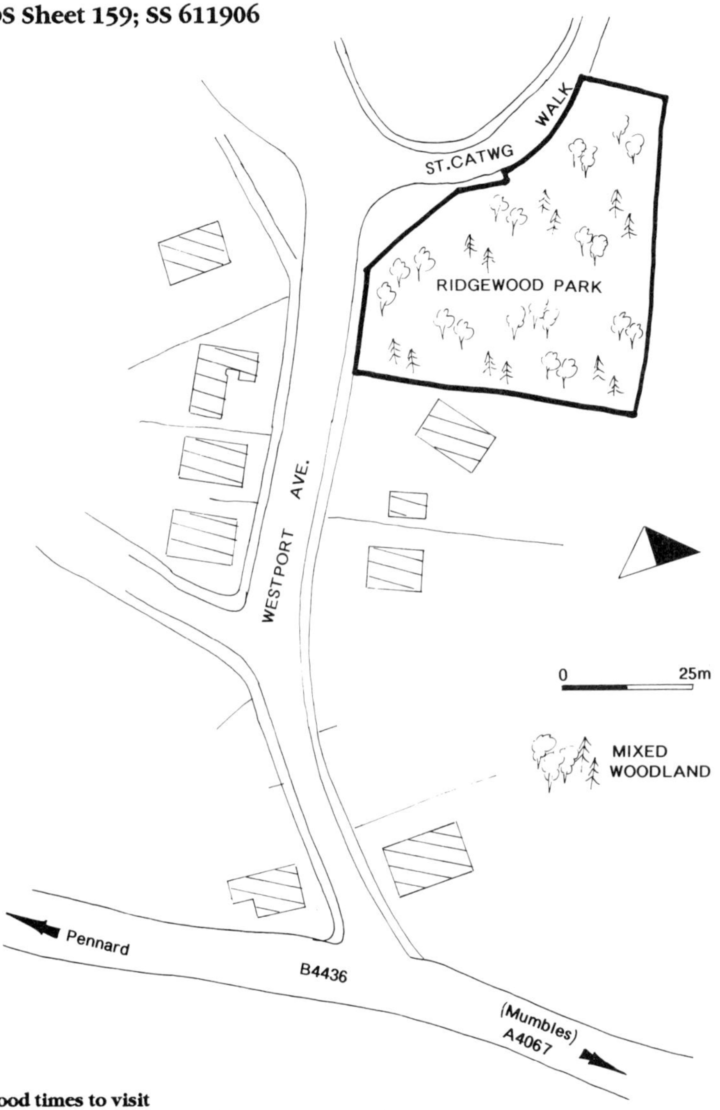

Good times to visit
April - June Spring woodland flowers; *May - July* Suburban breeding birds; *September - November* Fungi

Nearest Reserves
Gelli-hir Wood, West Glamorgan 5 km; *Kilvrough Manor Woods, West Glamorgan* 5.5 km; *Peel Wood, West Glamorgan* 4 km; *Redley Cliff, West Glamorgan* 3.5 km

SOUTH GOWER COAST – DEBORAH'S HOLE

Pilton, Gower

OS Sheet 159; SS 435862

Sea cliff, limestone grassland and heath, forming part of the Gower Coast Rhossili to Port Eynon SSSI. Area 6.7 ha (16.5 acres). The freehold of this reserve was purchased in July 1972 with financial help from Marks and Spencers plc. Managed by West Glamorgan Committee and the Port Eynon to Rhossili Coastal Management Group.

Location
2 km east of Rhossili, 3 km west of Port Eynon. Access to the Deborah's Hole nature reserve can be gained from the public footpath leading south to the coastline from Kimerleymoor, or via the Rhossili to Port Eynon coastal footpath.

Description
Deborah's Hole is named after a small inaccessable cave which during Nineteenth century archaeological excavations yielded Stone Age tools, which are to be seen in Swansea Museum.

The reserve has been partially surface quarried for limestone either as building stone for walls or for burning to produce lime for agricultural fields. This has left a broken surface and varied soil depth which has not allowed subsequent agricultural improvement, as has occurred to the cliff top immediately to the east.

The vegetation ranges from maritime limestone grassland with Common Rock-rose (5-9), Squinancywort (6-7), and Wild Thyme (5-8) on the thinner soils through to limestone heath supporting Heather (7-9) and Bell Heather (7-9) together with Gorse and Hawthorn scrub. The reserve also has nesting Rock Pipit and Linnet, with Fulmar and Raven nesting upon adjacent cliffs.

This reserve allows good views of the Knave, a small offshore stack with attendant Cormorants and Shags, and on a clear day, the Island of Lundy can been seen far out in the Bristol Channel.

Management Objectives
To maintain the present vegetation mosaic, and prevent the heath and grassland being over-run by scrub.

Wild Thyme

SOUTH GOWER COAST – DEBORAH'S HOLE

OS Sheet 159; SS 435862

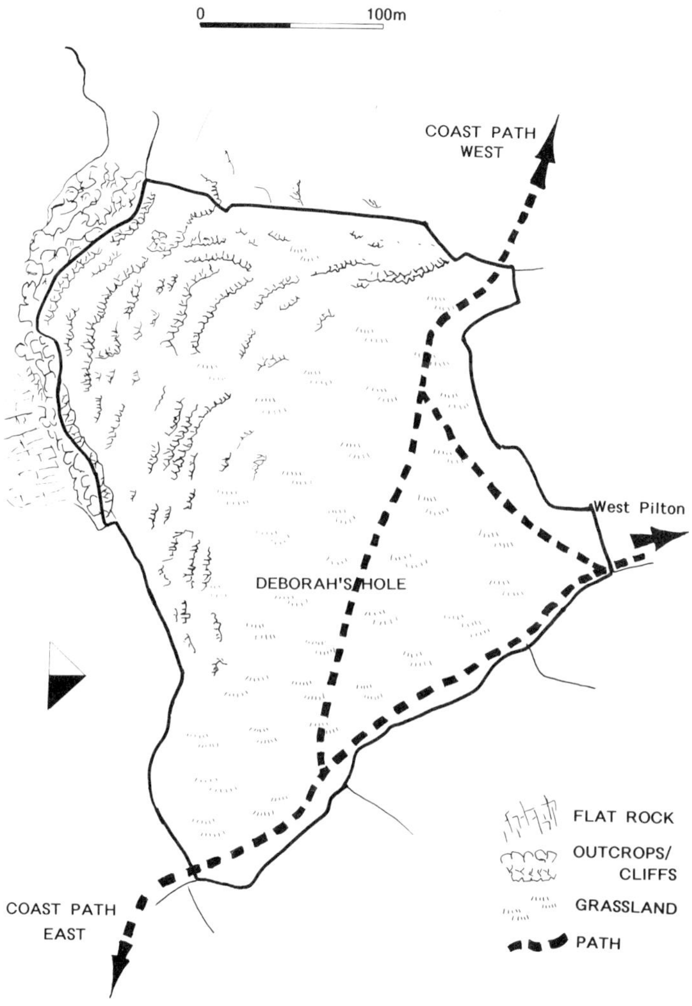

Good times to visit

April - July Spring coastal flowers; *May - July* Summer coastal breeding birds

Nearest Reserves

Berry Wood, West Glamorgan 4 km; Bun*ker's Hill, West Glamorgan* 2 km; *South Gower Coast - Long Hole Cliff, West Glamorgan* 1.5 km; *South Gower Coast - Overton Cliff, West Glamorgan* 2.5 km

SOUTH GOWER COAST – LONG HOLE CLIFF

Overton, Gower

OS Sheet 159; SS 450850

Sea cliffs, limestone grassland, heath and cave forming part of the Gower Coast Rhossili to Port Eynon SSSI. Area 20.7 ha (50.2 acres). The freehold of this reserve was purchased with financial help from BP Chemicals Ltd in September 1970. Part Registered Common Land. Managed by West Glamorgan Committee and the Port Eynon to Rhossili Coastal Management Group.

Location

1 km west of the village of Overton. The reserve can be accessed from the track that leads westward from the Village of Overton.

Description

Long Hole Cliff nature reserve is named after a small cave in the centre of the reserve which during Nineteenth century archaeological excavations yielded Stone Age tools and the fossil remains of Ice Age animals which are to be seen in Swansea Museum.

Part of the cliffs closest to the sea in the south-east corner of the reserve have been quarried for limestone, which was burned in the adjacent limekiln, the ruin of which is still visible, to provide lime for spreading on fields further inland.

The reserve displays a very clear difference in vegetation between the deeper cliff top soils which support Gorse and scrub and the thinner soils of the slopes, cliffs and scree with limestone grassland flowers. Spring brings a flush of blue to the cliffs as Spring Squill (4-5) flowers followed by a wide range of other flowers including as Bird's-foot Trefoil (6-9), Horseshoe Vetch (5-7), and Portland Spurge (5-9).

This reserve is also a site for plants protected under Schedule 8 of the Wildlife & Countryside Act 1981.

Management Objectives

The limestone grassland and scrub is maintained by a system of light sheep grazing.

Spring Squill

SOUTH GOWER COAST – LONG HOLE CLIFF

OS Sheet 159; SS 450850

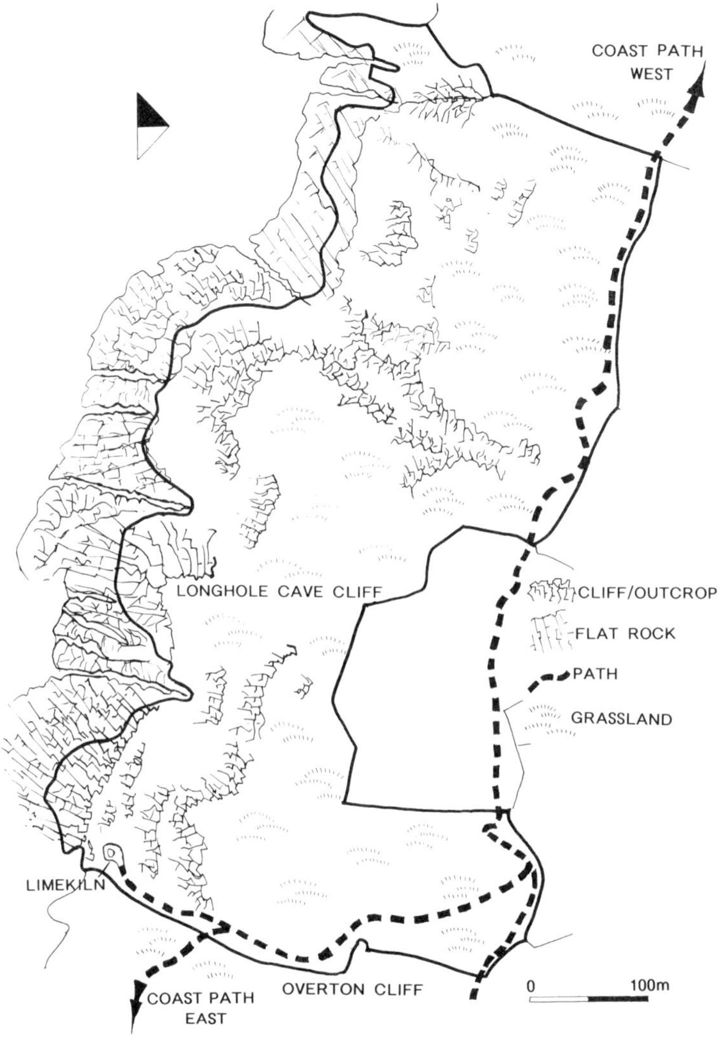

Good times to visit

March - June Spring coastal flowers; *May - July* Summer breeding birds; *November - March* Sea-watching

Nearest Reserves

Berry Wood, West Glamorgan 4 km; *Bunker's Hill, West Glamorgan* 3.5 km; *South Gower Coast - Deborah's Hole, West Glamorgan* 1.5 km; *South Gower Coast - Overton Cliff, West Glamorgan* adjacent to the east

SOUTH GOWER COAST – OVERTON CLIFF

Overton, Gower

OS Sheet 159; SS 458848

Cliffs, limestone grassland, heath and scrub, forming part of the Gower Coast Rhossili to Port Eynon SSSI. Area 9.4 ha (23.2 acres). This reserve was purchased in February 1964 with financial help and grant aid from SPNRs Nuffield Fund, the Pilgrim Trust and WWF. Managed by West Glamorgan Committee and the Port Eynon to Rhossili Coastal Management Group.

Location
0.2 km south west of the Village of Overton. The reserve can be accessed from the stile in the sout- east corner of the Long Hole Cave nature reserve in the west, or from the footpath adjacent to the seashore of the Overton Mere nature reserve in the east.

Description
Overton Cliff is relatively ungrazed and the vegetation is predominantly maritime limestone heath and scrub made up of a mixture of Common Gorse (3-6) and Western Gorse (7-9) with Heather (7-9) and Bell Heather (7-9) together with Hawthorn and Blackthorn. Because of the close proximity of the sea and lack of grazing, part of the grassland at the western end of the reserve which is dominated by Red Fescue has formed a thick mattress-like sward.

Early-purple Orchid (4-6) followed by Bloody Cranesbill (7-8) and Carline Thistle (7-10) adorn the grassland, while Wild Madder (6-8) climbs its way through the gorse.

Bloody-nosed Beetles are regularly to be found on the path in summer.

Feral Rock Dove and Herring Gull use the ledges on Overton Cliff to nest, while Jackdaws use the cave in its rock face. Green Woodpeckers are regularly seen foraging for ants amongst the anthills in the grassland.

Management Objectives
Monitor the vegetation and reinstate grazing if required.

Yellow Whitlow-grass

SOUTH GOWER COAST – OVERTON CLIFF

OS Sheet 159; SS 458848

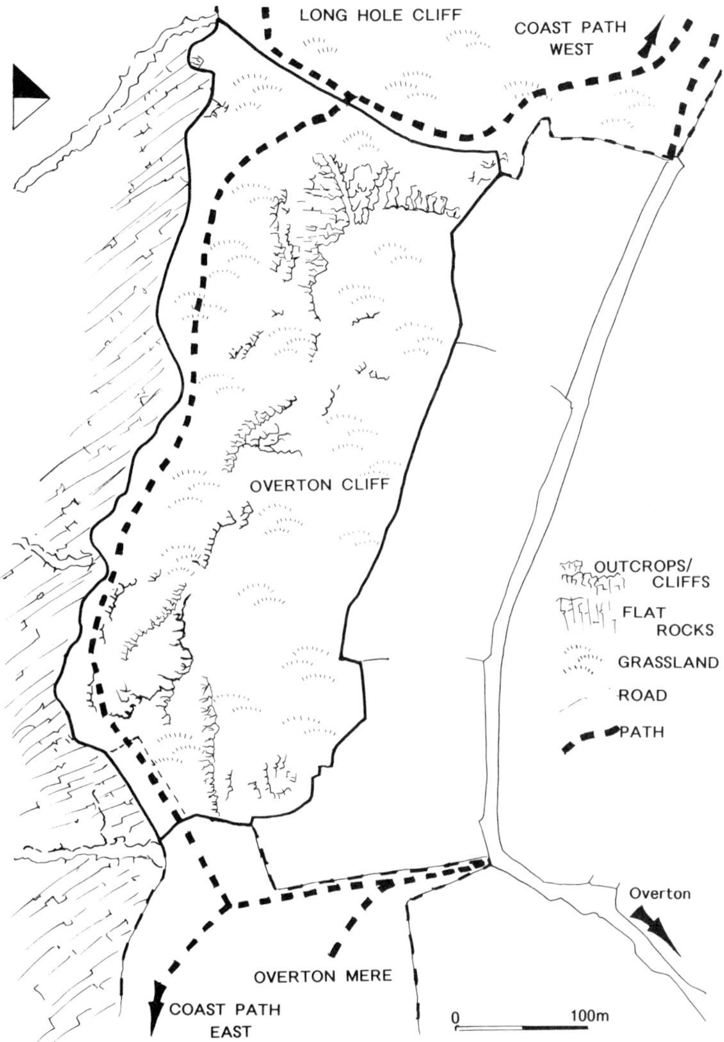

Good times to visit
April - June Spring coastal flowers; *May - July* Coastal breeding birds

Nearest Reserves
South Gower Coast - Deborah's Hole, West Glamorgan 2 km; *South Gower Coast - Long Hole Cliff, West Glamorgan* adjacent to the west; *South Gower Coast - Overton Mere, West Glamorgan* adjacent to the east; *South Gower Coast - Port Eynon Point, West Glamorgan* 0.5 km

SOUTH GOWER COAST – OVERTON MERE

Overton, Gower

OS Sheet 159; SS 462848

Limestone grassland, heath and scrub, forming part of the Gower Coast Rhossili to Port Eynon SSSI. Area 11.6 ha (28.6 acres). This reserve was purchased in December 1963 and March 1986 with financial help and grant aid from SPNRs Nuffield Fund, the Pilgrim Trust and WWF. Part Registered Common Land. Managed by West Glamorgan Committee and the Port Eynon to Rhossili Coastal Management Group.

Location
0.5 km south of the village of Overton. Access can be gained by way of the kissing gate adjacent to the first field gate on the left on the track leading out of Overton Village to the west, or by way of the coastal public footpath from Port Eynon Point.

Description
The reserve is named after the bay over which it looks. Overton Mere has almost the full range of South Gower Coast habitats ranging from Hawthorn and Blackthorn scrub, through mixed gorse and heath, open limestone scree, to improved and unimproved limestone grassland.

The areas of improved grassland are to be found on the plateau area closest to the sea shore which is a fossil raised beach dating back to the last ice age. The improvement came about when the previous owner ploughed these areas for potatoes, and they were subsequently reseeded with grass.

Lime-loving flowers such as Common Rock-rose (5-9), Milkwort (4-7), Eyebright (7-9), and Wild Thyme (5-8) flourish, while birds such as Linnet and Meadow Pipit search the grassland and scrub for food. Oystercatcher and other shore birds can be seen in the Mere at low tide.

Management Objectives
Continue to monitor the mosaic of vegetation and reinstate grazing if required.

Fulmer

SOUTH GOWER COAST – OVERTON MERE

OS Sheet 159; SS 462848

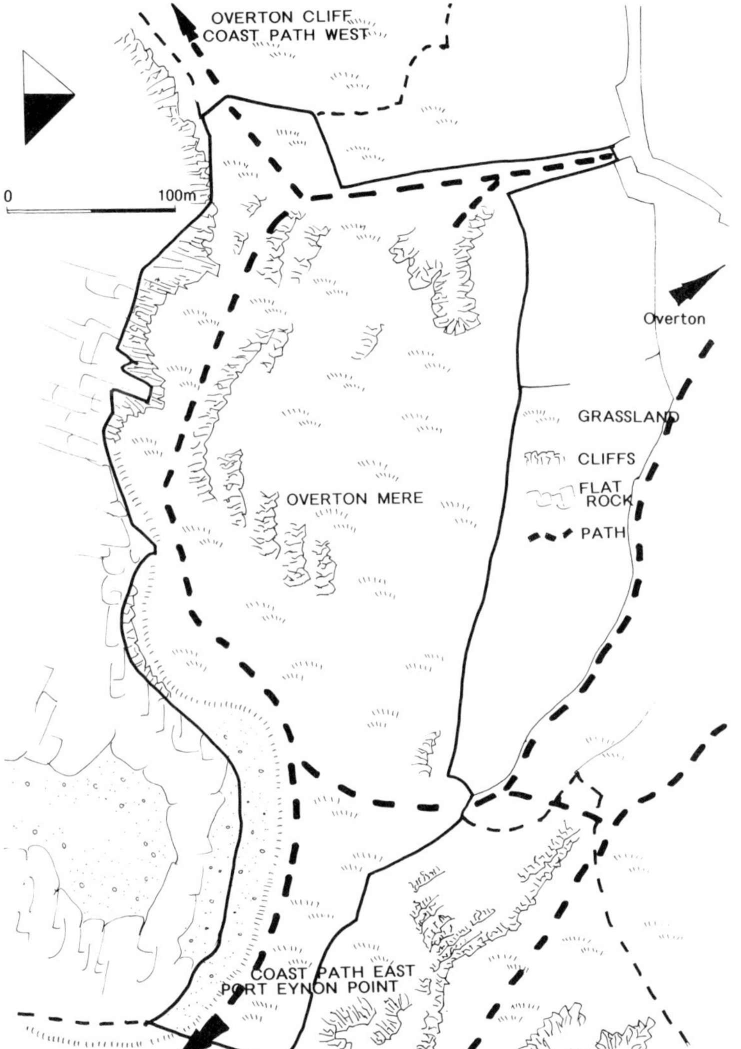

Good times to visit
March - July Spring coastal flowers; *May - July* Summer coastal breeding birds

Nearest Reserves
South Gower Coast - Long Hole Cliff, West Glamorgan 1 km; *South Gower Coast - Overton Cliff, West Glamorgan* adjacent to the west; *South Gower Coast - Port Eynon Point, West Glamorgan* adjacent to the east; *South Gower Coast - Sedger's Bank, West Glamorgan* 1 km

SOUTH GOWER COAST – PORT EYNON POINT

Port Eynon, Gower

OS Sheet 159; SS 465845

Sea cliff, foreshore, limestone grassland, heath and quarries forming part of the Gower Coast Rhossili to Port Eynon SSSI. Area 13.4 ha (33 acres). Acquired by leasehold for 60 years in February 1965. Managed by West Glamorgan Committee and the Port Eynon to Rhossili Coastal Management Group.

Location
Port Eynon Point is the headland dominating the western side of Port Eynon Bay. The reserve can be accessed from the footpath on the west side of Port Eynon beach.

Description
A large part of the reserve on the inland side has been used for quarrying and now provides a varied set of habitats for plants and animals, including foxes and rabbits and birds such as Stonechat and Rock Pipit.

Although part of the cliff top was ploughed during the last war, there is no indication of it in the gorse heath vegetation that now dominates it. There is a very clear limestone grass strip along the cliff top which is maintained by rabbit grazing and visitor pressure, where a range of flowers can be found including Thrift (4-10) and Sea Campion (4-10).

The reserve is regionally important as a sea watching site particularly in late July and Early August, though interesting birds are usually present throughout the year. January and February often bring Red-throated and Great Northern Divers. At the end of July and early August at day break, large numbers of of Manx Shearwaters, and Gannets may be seen flying past and often there are large groups of Common Scoter off-shore.

Management Objectives
Monitor the vegetation, and visitor pressure, and undertake management to maintain the present *status quo*.

Manx Shearwater

SOUTH GOWER COAST – PORT EYNON POINT

OS Sheet 159; SS 465845

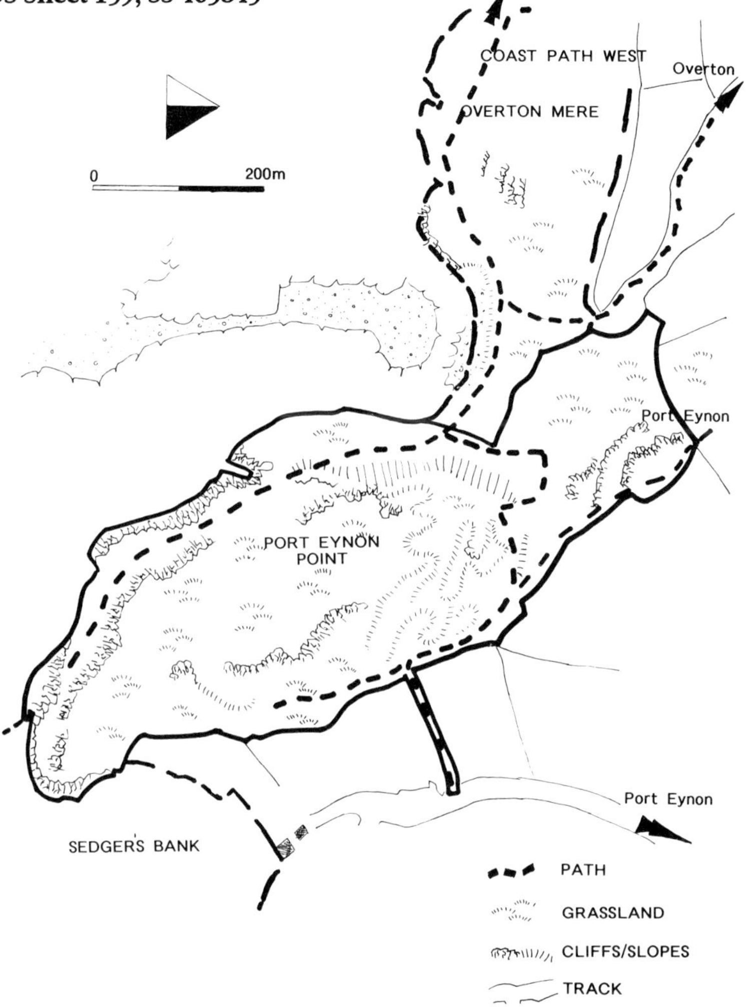

Good times to visit

January - February Birdwatching for wintering Divers, etc.; *March - June* Spring coastal flowers; *May - July* Summer coastal breeding birds; *Late July - Early August* Sea-watching for large scale seabird movements (NB For large numbers of seabirds in July/August, it is essential to be on site at day break.)

Nearest Reserves

South Gower Coast - Long Hole Cliff, West Glamorgan 1 km; *South Gower Coast - Overton Cliff, West Glamorgan* 0.5 km; *South Gower Coast - Overton Mere, West Glamorgan* adjacent; *South Gower Coast - Sedger's Bank, West Glamorgan* adjacent

SOUTH GOWER COAST – SEDGER'S BANK

Port Eynon, Gower

OS Sheet 159; SS 470844

Rocky foreshore, beach and relict sand dune grassland forming part of the Gower Coast Rhossili to Port Eynon SSSI. Area 35.1 ha (86.7 acres). The freehold of this reserve was given to the Trust in April 1966 by Mr C.P.M. Methuen-Campbell. Part Registered Common Land. Managed by West Glamorgan Committee and the Port Eynon to Rhossili Coastal Management Group.

Location
0.5 km south of Port Eynon village, at the western side of the beach.

Description
Sedger's Bank makes up a large part of the most westerly edge of Port Eynon Bay and the entirity of the nature reserve can only be seen on the lowest tides of the year.

The only area of the reserve which is above high water mark is made up of a small storm beach surmounted by a relict sand dune upon which Sea Bindweed (6-8), Common Rest-harrow (6-9), and Sea Spurge (7-10) grow.

The rest of the nature reserve is frequently covered by sea water depending on the height of the tide in the cycle between springs and neaps, and the limestone rocks provide shelter for the full range of shore life including Mussels, Whelks and Beadlet Anemones.

The reserve serves as a resting place for Purple Sandpipers and Shags at near high tide in winter, and is also a site where individual Grey Seals haul out having ventured this far up the Bristol Channel.

Management Objectives
Monitor for any marine pollution incidents.

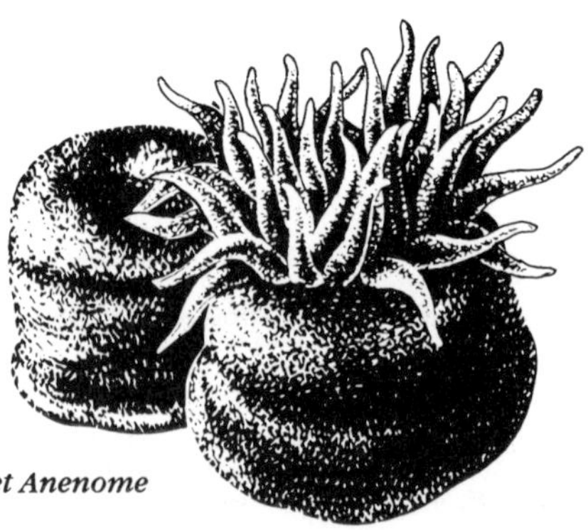

Beadlet Anenome

SOUTH GOWER COAST – SEDGER'S BANK

OS Sheet 159; SS 470844

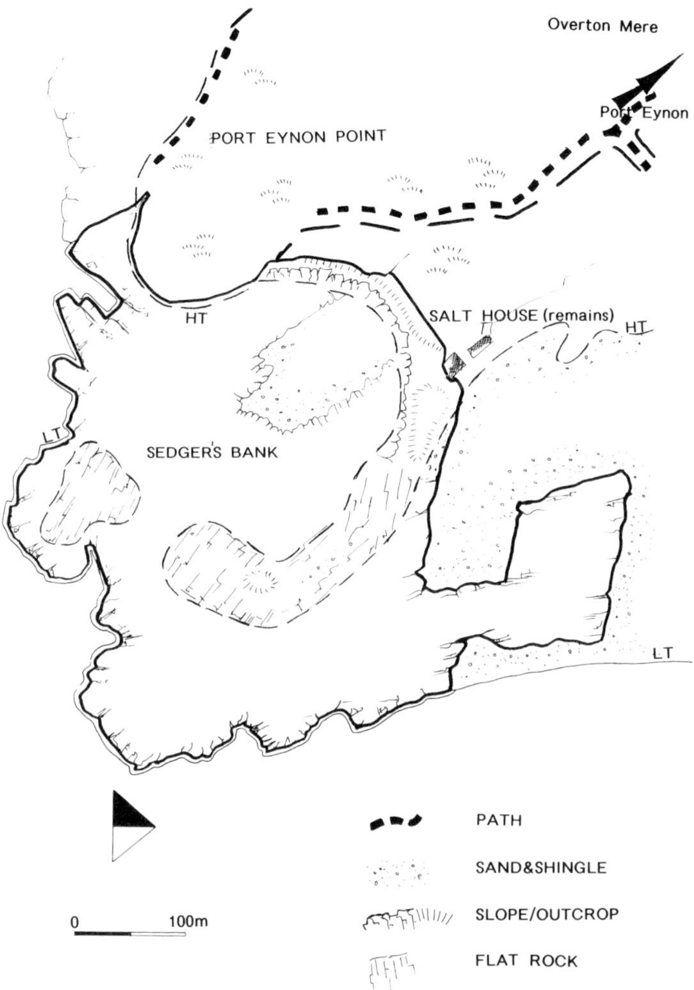

Good times to visit
At low tide to view sublittoral animals and plants; April - June Spring shore flowers; May - July Summer shore breeding birds; September - March Wintering migratory shore birds and Grey Seals.

Nearest Reserves
Berry Wood, West Glamorgan 4 km; *South Gower Coast - Long Hole Cliff, West Glamorgan* 1.5 km; *South Gower Coast - Overton Cliff, West Glamorgan* 1 km; *South Gower Coast - Port Eynon Point, West Glamorgan* adjacent to the west